THE PRIDE TRILOGY

3 Kyle Callahan Mysteries

Murder at Pride Lodge
Pride and Perilous
Death by Pride

MARK MCNEASE

Also By Mark McNease

Kyle Callahan Mysteries
Pride and Perilous
Death in the Headlights
Death by Pride
Kill Switch

Other Books & Writing
Outer Voices Inner Lives
(Co-Editor and Publisher)
Lambda Literary Award Finalist for Anthology

In Harmony with the Seasons
By Herbalist Cathy McNease (Publisher)
Stop the Car (A Kindle Single)
Rough & Tumble, A Fiction Short
The Seer, A Fiction Short

A Word About the Mysteries

A few things were true when I first had the idea for a mystery series featuring older characters, centered on a male couple who were my age, give or take a year. One was that I was writing it for the fun and experience of seeing an idea through to its end. The other was that if the first book, *Murder at Pride Lodge*, gained a few dozen readers I'd probably write a second one, and, if that was the case, I might as well make it a trilogy. Doesn't everyone write trilogies? So that's what I did, with a side trip to write *Death in the Headlights* as a sort of break, and to give Detective Linda her own story to lead.

I've now written five Kyle Callahan Mysteries. Kyle and I are four years older than we were when I took that fateful photograph of the empty blue pool at Rainbow Mountain Resort, the inspiration for Pride Lodge. Something about that picture and that forlorn empty pool in early winter made me say to my partner, "This would make a great place to set a murder mystery." For what else would you expect to find at the bottom of an empty swimming pool than a dead body? And that was that.

I wanted to provide the Pride Trilogy as a complete book, which is what you're reading. It makes it easy to flow from one book into the next, see how the characters develop and where the story arcs go. I hope you enjoy them collectively as much as readers have enjoyed them individually.

Will there be another one? I really have to leave that up to the characters. It's much more a matter of them being finished with me than me being finished with them. If they nag me enough, I probably won't have any choice. I hear them calling now ...

Thanks for riding with me on the mystery train.

Mark McNease
New York City

Murder at Pride Lodge

Who killed Teddy the handyman - if anyone killed him at all? Was it Sid, one of the new owners of Pride Lodge whose past gets darker the closer you look? Was it the woman whose name was once Emily, when she witnessed the murder of her parents in a burglary gone bad, and who has waited thirty years for vengeance? Was it young Happy Corcoran, promoted to bartender only to vanish three days before Teddy was found dead at the bottom of the empty pool? Find out as Kyle Callahan refuses to believe it was an accident, doggedly pursues the truth in his friend's death and does his best not to join him. Kyle and his life partner Danny Durban live in New York City, where murder never seems to be more than a subway stop away. In this first story, they head to Pride Lodge, their favorite getaway from the City, over what they expect to be a festive Halloween weekend. What they find instead is a web of murder, deceit, and revenge served cold as a knife blade.

Pride and Perilous

The Katherine Pride Gallery is the center of high art and low death in Pride and Perilous, book II of the Pride Trilogy and the second of the Kyle Callahan Mysteries. Kyle, an amateur photographer, is about to have his first exhibit at the gallery, in Manhattan's Meatpacking District. As time ticks away, bodies begin to fall and Kyle realizes somebody wants this gallery closed forever. Join the chase as Kyle and his partner Danny Durban reunite with Detective Linda Sikorsky from the New Hope, PA, police force. They met solving the murders at Pride Lodge, and Linda has come to town for Kyle's opening, only to find herself joining forces with him again to capture a killer ... before he captures them.

Death by Pride
The Pride Trilogy concludes with 'Death by Pride.' It's Gay Pride weekend, the most festive weekend of the year in New York City. Hundreds of thousands of partygoers arrive to show the world how to have a good time.

Stalking the party is the most successful serial killer the city has ever seen. He claims his victims in threes and has just begun his newest spree. Detective Linda Sikorsky comes to town to visit Kyle Callahan and his husband Danny Durban. It's her first Pride Parade and may well be her last. Harmless fun turns to terror in a frantic effort to stop the killer once the first body floats to the river's edge. This time it's personal, and this time one of them might not make it out alive

Murder at Pride Lodge

Book I

PROLOGUE

Los Angeles

S am Tatum was found flat on his back in a parking garage three blocks from the Glendale Galleria at three o'clock on a Wednesday afternoon. Had it started raining an hour later he would have parked on the street and died in a puddle, his face wet with drizzle and his eyes staring up, unblinking, as rain flushed the life from them. The garage had been fate's one courtesy, saving him the embarrassment of dying even more publicly than he did, insofar as corpses can be embarrassed. It was an ignominious death. While he'd expected to die from one too many lines of cocaine up his old man's nose, or murdered, even, in a fit of pique by one of the hustlers he'd been too fond of for too many years, ending his life on the concrete floor of a parking garage, his head in an oil stain, was too seedy even for Sam. Had he been able to think once he was dead, he would have found it a tawdry end to a tawdry life and been glad it was over.

The woman who found him, walking with her 12-year-old daughter to their newly purchased Prius parked three cars to the left of Sam's Camry, had worked as a nurse before marrying well and was familiar enough with dead bodies to make the call. The poor guy was old, out of shape, uncommonly pale, and obviously lived an unhealthy life. He was lucky to make it this far, she thought, more disturbed that her child had seen a corpse than that he was actually dead. She didn't know him, what was it to her? Mostly it was an inconvenience, since she had the decency to call an ambulance, knowing it was much too late to save the poor slob, and stay around to speak to the police. She'd considered making it an anonymous 911 call, since her daughter's ballet class started at 3:30 and this would mean missing it for sure. But something in her, that old nurse calling, that instinct to do the right thing, made her give her name and location and wait patiently for the paramedics who would try to resuscitate a man she knew was dead. His eyes were open, for godsake, and what life had been in them had slipped away some time ago. Anyone could see that.

She'd told her daughter Kelly to get into the car the moment she saw the man's feet come into view. Kelly, being a precocious, ballet-class-taking 12-year-old, wanted the full view and instead of doing what she was told rushed around ahead of her mother to get a good look. She had never seen a dead body before and she could tell by her mother's lack of urgency that the man was probably beyond help. After an inappropriate but predictable, "Cool!" she obeyed her mother and skipped ahead to their car. Once inside, she tweeted that she and her mother had found a dead guy, and waited for her friends' texts to start flooding in.

Sam's death was twelfth-page news, not more than a brief item for the curious, a paragraph about a man found dead near the Glendale Galleria. The reporter for the Glendale News-Press gave it a quick once-over, not bothering to call the coroner's office or find out any significant details about Sam Tatum's life and death. News had to flow constantly these days, and most of that was from wire services and Google alerts. Real reporting was a dying profession, and the News-Press hack was happy not to expend too much energy on dead old fat men in parking garages. If the death wasn't important enough to make the L.A. Times, why the hell should he bother with it? So it ran as a sidebar, a snippet, given about as much notice as Sam Tatum had been given most of his life.

There was one website, however, that specialized in unusual deaths, which Sam's turned out to be. *DeathWatchLA.com* had begun in the 1970s as a sort of gossip rag for the morbidly obsessed. Back then it was just a couple pages offering lurid details of murders both sensational and obscure, so long as they were noteworthy for their gruesomeness or peculiarity. An accidental decapitation could sell an extra thousand copies. Run of the mill heart attacks didn't make the grade; as it turned out, Sam Tatum's death was not run of the mill.

With the arrival of the internet the creepy little paper became a big attractive website, and even though its founder had died in a way befitting a banner headline—found stuffed in the trunk of a Lincoln town car—his sons knew a gold mine when they had one and turned the site into a million-hits-a-month bonanza. They expanded with sister sites (*DeathWatchNYC*, *DeathWatchCHI*, even a *DeathWatchMinneapolis*), death tours, both walking and by hearse, and planned to launch their own malt liquor in a few months. Meanwhile, they had content to keep up and readers to satisfy, and as much as one might not expect it, there were fans of the peculiar who found a parking lot death-by-ice pick as fascinating as a decomposed celebrity. For that is how Sam Tatum had really died: an ice pick (as close as the coroner could guess on a murder weapon) slipped quickly, almost expertly, into the base of his skull, shoved at an upward angle to ensure instant death and very little blood loss. It seems someone had wanted Sam dead and had found the perfect opportunity—the third floor of a parking garage with no more than a dozen cars parked in it and no eyewitnesses. How his killer came upon him was anyone's guess. There appeared to be no signs of conflict, not even a sign of alarm. Had it been someone he knew? Or simply someone he felt unthreatened by? No one would ever know, but *DeathWatchLA* certainly posed the questions.

Thus it was that someone on the other side of the country who happened to read *DeathWatchLA* took notice and knew that the email he'd gotten from Sam two weeks earlier was not the panic of a man who had used too many drugs and bought too many young men. Sam Tatum was dead. He had not been paranoid, but convinced someone was after them, and he had been right. Three months earlier there had been another death, a man named Frank Grandy, this one in Detroit. Neither of them had spoken to Frank in years, and it was only when Frank left Sam $2000 in his will as a very belated repayment of a loan, that Sam knew their old partner in crime was dead. No suspects had been named, no one identified, but the report mentioned an antique pocket watch Frank was selling on an internet auction site. The watch case was there, but the watch was gone. Robbery, they assumed, but the investigation had gone nowhere. That was what rang the alarm bell for Sam, the watch. He was surprised Frank had kept it all these years, but not surprised it had led to his death. The past, it seems, had been waiting patiently to find them, and it had.

The two deaths spoke not of coincidence, but of a plan, with a planner and only one target left. The *DeathWatchLA* reader logged off his computer, swiveled around in his desk chair and cheerfully took a cup of coffee from his partner, smiling as if nothing had changed and they were simply beginning another gorgeous day. Time to get started.

CHAPTER 1

PRIDE LODGE

Halloween weekend was the busiest of the year at Pride Lodge, with the Fourth of July a close second. Gay people like a party, and the Halloween parties at the Lodge had been legendary for twenty-five years. Rooms in the main lodge and the six adjoining cabins were sold out by mid-summer, all in anticipation of a fiendishly good time in the Pennsylvania countryside not quite like anything the guests would find elsewhere. It was city meets country in a unique and intimate setting far from the streets of New York or Philadelphia. Everybody knew everybody here, and among the delights for guests was seeing friends they hadn't hugged or shared a drink with since last Halloween.

Pride Lodge sits on ten acres along Pennsylvania's Highway 32, just 20 minutes from New Hope and a short walk to the Delaware River. Originally an old farmhouse, the Lodge had been converted into an inn in the early 1950s. Bed and breakfasts weren't all the rage then, and the idea of having an inn along a country road, surrounded by woods and farmland and catering to people who wanted something out of their way, was a novelty. So much of a novelty that the business failed and the original owners, well-intended but bankrupt, sold it to new owners, who sold it to newer owners. Finally, in the mid-1980s, the inn was dilapidated, its windows boarded up for longer than anyone could remember, and the last owner was selling the land. That was when Pucky Green and Stu Patterson, partners in life and whatever business venture they'd cooked up at the time, decided it was a perfect place for a gay resort. It proved to be the one stroke of genius and the one true success they ever had, aside from deciding to spend their lives together.

They renovated the old inn and re-christened it Pride Lodge. They added on to the main two-story building until it had eight guest rooms on the first floor and six on the second, along with what they called the Master Suite, where the two of them lived. The Lodge boasted a functioning restaurant and bar adjoining the main room, which everyone called the "great room," complete with fireplace, wide-screen television, three mahogany book shelves to give the space a library feel, and a check-in desk where you could buy the usual rainbow paraphernalia, along with a Pride Lodge sweatshirt and baseball cap, should you be in the market for souvenirs. Three years into the venture, when they realized it was going to succeed, they added a swimming pool, and two years after that they had six cabins built, each with two spacious "luxury" rooms that included kitchenettes and private baths. They had the inn's cavernous basement sound-proofed and converted half into a piano bar called Clyde's and half into a karaoke room. The combined entertainment had the effect of bringing in locals for dinner and a night out, helping to swell the numbers without having to add more rooms. The whole undertaking took five years, but once it was completed it was a sight to behold: a resort for gays, lesbians, bisexuals, and more than a few transgender visitors, well before the term had been officially coined. Back then everyone just called it a gay resort, with the knowledge that all were welcome, including the occasional, befuddled heterosexual couple who pulled into the driveway because they liked the name of the place. Most of them politely drove on once they got to the desk and realized there was something different going on here. Maybe it was the two slightly masculine women sitting by the fireplace, or the restaurant hostess with the Adam's apple, but now and then they stayed and were made to feel as much at home as any other guest.

Pucky was the ringmaster, the chatty, gregarious captain of this strange and colorful ship. A diminutive man at five-five, he had a habit of keeping his hair dyed strawberry blond and wearing a collection of eyeglasses to rival a young Elton John's. He wore Hawaiian shirts in the summer and high-end casual short-sleeved shirts the rest of the year, always with long pants. Pucky didn't like his legs; he thought they were too chickeny, as he called them, and he never exposed them in public. He was the face of Pride Lodge, the official greeter, taskmaster of a ragtag staff, and the table floater at dinner who went from guest to guest asking how their food was, if their rooms were up to snuff, and if there was anything at all he could help them with, excluding the sexual encounters some of the guests hoped for after an hour or two at the bar. That, Pucky discreetly let them know, was up to them. He was many things, with many hats, but a pimp was not one of them.

Stu had met Pucky when they were both in the United States Navy stationed at the Naval Air Station in Key West. Had it been up to Stu they would still be living there. He much preferred the tropical climate of the Florida Keys, but even more important to him was the man he'd fallen in love with and to whom he'd committed his life way back in 1972. A world away, a time removed, when Vietnam was still unresolved and an American president had yet to resign in disgrace.

Stu was silence to Pucky's noise, calm to Pucky's chaos. He stayed in the background, even though everyone knew who he was. Stu did the Lodge's books and looked after the financial end of things. He liked that. He was a thinker, a lover of novels and quietude. Running Pride Lodge might seem like an odd choice for a man who preferred the company of only one person, but it worked well for Stu. He had life in the country. He had Pucky to look after the guests and keep the occasional madness away from him. And he had a companion for life, his one great treasure. It made aging, going bald, feeling his knees begin to buckle and the weight slowly add to his once tall, slender frame, not quite so discomfiting.

One morning three years ago Stu was taking his dawn constitutional, as he called it, walking around the grounds as the sun was just beginning to rise. He would have a single cup of de-caffeinated coffee in the Suite's kitchen while it was still dark out; then he would put on his coat if the weather was chill, as it had been that September, and he would walk slowly around the cabins, along the periphery of the property and back up past the pool, climbing the stairs that led to the Lodge as the sun was ascended the morning sky. That was where they found him, on the stairs, almost at the top, as if, had he made it three more steps, he would still be alive. His heart had stopped, outlasted by his knees and every other part of him, as he made his way slowly up the stairs. The one small mercy was that Ricki, the long-time desk manager, night time restaurant hostess and summer pool boy—if you can call a 50-year-old man a boy—was the one who found him. Ricki slept very little, which helped explain how he managed to be so many things to so many people, and it was his habit to drive in from his home in Lambertville, across the river in New Jersey, and clean the bars first thing in the morning. When he parked his car that day he noticed what looked like a red jacket on the steps leading up to the Lodge. At first he assumed someone had had too much to drink the night before and lost their jacket, but then he noticed a pair of beige pants running below the jacket and an arm stuck straight out to the side, and he suddenly realized it was a person, lying face down and motionless. He rushed over to find Stu, dead with his glasses cracked on his face from where he'd hit the step, those stupid old black horn-rims Pucky had been on him for years to replace. He rolled Stu over and, not knowing the first thing about CPR, tried to save him anyway, stopping in the frantic effort to shout, "Help! Help! Somebody help!"

Pucky tried to carry on without Stu but everyone could tell it wasn't going to work. He stopped greeting people, he stopped paying attention to detail, and within a few months he stopped caring altogether. He decided to sell Pride Lodge and retire to Key West. The one other place he knew Stu loved and would probably have preferred to live, but he had loved Pucky even more. He would sell the Lodge, where his heart had stopped on those steps as surely as Stu's had, and he would go to the southernmost end of the country, buy a small condo, and live out his life with his memories.

Word spread quickly that Pucky was selling. Fear set in among the regulars that the famed and beloved Pride Lodge would end up in the hands of a developer who cared not a whit for its history, and the collective memory of all the friends and guests who had stayed there would quickly fade, blown away as easily and dismissively as ash.

That was when Sid Stanhope and Dylan Tremblay stepped in. Ten years apart in age, with Sid the older at sixty-two that year, they were long-time guests of the Lodge who drove in from their home in Long Branch, New Jersey, several times a year to spend long weekends. Sid was about ready to retire from his job as an assistant bank manager, having hoped the past five years not to be laid off; he saw this as a golden opportunity to get out before he was pushed out, despite the tragic circumstances that had the Lodge on the market. Dylan had never been content to begin with, job hopping his entire adult life until he found his job of the last six years selling men's clothes in a store whose only claim to fame was having survived in Long Branch. The boardwalk there had been built up over the last decade, with high-end condos along the shore. Life in Long Branch wasn't quite the depressing reality it had been, but the chance to get out? To buy Pride Lodge and live out their lives there, as Pucky and Stu had? It was just the sort of luck, that accident of timing, you could wait for most of your life. When it happened you had to act. Sid and Dylan acted, and two years later, as they decorated the Lodge for another Halloween, they still thought it was the best move they'd ever made.

CHAPTER 2

CABIN 6

Kyle Callahan and Danny Durban arrived at Pride Lodge late on Thursday night. This was their fifth Halloween at the Lodge and an event they both looked forward to months in advance. The couple had spent three long weekends each year there for the five years they'd been together, one for each season excluding winter. As lovely as the Pennsylvania countryside was, Kyle and Danny both found it too bare, too cold and stark in the winter months.

They'd found Pride Lodge by accident their first summer together, after Kyle suggested they go away for a weekend and began a brief internet search of gay bed and breakfasts within driving distance of their apartment in Manhattan. Pride Lodge popped up, just 90 minutes by rental car. While it was much larger than a traditional B&B, it instantly became one of their favorite getaways, and five years later they'd made the drive again as October came to a close and the Halloween festivities promised friendship, fun and an escape for them both from the pressures of their lives in the City.

Ricki was just about to go off desk duty when they arrived at nearly eleven o'clock that night. He knew all the regular guests and was delighted to see them, even though he'd known they were coming. Several other guests had arrived early as well and a few were having drinks by the fireplace as Kyle and Danny checked in and got the key for Cabin 6. They always stayed in Cabin 6. For one thing, it was one of the luxury rooms, with its own television, kitchenette and bathroom; it was also well away and just down the road, giving the roomers a greater sense of privacy. The cabins were surrounded by trees in back and a long private drive in front. Most of the people who stayed at Pride Lodge were older. It just wasn't the kind of place young LGBT travelers went to for a good time: too remote, too sedate, and too, well, old. The perfect hideaway for mature gay men, lesbian couples and singles looking to be comfortable exposing their 40 or 50 or 60-year-old bodies in a bathing suit, or sitting around a restaurant bar chatting with other people who remembered music from the 1970s when it was new and who would not likely be spending their time tweeting, linking in or obsessively checking their smart phones for texts and celebrity news flashes.

The other reason they always stayed in Cabin 6 was the painting: a beautiful dark-haired woman in a flowing red dress sitting at a black grand piano in front of a fireplace. She looked as if she were frozen in the 1940s, and appeared to be posing at the piano more than actually playing it. There was sheet music in front of her, but only one's imagination could decide what the music was. Classical, most certainly, given the elegance of the woman and the room. It was clearly a reproduction, something that must surely be hanging in thousands of homes and hotel rooms around the world, but Kyle had only ever seen it in one other place—above his mother's piano in the home he had grown up in in Highland Park, Illinois. His mother moved to a condo in Chicago after his father's death and she had taken the picture with her. Kyle, never a superstitious man, took the painting's presence as some kind of message, as if his parents were giving their blessing in a discreet but very unusual way. Kyle made sure he and Danny stayed in Cabin 6 every visit after that.

Kyle met Danny when both men were forty-seven, with just six months separating them. Danny, being the older of the pair, joked that theirs was a May-June romance. They stumbled upon one another, literally, at a photography exhibit at the Katherine Pride Gallery in Chelsea's Meatpacking

District. Kyle had gone because of his love for photography and his passion as an amateur photographer, and to support a friend who was having the exhibit. Danny had gone because the owner of the gallery, Katherine Pride, had recently become a customer at Margaret's Passion, the long-time Gramercy Park restaurant where Danny was the day manager. It was the kind of personal touch Margaret's was known for, securing in return a legendary loyalty to the restaurant and to Margaret herself. The only meat to be found in the Meatpacking District these days came on very high-priced plates at restaurants with names like Sacrosanct and Tiberius. The area had once housed butchers feeding the citizens of New York City; now it was all upscale eateries, art galleries and clothing stores. Danny had come around a corner, studying the photographs on the wall, and accidentally bumped into Kyle, spilling both their drinks. Their eyes met an instant before their smiles, and five years later they were still together.

Kyle was by most measures an average looking man: oval face, large nose, pale blue eyes. His hair had been blond as a child but had long since turned brown, and he kept it cropped close to his skull, in part to downplay a receding hairline. He dressed in slacks and button-down shirts, in and out of the office, not liking the heaviness of blue jeans even on vacation; and his one surrender to fashion was his glasses: progressive, transitional, bifocal Ray-Bans that just about everyone said were the coolest glasses they'd seen.

Danny was the more outgoing of the two. He was also six inches shorter than Kyle, who was not a particularly tall man. It was a height difference Kyle never noticed except when he saw pictures of them together. Danny was the talker, Kyle the brooder. Danny preferred shorts outside his job in all but the coldest weather, and would throw on a sweatshirt or sweater to compensate for a chill. He liked being as casual as possible outside the restaurant where he had worked for the past ten years. He was top talent, keeping Margaret's customers happy, familiar and returning. Margaret Bowman was a real person. Cheerful, birdlike and nearing 80, she seldom came down to the restaurant anymore from her apartment above it on East 21st Street, but when she did she always caused a stir. She would go slowly from table to table saying hello to people who had known and loved her for years. She asked how their children and grandchildren were; if there was a young couple dining she would remark on how lovely they looked together. If they were single, divorced, or even grieving the loss of a loved one, Margaret somehow knew and would say exactly the right thing. She had lost her husband Gerard to a freak traffic accident several years back and had no children, and she considered Danny the son she'd always wanted.

Kyle was the personal assistant to Imogene Landis, a high-maintenance, high-octane, high-profile television reporter whose star had been falling steadily for the past five years, which is exactly how long Kyle had worked for her. It seems she had found the best assistant she'd ever had—or at least the most persevering—just as her career began its slow slide into the tank of obscurity. Before Kyle, no one had lasted more than a year working for Imogene, and for that determination and loyalty she repaid him by being as needy, intrusive and inappropriate as she possibly could. Kyle suspected her current job, as a special English-language correspondent on financial affairs for Tokyo Pulse, a third-tier Japanese cable show produced by Japan TV3, was the last stop on this train. She'd be editing copy or selling Avon if she blew this one. He thought she knew it, too, which was why she leaned on him more than ever and why he allowed it.

"Please turn your phone off," Danny said as they rolled their luggage into Cabin 6. He knew the third person on every vacation they took was Imogene and he wanted her left in Manhattan; that included limiting her digital reach, ignoring her texts and letting her go to voicemail.

"Just let me check the emails, then I'll turn it off for the night. I promise."

"For the night? We're not just here for the night."

"She's at the Stock Exchange tomorrow morning, it's a very big deal for her."

"In the background! She's a prop, Kyle, she's not ringing the bell."

"Be kind. The show airs in Tokyo."

"A re-run at 3:00 am. On cable, with Japanese sub-titles. She doesn't speak a word of the language."

"Of course not, that's why they hired her! She's an English-language correspondent. Do I need to explain what that is?"

Danny glared at Kyle. "I know what an English-language correspondent is," he said slowly, causing Kyle to blush. "I know what a good one is, too."

Kyle started to protest in defense of his boss, but Danny cut him off with a wave of his hand. "It's great she's learning Japanese, it really is," Danny said. "She'll be able to tell her bosses to fuck off in their own language, maybe do a proper bow with it before they fire her."

"She's learned her lesson."

"Several times."

Danny saw the hurt on Kyle's face. "I'm sorry. I know you're devoted to her, but she's not the one you're marrying. And she'll get over the trauma of standing three people to the side, back row I'm sure, at the opening bell of the Stock Exchange. She can be your best man . . . or best woman or however it's done with gay people."

The two men had been talking about marriage since the law passed in New York. They'd been cautious, not wanting to get caught up in the emotions of the moment. They decided against rushing down to City Hall as they thought many couples had without really thinking it through. But they were in negotiations, so to speak.

Danny began hanging his shirts in the closet and putting his underwear, socks and sundries in the top dresser drawer.

Kyle rolled his suitcase into a corner by the nightstand on his side of the bed. He tended to vacation out of his suitcase and was never in a hurry to unpack. This was not their apartment, and he figured the task of hanging up shirts and pants could wait until morning. His real concern was his camera. He'd upgraded to a Nikon D3100. At $600 it wasn't all that top of the line, but it was the best he'd ever had and he was extremely protective of it, treating it the way a violinist might treat a Stradivarius. He had been in love with photography since his father gave him a new camera for his fortieth birthday. Late in life to find a passion, but not too late.

Kyle checked his camera to make sure he had the battery charger and the USB cable to upload photos to his laptop. He'd checked at home before they left, but these were the sorts of small details people tended to run through their minds over and over: Did I turn the stove off, did I lock the door? Once he confirmed he had not forgotten anything, he sat on the edge of the bed and took out his phone. He scrolled through his emails and saw that Danny was right, as he knew he would be. Seven emails from Imogene, all stealth with subject lines like, "HAVE A GREAT TIME!" and "TAKE LOTS OF PIX FOR ME!" She had never accepted that all-caps was bad form. And below the screaming demands that he enjoy himself she would type something frantic, urgent, or personal-time-interrupting. Kyle had been onto this trick for years but she still thought he fell for it.

He decided to keep his promise to Danny and leave Imogene's emails until the morning, when he could respond to them calmly, reassuring her that the earth had not shifted beneath her feet the past twenty-four hours. He was just about to turn off his phone when he saw the alert for a text message. Odd, he thought, looking at the time stamp. It had come in at 10:00 p.m. but they'd been on the road then. He hadn't heard any alert, and he never had his phone on vibrate. The text was from Teddy Pembroke, Pride Lodge's jack-of-all-trades. Teddy had been with the Lodge for fifteen years and was the only person other than Sid and Dylan who lived on the property.

The text read: "Let me know when u arrive. Things have gone wrong. Acceptance."

"Hmm," Kyle said, staring at the message, then looking at the nightstand: 11:30 p.m.

"What?" asked Danny, zipping up his now-empty suitcase and sliding it under the bed.

"Teddy texted me." He showed Danny the message. "Is it too late to call?"

"Yes," Danny said, glancing at the clock. "And what's with the 'acceptance'?"

"It's a quote, from the book they use in Alcoholics Anonymous. Kind of a mantra for him. I should call."

"It can wait. Let's just enjoy one quiet night away from everything and everyone."

Kyle smiled at Danny, trying to hide his unease about the text message. He'd befriended Teddy on their first visit to the Lodge and had kept in touch with him through the occasional email and a phone call now and then. Teddy had called him two days earlier to make sure they were still coming.

"It's Halloween," Kyle told him. "We never miss Halloween."

"Good," Teddy had said. He sounded nervous on the call, edgy. "I won't be staying at the Lodge much longer, Kyle. Something's going on here, something bad, we need to talk."

"What, Teddy? Just tell me."

"Not on the phone. I'm not even sure if I'm imagining some of this, it's confusing, but somebody needs to know. You're good at helping me sort things out, Kyle, it can wait two days."

Kyle had become Teddy's reluctant confidant, especially the last year. Teddy was close to Kyle's age but had never done much more than handyman work and odd jobs. Clearly once handsome, with chocolate brown eyes that were as seductive as they were sad, a mouth that had a habit of biting its upper lip, and still thin when most men his age were packing on weight, Teddy seemed as if he were from the coulda-been-a-contender school. Had he gotten more education, had he applied himself more intently, and especially had he not been an alcoholic. That was where Kyle had helped him most, connecting him with a local man Kyle knew was in Alcoholics Anonymous. Kyle wasn't in AA and had never had a drinking problem, but he was very good at finding sources and researching—it's part of what he does for a living—and after a few failed starts, Teddy had finally gotten sober six months ago. Maybe, Kyle thought, that's what this was about. Maybe Teddy had concluded he could no longer work at the Lodge and needed to move on for the sake of his sobriety. He had already stopped helping Cowboy Dave and Happy Corcoran in the bar. That's when it occurred to him this might be about love.

"Is there something wrong with you and Happy?" Kyle asked. He knew Teddy and the much younger Happy, who had started as a bar back the summer before, had been dating. *Young man breaks old man's heart*, Kyle thought to himself, *old man folds up his tent and runs away.*

There was a moment of silence on the other end. Then Teddy said, his voice lowered as if someone might hear him, "Happy's gone. Since yesterday, without a word. I'm afraid it's my fault."

"He's a kid," Kyle said, immediately regretting it. Happy was twenty-five or thereabouts and capable of making adult decisions. "A broken heart at that age . . . "

"That's not what I mean," Teddy said. "I told him things I shouldn't have told him, things that put him in danger. I should have known better, he's a talker. He can keep anything but a secret, and now he's gone."

"What secret, Teddy?" Kyle said, his exasperation showing. "What did you tell him?"

"Not on the phone." And then, with a sadness Kyle could feel from 70 miles away, "He wouldn't just leave me."

The call ended then, with Teddy not wanting to say anymore until they spoke in person. Whatever the problem was, it had Teddy itchy, sounding paranoid, and the sudden disappearance of Happy could only make it worse.

"You're sure it's too late?" Kyle asked, looking at the clock again.

"Let them man sleep," Danny said. "You'll see him at breakfast."

Kyle decided Danny was right. Teddy worked very long hours. He didn't need Kyle waking him up over a text message.

Kyle turned his phone off, waiting to make sure it actually shut down (it had a strange habit of coming back to life, as if it didn't appreciate being told what to do). He set it on the nightstand, then stood up and started to unbutton his shirt.

"I can do that," Danny said, motioning Kyle onto the bed. "I haven't forgotten how."

Kyle let it all go then, enjoying the touch of the man he was already growing old with.

CHAPTER 3

ROOM 202

She liked the idea of being a lesbian assassin and wondered if there were others like her, how they would go about finding one other, if they did. Maybe there was some sort of Facebook page for her kind, some site that required coded phrases and passwords to enter, but once inside she would not be alone in her singular mission, her only drive. It had been very lonely, and while she allowed her imagination its moments, she knew she did not belong in the company of killers. She'd had no choice in the matter, and was not really an assassin. Assassins were sent by others, were they not? They did the bidding of paymasters, while the assassin herself might have no stake in the matter at all. It was just a job, a high-risk paycheck. There was no comparison to be made. Hers was a mission of justice, of setting right a world that had been tilted wickedly out of balance thirty years ago when she was just a ten year old child hiding in a closet.

She had heard the men break into their home in Los Feliz, an affluent section of Los Angeles with its own boulevard snaking along past the Greek Theatre, east toward Glendale. She and her parents were supposed to be on a flight to London, part vacation, part present for her tenth birthday, but she had fallen seriously ill with a flu (there it was again, the guilt; it had been her fault somehow, another reason she must make amends and end these lives) and they had postponed the trip. Had they gone, had she not complained or registered a fever, her parents would be alive and her life would have had a completely different trajectory than the one leading her here, to this strange lodge outside a town she'd never been to or planned to see again.

Her childhood bedroom was on the second floor down the hall from her parents' room. She hadn't been able to sleep, tossing and turning, sweating with her fever, and when she heard the glass shatter she thought at first she had imagined or dreamt it. That's what fevers do to you. She sat up in bed and listened, hearing what to her was the distinct sound of someone in the house. She hurried out of bed in her nightgown and tip-toed quickly down the hall. Her father had always been a heavy sleeper, and her mother had the habit of using ear plugs to soften the sound of her husband's snores. Emily—that was her name then—went to her father and shook him awake.

"Daddy! Daddy!" she said, rocking him furiously. "There's somebody downstairs!"

Carl Lapinsky pulled himself from a deep sleep as quickly as he could, like a man swimming furiously up toward the surface. The alarm in his daughter's voice told him there was no time to waste, and he put his fingers to his lips to tell her to be silent. He'd heard her perfectly well, even blanketed by sleep, and he leaned up on one elbow to listen to the silence outside the room.

There it was, the sound of hushed voices. Carl cursed himself for not turning on the alarm. He'd seen a news report just the other day about the folly of having an alarm system you didn't turn on when you were home. Men especially thought they didn't need an alarm to protect a house they were in. Now, in the darkness with the sound of intruders coming up the stairs, Carl knew he would never make that mistake again.

His wife Barbara had woken up, disturbed by the commotion in her bed, and was taking out her earplugs when Carl told his daughter to get into the closet and stay there. She did as her father told her, rushing to the closet and hunching down below her mother's dresses, leaving the door open just a crack.

It was Carl Lapinsky's second mistake, and a fatal one. He owned a gun, but kept it in the closet, where he had just sent his daughter to hide.

He cursed himself for not thinking clearly, and wondered if he had time to rush to the closet and get the gun he kept in a box on the shelf. He would try, he had to. He made a gesture of fingers-to-lips, shhhh, to his wife, and swung his legs off the bed, about to dash to the closet when a man stepped into the doorway.

"What the fuck?" the man said. Clearly he had been surprised to find them there.

Carl turned and saw him: a squat man, thick with a barrel chest, but an intelligent face that registered, in that instant, curiosity as much as menace. Even in the darkness Carl could make out the man's appearance. He was wearing a blue or green flannel shirt, gray windbreaker, blue jeans, white sneakers and a belt with a ridiculously large silver buckle on it. One of those country-western type buckles you'd expect to find at a roadside honky-tonk holding up some fake cowboy's pants. It did not belong with the sneakers and windbreaker, and Carl was wondering why anyone would wear a belt buckle like that without boots when the man slid a gun from his jacket pocket and shot Carl in the head. Barbara was fully awake by then, staring at the scene as if she were still dreaming. She screamed for only a moment before the man shot her, too. Two people dead, just like that. Two people who weren't supposed to be there.

From inside the closet Emily heard sounds of footsteps rushing into the bedroom. More men, though she couldn't tell how many.

"What the fuck are you doing?" shrieked one man.

"They startled me," said the shooter. "What was I supposed to do?"

"Not kill them," said a third. "We don't kill people. We don't even carry guns. Why are you bringing a gun?"

"You're a moron," said the shooter. "We break into homes. Did it never occur to you that just such a thing might happen? And that we'd be the ones staring at the barrel of a shotgun? That's why I carry a gun, asshole."

"You're the asshole."

"No, you're the asshole. I just saved our lives!"

"By killing two people! That's life in prison! Jesus!"

Emily listened, terrified but alert. The man who had shot her parents sounded bright, an articulate murderer. She would remember his voice for the rest of her life.

"Where's the daughter?" said the second man. "They have a kid, you said. Where's the kid?"

"What difference does it make?" said the shooter. "Just grab what you can and get the hell out."

"I'm not grabbing anything," said the third man. "This is not cool, Frank, not cool at all. I'm outa here."

So off the third man ran, down the stairs and out the back door. Emily committed the killer's name to memory: Frank. Well-spoken, brutal, murderous Frank. Unconcerned with her whereabouts, for even if they found her, he would simply kill her as well.

"You running scared, too?" the man named Frank said to the second burglar. Getting no response, he said, "Just go through this room with me. There's jewels, I'm sure of it, money. Check the wall pictures, there might be a safe in back."

The two men began rummaging through her parents' room, opening drawers. There was a large jewelry box inside her mother's armoire, and she could hear him throwing it open, grabbing the jewelry inside. There was also a watch box where her father kept one of his prize possessions, an antique Waltham pocket watch his great-grandfather had owned. His great-grandfather had been a train conductor, and the watch had a steam engine engraved on it. He'd never had it appraised and considered its value to be sentimental, but the watch was authentic and, had he researched it, would have fetched several hundred dollars at the time. Frank had no idea of the watch's worth, but there was something about it that caught his eye, something that made him want to keep it, which is what he ultimately did and why he ultimately died.

Justice took its time, she thought, remembering the watch. Justice delayed was not justice denied, as the famous quote had it. Not at all. Justice delayed was justice perfected, savored like the taste of something one would only taste once.

The men might have found little Emily in the closet had a distant siren not spooked them. People intruding into other people's homes tend to be on edge, and when they heard the siren they glanced at each other, a wordless communication Emily did not see. They grabbed what few things they'd taken and fled down the stairs and out the door. She waited for what seemed hours, although it was only about fifteen minutes, then she crept out of the closet, walked to the phone on the nightstand and, standing numbly over her father's dead body, dialed 911.

Emily went to live with her mother's sister and her husband in Santa Barbara after "the tragedy," as everyone called it. She did not get along with her Aunt Susan, and was frightened by her Uncle Joseph, a man who was even more stern with his adopted daughter than he was with his own two. Emily always had the feeling living with them that she'd been thrust into their midst, taken in because, well, somebody had to, and that she was damaged goods. What they never knew—what no one else ever knew—was that she'd been in the closet and seen the cold-blooded murder of her parents. She believed the reason she has not told the police was because her life's mission had been set at the instant the first bullet flew; she would spend her life setting the scales back in balance, learning the skills she would need, from replacing her identity to firing a handgun with precision, to bring that circle to its fullness. She did not know when or how, but the time would come; she believed it as surely as religious people believed in God or their reward in an afterlife. Emily would prepare, remain alert, and wait with supreme patience for that fleeting opportunity, that chance of a lifetime, when the great wrong of her life could be righted. For that reason only she had told the police she'd been under her bed, in her own bedroom. For that reason only she had never told anyone about the gun she took from her father's closet when she was allowed back in the house to pack her things. The watch they knew about; its empty case was among the little evidence left behind by the killers. They'd not had enough time to take much more than jewelry and cash from her father's wallet and her mother's purse. And in exchange they had left nothing, no fingerprints, no hastily abandoned burglar's tools. All they'd left behind them was a trail that quickly went cold. But Emily knew: a man named Frank, her father's gun, and the watch no one would really think anything of. A few small things, but truly precious.

After graduating high school, Emily moved to St. Paul to live with her girlfriend at the time. Cassy was from Minneapolis and had met Emily through an ad in a small lesbian magazine. She was also twelve years older than Emily, who, at eighteen, was old enough to make her own decisions but not old enough to make wise ones. Against her aunt and uncle's wishes she packed up her used Mustang and drove to Minnesota, where she enrolled in the University of Minnesota's St. Paul campus and very quickly discovered that sometimes age mattered. Her relationship with Cassy only lasted a year, but Emily liked St. Paul; she enjoyed the distance of the place and the harshness of its winters, and she stayed there.

It was shortly afterward, on her twentieth birthday, she decided to disappear. She had no intention of moving, and it would be easy enough to tell the few friends she had that she was now someone else: changing one's name was not all that uncommon, and she had been telling people various versions of a made-up life since she'd moved to St. Paul. People did not want to hear that her parents had been shot in bed, it was definitely a downer, and the ones who did were beneath her contempt. That was how it came to be that very few people who knew Emily knew her past. She protected it from them, just as she protected her other secrets as she waited patiently to tell them to the only three people who mattered: three men who had intruded into her life and never left. For that, for privacy, for escape, for so many reasons, Emily Lapinksy became Bo Sweetzer. She didn't know where the name came from, only that it was on her lips one early morning as she awoke from a dream in which her father was standing over her and her mother was crying. "Emily," her father kept saying in the dream. He was disappointed in her. She didn't know how she knew that, or why he was disappointed, only that he was. "Emily," he said, shaking his head. She replied, "My name is Bo. My name is Bo." She awoke saying it, and just as surely added, "Bo Sweetzer." She was immediately convinced

her father had been disappointed because ten years had passed and no justice had been found. She would bring him peace, she knew then and there.
She would be Bo Sweetzer, and she would find a way to end it in the only
way it could be ended, even if it took her the rest of her life.

She dropped out of the University and started making jewelry, a pastime she'd had that she connected with the loss in her life. It became a passion, and, to her delight, her income. She had never been much for a 9-5
job and within a year she was running a business from a custom catalog.
Bo and Behold, jewelry made to order, quickly became a success, but never
a huge one. She didn't want the notoriety, nor the pressure of running a
business any bigger than could be managed from her apartment. Once the
internet came around she launched BoAndBeholdJewelry.com, and would
also sell her items on eBay and BidderSweet, online auction websites. It was
there, on BidderSweet, one Sunday afternoon as she was looking around,
that an alert showed up in her message box. She's had them set up on a
dozen sites to let her know when certain items she was interested in became
available. It had been a lot of work for nothing, sifting through hundreds
of ads for crap, some of them for treasure, but none of them turning up the
one thing she wanted. And then, that day, there it was: an antique watch for
sale. She looked at the photograph and couldn't believe her eyes. She knew
that watch very well, including the dent above the smoke rising from the
train's engine. She had caused that dent when her father had let baby Emily
hold the watch and she had promptly swung it, slamming it against her crib.
He had reminded her of it many times, as a way of saying, "See this? This
will always remind me of you as a baby. It's a great dent, I think, one of
those dents in life that means something."

The seller was an old man in Detroit by the name of Frank. Down on
his luck, as she imagined he had probably spent most of his criminal life.
But still an intelligent man, a man who knew enough about the value of a
watch to keep it. Desperate now, she knew, as he was selling it for a mere
$500, a third its current value. He either didn't know, or didn't care, and
she had to move quickly. She would not be the only one seeing it, so she
immediately emailed him from an anonymous account, one she had set

up for exactly this opportunity, explaining she ran a jewelry business and had a client looking for just such a watch. A wealthy client willing to pay $1000, cash. If that was agreeable to Frank from Detroit she would be there the following day. Yes, he wrote back, it was very agreeable, and he took the item down from the auction site. Bo smiled, something she did not do much, and she imagined her father coming to her soon in another dream, telling her she had done well.

She did not like losing herself in reverie. There was danger in the distraction of daydreaming—or in this case, late-night dreaming. She glanced at the clock: eleven forty-five p.m. She hadn't made any judgments yet of this Pride Lodge. She knew what history of the place she had read on its website and was aware the original owners had moved on, one to the hereafter and another to Florida. The only person she'd spoken to since arriving was the desk clerk, Ricki, who told her most people came the next day, Friday. All the better; she wanted to come in under the radar, to get herself into place so she could go unnoticed. She was not a killer, not really, and she had driven all this way (guns did not travel well by airplane) for just one purpose, to put an end to her late-night dreaming and her reveries and let her dead parents know that while little Emily had escaped, the men who did this had not.

She began unpacking the one suitcase she'd brought with her. She lifted out her father's gun, one she had practiced with a thousand times at a Minneapolis firing range and used in real-life, real-time, once in Detroit. It had served her well and she knew it as an extension of her hand. That's exactly how it had felt when she lifted it quickly and smoothly from her purse and aimed it at Frank Grandy. He had been so surprised, so flabbergasted. "You can take the watch. Take my money. I don't have much . . . "

"You don't remember me?" she had said.

He'd looked at her then, clearly not comprehending who she was.

"Oh," she said. "That's right. You never saw me. But I saw you. I was in the closet."

Then he knew. She could see it in his eyes as they widened and he whispered, "The little girl . . . "

"Yes," she said. "The little girl." After some brief negotiation in which he attempted to barter his life for information on his co-criminals, she shot him in the forehead. It hadn't felt good. It hadn't felt anything. She had not smiled. She had simply taken the watch from the case he had it in and left. It was the only thing the police reported stolen, and the very thing Sam Tatum read about that told him they had not escaped the past.

She wasn't sure if she would use the gun again. An ice pick had worked well in Los Angeles, and she may yet find a way to make it look like an accident. There were plenty of stairs here to fall down, a ravine or two to go tumbling into. Ways to die in nature as if nature were the cause. She put away her last pair of slacks, undressed, and slid beneath the covers of her double bed. She reached over and in the last gesture of a long day she turned off the night stand light.

CHAPTER 4

LONELY BLUE POOL

Kyle always beat the sunrise. He couldn't remember the last time he woke up and saw light outside. He thought it was a form of insomnia; while he had no trouble getting to sleep, his mind sometimes turned on at 3:00 or 4:00 a.m. and would not shut off again. He would try not to disturb Danny as he turned carefully from side to side, doing his best to remain still until the reasonable hour of 5:00, when he would slip out of bed, walk quietly into the kitchen and make his first cup of coffee. He'd used instant for many years but Danny had recently given him a Keurig single-serving machine for his birthday and Kyle had found a new love. So much that they now traveled with the cheapest version of the machines so Kyle could have one of a variety of his favorites wherever they went.

On this early morning Kyle lay on his back staring up at the ceiling. Their room had a picture window looking out on a hillside, and though it was still dark, Kyle could see the large tree outside Cabin 6 outlined against the slowly lightening sky. He was thinking of their life back in Manhattan and wondering if their cats, Smelly and Leonard, were nestled together in the empty space in bed where Kyle and Danny would normally be. The men slept entwined most nights, Kyle behind Danny, with a cat on each side. Smelly, Kyle's 6-year-old gray tiger, had been named as a kitten when he found her outside his Brooklyn apartment eating from a ripped trash bag. Whatever was in the bag had coated her fur, leaving her with a stench that gave her her name. She was just a tiny, scrawny thing then, a far cry from the 16 pound ball of love she'd become. Danny said she looked like a bowling ball with sticks for legs, and they both worried about her weight. Kyle was determined Smelly would not become diabetic, and after an annual visit to the vet he put her on low-calorie food with a fixed feeding schedule that, after six months, appeared to have failed. She'd lost a quarter pound.

A year after adopting Smelly he met Danny, who had been sharing his life with his three-year-old yellow tabby named Leonard. Leonard was as fit and lithe as a cat who'd spent his life outdoors, even though he had never ventured further out than the hallway. Danny adopted him from Spoiled Brats, a pet store on 49th Street that ran a cat shelter in the back. He had decided that summer he would never meet a man to spend his life with, and a cat was the next best thing. Maybe a better thing. He'd seen Leonard walking around the store trying to decide which of the customers should adopt him, and there Danny was, an obvious and easy mark. Leonard came up to him, just nine months old but already more confident than most humans will ever be. Now they were a family: two men, two cats, and a cursed aquarium where perfectly healthy fish went to die.

Kyle had lived in Brooklyn his thirty years in New York City. He had moved there from Chicago chasing a college sweetheart who had transferred to Columbia from the University of Illinois. David Grogan was his name, and he wanted to be a journalist. Columbia J-school, as it's called, was the top destination for anyone wanting to be a serious journalist. Or at least that's what David believed. Kyle had been studying psychology and English literature for no specific reason. He got his B.A., had no interest in either psychology or English literature, and didn't think twice about moving east with the man of his dreams. It was that love, in fact, that had prompted Kyle to come out to his parents. It had filled his heart to bursting and he had the need to declare it to the world, which wasn't something he thought could be done from a closet. His mother wasn't surprised or upset, and while she assured Kyle that his happiness was her only concern, she questioned the wisdom of moving to New York City. She didn't fight it, knowing Kyle would do what Kyle had set his mind to, but neither did she hide the bad feeling she had that youth was more at the bottom of it than love. Kyle's father simply remained as distant as he had always been with his only child. It wasn't so much that he didn't mind, as that he didn't care. For a man who had no other children, Bert Callahan had always been cool to his son. Kyle could never tell if it was because his father sensed something different about him, something he couldn't accept, or if he was simply one of those people who should never have had children. It made telling his father he was moving to New York City to follow a boyfriend a relief to them both.

Kyle soon learned that first loves are called that for a reason: they are not the last. He and David rented an apartment in the Carroll Gardens neighborhood of Brooklyn, and within six months David told him he was too young to give his life to someone; there was too much in the world to see (meaning, Kyle knew, too many men to sleep with) for him to be tied down at twenty-two, it just wouldn't be fair to Kyle. Yes, yes, Kyle said, thank you for thinking of me, I'll be moving out at the end of the month. He kept his promise. He also kept the friendship, and it was to Kyle David turned when his partner was dying from AIDS ten years later, and when David's mother passed away last spring. Their friendship had survived thirty years, and David had already been pegged as Kyle's best man when the time came. It was to Danny's credit that he wasn't jealous, that he understood time was the one thing of true value we can give to one another. He had welcomed David as part of their extended family and had even tried fixing him up a few times with men of their age who dined alone at Margaret's. Nothing had clicked so far, but Kyle and Danny were themselves proof that love did not discriminate by age.

Thirty years, Kyle thought suddenly, swinging his feet out of bed. Time to get a move on before it moves on! He was ready for his coffee.

Danny owned a two-bedroom co-op on the border of Gramercy Park and Murray Hill (also called Curry Hill for all the Indian restaurants on Lexington Avenue). He'd bought it with a loan from his parents twenty-five years ago. No mortgage, low maintenance, a second bedroom he occasionally used as an office, perfect for sharing with Kyle and one of the few pieces of furniture Kyle had kept when he moved in: his father's desk from Highland Park. It was an odd thing to ask for when Bert died and Sally Callahan decided to move to a condo on Chicago's Lake Shore Drive. Why he would want the desk of a man whose death he felt so little about was a mystery, but not one he was interested in exploring with a therapist. He simply asked for the desk and his mother gave it to him. It was pine with knots in the grain, deep sliding drawers and cigarette burns along the right side from when Kyle was a child and his father smoked. It fit perfectly into the spare room that became a shared office, in the apartment he moved into seven months after meeting Danny. His mother had not been surprised about that; Kyle still did what Kyle wanted to do, but Sally Callahan had no trepidation this time. She was as sure of this as Kyle was. Kyle gave up his apartment, gave away all the furniture since there was nowhere to put it in Danny's place, packed up Smelly and told her to get ready to meet her match, a yellow tabby named Leonard she would be sharing her life with, whether she liked it or not.

Kyle could see the sun beginning to rise, spilling early morning light across the landscape. He wanted to go for a walk to the Lodge soon, stopping on the way to see the empty blue pool. It was busy in the summer, a center of activity for Lodge guests, but emptied when the weather turned cold. The empty pool had provided Kyle with one of his best and most-loved photographs, one he called "Lonely Blue Pool." It had been an accident, really, one of those pictures he took as he strolled around with a camera slung over his neck, aiming and clicking at anything that might be an interesting shot. It was his method of capturing the surreptitious portrait, the off-guard expressions on people's faces, as well as some striking blurred photographs (he believed in the plasticity of art, the many ways in which it presents and the many ways a single instance of it can be viewed; he liked seeing people cock their heads at a picture trying to figure out not just what the image was, but how he captured it). The day he took the pool photo he'd been walking up the slight hill toward the pool and cabana, when he noticed it was empty and he quickly took several pictures. There were leaves collected at the bottom, gathered by wind and gravity into a brown patch, and there along the deep-end wall was a white ladder that Kyle had used himself to climb from the water last summer. It was happenstance, the luck of the shutter, and the picture had turned out so lovely many people thought it was a painting. But no, it was just Kyle taking one of the thousands of photographs he took. It was one of the first he put on his Tumblr blog, and two years later he'd had two dozen requests for it. He was so flattered by people liking his pictures and calling them his "work" that he didn't charge them—he would simply sign them in the corner and ship them off, asking the recipients to pay postage. But it had been his first inkling that someday, maybe, he could think of taking himself seriously.

Danny wouldn't be awake for another hour. He was an afternoon and evening person, while Kyle had his energy, ideas and focus in the morning. It was their routine that Kyle would get quietly out of bed and have his coffee. At home in their apartment he would leave the bedroom, pulling the door almost closed behind him (but never fully, as the cats did not like closed doors and would either scratch at them or cry all night until someone obeyed them and opened the damn door). He would head to their office room with a second cup of coffee and start in at his computer, either uploading pictures to his blog or sifting another two dozen he'd taken recently, or just reading websites and newspapers. He was also a news junkie, having become more so since he got into the business as Imogene's assistant.

There was no job to get up and go to when they traveled and Kyle had never been someone who could just lie in bed with his mind racing, so he would usually have a primer cup of coffee in the room, then slip out and head to a coffee shop downstairs or across the street from whatever hotel they were in. Here at Pride Lodge he could sit outside in one of the old wooden chairs that lined the walkway in front of the cabins, or he could head up to the Lodge and help himself to one of the newspapers they kept around and a cup of coffee they put out at 6:00 a.m.

This Friday he pulled on his khaki slacks and a sweatshirt, slung his camera around his neck, grabbed his smartphone (he could read his emails before Danny saw him and told him to stop) and headed up the road to the Lodge, by way of the pool.

That was when he saw the commotion. A police cruiser and what looked like an unmarked sedan were parked in the front driveway. Behind them was an ambulance that had made no noise, which struck Kyle as odd until he learned why, and a small crowd had gathered around the deep end of the pool. He hurried up the grass hill to the poolside, having the presence of mind to quickly slip off the lens cap and take several photos as he climbed toward the crowd. Ricki was already there; he may have spent the night at the Lodge, which he did sometimes when they had a busy weekend coming. Sid and Dylan were standing near the edge at the deep end, Dylan with his face buried in Sid's chest, Sid looking down into the pool. They both appeared to have just gotten up. Dylan's hair was disheveled and Sid's eyes looked red from sleep. Both men wore jeans, but Sid wore a pajama top under his black leather jacket. Two women Kyle didn't recognize were standing off to the side, one of them texting furiously on her phone. Or maybe she was tweeting whatever it was they'd witnessed. Nothing is private anymore, Kyle thought as he reached the top of the hill and headed toward them.

As the pool came fully into view Kyle looked down into it and stopped, his breath freezing in his chest. There at the bottom of the lonely blue pool, his neck bent so parallel to his shoulders it looked like a stalk that had been broken off, was the body of Teddy Pembroke. He was wearing blue jeans faded nearly white and a blue dress shirt. His tennis shoes were red, his socks black, and his hair had been recently died jet black, no doubt at Happy's suggestion. No 50-year-old man has jet black hair with a bald spot in back and a rapidly receding hairline in front. His horn-rimmed glasses he'd been so fond of now that they'd come back in fashion lay shattered a few inches from his face. His left arm was bent at the elbow, the hand nearly to his lips as if he had suddenly thought of something the instant he died, and there, just a few inches from it, a broken martini glass.

Teddy was the general handyman for Pride Lodge and had held different jobs there over the years. At one point he'd run the Karaoke bar, and he had done a year's stint as the desk manager when Ricki had to go home to Memphis to take care of his ailing mother. For the past two years he had been helping Sid and Dylan upgrade the property, re-carpet the rooms, fix the many little things that had run down over the twenty-five years Pucky and Stu had the place. He had also been Kyle's friend and reached out to him the previous year when he needed to talk to someone about his problems.

"You take a lot of pictures, Kyle," Teddy had said, one afternoon when they were alone in the Lodge's great room.

"I don't know why," Kyle replied. "I think I see the world in images. Even videos, which I don't much care for, are just thousands of single images flashing in front of you."

"Do you ever talk to them?"

"Pardon?"

"The people you take pictures of. I've seen you. Very sly, the way you do that."

Kyle had blushed, having never been caught red handed before—or in this case red faced.

"Well, no, I don't talk to them," Kyle said, waving Teddy over to the large couch in front of the bay window. Teddy came over and sat down, putting his coffee cup on a coaster on the side stand.

"The point of taking pictures of people when they don't know it, is that they don't know it," Kyle said.

"Yeah, but I bet if you asked them they'd say yes anyway. And then you could have a conversation, get to know them a little. The way you do it, you only ever know what you imagine."

Kyle saw Teddy in a different light after that. Not that he had ever assumed Teddy wasn't a man of substance, only that he hadn't considered him the potential friend he became. They were never especially close; that's hard to do when Kyle and Danny lived in Manhattan and Teddy lived at Pride Lodge. They only saw each other the few times a year when the couple stayed there, but they emailed and sometimes they spoke on the phone, as they had just two nights before when Teddy told him he would be leaving the Lodge soon but didn't want to discuss it on the phone.

Kyle walked over to the two women who had moved away from the pool's edge. The one busy thumbing the news of a dead body in a pool to her hundreds of Twitter followers didn't look up. She was squat, with a distinctly wide bottom in stone-washed jeans a dark green hoody. Her hair was short, red and curly, and she wore a pair of pink cat-eye glasses, the most striking thing about her. The taller woman had a more evolved sense of style, with navy slacks, a turquoise blouse and a gray p-coat. She stood tall, her posture impeccable, and Kyle pegged her as a professional woman, someone aware of her appearance at all but the least guarded moments. She did not wear glasses, as so many of the Lodge guests did (it went with the demographic), and her hair was just going gray, most of it raven's black and tied loosely back. She nodded at Kyle and extended her hand.

"Eileen," she said, shaking hands. "That's Maggie. Don't mind her, she thinks she's a citizen journalist. Or sixteen, I'm never sure."

Maggie seemed unaware that her companion was talking to anyone, or that Kyle had come into their presence.

"What happened?" Kyle said. "I didn't hear an ambulance."

"There wasn't a life to save, that's my guess," said Eileen. "I mean, he's dead, you can tell that."

Kyle looked down into the pool and just then noticed a woman—a detective, he presumed—kneeling by the body as one paramedic climbed down the pool ladder while a second eased a gurney along from the shallow end.

"It's horrible," Dylan said, coming over to them.

"You saw it?" Kyle asked.

"Nobody saw it! Sid was making his morning rounds and found him. I'm guessing he was drinking and slipped. I kept telling him to stop, you have to stop, Teddy, I just had a feeling it would end badly for him."

"Death by Appletini," said Eileen.

"I like that!" blurted Maggie, momentarily aware of her surroundings, then tweeting what she'd just heard.

Dylan looked at him and discreetly shook his head: this was not something to discuss further in front of Lodge guests. The death alone might mean a change in plans. He had to think, he had to talk to Sid and see what they should do.

Kyle watched as the detective stepped away from the body and allowed the paramedics to set up their gurney and go about removing poor Teddy from the bottom of the pool. He realized suddenly that the scene would soon change as the EMT workers removed the body; evidence that was there now might be gone or contaminated simply by being handled. He hurried over to the edge of the pool, aimed his camera down into it with a quick adjustment of the zoom, and took a half dozen photographs in rapid succession, moving very slightly each time to create, once he had the pictures in front of him, a wide, detailed view of the scene in the pool. As he was about to take a shot of Teddy's body being moved to a stretcher, he felt a hand on his shoulder, pulling his arm away from the camera.

"No photographs," said a cop, the one Kyle had not noticed in the turmoil. "You from the news?"

Kyle turned to the officer. He was older and heavy, probably not far from retirement, and Kyle wondered why he would still be a patrol cop. You didn't usually see men of his age out from behind desks. His patrol car identified him as being from the New Hope Police Department. His hair was a gray crew-cut, and his nose was red and pitted as if he'd had a few too many Appletinis himself over the years.

"No," said Kyle. "I'm not in the media. I'm staying here at the Lodge. I just take pictures."

"Well not today, not here," said the cop. And then, to all of them, "Don't go far. Detective Sikorsky is going to want to speak to everyone."

"Is this a murder?" asked Maggie, hoping for something juicy to share on her social networks.

"It's not for anyone to say," the cop said, "but frankly it looks like too many drinks and a step in the wrong direction."

This, Kyle knew, was not the case. At least, he was as sure of it as he could be, given Teddy's history and the personal things he had shared with Kyle over the last year. Kyle hurried away from the group, back down the hill to Cabin 6 to get Danny out of bed and tell him what was happening. The lonely blue pool wasn't lonely anymore.

CHAPTER 5

ROOM 202

The woman whose name was once Emily watched the scene play out poolside from her second-floor window. The sound of the ambulance and police arriving had woken her fully up, even though no sirens had blared. Before then she'd been lying in bed in a half-dream state, remembering the shock on the man's face in Detroit and how sorry he had professed to be, so very sorry for what he believed had been a momentary lapse in judgment. It seemed he considered killing her parents while she cowered in a closet a bad split decision. So convinced was he of his own powers of persuasion that he readily gave up the names of the other two men, and while not all three had stayed in contact the connection had never been completely lost. Tracing one to the other would not be difficult and he would in fact be happy to help her, something for which he would need to be alive. She thanked him for the offer and shot him in the head.

"Oh," she said to his corpse on the couch, his head thrown back with a bullet hole above the left eye, as she slipped her father's watch into her pocket, "I kept the gun, too."

She wished she could say that killing a man was the last thing she could imagine herself doing, but it was the one thing she had imagined every day for thirty years. She had fantasized it, prepared for it, and now, in a shabby apartment in a dilapidated city, she had done it. The only thing that surprised her as she collected her things and wiped down what few fingerprints she may have left, was how plain it felt, how anticlimactic. It was, she realized sadly, as cool and unemotional as it must have been for the man she'd just killed to murder her parents. At least she knew now she could do it, and would do it twice more.

She shook off the memories and made a cup of coffee with the machine in her room, then stood by the window and watched the commotion at the pool, standing to the side so no one looking up would see her. She had heard no argument outside the night before or in the pre-dawn, no noise at all, and she wondered how the man managed to die at the bottom of the empty pool without making a sound. She guessed it would be seen as an accident, but she had her doubts about that. It was so clean and neat, with a feeling of deliberateness about it. Could it possibly have something to do with her mission here? Might the hunted be doing some hunting himself? If that was the case, then he knew about his old friends in Detroit and Los Angeles and he was making moves of his own. Good, she thought, blowing on the hot coffee. Let him worry. Worried men make mistakes.

She set her cup on the dresser top and headed to the closet, taking out her clothes for the day, meditating on what an interesting weekend it was going to be.

CHAPTER 6

CABIN 6

As much as Danny prodded Kyle to leave Imogene and the job behind, he was guilty of always being on duty himself, even if it meant only *thinking* about the job. He sat at the small round table provided in each room, sipped his own single-serving cup of coffee and reviewed plans for a very special private luncheon at Margaret's Passion the following Wednesday. Margaret was turning 80 and a select who's-who of city politics, entertainment and culture were on the guest list. There would be toasts from Broadway legends as well as the mayor, and the cake was being made by culinary icon Billy Cervette himself, repaying the loyalty he'd had for Margaret since she gave him his start twenty years ago. The list was short—only sixty people—and already there had been rumblings of displeasure from the names left off. Each of them would receive a sincere apology from Margaret, written and sent out by Danny, explaining that it was a space issue, no offense was intended. Margaret's Passion had been famous for years for how difficult it could be to get into, since it only had ten tables of four and ten of two: the math was easy enough, and there was simply no way to accommodate more, as much as she wished there had been since each and every one meant so very much to her. Danny had crafted the apology with exceeding care; it did not do to offend anyone at any point in their career, since a year from now they could be nominated for a Tony or taking an oath of office.

He'd just finished his coffee when Kyle came into the cabin, his manner flustered and urgent.

"He's dead," Kyle said, taking the camera from around his neck and dropping it onto the bed.

"Who's dead?" asked Danny. "What are you talking about?"

Kyle crossed around the bed and sat on the corner nearest to Danny.

"I should have called him last night. He wasn't right, something was going on, he told me that. Why didn't I just pick up the phone and call?"

"Is this Teddy you're talking about? What do you mean, he's dead?"

Kyle stared out the window into the woods beyond. He felt as if he were still trying to wake up, that the morning's events had been a dream and if he just closed his eyes tightly enough he would open them to a different reality, one in which he and Danny were having their usual weekend at Pride Lodge and death was no part of it.

"Yes, Teddy," Kyle said. "At the bottom of the pool."

"Drowned?!"

"No! There's no water in it this time of year, they empty it for the winter."

Danny imagined poor Teddy falling twelve feet into an empty concrete pool. "That's terrible."

"It wasn't an accident," Kyle declared, standing up suddenly and going to the coffee machine. "That's what they'll say, but I don't believe it."

"You're getting way ahead of things," Danny said. "Why would you think it wasn't an accident?"

"Because of the martini glass," Kyle said. He held his camera out and scanned the photographs he'd just taken at the pool until he found the one that struck him. There at the bottom of the pool, near the drain that had collected leaves, was the broken glass. He hadn't realized what was off about it until he was on his way back to the cabin. "Teddy didn't drink anymore, and he never drank martinis. He was a bourbon man, Danny. If he was going to take a dive off the wagon, he would have done it with something he liked drinking. It just proves that he didn't!"

"Oh," said Danny. He knew about Teddy's struggles with drinking and hated to disillusion Kyle.

"He stopped drinking six months ago," Kyle continued, "precisely because of this sort of thing. He didn't want to die an alcoholic's death. Drunk behind the wheel of a car, killed by someone he picked a fight with in a blackout . . . dead at the bottom of an empty swimming pool. He saw it coming if he didn't stop. Those were his exact words to me. 'I see it coming, Kyle, and it's ugly. I've had enough ugly in my life, I don't want it to end that way.'"

Danny walked over to Kyle and gently put his hand on his shoulder. "I don't want to disappoint you . . ."

Kyle knew what Danny was going to say and stopped him. "He did not relapse, Danny, I know he didn't. He had support, he had his AA meetings, and when he called me the other day about coming here he was still sober. I even asked him, Danny. I said, 'You're not going to drink over this, whatever it is, right?' No, no, he was sure of it, he needed his wits about him, he said. I know he didn't drink."

"Can you at least allow for the possibility?" Danny said carefully. "Maybe that was the big news he had and he couldn't bear to tell you on the phone." He saw the hurt in Kyle's expression and wished he didn't have to say this. "I never had anything against Teddy. I didn't know him, and you know I don't make judgments about people I don't know. But he was an alcoholic, Kyle."

It was true. Not only did everyone know Teddy from his years at the Lodge, but they all knew Teddy was a drunk. He would get his work done well enough, and the man was universally liked, but there was also an element of pity to how people felt about him. He most often greeted guests with a telltale whiff of bourbon on his breath, and too many times he'd been found passed out on one of the sofas in the Lodge's great room or downstairs in one of the bar's green leather booths. Then, after reaching out to Kyle and confronting his problem, he started to get sober. It took time, with a few false starts, but Teddy had been abstinent for six months when he was found dead that morning. Kyle was convinced of it. Teddy had turned a crucial corner and there was no way in hell he was going to end his life with a broken neck and a shattered martini glass next to him, unless someone else ended it for him.

"I don't really want to go over this again," Kyle said. "I know you didn't like him calling me in the middle of the night—"

"He should have been calling his AA friends at that hour. His sponsor, whatever. You're not part of that circle."

"I was his friend. That was enough. At least until last night."

"This is not your fault," Danny said. "It was late, too late to return anyone's phone call, they wouldn't expect it."

"No one but Teddy."

"Listen, if you want to beat yourself up over this you can, it's one of your favorite pastimes, but you did not have any part in Teddy's death simply because you didn't call him back last night."

"Fine, fine," Kyle said. "We should get ready and go."

"Where?" asked Danny, thinking for a moment that Kyle wanted to check out and return to Manhattan.

"Up to the Lodge. There's a detective up there. She wants to talk to the guests and staff, anyone who was here when it happened."

"They know when it happened?"

"It happened," Kyle said, taking his coffee cup and heading toward the bathroom, "when Teddy needed someone most and no one was there."

Danny sighed and let it go as Kyle closed the bathroom door behind him. He knew there was no changing Kyle's mind once he had decided to believe something against all evidence—in this case that he could have prevented Teddy's death with a phone call. He knew, too, that Kyle would not stop chewing on this bone until he got to the very marrow of it.

Danny put away the seating chart and menu for Margaret's 80th birthday luncheon and set about preparing for what he suspected was going to be a very long weekend.

CHAPTER 7

DETECTIVE SIKORSKY

Detective Linda Sikorsky was the only detective on the New Hope police force. The town's population was a mere 2,525 in the latest census, though it was a well known and popular tourist destination (some who lived there would say trap), and the actual number of bodies in town increased several fold on warm sunny days. Linda had endured the initial resentment from her colleagues after being promoted into the position two years earlier, following the retirement of the city's last detective. A few of the others on the force didn't take to the idea of a less senior member of their ranks stepping into a job they thought should go to one of them; add to that some unspoken resentment over the job going to a woman and she had her challenges, to say the least. No one dared say aloud that her gender played a role in any opposition to her, but Linda Sikorsky was no fool. She had a lifetime of experience as a woman in a world that in many ways was still a man's and knew well the subtle discrimination that went on, the doubts and silent skepticism men had about their female colleagues, especially their female superiors.

Some things never change, she thought, finishing notes from her last interview with the desk clerk Ricki . . . what was his last name, she wondered, flipping back through her notepad . . . Hernandez. Ricki Hernandez. Skittish man, she thought, but not in a guilty way. More hyper than anxious, a subtle but distinct difference. It probably made him good at his various jobs. It must take a tremendous amount of energy, she thought, to be a desk clerk during the day in a busy hotel, or resort, or whatever they called the place, and a restaurant hostess at night. He had explained to her that he was not a drag queen, necessarily, and not transgender or transsexual. He had leaned over and whispered, glancing around to make sure no one could hear him, "I'm a transvestite. I know I'm not supposed to say that, it's very politically incorrect these days, but I like the word. It comes from vestments, clothes, you see. Trans-clothes. It's elegant, really, I don't know why people think it's some kind of bad word." He explained that he liked the particular character he'd made up as the hostess, also conveniently named Ricki. He had invented her, he said, after the woman who used to do the job went ex-gay and just stopped showing up for work. (He knew about the ex-gay part because she had gone on to write a book and cash in as a motivational speaker for self-hating gay people, despite continued sightings of her at Manhattan's Wild Orchid and other well-known lesbian hotspots on the East Coast.) Her name was Leslie and she went by LaLa until she was saved from the homosexual lifestyle and went on a book tour. One afternoon Leslie/LaLa resigned with an angry phone call to Pucky, after not having been to work for a week, and warned him of the danger to his soul. He thanked her and asked Ricki to fill in at the restaurant. Ricki had the idea then and there to do the job as a hostess and had been doing it ever since.

Linda Sikorsky was tall, nearly six feet in flat shoes (another reason some of the men at the precinct had been intimidated by her). She was also, as her grandmother would say, a big-boned gal. She was a formidable foe to any criminal who thought New Hope and its citizens were easy marks. She wore minimal makeup, having always thought it must have been invented by men as a form of torture; her hair was dark blonde and had once been long, but she'd learned to keep it short in police work—one less thing for a bad guy to grab hold of. She wore glasses, but only for reading, and she pushed them up on her nose as Kyle walked over and took the seat across from her.

She'd been interviewing guests and staff at an out of the way table in the restaurant she had chosen strategically for its window view of the pool below. She wanted to gauge the reactions, subtle or obvious, of people who sat across from her and could see where the death had taken place. A lot could be learned from how some averted their gaze, or how hard they tried not to. Normally the restaurant would be serving breakfast, but Dylan had told the twins Austin and Dallas, who had both worked at Pride Lodge since their days of filling in for summer work, to offer people a continental breakfast in the great room. Now in their mid-twenties, their youth was less a novelty than the fact they were identical twins, providing ornamentation as much as table service.

"Please, have a seat," she said to Kyle, motioning to the chair opposite her at the small table for two. She did not stand or offer her hand. "And you would be?"

"I'm not sure who I would be," Kyle said dryly, "but I am Kyle Callahan."

She smiled so slightly Kyle wasn't sure she had.

"Not the best view," he said, nodding at the window and the pool below. He had brought his camera with him and set it on the table. "It's only been an hour and a half since they took poor Teddy away. Death by shove? Assisted falling?"

"Well, I'm not convinced there's a lot going on here. A man drinks too much near an empty pool . . ."

"It wasn't an accident," he said, and he motioned for Dallas, who had been standing near the entry trying to eavesdrop. "Could I get some coffee?" And to Sikorsky, "Do you mind?"

"Not at all. Then he'll be free to leave the room," she said, tapping her ear to indicate the young man had been listening in.

Dallas scurried away to fetch Kyle's coffee. Kyle wanted to get a good look at this detective, scan her, so to speak, and see what conclusions he might draw, but she wouldn't look down or away. He quickly experienced her unnerving habit of looking directly at him. He assumed she did this with everyone and that it was some kind of interrogation technique meant to unsettle the people she spoke to.

"Mr. Callahan," she said, "why are you so sure this wasn't an accident? Everyone else I've spoken to, including some guests whom you would think didn't know things this personal, has told me he was a drinker. A lush."

"An alcoholic. 'Lush' belongs in the lyrics of a song, not as something to call another person. Teddy was a good man, and he had turned his life around this past year. Well, six months, actually, that's how long he'd been sober. He went in and out of Alcoholics Anonymous for a few months before that."

Linda was not unkind. On the other hand, she was too world-wise and experienced to let emotion and attachment influence her critical thinking.

"People relapse, Mr. Callahan," she said as gently as possible. Clearly this man had been friends with the dead man, and she did consider it an accident at this point, having discovered neither evidence nor motive to think otherwise.

Dallas came gliding up with Kyle's coffee, ending their conversation just long enough for Kyle to nod his thanks and wait for Dallas to head away. When the young man tried to take up his position by the door, Kyle waved at him to keep going, completely out of the restaurant.

"Teddy didn't relapse," he said, leaning in as if Dallas might still be able to hear them. "I know he didn't. We spoke every couple of weeks. He called me just a few days ago very disturbed, saying he was leaving Pride Lodge."

"Maybe he was upset about breaking up with—" and she quickly referenced the notes she'd been taking from interviews—"Happy Corcoran."

Kyle studied her a moment. "I just don't believe Teddy would go over the deep end about Happy. He knew the odds. Teddy was fifty, Happy's just a kid."

"Twenty-five, I believe," she said. "That makes him an adult. What other people think of a twenty-five-year-old being involved with a man twice his age is irrelevant. I was told by more than one person that Happy, whose real name was Happy, by the way, took a liking to Teddy Pembroke not long after he started working here, as a bar back I think."

"Yes, a bar back."

"It sounds more like a kid's summer job to me, but it became a permanent one. Whether their affair was on the rocks or not, I don't know. I do know that Happy has not been seen for three days."

"Surely there's no connection," Kyle said, sounding uncertain.

"We'll have a better idea of that when Happy shows up," said Linda. "Until then I think we're about through here."

"But you haven't asked me anything."

"I don't think you have much to tell me, Mr. Callahan."

"Kyle. And I may not have much to tell you, if you consider a distress message from a dead man last night 'nothing.' He texted me, he was getting frantic. If that's nothing, fine then, but I do have something to *show* you."

Kyle picked up his camera, held it out for the detective to see the photographs he'd taken, and showed her the zoom-in of the martini glass."

"And?" she said, unimpressed with the evidence. "Are you suggesting this was a murder weapon, a martini glass?

"Yes, and no. It wasn't used to kill him, but it tells me somebody did. You see, Detective, this 'lush' didn't drink martinis. I doubt he'd ever had one in his life. He was a bourbon and whiskey kind of man. Whoever pushed him into the bottom of the pool obviously didn't think anyone would notice and threw the glass in as misdirection."

"I'm trying to be fair here," she said, handing him back the camera. "I've known alcoholics, my uncle among them, who would drink Listerine to get high if nothing else was around. I just can't see this as anything significant. Maybe he had bourbon in a martini glass, maybe that was the only glass on hand when he took it. Did that occur to you?"

It had not occurred to him and Kyle blushed, feeling exposed. He didn't for a moment think Teddy, a creature of habit like everyone else, would grab a martini glass when he'd been drinking from tumblers for thirty years. She was right, though; all he had were strong suspicions that would not go away as easily as this detective was dismissing them.

"I'm a detective, not a guest here," she said, deliberately softening her tone. "You were friends with Mr. Pembroke, who by all accounts had a serious drinking problem. From the looks of things he fell off the wagon and into an empty swimming pool. I'm sorry your friend is dead, but I've got nothing here to say this was anything but a tragic accident."

"I've told you it wasn't."

"That's not how these things work," she said, closing her notebook and making it clear she was about to finish up and leave. "Aside from his boyfriend taking off, which is likely what happened with this Happy, nothing indicates foul play. It's a terrible, lonely way to die, although I'd guess it was instantaneous."

Kyle had noticed throughout their conversation how nice she seemed, despite keeping a professional distance. He thought, incongruously, that he would like to meet her under different circumstance, to speak to her and photograph her.

"That's it?" he said. "You're just going to call it a day, case closed?"

"Yes and no," she said, standing from the table. "I'll be heading out now, but I won't close the case, not yet. The medical examiner needs to determine the cause of death. If it's anything other than from the fall . . . say, drowning in an empty pool . . . that's another story. Even if it is the fall, if some new information comes up, the boyfriend confesses or we find another body, then that's a different ballgame. As mundane as it sounds, an intoxicated fall into a swimming pool may be the final explanation as well as the simplest one, we'll have to wait and see."

Detective Linda Sikorsky then gathered her notebook and pen, about to leave the resort she had driven past many times but never been to. "By the way," she said, as if a thought had just occurred to her. "How much do you suppose a place like this costs? To buy, I mean."

Kyle thought it was an odd question and wondered if she might be looking for an investment opportunity at a most inappropriate time.

"I've never bought property, I wouldn't have any idea. Dylan and Sid could tell you, they bought it two years ago. Maybe a couple million?"

"Around that," she said, as if she had the figure in mind all along. "Anyway, thank you," and this time she reached out to shake his hand. "Enjoy your stay."

She left him sitting at the table with his coffee and his thoughts. Her parting words, "enjoy your stay," seemed off the mark, given the circumstances, but the situation was awkward all around. Everything about the morning had been either awful, confusing or awkward. What does one say at the end of a brief police interrogation that could hardly be called an interview? And now, the weekend was ahead of them. The ultimate in awkward: a man had died here, in the pool just below the window Kyle was looking out now. Someone known and loved by all (although, if Kyle's instinct was correct, seriously un-loved by someone). What would Sid and Dylan do? Would they send everyone home? Would they cover the front porch in a black mourning sash, or lower the rainbow flag to half-mast? What would they tell people? Surely they *would* tell people, surely they would cancel the Halloween festivities in honor of Teddy? The one thing Kyle knew for certain was that he and Danny would not be leaving for the City. They would stay here as planned, and Kyle would not rest until he could prove to others what he knew for himself: Teddy Pembroke had been murdered.

CHAPTER 8

ROOM 202

Bo Sweetzer had wondered about the detective during their interview. Linda Sikorsky was a looker by anyone's standards, what might have been referred to as Amazonian in less politically self-conscious times. Bo had tried to drop hints, mentioning a local lesbian hangout she'd read about in the New Hope Gay Guide. There had been no reaction from Sikorsky, no telltale glance. Maybe people were so much more open now that code between gay people was a lost language. Or, more likely, Sikorsky was straight and didn't know she was being tested. She acknowledged having heard of the bar but never having been there, and she suggested to Bo that an inquiry at the front desk would be more informative. No nonsense, that one, Bo thought, standing at her window and watching the unmarked car drive away.

She had never had a real relationship, including the one that had gotten her from California to Minnesota. That had been puppy love with fangs and had finished the job of hardening her heart. She knew from a few years of therapy in her twenties that her inability to feel was a direct consequence of the trauma she'd experienced watching her parents killed in cold blood. Not the least of it was survivor's guilt: why should she be allowed to go on living when her parents had been brutally murdered? Indeed, she wondered, turning from the window and heading to the clothes closet, exactly who would have allowed it or disallowed it? God? She snorted derisively at the thought. She did not believe in God and had little use for those who did. God had ceased to exist for little Emily the moment that trigger was pulled and she glimpsed her father flying back on the bed. God went silent at the sound of her mother's sudden scream, cut short by a second gunshot. God was for fools and cowards, and she was neither.

She was looking forward to seeing more of this Pride Lodge, of smiling and chatting and blending in as she wove her way into the tapestry of the place. Most of the women here were in pairs, she'd already noticed that. Pairs or groups. It might be the only thing that set her apart: she was a woman alone, a solitary assassin (again she smiled at the word) with only one objective. When she had accomplished that, the mission would be over. There were no other names on her hit list. She had no grudge toward anyone who did not deserve her vengeance, and only three men fit that description. Three men who had broken into her home when she was just ten years old and robbed her of any semblance of a normal life; three men who would pay with their lives. It was that simple, that necessary.

She chose a beige cotton blouse appropriate for the fall weather, and a light gray sweater that would suffice if she decided to walk the property—which she surely would, wanting to refine her plans, to identify places and opportunities. Jeans and black penny loafers finished the outfit, making her look like most of the other women here, and the men, too. Casual wear was like that nowadays, very little gender difference, and that was fine with her. She wanted to be just another flower against the flowered wallpaper.

She laid her clothes on the bed and padded barefoot into the bathroom to get ready for the day. She had completed her interview with the intriguing Detective Sikorsky in the same clothes she'd arrived in the night before; she hadn't expected to be interviewed at all and had not gotten ready before Ricki, the desk clerk, knocked on her door to tell her the detective wanted to speak to everyone who was at the Lodge that morning.

"Do I have time to shower and change?" she'd asked, not opening the door wide enough for Ricki to enter or even get a good view.

"I can't say that," he'd said, clearly wanting to move on to the next guest.

Rather than risk losing her turn in line, if there was one, she had simply slipped on her slacks and windbreaker and headed downstairs. It had been a smart move, as she found herself immediately sitting across from Linda Sikorsky, wondering if, had circumstances been completely different, she might ask the woman out.

The killer and the cop. The thought amused her, even as it reminded her of her essential loneliness. She sighed at life's absurdities, the contrast often found between what was and what one wished could be, and she stepped into the shower.

CHAPTER 9

THE SHOW GOES ON

Sid and Dylan both insisted it's what Teddy would want, that canceling the Halloween party and sending the guests home would only make a tragic situation worse.

"We don't even have to tell people," Dylan had said when the two of them were discussing it alone in their suite.

"Excuse me?" Sid had replied, startled at the suggestion they hide Teddy's death. "You honestly think no one who was here this morning is going to talk about it?"

"No, no," said Dylan. "I know they will, they've probably already got it on their Facebook pages. I just mean we don't have to make a signature issue of it. Teddy wouldn't want that any more than he would want us cancelling. It just draws attention to how he died . . . the booze, I mean."

The two Lodge owners then met with the staff mid-morning and everyone agreed the show would go on. They would not refuse to discuss Teddy's death, and they certainly wouldn't pretend that nothing had happened, but they would leave it to anyone arriving to ask about it or wonder where Teddy was. The guests would make sure they knew anyway. There was nothing they could do to keep them from talking. But they would carry on. This was Teddy's favorite weekend at the Lodge, and to cancel it all, to hang the place in black bunting or some such thing, would only bind the annual weekend to his passing.

"Maybe they're right," Danny said, sipping a hot chocolate as he sat in one of the great room's overstuffed chairs. There were two of them, both a soft, sinking beige, with a matching couch given more color by a large green plaid sham thrown over its back. An empty brown recliner faced the television mounted high in a corner.

Kyle was sitting next to Danny, the chairs angled slightly to face each other, as he watched more guests check in. He had been doing his usual surreptitious picture-taking, the camera at chest angle so no one looking would know he was taking their photograph, the zoom set just right for getting snapshots of incoming guests at the front desk.

"Yes and no," Kyle said, just then clicking the shutter for a shot of two middle-aged men checking in. Kyle didn't know them, but judged from their easy way with each other they were a couple. "I mean, it's kind of unnerving. It's not even noon and everything's back to normal, if you don't count a death, interviews with a homicide detective and a staff meeting to see if they should close the place down."

"Teddy wouldn't want that."

"Does anyone really know what Teddy would want? Maybe it's Sid and Dylan who don't want to lose the money."

"That's cold."

"And having a Halloween party after the death of someone who's worked here for fifteen years isn't?"

"Not the way they see it," Danny said. "Not the way most of the people here are going to see it."

"Right. The show must go on."

"Why are you being like this?" asked Danny. He didn't like it when Kyle was surly, and while the morning's events were more than unsettling, there was nothing anyone could do about it, no way to bring Teddy Pembroke back from the dead.

"I'm being like this because my friend is dead and everyone thinks he took a drunken fall and I don't believe it for an instant."

"Leave that to the police."

"She thinks he fell, too! And if it were true—which it's not—it only makes the whole thing more unseemly. Oh, let's have a party so everyone can get drunk and raise a toast to poor drunken Teddy, poor dead Teddy, the lush at the bottom of the pool."

"We could just leave, you know. We'll check out, tell them it's not for us, and be back to the City by mid-afternoon. Smelly and Leonard would be thrilled. She's gotten too fat, Smelly has, have you noticed?"

"She's always been fat. But fatter, yes, we'll have to watch that. Cats get diabetes just like people. And no, I don't want to check out."

Kyle turned and angled the camera for another quick shot, this one of Diane Haley and her girlfriend, just arrived in an Escalade Kyle had watched them park in the side lot. Diane was in her mid-40s, tall and on the butch side with a platinum crew cut and an impeccable turquoise pantsuit. Over-dressed, but then Diane always was. She owned a very successful hair salon in Princeton called Diane's, of course. You couldn't step through the door for less than $200. She'd been coming to Pride Lodge for years and, Kyle noticed, had managed to stay with the same woman for two of them. Her girlfriend, Cecelia-something, was what used to be termed a lipstick lesbian. Just a few years younger than Diane, she still looked like the high-priced runway model she once was. This was a pair who could not enter a room unnoticed.

"We're staying," said Kyle, clicking the photo and waving as Cecelia instinctively turned toward him at the sound of a camera. "I'll leave when I know the truth."

At that Kyle shifted in his chair and stared out the window. More people would be coming. Linus Hern, Danny's nemesis in the restaurant business. Linus's favorite person was Linus. He amused himself, entertained himself, engaged himself in intellectual gamesmanship, and thought nothing of saying that Margaret's Passion was on its last table leg, so to speak. Linus had started and sold a string of restaurants, none of them remarkable, all of them profitable enough at sale to leave him floating in cash. He frowned at what he considered boutique establishments like Margaret's, and when it was confirmed he had not been invited to her very high-profile birthday luncheon he'd sniffed, "I didn't know she was still alive." He would be checking in later with a current-issue boy toy and a sycophant or three. The group always booked a cabin, one side for Linus and his "mentee," as he called whatever young man he brought with him, and one side for his yes-men. Fortunately it was the cabin furthest from Kyle and Danny's.

Cowboy Dave, the bartender, would be there by sundown. Marti Martin always came for the big holiday weekends, Fourth of July, Halloween, even Valentine's Day, despite being alone. "What better time to meet a Valentine?" she had said to Kyle last February.

There would be others, filling up every room the Lodge had to offer. The basement would be turned into one big party space with pumpkins and witches, cobwebs and plastic zombies. Cowboy Dave would serve an endless flow of drinks, assisted by one of the other staff stepping into Happy Corcoran's place; there was always someone available, one of the twins maybe, or Elzbetta when she got off shift waiting tables. Kevin, aka Kevin the Magnificent, karaoke master of ceremonies and tireless self-promoter, would oversee the festivities, and they would all dance the night away.

Kyle sipped his coffee gone cold and watched as Ricki provided just the right amount of professional fawning to guests, smiling and nodding, careful not to be too familiar even if he knew all their secrets. Kyle made a mental note to have a private conversation with Ricki when things slowed down. Ricki may well know something he didn't realize he knew, for unless the killer had already left—and Kyle had reason to believe he had not—he would be there among them this weekend. By the time he and Danny left for New York City, Kyle intended to identify a murderer and gain vindication for his poor dead friend.

CHAPTER 10

AN OFFHAND REMARK

It was an offhand remark, the kind no one noticed and that would have been forgotten had it not jarred something in Kyle's memory

He had planned to read and take a nap after lunch. That was his preferred agenda on weekends, holidays and any other day he wasn't working. It had nothing to do with getting older; he had been an avid napper since childhood. First came a good meal, then twenty minutes or so of reading, and finally drifting off to a luxurious sleep.

The pleasure of napping eluded him this Friday afternoon, as did the ability to focus on his book. The anxiety had started that morning with Teddy's death and escalated during lunch, when Kyle and Danny found themselves sitting at a table with the lesbian couple from the pool that morning. There were plenty of other places to sit, no reason whatsoever for the four of them to eat together, but the women walked into the dining room, saw Kyle and Danny looking at their menus, and the tall one, Eileen, said, "Afternoon, gentlemen, mind if we join you?"

Kyle was quickly trying to think of a reason to say no when Danny motioned at one of the two empty chairs at their table and said, but of course, they'd be delighted.

"We don't know them," Kyle whispered.

"That's what makes it interesting," Danny said, just as the women made it to the table.

Kyle noticed that the shorter woman, Maggie, wasn't tweeting or texting at the moment, but she kept her right hand poised just above the cell phone hooked on her belt, as if it were a gun holster and she was prepared to draw quickly, firing off messages with the speed of bullets. Both women wore jeans and what looked like plain light blue men's shirts. Kyle noticed Maggie wearing lace-up work boots, better used to walk along metal beams in the sky than hiking hillsides in Pennsylvania. Combined with the pink cat-eye glasses it made for quite a look.

"Where you boys from?" Maggie said, un-holstering her smart phone and setting it on the table as she sat down.

"New York City," Danny said. "How about you?

The women were seated now and Elzbetta, on duty for lunch and dinner, hurried over with two more menus. Elzbetta had the appearance of a young woman who never expected to work where appearances mattered: twenty-eight years old, mid-length yellow hair (for it could not be called blonde) with purple streaks in it, five tiny gold hoops rimming her left ear, a nose stud, and all black clothing: black jeans, black shirt, black shoes.

"I'm Elzbetta," she said to the table, "and I'll be your server today. Probably every day you're here, unless you stay past Sunday. I don't work Monday or Tuesday, in case you were wondering, which I doubt. And no, it's not a nickname for Elizabeth. It'd old-country, Slavic or something. You'd have to ask my mother which old-country, but she's dead and never did tell me. Drinks for anyone? Bar doesn't open 'til two."

The four looked at each other, wondering as much about the overload of information from their waitress as they were about what to order.

"Tomato juice please, Elzbetta," answered Eileen, putting just a slight emphasis on the name. "With ice."

Maggie said water was fine, while Kyle and Danny both asked for coffee. Elzbetta turned on her heel and hurried off, writing the drinks down on her order pad.

"Philly," Eileen said, turning to Danny as if there had been no interruption.

"Now we are," Maggie added, sounding none too happy about it.

"Maggie's from a small town in western PA," Eileen explained. "She thinks Philly is the big city. Which it is, but c'mon, New York City? I can't get her to go there with me and we've been together for thirteen years. She's convinced we wouldn't get out alive. And the subways? Like being buried alive, she says, as if she'd know. I miss the Big Apple."

"Does anyone still call it that?" Kyle mused, starting to warm to their company.

"Not for a while, I don't think," Danny said. "It was part of an advertising campaign, like those 'I Love NY' coffee cups with the heart on them. Back in the 70s or 80s when the place was going to hell."

"Well," said Eileen, "Maggie thinks it went to hell and stayed there. I told her it's run by Disney now but she won't believe me."

"What'd you think of that dead guy?" Maggie blurted, abruptly changing the subject. Either she didn't like her phobias being put on display or she had very poor social skills. "There hasn't been anything on the news about it." At that she glanced at her phone, as if news of any importance would set it vibrating.

"Who's going to report it?" asked Eileen. "It was six hours ago."

"To answer your question," Kyle said, "I knew the dead man. He worked here for many years and was a friend of mine, at least the last year or so."

"My mother was an alcoholic," Maggie said. "No good comes of it."

Kyle was wondering what made Maggie think Teddy was an alcoholic and why she would offer up such personal information, when Elzbetta arrived back with their drinks.

The now-foursome placed their lunch orders and continued with their conversation, the rest of it light, about the unseasonably warm weather and the pleasures Philadelphia had to offer, since it was the only place all four of them were familiar with. They watched as the restaurant started filling up with guests from the night before and new arrivals. Much to Danny's displeasure, Linus Hern swept into the room halfway through their meal, deliberately talking loudly so no one would miss his entrance. He had a young man in tow—not the same one he'd come with last year—and only two acolytes this time, fawning over Hern and glancing around to be sure they were looked at.

Linus was an imposing figure even without the ego. He stood six-three and carried himself like a man ten years younger than his sixty-two years. He wore his thinning hair a natural gray and swept back, no doubt the better to expose his face. Danny suspected contacts, since he had never seen Hern with glasses and knew that weakening vision was simply a part of aging. Today Hern was wearing cream cotton pants and a light blue jacket over pink shirt, something that looked more appropriate to spring than fall, but it wouldn't surprise Danny for Linus to expect the seasons to adjust to him and not the other way around. The young man gliding close to him was almost an afterthought, but a handsome one. Tanned in October, in tight sky-blue jeans and a Pride Lodge sweatshirt Linus had no doubt bought for him. The party moved en mass to a table well away from them, much to Danny's relief. He knew he would have to encounter Hern face to face at some point this weekend, but the later in their stay the better.

The twins, Austin and Dallas, had changed into their waiter clothes and were working the quickly-filling room.

Diane Haley and her beautiful partner took a seat by the window, Diane waving slightly at Kyle. The male couple they'd seen checking in were missing, and there was one woman who had come in and taken a seat by herself. Kyle remembered seeing her pull up in the parking lot last night as he and Danny walked down to the cabin. Something about her struck him: she seemed to be intensely observing everyone and when she saw him looking at her, she looked back, staring until he blushed and looked away.

"We haven't seen you here before," Danny said, continuing the lunch conversation as their food arrived. "Is this your first time?"

"It is indeed," said Eileen. "I knew Dylan back in high school. We were both in the closet, but we knew, ya know? We ended up coming out to each other but no one else, not until our senior year. He took the plunge first, God love him. This was in Philly, he's from there, in case you didn't know."

"I didn't," said Kyle. "I knew he and Sid lived in Long Branch, New Jersey, and they've been together for ten years. They had a big anniversary party last spring. But other than that, no."

"Did pretty damn well for himself," offered Maggie, looking around the room to indicate she meant the Lodge itself.

"I'd say he married well," Eileen said. "Or luckily. Anyway, we lost track for, what, thirty years? And then, Facebook! Just a couple months ago I got a friend request."

"They're not your friends, most of them," said Maggie with slight but noticeable resentment.

"Says the woman who tweets to four hundred followers, perhaps a dozen of whom she actually knows."

"It's a completely different social media."

"Maggie dropped off Facebook," Eileen explained. "A falling out with someone, so she declared it a diabolical corporate plot to get as much information about us as possible and she deleted her account."

"Which is never really deleted," said Maggie. "Nothing's ever truly deleted. It's all data mining."

Eileen rolled her eyes and continued. "Dylan and I have been in touch since then, sometime in the summer. He told me about Pride Lodge, I looked it up and it seemed like a great place to visit."

"And he gets to live here," Maggie said. Then, to Eileen, "You're welcome to buy me a resort."

"I'll be happy to, as soon as the rich aunt I don't have dies and leaves me a couple million dollars."

"Is that what happened?" Danny asked. "Dylan inherited from an aunt?"

"On, no," Eileen said. "Not Dylan. Sid. Bought the place for cash, Dylan said. And just in time! Who knows what a developer would do with this land."

Elzbetta appeared seemingly out of nowhere. "Finished with these?" she said, as she took their empty plates without waiting for an answer.

"I'm still working on mine," Kyle said playfully, his plate empty.

Elzbetta gave him a weary smile and headed off again, her arm piled with dishes.

"Will we see you at the pumpkin carving?" Eileen asked. "I'm told it's the official start of the Halloween fun."

Kyle wondered what fun there could be, considering the day had begun with a man's death. He started to say as much, thought better of it, and just said yes, they would be there that afternoon for the pumpkins, they wouldn't miss it.

You're welcome to buy me a resort. An offhand remark, a few words, information Kyle would probably never have known without that chance encounter. He gave up any hope of taking a nap and turned to Danny, who'd been reading the current issue of New York magazine in bed next to him.

"It's funny . . . " he said.

"I'm waiting," Danny replied, not taking his eyes off an article on the slate of Oscar hopefuls opening in December.

"The detective asked me an odd question, about how much I thought this place would cost. I didn't give it any thought until lunch, when they said Sid paid cash for it."

"That he inherited from an extremely generous aunt just when Pucky was selling the Lodge. Timing's everything, they say. I imagine Linus Hern would concur. The man has the most uncanny timing—he gets out with the money just in time. Whatever sap he sold the restaurant to goes out of business three months later, and it's nothing to Linus, he's on to the next venture. You'd think investors would have learned by now."

"You're not listening to me," Kyle said. "You're fantasizing a terrible end to a man you shouldn't be wasting your resentment on."

"He's had his eye on Margaret's Passion for some time, you know. He circles, like a vulture."

"What if there was no rich aunt? What if the money came from somewhere else?"

"And Teddy found out and was about to blow the whistle, so they silenced him."

"Yes, exactly!"

"You should take that nap. Your brain's tired. It's got you imagining things."

"Should I call her?"

"Who?"

"Detective Sikorsky."

"I imagine she's pretty good at finding these things out on her own," Danny said. "For that matter, she may already know. After all, she didn't ask how someone could afford to buy Pride Lodge, just how much it might cost."

"Ah, but that's the question, isn't it? How could someone who worked as a bank manager save up a couple million dollars to buy property? And why make up a relative who gave you the money?"

Danny tossed his magazine aside and swung his legs around off the bed. "You could ask them yourself in about twenty minutes. It's almost pumpkin carving time."

Kyle glanced at the dresser clock. Almost two hours had passed since lunch. He would not be taking a nap this afternoon. He sighed and slid off the bed, hoping for answers but still not certain what the questions were.

CHAPTER 11

A TABLE FOR ONE

For a moment she thought the man staring at her knew who she was, then she realized it was impossible. She was a stranger to everyone here, and everyone here a stranger to her. It must be the way she dressed, common enough in a resort filled with gay men and lesbians; or, more likely, she reminded him of someone he knew. That happened a lot. She'd been born with one of those faces that could serve as a template for at least one person in everyone's life. It had happened to her as a girl in Santa Barbara, and again in St. Paul. Anywhere she went, really. Every few months someone would stop her and say, "Don't I know you?" She was the spitting image of their cousin or an old classmate. Once in a great while they actually did know her, and she would lie. "No, sorry, my name's Bo," she would say after they insisted she reminded them of an old acquaintance named Emily. "Bo Sweetzer." She liked the name. Bo. One syllable. Gender-neutral. She knew people assumed it was a nickname, some diminutive of "Barbara" perhaps. It added to the fun.

She glanced at the table for four and saw he had turned his attention back to one of the women. Yes, she assured herself, he could not possibly know anything about her. Nonetheless, there was something about him, a curiosity she found threatening. She would have to keep an eye on him until she was safely away.

"My name's Austin," the young waiter said, startling her. He'd come up from behind her, but she chastised herself for not staying fully aware of her surroundings. She resolved to stay vigilant, even as she turned to him and did a double-take.

"I thought your name was Dallas," she said.

"We're twins. But we don't dress alike and he wears his hair shorter. He's also ten pounds heavier than I am, which should be obvious. Are you ready to order?"

"I'll have the usual," Bo said, toying with him.

Austin stared at her, even less amused than he had been, which was not at all. "Maybe my twin brother knows what your usual is, but I'm not him, which I just explained."

"Ah, yes, he's ten pounds heavier. Sorry. Just two eggs over easy, wheat toast, no potatoes. Coffee when you have a chance."

Austin jotted down the order and hurried away, rolling his eyes: another comic.

Pride Lodge, Bo thought. They should have called it Pride Circus. The man Dylan was the ringmaster, she'd seen that already, with the old guy Sid hanging back. Dylan fussed over everything, especially the guests. He told the staff what to do and when, but in a nice way, she'd noticed. Pity.

There was that desk clerk Ricki who looked vaguely familiar from photos she saw on the Lodge corkboard, except in those he was dressed as a woman and holding a restaurant menu. Maybe he, too, had a twin, the place seemed to attract them. She'd met Dallas and Austin and she had watched Elzbetta dashing here and there. Elzbetta had introduced herself briefly when she took Bo to the table, and already Bo was wondering, since it obviously wouldn't work out with the lady cop, if this waitress might be available for a drink. One last for the road, so to speak, when her work here was done. She smiled at the daring of it even as she knew it would be a mistake.

Bo was a lonely woman. She didn't dwell on it; it was her lot. She had prepared for this mission since she was ten years old and nothing, least of all entanglement with another woman, could interfere. It almost had once, with Cassy and her move to Minnesota that had left her in that cold, bitter landscape, and yet she had stayed. As if fate had intended it all along. She understood cold and bitter. They were what gave her solace through the years as she knew somehow the day would come for action, and it had. She was prepared, and she was remorseless.

She finished her coffee and watched the foursome leave. The man who'd seemed curious about her looked at her again, saw her staring back and quickly looked away. The two men were a couple, that was obvious, as were the women. Bo had noticed Pride Lodge attracted a particular clientele: older gay men and lesbians, many of them coupled. She allowed herself a moment of self-pity, mourning a life she would never know. But it was only a moment's reflection; she did not cry over wistful fantasies, and regret was something she had promised herself never to indulge in.

She thought again of the man who had just left and his unexpected interest in her. Was he a danger in any way? Did he recognize her from somewhere? She doubted both, but would see what she could learn from casual gossip with the desk clerk Ricki. Nervous people eager to chat were always an opportunity. She made a mental note to stop by the desk soon and properly introduce herself, then she left four dollars on the table and headed for her room.

CHAPTER 12

THE MASTER SUITE

Sid Stanhope sat as his desk looking out on the pool below. Some days he felt his age more than others and this was one of them. He would be turning sixty-two next spring, and unlike most people who wondered where the time went, he wondered why it took so long. That can happen to a man on the run, a man with a past who could never be sure it would stay hidden. He thought it had. After the first year, when the three of them hadn't been caught, they all breathed just a little bit easier. Then five years, then ten, until it really did seem this cold case would stay frozen, buried deep where it would never see the light of day or the warmth of the truth of what they had done. What Frank had done. It was an accident, as much as one could call the killing of two people an accident. The family wasn't supposed to be home. They had stopped their mail delivery, which was how Frank picked the houses to break into. His girlfriend worked at the post office and kept him informed of the families on Los Feliz Boulevard and its surrounding streets. The whole criminal enterprise was only supposed to last a few months, until they had enough between the three of them to move out of law breaking as quickly and quietly as they had moved into it. It was a cash flow problem, nothing more, and no one was supposed to get hurt. The Lapinsky woman had put a hold on the family's mail. She'd been telling everyone they were taking their daughter to London for her tenth birthday, all of them were excited. Then something changed. They were home, in their bedroom. They woke up, and Frank shot them.

Sid found out from the newspaper reports that the daughter had gotten sick. As simple and as dreadful a twist of fate as there could be. She had some kind of bad flu or something and the mother, being a mother, called off the trip. London could wait, she wouldn't drag her poor baby across the Atlantic in a plane, probably making everyone else sick along the way.

The police had already dubbed them "The Los Feliz Gang," even though they didn't know how many men were involved, or if they broke into homes in other neighborhoods. They'd had a successful streak of six houses, with the Lapinsky's being unlucky number seven, and once murder was part of it, everything changed. The burglaries stopped as the three men separated. Frank went East, to Bloomington, Indiana, then moved every few years until he ended up in Detroit. His girlfriend went missing; Frank said she'd gone into hiding, Sid always suspected her bones would never be found. His opinion of Frank had changed from one colored by friendship to one colored by fear. Sam Tatum stuck it out in L.A., keeping his head low and watching over his shoulder a little less every year. And Sid Stanhope went as far east as he could without leaving the continent, first to New York City where he vanished into the seemingly limitless anonymity that great metropolis provided, then, some years later when it felt safe, to New Jersey.

He had been planning on collecting social security next year. The Lodge was bought and paid for, the one truly lucky break of his life. And now all of it was threatened. But by whom? Frank had certainly not robbed and shot himself, and Sam Tatum did not put an ice pick in the back of his own head, much as Sid thought it was about time somebody did, given the seediness of the life Sam had insisted on living. He'd been in a state of rising panic after Sam's death. He needed a plan but had none, with no idea how to protect himself. If he knew who was coming, or even if he could be certain why, he could determine a course of action. But he had no way to be sure if this was connected to the murders in that bedroom thirty years ago. He had searched his memory for any other connection between the three of them, but there wasn't any. And surely no one would be coming after them all these years later for a house they'd simply freed of the few things they could carry? This was revenge, but by whom? And why after all this time?

Sid and Dylan had moved into the set of rooms their predecessors called "The Master Suite" when they relocated to the property shortly after the signing. It wasn't where Sid would have preferred to live: there was something haunted about it, and even after painting and completely redecorating the three joined rooms and installing a new, larger bathroom, he could still feel the presence of Pucky and Stu. Especially Stu. He had concluded the old man's ghost had moved from the steps where they found his body, back into the comfort of the Suite where he had spent so many years puttering and overseeing the business. Sometimes Sid could swear he'd seen Stu standing in the bedroom doorway, but when he blinked the apparition was gone, leaving only a shadow outline that could be explained away as the swaying of an overhead tree limb outside the window or the passing of a cloud.

Whatever the case with Pride Lodge, Sid knew the real haunting was his. He had thought for so long he had escaped his past. There had been no indication for any of them that a case grown so cold had warmed again. No one came around asking questions, no one looked at him too long at the bank or the grocery. The only thing chasing him was his own guilt, and that had dulled over three decades until it was more mild regret, wishing things had not gone wrong that fateful night, but never taking responsibility for those people's deaths. He hadn't brought the gun, hadn't pulled the trigger. He was just a burglar in the wrong house at the wrong time. They had left the girl alive. And the thought literally struck him, like an epiphany or the sudden realization he'd taken a step too many and there was no ground beneath him. He stumbled into it: the girl. But she was ten years old at the time. By now she would be forty, married with a family. Could she have found them? Could she have hired someone to take revenge after all this time? He was trying to get it clear in his mind, trying to envision connections leading from that bedroom thirty years ago to this weekend, when Dylan entered the room.

"Everything's set up," Dylan said, meaning the tables, pumpkins and whatever utensils people needed to carve.

Sid swiveled around in his chair. Sweet Dylan, he thought, watching as the man he called his husband busied himself in the main room. Cheerful

Dylan. Accommodating Dylan. Doting, loving, gullible Dylan. Sid felt his usual but brief twinge of guilt thinking of how useful Dylan had been these last ten years. Sid had grown to love Dylan but it had not started out that way. He hadn't wanted to be alone in his old age, and along came Dylan. By that time in his life he was willing to be flexible; that's how he considered it, too, not "settling," but simply being open to whatever shape their relationship took. After ten years he didn't even think about their differences, and it brought him great sadness, sitting there, to know he might be leaving soon, disappearing once again for a last time.

"Is that what you're wearing?" Dylan asked, nodding at Sid as he got up from the desk.

Sid was in sweat pants and a Pride Lodge t-shirt, both gray and worn. Dylan, meanwhile, was in crisply ironed jeans, black loafers and a green plaid shirt with the cuffs buttoned. Dylan was the more style conscious of the pair and took pains to always look good, however casually he was dressed. At five feet six inches, he was a good two inches shorter than Sid and easily forty pounds lighter. Where everything about Sid was large— his hands, his feet, his head, his shoulders—everything about Dylan was medium-scale. He had taken to dying his hair brown to keep the gray out and he swept it back with gel, giving him an open, inviting face framed with silver half-rimmed glasses. He blinked frequently, the result of a dry eye condition, and it made him seem perpetually curious.

Innocence, thought Sid; that's what I think of when I look at this man. Innocence. He dreaded the thought of breaking Dylan's heart, leaving him alone in rural Pennsylvania, but he was first a survivor and would save himself whatever the cost.

"I don't do pumpkins, you know that," Sid said. "But no, I wouldn't go downstairs dressed like this. Do I ever?"

"I'm just reminding you," said Dylan as he straightened magazines on the coffee table. It was part of a fastidiousness bordering on obsession. He turned to Sid suddenly and asked, "Are we doing the right thing? After Teddy, I mean? Is this all too unseemly?"

Sid went to Dylan and put his large, comforting arms around him. He felt Dylan slump into him, letting his body lean against the older, bigger man.

"Teddy would be completely disappointed if we didn't," Sid said. "And really, do you think he'd want us bringing even more attention to how he died? Some alcoholics just can't make it."

"Most, from what I've read. I just feel so bad for him."

"We all do."

"Oh my God," Dylan said, pulling away. "Who's going to tell Happy? They'd broken up, but still . . . "

"Nobody knows where Happy is," Sid said. "It's not something we can worry about. He'll find out however he finds out. Now let's get ready and go downstairs. I won't carve, but I can watch."

Sid headed for the closet to pick out something appropriate for joining his guests. As he stood flipping through his slacks, he reflected on the timing of it all: Sam's death, someone coming after him, Teddy's drunken fall into the pool. And Happy, of course, but Happy was young and impetuous and had probably just run off for a few days.

Sam's death.

Someone coming after him.

Teddy's drunken fall into the pool.

Sid wondered if there could possibly be a connection, and if anyone else was making it, too.

CHAPTER 13

ALL THE JACK-O-LANTERNS

There were two main events required for the success of the Halloween week-end at Pride Lodge. One was the costume party on Saturday night, when the lower level karaoke room and the adjacent piano bar were turned into one large dance floor with the busiest bar of the year, and the other was the annual pumpkin carving held in the Lodge's great room. Tables, carvers and pumpkins would spill over onto the porch in good weather or into the restaurant if it was raining. And while some of the guests skipped the pumpkin carving, most showed up and picked out one of several pre-drawn pumpkin designs or, if they were really in the spirit, brought their own pattern.

The pumpkins were lined up on temporary tables set out in a U-shape jutting from the fireplace. There wasn't any fire yet—that would come later in the year—so no one was in danger of running out of the door in flames. Next to each pumpkin was a small serrated metal stickpin used to saw along the lines of the Jack-O-Lantern pattern. There were also several X-Acto knives for the more experienced and determined. Dylan, who oversaw the carving (which was also a contest with first prize being a weekend for two at the Lodge), warned everyone to only use an X-Acto knife if they knew what they were doing and if they were prepared for the loss of blood—the Lodge assumed no liability.

Ricki had displayed the paper patterns along the top of the check-in desk and was offering them up with the occasional suggestion. "That's not you, really, try the witch," or, "This might be a little too complicated for someone of such simple tastes. Here's a cat, it has your name on it." Ricki loved Halloween more than any other time of year at Pride Lodge, so much that he'd temporarily forgotten about poor Teddy and the horrifying events of the morning. He had meant to call that detective and tell her about an argument he'd heard the night before between Sid and Teddy, but it surely meant nothing. Besides, he'd mentioned it to both Kyle and that strange woman, Bo, when each had stopped by the desk after lunch. He had the feeling they were pumping him for information, though he couldn't imagine why, and all he really had to say was that Sid and Teddy had argued. That was nothing new; Sid didn't really like Teddy and only kept him around because of Dylan and the fact Teddy had worked there so long. From things he'd overheard—you can't work the front desk of a place like Pride Lodge and not hear things—Sid thought Teddy was a sloppy drunk and Teddy thought Sid was using Dylan, though he couldn't say for what. In the end it was all just scuttlebutt and didn't matter now anyway, in light of the circumstances.

"Linus!" Ricki said, pulling himself back from his thoughts. "How nice to see you!"

It wasn't, really. Nobody who knew Linus Hern was happy to see him, unless they were being paid . . . which, frankly, Ricki was. He proceeded to glance at the pumpkin patterns, deciding which would be the best suggestion for Mr. Hern.

Back in the cabin, Kyle had finally been able to sleep for about twenty minutes before being startled from his nap by a call from Imogene, apologetic to be disturbing him on a vacation but not so bothered as to refrain from it. She swore yet again it was something she would only do in an emergency. Kyle and Danny both knew the definition of "emergency" when it came to Imogene had a significantly lower threshold than it did for most people. It might be anything from misplacing her iPhone to needing a sudden flight to Chicago, which she had shown herself incapable of arranging on her own. This afternoon it was for advice—something she relied heavily on Kyle for and as often as not ignored. She had been approached about a job in Seattle and couldn't decide if she should consider it or dismiss it out of hand.

"You've been with Tokyo Pulse for what, nine months?" he said, waving at Danny to stop rolling his eyes. Kyle had started working for her when she was still with Channel 6 doing woman-on-the-street segments no one watched or cared about. Then came a year of freelancing while she burned through her savings, and finally the last-chance job with Tokyo Pulse.

"'*We*,'" she told him. "*We* have been with Tokyo Pulse nine months. You're not thinking of leaving me, are you?"

Her insecurities challenged Kyle more than anything else about her. "Fine, 'we,'" he said. "It's too early to make another move, that's all I meant. And I will be leaving if you move to Seattle. That's not an option for me, not anymore."

"Since I shackled you," Danny said, getting up from the table and heading to the bathroom.

"That's my answer then," she said. "No Kyle, no Imogene."

The comment both touched and alarmed Kyle. The thought of her making decisions based on his ability to stay with her was more responsibility than he wanted.

"Be sure to thank them anyway," he said. "Just to keep that door open, you never know. Forward the email to me so I can add them to your contacts, for when you're ready to part ways with me."

He ended the call with her knowing it had been completely unnecessary, and knowing it was one of the things than endeared her to him. He allowed himself an image of the two of them in twenty years' time, Imogene tamed by age but still rebellious, and himself listening to her demands through a hearing aid.

Bo wasn't very good in crowds and intended to avoid them at the Lodge as much as possible. She fidgeted behind her neck with a small gold crucifix her mother had given her for her sixth birthday. It was among the very few things she had kept throughout her life. She had always believed we leave everything behind anyway for someone else to sort and dispose of; the fewer things we hold onto, the less we'll have to fear losing when the time comes. And the time comes for everyone.

After the murders of her parents everything had moved so quickly. Her aunt had come to Los Angeles to identify the bodies, something young Emily thought was ridiculous. Who else would be dead in her parents' bed? Many things were mysterious to her then, including the complete disregard for what a girl of ten may or may not want. She did not want to live with her aunt and the uncle who made her skin crawl. She did not want to be the live-in orphan, which is how she felt and how her new step-sisters treated her. Her mother and aunt had never gotten along, and Emily knew her mother would be upset to know her only child had been shuttled off to Santa Barbara to live with her sister and *him*. That's how her mother referred to her brother-in-law, simply as "him." Never Joseph, never with anything that could be confused for affection or even respect. Her mother always had suspicions about the man, about how he made his money and his dictatorial way of being a husband and father. Unfortunately, Barbara and Carl Lapinksy thought they had all the time in the world and had neglected to make legal arrangements should something happened to them, which it did. Now they were gone and one of the few things that remained of their ever having been on the earth was the small gold cross Bo fastened around her neck.

She had been wearing the necklace the night they were killed. Even as a child she only took it off to bathe, and her father jokingly said he was concerned she would become a nun. He mistook her attachment to the crucifix for a devotion to the cross. Emily did not understand the whole Jesus thing and never considered the two to be connected, even though she knew many people wore crucifixes as professions of their faith. She had no faith, and she was not a nun. She was a killing machine that had been oiled and ready for three decades. Her surrender to the cross was her surrender to the memory of her parents, in this case her mother, and her complete acceptance of the commitment she had made as she watched the men flee from their home: I will kill you. As odd a thought as that seems for a ten year old cowering in a closet, it was the thought she had and the promise she made. I will kill you. I will find you. I will hunt you down.

Here she was at last, having never known for sure it could come to pass. She had believed it would. She had kept things in place, ready to act. But until she saw the watch for sale she could not have sworn in a court of justice—for that is where she now found herself—that the opportunity would present itself and all her preparation would have been for good. What she was doing was good. What she was doing was right. No innocence would be violated; they had forfeited any claim to innocence when they left two people dead in a bedroom. She had carried out the Court's decree with the men Frank and Sam, and now, once she was finished here, she would return to anonymity. She would replace the smile on her face, so familiar to her friends in St. Paul. She would tell them what a lovely time she'd had in Hawaii, her first trip in years but definitely not her last, so wonderful and relaxing and tropical. And she would close the lid at last—the lid to her past, to her parents' coffins, to the hatred that had fueled her nearly her entire life.

She slipped into her comfortable black loafers, adjusted her expression to be as soft, welcoming and unremarkable as possible, and headed downstairs.

Dylan wasn't able to have a seating arrangement at the tables, that would have been too formal, too deliberate, but he could steer people in the general direction of where he wanted them to be. The real challenge with a group like this was knowing who to keep apart, not who to seat together. Diane Haley, for instance, had been in a Cold War state with Marti Martin for years, ever since Marti stole Diane's girlfriend so long ago neither of them remembered her name. Bad blood tended to stay bad, and no infusion of good will or forced togetherness would change that. The same might be said for Linus and Danny, although Danny wasn't really the grudge holding sort. His dislike for the stuffy restaurateur didn't cross the line into open warfare, but it would still be best not to have them next to each other. Linus enjoyed provocation and could be counted on to throw a flame or two regardless of the best intentions or efforts to ignore him.

As the guests filtered in, Dylan accomplished his manipulation by carrying their Jack-O-Lantern patterns to the tables for them, chatting as he led them to where he thought they should be. He had planned it out ahead of time, knowing, for instance, that Linus would insist on the largest pumpkin in the room while Kyle would want something front-lit for the photographs he was always taking.

Drinks were served to ease the social interaction. Austin, Dallas and Elzbetta saw to that, working on a single pumpkin for the three of them while taking turns filling drink orders. More than one person had said to Dylan that alcohol and knives were probably not a good combination.

By the time Kyle and Danny arrived, Kyle with his ever-present Nikon slung around his neck, everyone was in place and already starting to carve. Diane and Marti were separated by an elderly gentleman from Long Island, a regular customer named Jeremy Johnston who took a bus to the Lodge twice a year for a week's stay. Jeremy was the last person to retire at night, given special privilege to watch the great room's wall-mounted television set well past midnight to accommodate his insomnia. He also had the odd habit of pushing a walker with him everywhere, which would seem natural for a man of 82 if he actually needed it to walk. For Jeremy it was a prop, like a cane might be for a man of an earlier era.

"How you doing, Jerry?" Marti asked when he first approached the table. Marti Martin ran a travel agency that was barely hanging on. Her hair was gray and cropped short, almost military style, and she wore incongruously large, red plastic eyeglasses that made her head look more like a baby's than a grown woman's.

"It's Jeremy," he replied. "You know that, Marti Martin."

"Yes, I do. I'm just checking to make sure you're paying attention."

The old man was indeed paying close attention. That's what he did: he watched everyone. He enjoyed the ruse of the walker. He needed it, to be truthful, since he sometimes lost his balance, but mostly it served as a form of misdirection. People would be paying attention to the walker while he was paying attention to them.

Linus and his man-child were at the end of one table, near the fireplace. Next to them were the two sycophants. Danny recognized one of them and had in fact fired the man from Margaret's Passion just that past June. He had been a new nighttime maitre d', and even though Danny was the day manager, Margaret relied on him for the unpleasant tasks as well as the pleasant ones. The man's name . . . what was it? . . . Fidel? Filio? Filo? . . . Filo had given it his best try but it wasn't good enough. He had been short tempered with some of the diners and had an unwelcome air of superiority the other staff didn't like, even leaving one waitress in tears. He had to go, so off Danny went to the restaurant late one night to tell Filo he wished him well in his future endeavors.

"You remember Phineus!" Linus shouted at Danny as he and Kyle took their seats. "You fired him!"

Phineus was clearly embarrassed and simply smiled in Danny's direction.

Kyle took a few quick photos of the tables with all the guests seated. He saw Maggie and Eileen, the twins, Elzbetta, Ricki at the desk, Dylan hurrying around making sure everyone was in place. There were some other guests on the porch, a few Kyle recognized and some he did not. There were also several empty spaces: the pumpkin carving took place on Friday afternoon when people were still arriving. It was a tradition; it had always been on Friday. It also allowed for the judging that night and the Jack-O-Lanterns to be displayed for the rest of the weekend.

Just as Kyle was about to take a picture of the pumpkins on the table in front of them, the woman he'd seen eating alone at lunch took the empty place to his left. She had short, curly brown hair that reminded him of the late Phoebe Snow. Unlike most of the others at the Lodge she was not wearing blue jeans, instead having on rather elegant black pants, a cream blouse and a gray sweater. He glanced at her and saw she was wearing a crucifix around her neck.

"Hello," she said, seeming to enjoy the sizing up. She extended her hand. "My name's Bo. Bo Sweetzer. You must be Kyle."

He shook her hand and she could tell he was puzzled that she knew his name.

"I asked the desk guy."

"Ricki."

"Yeah, Ricki. I saw you this morning at the pool. My room's above it on the second floor. You're good with a camera."

"Not as good as I'd like to be," Kyle said.

"Yes, he is," Danny interjected. "He's just falsely modest."

"I've never sold anything."

"Because you've never asked to be paid!"

"He's right," Bo said. "You could sell your photographs, absolutely. I've seen your website."

This got his attention. He knew how many people visited his photoblog on any given day; he could track the statistics. If 500 people looked at AsKyleSeesIt in any 30-day period, he was doing well. That this stranger, here for a weekend at Pride Lodge, had not only asked Ricki about him, but taken time to look at his site, was something out of the ordinary. While it was flattering, it was also a little unsettling, as if he'd finally acquired a stalker.

"I used the Lodge's laptop," she said, nodding toward the old battered Dell that was always on a table by the checkerboard. "I'm impressed. Maybe I'll be your first customer."

"First paying customer," Danny said. "He's had quite a few customers." And to Kyle, "You see? It's time to take it—"

"Please don't say it."

"To the next level."

"I hate that phrase. Along with a few others: next level, same page, bandwidth. Do you think we have the bandwidth to carve these pumpkins?"

Elzbetta suddenly appeared between Kyle and Bo. She'd got into costume for the weekend and was dressed this year in a French maid's outfit with an enormous Marie Antoinette wig. The studs were still in her nose and ears and her fingernails were painted black with tiny witches in the middle of each fingernail.

"You did that yourself?" Danny asked, indicating the intricate paintings.

"Kevin," she said, meaning the karaoke host. Kevin McGill had been running the evening entertainment at Pride Lodge nearly as long as the Lodge had been in business. He didn't show his face before mid-afternoon, which made Elzbetta's fingernail painting this early in the day something of a rarity.

"He just got in after lunch, " Elzbetta said. "He'll be down for dinner. What can I get you to drink?"

"I'll take a martini, vodka, straight up," Danny said.

"There is no such thing as a vodka martini," Elzbetta said. "A true martini is made with gin."

"Then I'll take a fake martini, vodka, straight up. And not the house swill, either."

"I'll have Scotch and water," Kyle said. "Plenty of ice. And whatever Bo's having, our treat."

"Why thank you, that's very nice of you! I'll have club soda, please. Make mine neat."

Elzbetta nodded and hurried off.

Watching her go, Bo said, "Not the costume I'd expect with someone so deliberately rebellious."

Just then Dylan interrupted with several loud hand claps. "Listen up, everybody!," and when a few of the guests kept chatting, "'Everybody' is self-explanatory! It means every single person who can hear me!"

"Does that include Staten Island?" Linus said, to approving laughter from his mini-entourage.

"Each of you has a fresh pumpkin in front of you and the pattern you've chosen or been provided. These pumpkins are sacrificing their lives to provide us with a fabulous weekend, so don't disappoint them! Next to each pumpkin you'll find . . . "

Kyle let Dylan's voice fade into the background, much like the sound of a flight attendant giving survival instructions from the aisle of a crowded plane. He realized he needed *before* photos of the pumpkins to contrast with the *after*. He quickly picked up his Nikon from the table and set about taking pictures. He wasn't worried about Dylan calling him out for not paying attention; the man was completely self-absorbed in his own central part of the afternoon's drama. Kyle and Danny would carve one pumpkin together, leaving an extra one. This happened with most of the couples, whether they were involved or just friends. There was something about carving a pumpkin with someone that made it more enjoyable and less tedious. He snapped a photo of their pumpkin, then angled his camera for a shot at Bo's. He noticed she had one of the X-act knives resting to the left of her pumpkin.

"I see you're a southpaw," Kyle said to her, commenting on her left-handedness. "And a pro at pumpkin carving! I'd probably cut my finger off using one of those."

"It's for the details," she said, holding up her pattern. It was an intricate sketch of Cinderella's pumpkin carriage being pulled by two horses. Once it was finished and a candle placed inside, the flame would shine through the carriage's windows. "I'm used to detail work. I make jewelry for a living. I also restore old watches."

She reached into her pocket and pulled out her father's pocket watch. Kyle had noticed the gold chain running up out of her pocket to a belt loop.

"This one is very special," she said, showing it to him. "It belonged to my father. I'd have to say it's been my inspiration since I was, oh, ten years old."

Kyle peered at the watch. Even someone not schooled in watches or engraving could see it had been made with care. There was something delicate yet masculine about it, and it made him wonder, as he looked at the fine lines of the train station, how much of the little boy remains in a grown man: trains were something a child played with when he was ten, and built when he was thirty.

"It's lovely," he said. "From what you've said, I take it your father's passed on."

"Oh, yes. He and my mother both. At the same time. A freak accident." She put the watch back in her pocket. "It's not something I talk about. You can see some of my jewelry at my website, if you're interested.

BoAndBehold.com. Maybe we could barter, it's the future of commerce, if you listen to twenty-year-olds obsessed with their carbon footprints. Something of mine for a photograph of yours. You could use it to get used to the idea of being paid."

Kyle was beginning to enjoy this woman's company. There was something both inviting and off-putting about her, an unusual combination. He was a people watcher. He had always attributed it to a mix of introversion and curiosity, the essence of a photographer even before he'd ever held a camera . He saw the world, and life, as a series of images, instantaneous and continuous while constantly changing. Almost like one of those small picture books where the image moves as you flip through the pages. Kyle was always watching the image, always observing one moment's connection to the next.

Danny broke his reverie by saying, for the third time, ". . . Earth to Kyle, hello, Kyle?"

Kyle shook off his thoughts and noticed that everyone had started carving, including Bo, who was holding her pattern against her pumpkin and poking pinpricks along the line drawing. Slowly, steadily, one quick saw at a time. Everyone was doing it now.

"You hold the paper, I'll cut," said Danny. "When we get to the witch's broom it's your turn."

A half hour later Danny and Kyle were finished, the table in front of them littered with pumpkin bits. Kyle looked around the room and saw the others either finished or nearing it. Bo had moved on to the X-Acto knife and was painstakingly slicing out the finest details of her carving.

"It all looks amazing!" Dylan said. He was holding a drink by this time, and while he wasn't someone who would indulge too much (bad for his image as well as his business), he wasn't opposed to joining the Lodge's guests in an afternoon cocktail. It was a holiday, after all, or at least as close to an official gay holiday as the year provided.

"Now," Dylan continued. "If I can get everyone to take their pumpkins and line them up around the porch railing—it's wide enough, don't worry—we can get the candles in and as soon as the sun goes down, we'll be a proper haunted house!"

"The ghost of Teddy," Ricki said morosely and not too loudly.

People started gathering their pumpkins for the short walk outside.

"Let me get some after photos," Kyle said, and he grabbed his camera off the table. He quickly snapped pictures of his and Danny's pumpkin, which, if you tilted your head at a certain angle and closed one eye, looked like a witch on a broom flying across the moon. Then he turned and took a photo of Bo's pumpkin, which reflected her artistic expertise. He knew looking at it that her jewelry would be even more impressive: there was no need to close an eye or cock your head to tell what she had carved. Cinderella herself would ride in this pumpkin! He was about to compliment her when Dylan came quickly up to them, a pumpkin in his arms even though he had not carved one, and said, "Kyle, you've got an eye for these things—come with me and help me arrange all these pumpkins."

Kyle had never been asked to do this before and looked at Danny for his reaction. Danny shrugged and carried their pumpkin himself as the Lodge guests all began to file outside.

The porch was spacious and not closed in. Pucky and Stu, then Dylan and Sid after them, had considered enclosing it so people could sit out in inclement weather, but having it open to the air and the hill gave it a sense of flowing into the surroundings. There was a porch swing on each end, a bench along the bay window looking into the great room, and two small tables with deck chairs. A waist-high railing encircled it all. People were setting their pumpkins along the railing when Dylan took Kyle by the arm and led him out into the yard.

"We'll get a better perspective from a distance," he said. "You're a photographer, you know all about perspective."

Kyle followed along as they stepped away from the crowd. It was late afternoon and the sun, while not down, was giving it up for the day. Another hour and they would be lighting the Jack-O'-Lanterns.

Once they were out of earshot of the other guests, Dylan, keeping his eyes on the porch, said to Kyle, "I need to speak to you privately, Kyle. It's about the Lodge. About Sid."

"Why me?" Kyle asked him, uncomfortable with the intimacy. He had known Dylan for the five years he and Danny had been coming here, but they had never been more than cordial.

"Because Teddy trusted you." And then, without looking at Kyle, "I don't believe his death was an accident."

"Nor do I, Dylan, but you can't take conjecture to court. If you know anything, you should call the police, speak to that Detective Sikorsky."

"I don't know things for a fact. That's the problem. I only have suspicions at this point, and I wanted to speak to you first. I think I know what Teddy wanted to see you about."

Kyle's head was spinning. He wanted answers as much as anyone, but he'd never thought they might come from Dylan. What benefit could he have in proving a murder on his property? It was the sort of thing that might make people think twice about staying there.

"Come to Clyde's," Dylan said, referring to the downstairs piano bar. "Tonight."

Before Kyle could protest or ask him anything, Dylan headed back toward the porch. "Cinderella in the middle," he said loudly for everyone to hear. "We'll work out to the left and right from there. You're all looking amazing! And don't forget to pick your favorite, Ricki has ballots at the front desk!"

Kyle watched him begin to fuss with the pumpkins, as if they had actually just discussed arranging them. He was again struck by the imposition of intimacy, the sharing of a confidence, or at least promising to, that should be shared with the authorities. He decided he would hear Dylan out that night, and depending on what came of it, he would call Detective Sikorsky in the morning. He doubted very much she took weekends off in a homicide case.

CHAPTER 14

STANLEY AND OLIVER

Kyle was Stanley Laurel, being the taller of the two, and Danny was Oliver Hardy, which he was none too happy about: Hardy was the fat one.

"Just tell yourself he went on Weight Watchers and lost forty pounds," Kyle said, adjusting his bowler hat in the mirror.

"There was no Weight Watchers then," Danny said, applying a moustache while he glanced at a photograph of the old comedy team.

"You're missing the point. There's nothing insulting about going as Oliver Hardy. You're not really him! You're a . . . thinner Oliver Hardy."

"Thanks," Danny said, having caught the hesitation in Kyle's voice. He was a thinner Hardy, for sure, thin enough he had to pad the suit with a pillow tied around his mid-section, but not thin enough to make the costume ridiculous.

About half the guests would dress for dinner, creating a mix in the dining room of people in casual clothes eating their meal with people in Halloween costumes. Some of them were as simple as a magician's cape and wand, while others were elaborate and probably took an hour or two to prepare. The previous year Kyle had come as a scarecrow and Danny as a sultan, complete with a sultan's multi-colored robe and a turban. Kyle had hated his costume and cursed his decision: it was made of straw and burlap, purchased on the internet, and it itched fiercely.

"I'm so glad we're not in the City," Danny said. "I'd have been roped into working Margaret's for Halloween crowd control and you'd be dealing with Imogene fretting over every sequin on a fairy costume."

"She's a tube of lipstick this year," Kyle said.

"You know what I mean. If you weren't at her apartment helping her, you'd be on the phone offering reassurance."

The two men were just about ready. Their plans for the night were simply to have dinner, after which Danny would return for some quiet time before bed. He was a people person when he was paid to be, at the restaurant especially, but when they managed to get away by themselves, he preferred to enjoy time reading, or even watching television, anything away from the crowd. Crowds were central to his job and, to some extent, to his identity. He needed to keep the boundaries clear, to remind himself that he was not what he did for a living. There was a risk in confusing your work with who you are.

"Danny?" he heard Kyle say, and he realized Kyle had been speaking to him while he sat thinking on the edge of the bed.

"What?"

"What do you suppose Dylan found out, and why would he want to talk to me? I told him to call the detective."

"He's probably not sure enough to do that," Danny said. "It's probably still conjecture for him."

"Suspicions."

"Exactly."

"But about what?"

"Well, that's what you're going to find out, Mr. Laurel, when youse 'av yourself a propah convahsation with the man."

Kyle walked over to Danny, leaned down and kissed him. "That's the spirit."

"I hate Halloween."

"You don't hate Halloween, it's your favorite time here, you're just being contrary. Now let's go eat."

Kyle retrieved his camera from the dresser and the two of them headed to the Lodge.

CHAPTER 15

HAPPINESS IS A WARM GUN

Bo sat gently rocking back and forth in the old chair in her room. It wasn't a rocking chair, but she took comfort in the motion. It reminded her of being in her father's lap so many years ago, when he would rock her and tell her stories before putting her to bed. Now, over thirty years later, it was his gun she took comfort in, caressing it with the fingers of her left hand. Her shooting hand.

It's funny, the things we forget in a moment of crisis and chaos. Her father had kept the gun in a case in the closet, yet when he needed it he neglected it, choosing instead to hurry his daughter into hiding, to protect her and take his chances hand-to-hand. She supposed he had never expected to have to aim a gun at anyone, much less pull the trigger. He wasn't a gun man. He'd simply had it as a precaution, like a life preserver that gathered dust inside a boat and was never worn. She had no idea what had gone through his mind in those seconds, or if he had suddenly remembered the gun was in the closet with his ten year old child and it was too late; he would not risk exposing her to get the one thing that could have saved them. And the timing, too, all of it happening so fast. Bo watched in horror as the man stepped into the bedroom and promptly shot her father, then her mother. Bang, bang, just like that. She didn't know why she hadn't screamed, or at least sucked her breath in so loudly it would give her away. But she hadn't. She had stayed fixated on the horror. And then, when she was gathering her things to move to Santa Barbara and be raised by strangers called a family, she had taken the gun. The police hadn't found it; they hadn't been looking for any such thing. This was a burglary gone wrong; what you saw was what you got. So the gun had still been in the closet when she came to pack, and she had kept it with her all these years. Not only kept it with her, but learned to shoot it, and shoot it well. Which made it that much sadder knowing she would have to discard it, leave it rusting at the bottom of the Delaware River when she left this place, having put it to its only good use.

Bo believed in coincidence. She had no patience for people who said there was no such thing. Thus, had she not been paying attention that day, she would not have seen the watch for sale on BidderSweet. Had she not seen the watch, she would not have made her way to Detroit and used the very same gun she now felt pressing lightly on her lap. For that matter, had she not gotten sick, she and her parents would have been on a flight to London that night and everything about her life would be different. Surely this is the very definition of coincidence, with all its good fortune and its tragedy.

She stopped rocking. She got up and carefully slipped the gun in a dresser drawer, beneath her sweater and jeans. She would head downstairs for dinner soon. She didn't want to go and would prefer to focus on her objective, plus her appetite had vanished as her anxiety slowly increased, but she knew appearance was reality. She had another day and night to go before slipping away; not showing up was the very way to draw attention to herself. She didn't know if it was usual here was to wear costumes for dinner and she didn't want to do that anyway, so she would join the other Lodge guests as herself, the best mask of all. For Saturday night's main event she had brought a cat costume that she purchased for $40 at a store along the way from Minnesota. It came in a box, that's how cheap it was and how easily thrown away when this was over. Cats were patient, cats were predators, and as silly as it seemed, she took some pleasure in being a cat that had come to claim the canary. The old man, the one named Sid.

Well, Sid, she thought, glancing out the window at the night sky, I'm here, and the cage you've been hiding in won't save you.

CHAPTER 16

THE MASTER SUITE

Sid was disappointed with himself; he was not a man to panic, he never had been. Even when the heat had been greatest, just after the murders, he'd been the one to remain calm. The fool Frank had shot that couple and the next day it was all over the news. *Monsters Kill Parents, Leave Little Girl Alive!* They shouldn't have killed anyone, but if that was the way it played out they should not have left a witness. Not that she'd done the cops any good. All they had to go on were three anonymous men and a dead couple. They'd been very careful up until then, no fingerprints, nothing to trace. The mail connection, sure, but by the time the police put that together in some little "ah-ha" moment, the three of them would be long gone and Frank's girl-friend from the post office would be as well. Sid felt bad for her, even though there'd never been any proof Frank got rid of her, but if you play with fire you will surely be burnt. She had cast her lot with a sociopath, they all had, and look what it had cost them. Leaving his life a second time, van-ishing again, would be emotionally difficult but not impossible. He didn't have that many years left and he was not about to spend them behind bars or, worse, in an early grave.

He had no idea who was after him but he knew it was connected to the girl. She was behind this. She must have hired someone to hunt them down. An expensive proposition, given the amount of money someone this professional would charge. Two murders with a third on the way? Could it be? Might the little girl they'd missed while she cowered in her parents' closet have found them thirty years later and still hated them enough to send a killer after them? Or had she simply never stopped hating them and bided her time until an opportunity came, the recognition of a face in a crowd . . . or a watch.

He was sitting at his desk as the sun slowly set to the west. It was that time of day, the gloaming some called it, when the landscape fell to the slowly lengthening cape of night. His knees were bothering him, especially the left one. He wanted to beg off dinner but knew Dylan would be disappointed. Appearances, Sid, appearances. They all come here, they pay good money, we want them coming back. Passing on the pumpkin carving was okay, but joining for dinner was a must. In a few minutes he would change into his nice slacks and a cardigan, slide his feet into his tan penny loafers, the ones with dimes in them, and make his way downstairs. But first he wanted to see something.

He went online and typed in the dead couple's name. "Lapinksy murder Los Feliz 1981." News that old might not be online, but a dogged reporter with nothing better to do had written a "where are they now" piece for the Los Angeles Times over a decade ago: where was the little girl now, on the twentieth anniversary of the unsolved murders that had rocked the tony neighborhood of Los Feliz. He began to read the article, only available because it had been referenced from another website, and saw that the reporter had been stymied as well. Emily Lapinsky had ceased to exist. She'd left Santa Barbara for Minnesota and vanished.

Minnesota . . . Minnesota . . . didn't he hear Ricki talking to one of the guests who said she was from Minnesota?

He read on and was thankful the reporter was as determined as she had been. She found Emily living in St. Paul, designing jewelry she sold on the internet. Her name was now Bo, Bo Sweetzer. Bo did not give interviews, the reporter discovered. Bo denied being or knowing anyone named Emily Lapinsky.

Interesting, Sid thought, as he scanned the now-forty-year-old woman's website, BoAndBeholdJewerly.com. Very good at what she did. The pieces on display were stunning and clearly custom made, as well as very expensive. Also of considerable interest, she was good at not having photos of herself, anywhere. There were none on the website, and it was only by spending ten minutes jumping from one hyperlink to another that Sid finally found a picture of young Emily, now all grown up and named Bo. She was at an art gallery opening, part of the background, but she'd been identified in the text and that is what snared her. It wasn't a great photograph, but it was good enough for Sid to recognize her as the woman in Room 202.

So she hadn't hired anyone, he thought, feeling a newfound respect for this woman as well as a growing apprehension. And while it was only conjecture at this point, he pondered how much determination it must have taken to vanish, to become not only another person, but a person on a mission, to wait and plan and when the chance came, to strike.

He erased his search history, something he'd been doing since that snoop Teddy started looking into things that were none of his business, and turned off his computer. It was time for dinner, time to greet the guests with a particular one in mind.

CHAPTER 17

AN INTIMATE ENCOUNTER

One of Dylan's greatest strengths at running the Lodge, a strength he would otherwise never have known he had, was his insistence on treating the guests as if they were visitors to his own home, which they were. This was just a very large house and the visitors numbered in the dozens. Fifty-six to be exact, not counting the staff and the locals who came for dinner and the downstairs bars, swelling the annual Halloween party to well over a hundred. Dylan would accommodate anyone who wanted to dine with just a special someone, or friends who'd come together, seating them at a table for four, but he also enjoyed setting up tables for six or eight and mixing it up. He got the idea from a cruise he'd taken with Sid some years before, where passengers sit with people they'd just met at the dining table their first night and get to know one another over the course of the cruise. Granted, it didn't always work out perfectly, and occasionally table mates didn't like each other, or they would stop coming to the main seating and eat elsewhere on the ship, but for the most part it was an effective social mixer, and that's what Dylan was all about. Mixing it up, keeping it interesting for the guests, doing everything he could to make sure they'd be back.

Friday night in the dining room was always busy, and on a special weekend it could become chaotic, at least for the wait staff, cooks and extra help that had to be brought in. Ricki had transformed himself into a hostess in a shimmering red sheath dress and red hair bigger and wider than his shoulders. When Kyle and Danny made their first visit to Pride Lodge, neither one of them had realized that Ricki who had checked them was the same Ricki who seated them for dinner. He wouldn't stay that way all night, changing back to jeans and a sweatshirt before heading downstairs for a nightcap and a song at Clyde's piano. The music was provided by one of two or three local musicians who took turns headlining. Legend had it the bar was named after the first piano player in the joint, an old woman who called herself Clyde and who died at the piano one Saturday night from an aneurism.

Also in attendance tonight was Kevin the Karaoke host and general emcee, rested from an afternoon nap. He lived in Stockton with his mother in a house along the Delaware River she'd owned with her late husband since the 1950s. It wasn't grand, but its view of the river was spectacular, and, since Kevin was the only child, he saw no reason to move away. Mom was close to 90 and Kevin expected to soon be living alone. So there he stayed, and every weekend he would check into the Lodge, same room that he sometimes shared with one or two of the staff if things went on too long or they drank too much to drive home. Most recently his roommate had been Happy, and Kevin, though he'd not said anything, suspected something ugly had happened to him. Happy was a good kid, with the emphasis on 'kid.' He was legally an adult, but most people were still wet behind the ears at that age, still inexperienced in the survival techniques that saw one into one's 50s and beyond.

Kevin was filling in at the main desk while Ricki seated people. It wasn't his job, nor had he been asked to help out, but he was in a good mood and this was the busiest weekend of the year. He was wearing a sheep costume with a Bo-Peep doll under his arm. Kyle waved as he and Danny came into the Lodge. The temperature had dropped considerably from the night before, and it had made Kyle think of something that had slipped all their minds that morning: Teddy hadn't been dressed for a chilly October night. Even someone who was drunk—if that had been the case—had the sense to put on a sweater or a jacket in late October. But they'd found him at the bottom of the pool in loafers without socks and a button-down blue striped shirt, with a shattered martini glass by his hand. It made no sense, none of it did, and Kyle hoped his meeting with Dylan later that night would clear some things up, or give him enough reason to call the detective. Forty-eight hours, wasn't that what they said on all those cop shows? Forty-eight hours and the case begins to go cold. He wouldn't be here forty-eight hours from now; things had to move quickly if they were going to move at all.

Danny knew Dylan's modus operandi by now and when Dylan came over to seat them Danny deliberately waved at Eileen, who was sitting by herself at a large table near a window. Ricki had his hands full with a group of women who'd already started drinking at the tiny restaurant bar and kept commenting on people's costumes, very loudly.

"Eileen!" Danny called out, "How about some company?"

Dylan frowned. He had wanted to seat them with some newcomers, determined to replicate his cruise experience regardless of its effectiveness on dry land.

"Please," Dylan said to them, declining to walk them over. "Enjoy."

Kyle and Danny made their way over to the table for six where Eileen was halfway through a glass of white wine. She was dressed as a scarecrow, and it looked like the exact costume, burlap and all, that Kyle had worn the year before.

"Ouch," Kyle said, taking a seat to Eileen's right, with Danny between them.

She knew he was talking about her costume, and said, "Never again. The scarecrow was the one without a brain, right? He'd have to be brainless to wear this damn thing."

"But it was cheap," they both said, and laughed.

"You get what you pay for," Kyle said. "Where's Maggie?"

"I think her battery went dead. You spend that much time on a smart phone or iThing or whatever and you don't last long, constantly re-charging. So that's what she's doing, watching CSI or NCIS or XYZ-something reruns on television. Which one of you is Laurel, by the way? I never could keep them straight."

"Oliver Hardy was the short, fat one," Danny said, "Does that help?"

"Hardy was taller, actually," Kyle said, "and you're not fat. There's a pillow in there, remember."

Dallas—or was it Austin?—suddenly appeared across from them with a pen and order pad in hand to take their drink orders. He was dressed as a Chimney sweep, with black high-water jeans and a t-shirt streaked with charcoal, as was his face. He had on red suspenders, which Kyle didn't think were part of the chimney sweep look, but it didn't matter. He looked at the waiter a moment too long.

"Austin," the young waiter said, knowing Kyle was trying to decide which of the twins he was. "You'll have an easy time of it tonight. Dallas is David Bowie with the lightning bolt on his face. I think it's so forty years ago, but whatever. "

"Sure," Eileen said. "Chimney sweeps are so . . . a day ago."

"Timeless is the word. What can I get you to drink?"

Kyle ordered a Bloody Mary and Danny a vodka martini, dirty with olives. Austin hurried off as quickly and quietly as he'd arrived and the three of them got back to their conversation.

Just then Linus Hern showed up, and, like Kyle and Danny, he ignored Dylan's attempt to seat him, his boyfriend and his two hangers-on at the large table for eight. Danny thought it was odd, since the biggest table in the room had the appearance of being where the captain ate—whoever that captain was and whatever ship he was sailing. For Linus to turn down a place at the center of attention seemed unlike him, until Danny remembered that Linus was always the center of attention, it mattered not where he sat.

The group's trajectory brought them past Kyle and Danny's table. Linus was dressed as someone out of the Matrix movies, complete with sweeping black coat that ran from his buttoned collar down to his black boots. His boyfriend was wearing a collar as well, but studded, and Danny took it as an indication of what the pair did behind closed doors. Aside from the collar, the handsome youth was wearing a suit, as one might to a fine restaurant. The two sycophants appeared to be Munchkins representing a Lollipop Guild from Hell.

As they floated by the table Linus stopped in front of Danny. Danny eyed him quickly and said, "No costume this year?"

Linus chuckled. "You're very amusing, Mr. Durban. This," he said, indicating his companion in the studded collar, "is Carlos, remember the name. Phineus you've met."

"I fired him, as you told the room earlier."

"Yes, you fired him. And this is Henry. Not nearly as distinct a name as Phineus, but with its own rich history. Now if you'll excuse us, Carlos is a feng shui expert and said this table's toxic."

"It's nice to meet you all," Kyle said. He secretly enjoyed encounters between Linus and Danny.

"The pleasure's all yours," Linus said dryly. Then he leaned down just a bit and said to Danny, "Tell Margaret happy birthday for me. Eighty is quite an accomplishment. She can't have many left."

"I'll give her your regards," Danny said. "I know how much you mean to her."

"So much I wasn't invited."

"It's a small venue, nothing personal."

"Not at all," Linus said. "Not at all. I'm sure she'll remember me for her ninetieth. Or maybe not."

The Munchkins chuckled slightly. Carlos the collar boy didn't seem to get it and just looked bored.

"We'll see you later at the bar?" Linus said.

"He'll be asleep," Kyle interjected. "Beauty rest, Linus, something you could use more of."

"Oh I did forget you're just about as entertaining as your husband. You are married, aren't you? New York permits it now."

"It's in the planning," Danny said. "Don't worry, you'll be the last to know."

The sparring had run its course, the verbal fencing having left a prick or two but drawn no blood. It was time to get on with the evening, something they all realized and silently agreed on as Linus nodded goodbye and took his troupe to a table in the corner.

"Who was that?" Eileen asked, having stayed quiet through the exchange.

"The Creature from the Chelsea Lagoon," Danny replied. "No one to be concerned with."

The restaurant was filling up by then and Kyle was wondering if they might be joined by some strangers when Bo walked into the restaurant, spotted them and came over. "May I?" she asked.

They all nodded. Kyle knew people often formed clusters at extended gatherings. It seemed natural to gravitate toward a few other guests as a way of increasing the comfort level and having reliable conversation partners when they all knew they would be there for a weekend.

"To costume or not to costume," Bo said as she took one of the two remaining seats. "I decided not to. I'd rather surprise everyone tomorrow night and walk away with the prize."

"There's a prize?" Eileen asked, waving across the room at Austin to let him know they had another person at the table.

"The prize is for the pumpkin," Danny said. "I don't think they give another one for costume, do they?"

"We haven't stayed that late to find out," Kyle said.

"We should this year."

"Fine. You'll be sleeping in a booth by then but we can set our sights high."

Bo picked up one of the menus and glanced at it. It hadn't changed since Kyle and Danny had been there in the spring, or, for that matter, since Pucky had sold the place to Sid and Dylan. They'd hired a new chef and made a few changes, but they had kept the Lodge's long-time success in mind and not fixed what wasn't broken. There were lamb, chicken, fish and vegetarian lasagna dishes as entrees, supplemented with a half dozen choices for sides and appetizers.

"How's the food here?" Bo asked.

"Above average," Danny said.

"He'd know, too," said Kyle. "He manages one of the best restaurants in Manhattan."

"But homey, don't you think?" Danny added. "Margaret's—she's a real person, by the way—it's high-end but not uncomfortably so."

"True, anybody would feel welcome there, providing they can spend a couple hundred dollars for dinner."

"So they come for lunch and only part with half that. It's a bargain."

"You think it's a bargain because we get to eat there for free."

The two women watched, amused, as Kyle and Danny mildly bickered over Margaret's Passion.

Eileen suddenly jumped at a hand on her shoulder. Sid had come up to the table unseen and unheard. He was wearing gray trousers and a navy jacket over his sweater, looking unusually dapper, like the proprietor of a guest lodge he was.

"Kyle," he said, his voice low and full. It had a soothing depth to it, and Kyle sensed that Sid had deliberately adjusted his voice.

"Sid," Danny answered, "The weekend's going great, you look full."

"Me or the Lodge?" Sid said, following it with an affected laugh. "Halloween is the big event here every year, you know that. It was falling off some in Pucky's last year, he just wasn't up to it and it made people . . . sad, I suppose. Quite a few stayed away last year, but it was so good you and Kyle came. I know it meant a lot to Pucky. I heard he might be coming."

"Really?" Kyle said, pleasantly surprised.

"Yes, but not staying here. We'd know, of course. Too painful for him I'd guess."

"Who's Pucky?" asked Bo. She was smiling, but it was as artificial as Sid's voice. She was staring at him and something told her he hadn't come to their table by chance.

"May I?" Sid said, nodding at the last available seat. No one objected, and in a moment Sid was sitting with them, next to the woman who had come here to kill him.

"Pucky Green was the owner of Pride Lodge, along with his partner Stu Patterson, for twenty-three years? Twenty-five? They built it up from an old Inn that was about to be torn down. Then two years ago poor Stu died from a heart attack on the steps to the pool."

"That's a very unlucky pool," Bo said. "Maybe you should fill it in."

Kyle noticed a tension between the Lodge owner and the jewelry maker. There wasn't any reason for it he knew of, and he wondered, watching and listening to them, if Bo was someone who simply didn't care for men. But that didn't jibe, since she'd been very friendly with him. And then he thought it might simply be a case of clashing personas; if there was love at first sight, there was certainly dislike at first sight.

"Do you suppose that detective will come back?" Bo asked. "For follow up questions?"

"Why, Bo, it sounds like you're interested in Ms. Sikorsky. Plenty of couples have met here over the years, but I'm not sure she's even family."

Bo blushed, having been seen through so easily, and just as quickly realized he had called her by name. They'd not spoken since she arrived.

"Who mentioned my name to you?"

Sid smiled with all the warmth of a lizard eyeing its meal, and said, "Oh, I make it my business to know all the guests' names. It's the right thing to do." He put his hand out at last, "Sid," he said. "Sid Stanhope, I own Pride Lodge, along with my husband Dylan."

She shook his hand and held it, staring into his eyes. Two could play at the predator game.

"Let's have a table photo," Kyle said. He took the camera from the table and walked around to get a shot of the others.

"But you're not in it!" Eileen protested. "And my hair looks like straw!"

"It is straw," Kyle said. "Besides, I don't take pictures of myself. So everybody just squeeze in a little and smile when I say so."

Sid slid his chair in from one side, Eileen from the other. Bo found herself being pressed against by a man who had been in her house thirty years ago and seen the bodies of her parents, dead in their bed with bullet wounds in their heads. She at once wanted to move away, fearful she would find a knife blade slipped between her ribs, and to move closer, ever closer, to feel his breath on her face as she watched him die.

"Cheese!" Kyle said. They all smiled reflexively and he snapped the picture.

"I should say hello to the others," Sid said, easing back to his place and rising from his chair. "I'm not supposed to play favorites." And then, to Bo, "Not even with someone so charming as yourself. A jewelry maker, no less."

"Yes," she replied, her voice cold. The game was clearly up. "I specialize in pocket watches."

"So I'm told," Sid said. "Well, everyone. I'll head off now and do the meet-n-greet. See you all at the party tomorrow, if not sooner. And don't forget to vote on the pumpkins. There's a high-tech basket with pencils and paper on the front desk. I'm partial to Bo's Cinderella, but I mustn't given anything away, it's not fair."

Sid glanced at her one final time, adjusted his smile, and walked away from the table.

Both Kyle and Danny wanted to say, "What was that?" but neither did. Instead they turned to find Austin back at last with their drinks. Animosity still hung in the air, and Kyle waved it away, telling himself it had just been a strange encounter, nothing more. He put his camera back on the table and sat down.

CHAPTER 18

A LITTLE NIGHT MUSIC

As Kyle knew he would, Danny declined to go to the bar that night, once they'd settled back into their cabin after dinner. It had long been Danny's habit to retire to their bed shortly after dinner and read books or magazines with the television on low volume.

This night Danny found a Frasier marathon on the Hallmark Channel. He'd undressed, slipped into the gym shorts he slept in along with his t-shirt, and nestled under the covers to watch the reruns and eat from a box of chocolates every guest at the Lodge found on their beds when they checked in.

"You're going dressed as Laurel?" Danny said, watching Kyle get ready to head to the piano bar.

"Why not?" Kyle said. "It's more trouble to change clothes. I don't plan on staying long anyway, once I hear what Dylan has to say."

"What do you think's going on? And why get involved? This is something for the police."

Kyle had been lying next to Danny, resting up after dinner, but had got up and started adjusting his clothes in the dresser mirror. "I agree with you, and I have every intention of calling Detective Sikorsky myself if this is more than lurid speculation. He can be lurid, you know. Dylan's got a dramatic streak."

"Death is dramatic."

Kyle glanced at Danny in the mirror.

"There was a death, remember?"

"Of course I remember. And it was a death that might have been prevented if I'd picked up the phone and called Teddy last night."

"Have you thought about that?" Danny asked.

"About what?"

"About what if it was an accident? What if Teddy fell off the wagon and ended up falling in the pool?"

"I don't think that's what happened."

"Because you don't want to think it, Kyle."

"He was sober, I believe that."

"Just don't believe it against the evidence, whatever that turns out to be."

Kyle sighed, knowing Danny was right. He didn't want to believe Teddy had gone over the edge, that he'd thrown away six months hard-earned sobriety. But it happened all the time. Addiction was merciless, and all it took was one sip from a glass or a bottle and someone like Teddy could find himself right back where he started—or even where he ended.

The Lodge was emptying out by the time Kyle got back. He'd lingered in the cabin longer than intended, and when he walked back in he saw the twins and Elzbetta closing up the restaurant. It was after 10:00 pm, and the restaurant had seated its last guest at 9:00. Ricki had changed back into his civilian clothes and was fidgeting behind the check-in desk. Few people would still be arriving at this time of night, but a few did and the desk was staffed until midnight. Grueling hours, Kyle thought, as he walked into the great room and saw a couple of stragglers playing checkers at a table, and Jeremy Johnson, the ancient sentry, settled in for his night of television watching until well past the witching hour. Jeremy would be the last person standing—or in his case sitting—and was so much of a fixture during his stays that people tended not to notice him; he, however, noticed everything and everyone.

Kyle regretted having kept his Stan Laurel costume on. The suit didn't fit well and the bowler hat was at least a size too small, making it perch on his head rather than fit it.

"What's on tonight, Jeremy?" he said to the old man. Jeremy was wearing pastel striped pajamas, and it was not a costume. This is how he dressed after dinner, for his long stay in the easy chair.

"A couple of Christopher Lee Draculas," Jeremy replied. He had a snifter of brandy sitting on the small stand by his chair. Kyle knew it would be top-of-the line and supplied by Jeremy himself. The old gent may love his visits to Pride Lodge, but there were some things even he was too particular about to leave to his hosts.

"They scared the shit out of me when I was a kid."

"Me, too!" Ricki said from behind the desk. "Maybe I'll join you."

"Off to the bar?" Jeremy asked.

"Normally no, not by myself," Kyle said. "But I thought a nightcap was in order. Danny's asleep right about"—and he looked at his watch—"now."

"Have fun. The kids are a little wild for me, as you know."

By 'kids' Jeremy meant anyone under the age of sixty. Kyle waved to him, noticing the two men playing checkers had never looked up during the exchange, and made his way downstairs.

"Basement" wasn't really a word that described the below-ground level of Pride Lodge. It usually conjured images of house basements with family rooms or exercise setups, washers and dryers and boxes stored away never to be opened. The basement of the Lodge was cavernous, as long and wide as the Lodge itself, and Pucky had had the idea to gut it, renovate it, and launch it as two clubs in one: a piano bar reminiscent of his favorites in New York City, and an adjacent karaoke club.

The following night the clubs would be combined for the annual Halloween blowout, but tonight they still maintained separate identities. He glanced into the karaoke bar, christened "Club K" (not, he presumed, a reference to the infamous club drug Ketamine, but to "karaoke"), and saw a dozen people sitting at booths around a central stage area where Kevin was announcing the next singer.

He headed past it down the short hall and was immediately met with the sounds of Pete the Piano Guy playing and singing "Come In From The Rain," the Melissa Manchester, Carole Bayer Sager collaboration that always gave him goose bumps. It was a melancholy song and he knew there wouldn't be too many of those played this weekend.

He entered Clyde's and glanced around. The decor consisted of love-seats, sofas and overstuffed armchairs accompanied by small tables for drinks; a bar area with a dozen stools, and in a corner a baby grand where Pete held court with just his voice, his music sheets, and a giant snifter as a tip jar. Kyle knew nothing about Pete except that he'd been the main entertainment here since Clyde herself passed on some twenty years ago. He rotated now and then with other local musicians, but Pete was the main headliner. The fact that so many of the Lodge's staff and guests had been there for many years made it that much more welcoming. It was, Kyle knew, an old friend to many, and he nodded at Pete when he entered. He noticed Pete had lost weight: the piano player wore a tuxedo, his own gimmick, but Kyle saw it was a much smaller tuxedo than it had been the last time he and Danny were here.

There were probably twenty people in the bar, as Kyle made a quick headcount. Cowboy Dave was bartending, named so for his habit of wearing a cowboy hat even though there was nothing else cowboy about him. He, too, had been a regular presence at Pride Lodge for some years, certainly since before Kyle and Danny had been coming there, and Kyle said hello as he stepped to the bar and ordered a diet cola. He wanted his senses about him tonight and wouldn't allow himself so much as a beer.

"How's it hanging, Kyle?" Dave asked, sliding the soda across to Kyle.

"You'd have to ask Danny that," Kyle said, winking.

"Good to know it still works at our age, ain't it?" Dave said.

Kyle wasn't sure how old Dave was, and he couldn't tell if there was hair under the hat or not; he'd never seen Dave without it. But he looked to be about fifty, and a well-kept fifty at that. The kind of older man who did a hundred sit-ups in the morning while he watched the news.

"Sorry about Happy," Kyle said, sipping his drink.

"Oh, he'll come back," Dave said, and Kyle saw a distress on Dave's face that made him think the older man and the younger one had been more than co-workers. But he knew Happy and Teddy had had something going. In fact, that was what he thought Teddy wanted to talk about and why he was leaving the Lodge. Relationships get very complicated in close quarters.

"I'll have help tomorrow night," Dave said. "Elzbetta for some lesbian vibe, it's always good to have, and the twins. Ricki gets the night to party, it's his turn this year."

Kyle marveled at the planning, execution and sheer work of keeping an operation like the Lodge going. Someone on duty almost twenty-four hours a day. Bartending, the restaurant, it really was quite a daily undertaking.

"I never expected to see her here," Dave said, indicating someone along the wall behind Kyle. "Maybe she's curious. It happens."

Kyle set his drink down, turned around, and was surprised to see Detective Linda Sikorsky sitting alone on a leather loveseat under a low-lit sconce. She saw Kyle looking at her and waved slightly. Kyle took it as an invitation, whether it was or not, and headed over to her.

She looked handsome dressed in civilian clothes. Sky-blue jeans Kyle guessed had been made to look that way with some sort of stone washing; a tan blouse with just a slight frill down the buttons; brown leather loafers. Even in street clothes she projected calm and confidence, and Kyle noticed for the first time her green eyes, made more startling by their obvious intelligence and curiosity. This was a woman who did not miss anything, and he suddenly understood that that's why she was here: the good detective was interested in what she could learn from coming closer to what could be the scene of a crime.

"Mr. Callahan," Linda said, patting the cushion next to her. "Have a seat."

Kyle sat down and placed his drink on a side table. "Here for an after dinner drink?" he asked.

"What else would I be here for?"

He saw she was being mischievous.

"I'm not gay, not officially," she said. "But I'm thinking about it. Which is still not why I'm here. I wanted to get a feel for things."

"In a piano bar full of mature patrons."

"At Pride Lodge," she said. "The place has quite a history. I've been reading about it. Did you know it was a farmhouse in the early 1800s?"

"I had no idea."

"Yes, and the man who owned it lost two children and his wife in rapid succession. Influenza. He was heartbroken, left the farm to decay and was never heard from again."

"That explains the whispers of haunting."

She arched an eyebrow and reached for her glass of white wine on a coffee table in front of them.

"Ghosts on the moors, you know."

"More recently," she continued, "what came to be known as 'Pride Lodge' was sold to Sid Stanhope and Dylan Tremblay. Or more accurately sold to one of them with the money to buy it."

"Let me guess," Kyle said. "Sid."

"Yes, Sid," she answered. "Who, most astonishingly, paid cash with the explanation he'd recently inherited it."

"Lucky man, unlucky relative. Nobody wondered about such good fortune?"

"Cash is still king. Questions have a way of never being asked when there's a million dollars on the table. Make that a million-five."

Kyle was as torn as he was intrigued. He considered telling her about Dylan's aside during the pumpkin carving. But if he told her she would likely get involved, or want to somehow listen in. He thought he should wait and hear what Dylan had to tell him, then decide what to do with the information.

"You don't think Teddy fell into the pool by accident, either," he said, feeling a sadness as he remembered how the day had begun. "That means a lot to me."

"As much as I'm starting to like you, my interest is in justice."

He nodded, understanding. It wasn't about what Kyle wanted or needed to be true, but what Teddy needed to be known.

It was then he saw Dylan in the hallway, looking at him. The two of them exchanged quick nods, as Dylan disappeared to the men's room and Kyle got up to follow.

"Be careful, Detective Callahan," she said.

No, Kyle thought to himself, she didn't miss a thing.

"Isn't meeting in a bathroom a little . . . I don't know, B-movieish?"

Kyle was leaning against the wall while Dylan poked his head out the door a last time to make sure no one was coming.

Dylan bent down and looked under the stalls: no one there, the coast was clear.

"I can't risk being overheard," he said, in a voice so low and soft he assured he would not be.

"Dylan, listen —"

"I saw you with the cop lady. She shouldn't be here."

"You run a public establishment. Besides, she'll be a lesbian soon and she has to start somewhere."

"Can we not joke for the moment?" Dylan said, and Kyle realized he was truly afraid.

"What's going on here?"

"I don't know!" Dylan said, his voice rising. "I don't know! That's the problem. I think Sid stole the money to buy this place."

"I thought he inherited the money from an aunt."

"That's what he said, but why is it I never met this aunt? And when I went searching . . . nothing, Kyle. If there was a rich aunt he never mentioned, she did a very good job of taking any trace of herself to the grave. No, I think he stole the money, and I think Teddy found out."

"A fatal bit of information, so it seems."

"Please, I so much don't want to think that. We've been together for ten years. I know Sid, he wouldn't hurt anyone."

Kyle waited a moment, hoping Dylan would relax enough to have a conversation that wasn't infused with panic.

"So he wouldn't hurt anyone, but he would steal a million dollars, or whatever the Lodge cost . . ."

"Most of it's the land. And yes, I'm afraid he would. But I can't say for sure he did! He told me it was an inheritance."

"Good timing."

"Good timing, indeed. I never questioned him. There wasn't any reason to, and . . . no desire to. I mean, this was the chance of a lifetime, a dream come true."

"Where would he get his hands on that kind of money if it wasn't inherited?" Kyle asked.

"He worked at a bank," Dylan hissed, and it was suddenly clear. If Sid had stolen the money, he had embezzled it; a large sum of it, which could not go unnoticed forever.

"You need to speak to the police," Kyle said. "And they need to speak to the bank."

Dylan was crestfallen, his face expressing pain and indecision. This was his partner, his husband, the man he planned to spend the rest of his life with.

"I can't," he said.

Suddenly Kyle knew why they were having this conversation: Dylan wanted him to be the one to go to the authorities. He'd been able to reveal his suspicions to Kyle, but not to take it further, not to put his prints on a noose that might soon be around Sid Stanhope's neck.

"I have to tell her," Kyle said, meaning Detective Sikorsky. "I'm not in a position to do anything else with this information."

Dylan nodded, having accepted as much.

Kyle felt terribly for this man whom he could at best call an acquaintance. They'd never had a long conversation, never shared a meal, but he thought of what it would mean to him if Danny faced a crisis that could separate them. Danny, of course, would never commit a crime, let alone murder, but life had a way of dropping boulders on the unsuspecting.

"I don't know why I told you this," Dylan said, regretting his decision to speak to Kyle.

"Because you have a conscience," Kyle said, and he started to leave.

Dylan grabbed his arm. "He's not a killer. I don't know how Teddy ended up in the pool, but Sid didn't put him there. I refuse to believe that."

Kyle believed him—not that Sid was incapable of killing someone (a million-five was a serious motive), but that Dylan loved him enough to deny it. He patted Dylan's hand, gently removed it from his arm and headed back to the bar.

Pete was singing Billy Joel's "The Piano Man," joined in the chorus by a half dozen guests ringing the piano. Kyle walked back in and looked to the sofa, only to see it was empty. He wandered to the bar instead.

"She left with someone," Cowboy Dave said, knowing who Kyle was looking for.

So she wasn't such a novice after all, and while she may not have come there looking for a date, she'd had no trouble accepting one.

"That Bo chick," Dave said, as if Kyle must know who she was. His use of the word "chick" seemed dated and quaint, given that few women at Pride Lodge would consider themselves chicks.

It struck Kyle as odd; Bo had told Sid and the others at the table she would not be going to the bar later that night. He wondered if she'd simply had a change of heart, or if perhaps she hoped to get lucky. Rural Pennsylvania can be a lonely place at night, even at Pride Lodge.

Good for her, he thought, reflecting on the detective meeting up with the loner from St. Paul. Maybe fate would treat them well, at least for a weekend.

He waved goodnight at Dave and Pete, smiled at the enjoyment everyone was having at another Halloween weekend at Pride Lodge, and headed upstairs. As he came into the great room he saw old Jeremy in his chair, alone now, watching his Dracula movie in the dark.

"Good night, Jeremy," he said, crossing in front of the television.

"Good night, Kyle," Jeremy replied, never taking his eyes off Christopher Lee. The vampire was just about to feed.

CHAPTER 19

NATURAL CAUSES

Kyle was surprised to find Danny awake first on Saturday morning. He discovered it when he reached across the bed, half asleep, and found an empty mattress next to him. He looked up, focused, and saw Danny sitting at the small table with his restaurant notes and a reading flashlight.

"Why don't you turn the light on?" Kyle said, his voice thick with sleep.

"I didn't want to wake you," Danny said. He was wearing just his boxer shorts and t-shirt.

Kyle rolled back, facing the ceiling. "I thought you weren't going to work this weekend."

"I'm not working."

"So what's on your mind? You're never up at—" and he glanced at the clock on the nightstand—"six-thirty! On a weekend?"

Kyle remembered getting back to the cabin after midnight. "What's troubling you?" he said, knowing from his years with Danny that the only thing that would have him out of bed this early was worry.

"She's going to be eighty next week. That's old, you know."

Margaret Bowman was a second mother to Danny. She'd taken him under her wing and nurtured him along, and had hinted more than once to him that he was her heir apparent. With no children of her own, and no nieces or nephews who were interested in the business, even if she had been inclined to leave it to them, she worried Margaret's Passion would die with her. Then along came Danny and it seemed fated that they would form the sort of mentor/parent bond they had. The thought of Margaret coming to the end of her years weighed on him.

"She's sharp as a tack," Kyle said. "And she still gets around very nicely. She comes down and talks to people in the restaurant. Why are you thinking about this?"

"I don't know. I just feel time passing, that's all." And then, suddenly, "We should get married next year."

They'd talked about marriage ever since New York passed a bill making it legal. At first Kyle had wanted to make the trip to City Hall quickly, seeing the rush of excitement and the sight of history unfolding on television. He thought their fifth anniversary, which was only a month away at the time, would be an ideal date to get married. But the thrill quickly died down and both men decided to take an informed approach: what does marriage mean, what are the legal ramifications, what is the hurry? They knew they would do it, but they would do it in their own time. And now, unexpectedly, Danny was pushing to make it official: to be husbands in more than name only.

"Well," Kyle said, "a wedding takes time. It's October now—November, really—so maybe next summer . . ."

"Next year, for sure," Danny said. Then, glancing at the seating chart for Margaret's birthday luncheon, "I'm sure she'll make it another year. Hell, another ten. She's a tough old bird."

Kyle wasn't comfortable when Danny became melancholic. He picked up the television remote from the nightstand and turned on the TV, wanting to watch the news and change the subject.

There on the local channel was a young woman reporter, dressed warmly for the weather but still television-pretty with strawberry blonde hair and a face perfectly made up at six o'clock on a Saturday morning. Her breath was coming out in clouds, which told Kyle it was colder than it had been yesterday. Wetter, too, as it appeared to have been raining where the woman was. Identified on the screen as Ellie Cameron from Philly6, she stood in a wooded area while several policemen moved around behind her.

"The body found in Chester Creek has been identified as Happy Corcoran."

"What?!" Kyle shouted, sitting up in bed.

"A neighbor of Mr. Corcoran's from Stockton, New Jersey, responded to our earlier report on a body found in the woods and called authorities. Apparently Mr. Corcoran has been missing for several days and the neighbor thought the description was familiar. The coroner is declining comment on a cause of death until an autopsy's been performed. As you can see, police continue to search the area for evidence of just what happened here, and when. If you have any information about Happy Corcoran and his movements, please contact the Sheriff's Department immediately. All calls are kept confidential. This is Ellie Cameron from Philly6, back to you, Carlton."

Kyle hit the mute button. He and Danny both stared at the television, stunned.

"That reporter's a long way from Philly," Danny said. "I think. I mean, where the hell is Chester Creek?"

"Far enough from civilization that a body could lie there for days without anyone seeing it. And a body in a creek is news for a local Philadelphia station. It's only an hour from here."

"This isn't going to go well," Danny said, and Kyle knew he meant at the Lodge. "We can't be the only people who saw this. Poor Cowboy Dave. They had a thing, you know. Before Happy and Teddy. Or maybe at the same time, kids are like that."

"I didn't know, but I guessed. The way Dave talked about him. So sad. And so mysterious. I mean, think about it. Happy goes missing three days ago. Teddy dies at the bottom of the pool yesterday."

"Do you want to check out?" Danny said. "Go back to the City?"

Kyle looked at him, surprised. "God no, not now. I want to know what's going on here. I want to talk to Detective Sikorsky." He swung his legs around and sat up on the edge of the bed. He was wearing the red plaid pajama bottoms he always slept up. He slid his feet into the slippers Danny had given him. "And I want to do some research. Something about the exchange at dinner between Sid and that Bo woman, it was odd. And she said she wasn't going to the bar last night but did, and left with the detective! I don't know, I'm just curious. Please tell me you brought the laptop, I haven't seen it out."

"It's in the suitcase," Danny said. "Have I ever forgotten it?"

"Yes, in Key West."

"And you'll never let me forget it. All those amazing photographs that had to wait for you to post on your blog until we got home. Consider it a lesson in patience."

Kyle got out of bed and walked over to the suitcase. He wanted his morning coffee and some time with a search engine.

"You want the sound back on?" he asked.

"Leave it off," Danny said, sliding his papers to the side. "We've had enough excitement for now, and a lot more waiting up the hill."

CHAPTER 20

ROOM 202

*T*he moon was *so large the sight of it took Bo's breath away as she glanced across the bed, out past the window into the night sky. The blackness of the heavens in the Pennsylvania countryside had struck her the first night here; before that, even, as she'd driven from St. Paul along back roads, far away from city lights that stole the majesty of the stars. They were bare and innumerable here. She likened them to the beauty of the woman lying next to her, breathing gently in her sleep. She chose to ignore the irony of sleeping next to the very woman whose choices in life were her polar opposite: Linda Sikorsky, detective, seeker of facts, if not truth, justice personified as she followed and tracked and peered into puzzles, with her one goal of solving them and stopping even some small evil in the world. Bo Sweetzer, Emily Lapinsky as a child, a good person from all appearances, a woman set on revenge behind the goodness. She didn't fool herself; while many people would say the men she'd killed had only got what they deserved, she knew she was a murderer. There were no degrees of murder and those who commit it: killing was killing, and here she was, watching someone she could so easily love, asleep and dreaming beside her, who would not hesitate to see her sentenced to a life behind bars.*

What was an assassin to do? Should she slip away now, so soon after first light? Should she abandon her mission, let the old man live, and try to build a life with this policewoman? A life of secrets and lies? Or should she—and this she knew to be the answer—complete the one true objective of her life: to silence the voices that had haunted her for thirty years, to put an end to the screams of a child watching her parents be coldly, brutally murdered. For a handful of cash. A watch. She sighed, knowing what she had to do, that she would be taking one life while setting free another, and that after the coming day she would never see this woman again, this woman whose shoulders she now leaned over gently and caressed.

Bo rolled over in her empty bed and stared out the window, seeing it would be a sunny day. The clouds had moved on and left in their place a startling blue sky. She let the fantasy of love with Linda Sikorsky go, evaporate like morning dew. She was both amused and troubled by her willingness to think the unthinkable. Nothing had happened between them except in her imagination. It was just as well, since her imagination had always been a dark and lonely place. Only the men she exacted revenge upon belonged there.

They'd had coffee and pie at the Eagle Diner in New Hope. Bo admitted to herself she wanted more—expected more, in the way we sometimes allow ourselves to think we are entitled to something simply because we wish it—but Sikorsky had not promised anything at all, spoken or unspoken, and she had not led Bo to believe their trip away from the Lodge was anything other than a friendly ride to a nearby diner for a private chat. That was something almost charming about people unsure of their own sexuality: they often didn't realize there might be something suggestive in simply asking someone out for coffee. By the time they'd finished, however, Bo wasn't so sure the detective was just curious, or that she hadn't meant to send signals.

It had started simply enough: Bo had been unable to sleep. After two hours of lying in bed in a dark room, staring at the ceiling, she decided to head to the piano bar and have something to drink. Non-alcoholic, since she seldom drank and had committed to abstinence while she carried out her mission. But anything would help, and she'd hoped that being in the bar would distract her mind enough that after a while she could return to her room and sleep.

She had never been a bar-goer. Bars unsettled her. They upended her sense of the world as essentially a lonely place. Bo had loved only once, and that, she'd come to know, was a mistake. As for companionship, it was dangerous. Even someone as tightly controlled as she was could let something slip; it was much better never to court error. But there she was, sitting on a stool at the Lodge's bar, watching as some guests chatted and mingled in costumes, others in their street clothes. She recognized the lesbian couple Eileen and Maggie. Eileen didn't notice her, and Maggie was busy once again reading something on her cell phone. The man Danny had so disliked—Lionel? Linus?—continued to hold court, this time around a small table with the two disciples who'd been at each arm since he arrived. The young boy-toy was nowhere in sight.

She was halfway through her Ginger Ale when she felt someone come up behind her. She didn't believe in a sixth-sense, but that we feel shifts in the air, or we manage to connect very distant dots and determine their destination point before they get there. Mysterious, yes, but not inexplicable. She just knew someone was behind her, and she swiveled around on her barstool. Much to her surprise she found Detective Linda Sikorsky not more than two feet away, as startled to have Bo turn around just then as Bo was to see her there. She was wearing jeans and a blouse, Bo noticed, looking much less like a cop and much more like the kind of women she imagined sought one another out in the bars she did not go to.

"Hello, Ms. Sweetzer," the detective said. She didn't extend her hand, and already Bo could tell she was nervous, unsure if a handshake was called for or if withholding it would be rude.

"I prefer 'Miss,' actually," Bo said. "I've never been a missus and the whole 'Ms' thing is too much of an artifice for me. Call me old-school."

Linda smiled, and Bo couldn't tell if she was amused or pleased; possibly both.

"Well, then, Miss Sweetzer, how are you enjoying your evening? Have you been here before?"

Bo was suddenly suspicious. She'd told the detective in their morning interview that she had never been to Pride Lodge. She wondered if the approach was just part of the job, or if Linda Sikorsky was trying to trip her up for some reason.

"Oh, wait, you told me that," Linda said, shaking her head at her own forgetfulness. "Even cops forget things."

And she's a mind-reader, too, Bo thought. I like this woman.

"I tried to go to sleep," Bo said. "I'm not really a party person, or a bar person, but I am an insomniac on occasion. I figured a drink might settle my mind down."

Linda looked at the half-empty glass on the counter in front of Bo. "May I get you another?" she asked.

"It's only soda. Not the sort of thing that makes you want more."

There was a moment of silence that quickly grew awkward, and Bo realized that Linda wasn't very skilled in these situations. Chasing down criminals she could do very well, but striking up and maintaining a conversation with another woman in a gay bar? Not so used to that.

"How about some coffee?" Linda said.

Bo burst out laughing.

"What? What did I say?"

"You just asked an insomniac if she'd like a cup of coffee."

"And I forgot you'd never been here," Linda said, embarrassed. "Strike two. But maybe I meant decaf. Yes! I meant decaf! And a piece of pie . . . unless sugar keeps you up, too."

Bo thought about it a moment.

"Not here," Linda said. "The kitchen's closed down anyway. But there's a restaurant not far from here, the Eagle Diner. Twenty-four hour place. It'd give you a chance to see a little more of the area."

"In the dark."

"Well, yeah. But that's not a bad way to see it. We could come across some deer in the headlights."

Bo wondered who was the deer, and who was the headlights. Sikorsky was clearly a very intelligent woman, and she might yet have questions in mind to ask Bo that Bo would not answer truthfully. But she couldn't sleep, and she found the detective attractive, and she was very skilled at only revealing what she wanted people to see. So why not?

"Let's go," Bo said, sliding off the stool. "I can't think of anywhere I'd rather end the night than at the Eagle Diner. Unless that's not where it ends."

She saw the sudden flush in Linda's face: Bo had her number, and the detective knew it. "Relax," she said. "I was just having some fun. Now let's go get that pie! They have ice cream there?"

"It's a diner," Linda said. "Of course they do."

The two women headed out of the bar. Cowboy Dave watched them go and smiled: another romance blossoming at Pride Lodge. He'd seen more than a few.

The Eagle Diner was on Highway 202, a stone's throw from the Giant grocery store and just up the road from the Raven, a gay hotel, restaurant and gathering place that had been there for decades, with the occasional interruption. They knew each other, of course, the Raven and Pride Lodge, and had remained friendly as long they'd both been in business. Pride Lodge was more out of the way, and people who stayed there tended not to be the same customers who would stay at the Raven. There had never been any real rivalry between the two: there were enough gay, lesbian, bisexual and transgender patrons to keep them both operating this long. Throw in the Q's, I's, and any letters not yet added to the acronym, and business should stay brisk for years to come.

Bo's suspicions that Linda Sikorsky was somehow on to her vanished quickly enough once they were seated in a booth. The diner had quite a few customers even this close to midnight, and the two women did not stand out in any way. They'd each ordered apple pie and coffee (Bo had started to suggest one pie, two forks, but thought better of it) and were several bites in when Sikorsky made her motives known.

"I've lived in this area all my life," she said, glancing around nervously to make sure no one was eavesdropping. She was known well enough in New Hope that she had to always be aware someone might recognize her. "I'm thirty-six years old. Everybody knows me."

"And everybody thinks you're a lesbian," Bo said.

Linda stared at her, taken aback. While she wasn't going to state it that way—unsure exactly how she would state it—that's what she was thinking and trying to articulate.

"But you're not," Bo continued. "Or you're not sure, and what better way to crystallize it for yourself than ask a real one out for coffee and advice."

"You're either a cop," said Linda, laughing nervously, "or a psychic." She paused a moment. "I don't suppose you're wondering, why you?"

"I know why me. Because I'm cute! Shorter than you, about the right age, Minnesota nice, and, from your own notes, I'm sure, single."

"I've never dated a woman," Linda said. "I've thought about it. My father's dead and my mother lives alone in Philly. It's not like I have to worry what they'll think of me. Who the hell cares if I'm a lesbian? Which I'm not saying I am, since it's hard to say when you've never done anything but imagine it."

"Well," said Bo gently, "you're free to imagine it all you want to with me. I won't ask you to act on it." She winked. "Not tonight."

Linda visibly relaxed. She had fantasized for years having this conversation with someone, but she had honestly never thought the right time— or the right woman—would come. If she were simply blunt with herself she would say yes, Linda, you're attracted to women, and that pretty much makes you a lesbian, but she had not been honest. She had clung to uncertainty as a way of avoiding having to come clean: to her friends, who probably already knew, to her neighbors, and to her colleagues—the people she dreaded telling most. It was a small force, and she knew they would think just as highly of her after she came out as they had the moment before, and that they would probably start trying to line her up with dates.

"You're here until when?" Linda asked. "Just in case I have a few more questions about the investigation, of course."

"Of course," Bo said. "I'm set to check out Sunday, but who knows, I kind of like the place, I might want to stay a few days and see more. If it's got an Eagle Diner, I can only imagine what else is going on here."

The two women laughed. Bo felt her heart sink, suddenly, painfully conscious of the lie she'd told and what it meant. She would never see Linda Sikorsky again after tonight. She intended to see her mission through to its deadly conclusion and be gone well before Sunday's first light flooded the sky. Unless . . .

"Are you coming to the party tomorrow?" Bo asked. "The Halloween party?"

"I wasn't planning on it," Linda replied, and she waved at the waitress for the check. "But now I'm thinking maybe. I don't have a costume."

"Come as Cupid," Bo said, smiling. "It's a natural fit."

Bo wondered why she was doing this to herself, asking a woman she clearly desired to come back the next night, the night she planned to claim her final revenge and go. You're slipping, Bo, she told herself, all the while smiling as Dottie, the waitress, left the check on the table between them. Maybe you don't have the heart for it, maybe you want a happy ending after all. She felt a sting in her eyes—an unfamiliar fall for a woman who had not cried in thirty years, and she quickly looked away. It wouldn't matter if the cop came, it wouldn't matter how she felt about Bo or how she made Bo feel. The die had been cast in that bedroom three decades ago, and there was only one roll left. So let her come, let her think Bo had made a fool of her as she vanished in the night, let her never know the truth and how high its price.

Linda slid out of the booth and started to reach for Bo's hand. She happened to look over and see and old straight couple she had known for years, used her hand to wave to them instead, and led the way out.

CHAPTER 21

THE PAST CATCHES UP

Kyle hit a dead end in his internet search. He'd been unable to find anything about Sid Stanhope until he ran across a group picture from a bank office in Newark. It was Sid alright, fifteen years younger but identifiable. And years later the items about Pride Lodge. Kyle realized Sid was not the type to spend much time online. He doubted he was on Facebook and he probably thought tweeting was something baby birds did when they were hungry. He was stymied until he started thinking again about the odd, tense exchange between Sid and Bo at the restaurant. Maybe he was looking in the wrong direction, for the wrong person. Maybe *she* was a better lead to follow. Letting his hunch take him where it may, he started looking into Bo Sweetzer. BoAndBehold, pleasant jewelry designer from St. Paul. Ten minutes into his search he found the same article Sid had found and his breath stopped. Bo Sweetzer was not who she had always been. Once upon a time she'd been a young child named Emily Lapinsky, living far from St. Paul.

Kyle's pulse accelerated as he jumped from one link to the next, one dot to the next, connecting them at digital speed. He was reading what little he could find from so long ago when up popped a website called *DeathWatchLA*. At first glance it appeared to just be lurid, tabloid fodder: morgue photos of dead celebrities, macabre stories of people murdered in sudden, gruesome acts of violence. It wasn't until he read the "about" section and saw that there had been a print predecessor, that in fact the website was based on a cheaply produced throwaway newspaper that hadn't been much more than a flyer in the 1980s, and that there were scanned PDF copies of the old issues available for $4.99 each (PayPal or credit card accepted), that he knew he might be onto something. He quickly got his Visa and randomly selected a dozen old issues, dating back to 1980. He was halfway through them, having read six without finding anything that struck him, when he came upon the Lapinsky murders. A burglary gone horribly wrong, involving a trio of thieves. The Los Feliz Gang, as the media dubbed them. Three men, a dead husband and wife, and a daughter who had escaped execution by hiding in the closet. There was a photo showing her in a Catholic school girl's uniform.

Kyle stared at her.

"Look at this," he said to Danny. Danny had been resting in bed reading an old New York Post he'd brought with them. Kyle never understood why Danny liked reading that paper, given its politics, but he knew it was a guilty pleasure, like watching a reality TV show that wasn't real in any way and that made the human race seem doomed.

Danny got out of bed and walked over to the table where Kyle was sitting with the laptop. He peered at the old photograph. "It's a girl," he said.

"Well, yeah, but does she remind you of anyone?"

"I can't say she does, sorry."

"Look closer."

Danny leaned down and peered at the photograph.

"Oh my God."

"Yes," Kyle said. "Our table mate from St. Paul." He slid the laptop away and started to pace. "I need to get into that room."

"Her room?"

"No, Teddy's. I need something solid to take to Detective Sikorsky."

"Isn't this enough?" Danny asked, nodding at the article on the laptop.

"No, it's not. But I think there's something to be found . . . and I think Teddy found it. Maybe Happy, too. Or Teddy told him, or something like that. Their deaths are connected, I'm certain of that. And if we trace the line back, and back some more, we can trace it all the way to a house in Los Angeles thirty years ago."

"You should call Sikorsky now," Danny said. "This is dangerous territory. You could get hurt."

"I won't get hurt. And I will talk to her, soon. Dylan will help me, he's already panicking over these suspicions he has. He'll let me in Teddy's room and I'll find something there, I'm sure of it. Then I'll call the police."

"You have to promise me."

"I promise," Kyle said. "Cross my heart . . . "

"Don't finish that! Nobody hopes to die, it's an awful expression. You know, Kyle, life is so much simpler when you just take pictures."

Kyle stopped pacing and shut the laptop. "Let's go have breakfast," he said. "I hear murder's on the menu."

CHAPTER 22

BREAKFAST AT EPIPHANY'S

Most of the dozen or so people having breakfast didn't know who Happy was and hadn't heard about his death. Unlike many of the staff, he'd only been around a few months and seemed to have made the biggest impression on the two men he had dated, Teddy and Cowboy Dave. The other staff, on the other hand, had clearly gotten the news about the body found in a creek, and it made for a strange emotional mix: guests chatting about their plans for the day and wondering if the good weather would hold out, while Ricki manned the desk with a dazed expression on his face and Elzbetta, on table duty, only spoke when spoken to as she took their orders. Dylan, meanwhile, was visibly pale, with a fear in his eyes that couldn't be hidden by his wooden smile.

Kyle and Danny showed themselves to a table by the window overlooking the road.

"No camera this morning?" Danny asked, used to seeing Kyle with his Nikon slung around his neck. "It looks like a good day for photographs."

"I may need to move quickly," Kyle said, his voice low. "I can't worry about leaving a camera sitting around or having it swinging on my neck."

Just then Elzbetta came up to them. She was more sullen than usual, and appeared to have been crying.

"You heard about Happy," she said, posing it as a statement, as if everyone must have heard.

"We saw the news, yes," Kyle said.

"We were . . . friends."

"I'm sorry."

"We were going to go away, to the Rocky Mountains," she said. "Denver. He had family there."

Kyle and Danny exchanged glances: apparently there weren't many people young Happy did not sleep with.

"He didn't kill himself!" she blurted out.

Danny was startled. "Who said . . . "

"They speculated, the news guy I saw, he said they hadn't ruled out suicide, which means they've ruled it in!"

"Reporters don't know much," Kyle said, trying to reassure the distressed waitress. "That's why they're reporters."

"It's just fucked up. Seriously fucked up, like everything around here. This place is cursed, I can't stay. What did you want for breakfast?"

They placed their orders and were relieved to have Elzbetta finally walk away without saying anything more.

"Do you believe her?" Danny asked. "That Pride Lodge is cursed?"

"Don't be stupid," Kyle said, immediately regretting his use of a word Danny hated. Danny was not stupid by any definition, but somewhere in his life, probably his childhood, the word had been used to great effect against him. He glared at Kyle.

"I'm sorry," Kyle said. "I just meant it's preposterous. The Lodge has been a going concern for almost thirty years, and suddenly it's cursed?"

"Stu died from a heart attack on those steps right there," Danny said, nodding toward the stairs that led down the hill. "Not to mention the first owner's wife and children. Curses have to start somewhere."

"In our fevered imaginations, that's where."

Their conversation was interrupted as Bo Sweetzer came walking through the dining room and approached their table. They'd formed their own small group the last two days and it seemed natural to her to invite herself to join them. Kyle looked behind her, noticing she was alone.

"Looking for someone?" she said, smiling. She knew her departure the night before with the beautifully sturdy detective had not gone unnoticed.

Kyle blushed at his own transparency. "I thought you might be dining with someone else this morning."

"Dining," she said. "I like that. You don't usually think of people dining at breakfast."

Bo was in very good spirits. She either hadn't heard the news about poor Happy, or, more likely, she had no idea who he was. Most people relegated the deaths of strangers to the general news feed of their day.

"We only had coffee and dessert," she said, quelling Kyle's curiosity.

Danny hadn't been all that interested to begin with and was hoping their food would arrive soon. He reached for his water glass.

"She's questioning," Bo continued.

"And a sucker for a California girl, I'm guessing," Kyle said.

Danny nearly choked on his water.

"Oh, I'm sorry," Kyle corrected himself. "You're from Minnesota. St. Paul. My mistake."

The smile on Bo's face remained, but took on a rigid quality, as if it wanted to fall but she was keeping it in place by force of will. "It must have been the accent," she said, knowing there was no such thing as a California accent. "I did live there for a few years, when I was a child."

Danny carefully watched the two of them, worried Kyle had tipped his hand too readily.

"We've been there a few times, haven't we, Danny?"

Danny nodded, hoping the subject would change.

"We stayed with friends in the Los Feliz area. Did you live anywhere near there?"

And now she knew. Kyle had all but told her who he thought she was. Unfortunately for him, she was close to her endgame and losing her need for concealment with each passing hour. She had come to believe, since her time with Detective Sikorsky the night before, that while she would see an end to her mission, her mission would also be the end of her. If she made it away from Pride Lodge, having fulfilled the promise she had repeated to her parents' ghosts for thirty years, she would have to abandon Bo Sweetzer as completely and easily as she had abandoned Emily Lapinsky. Sid Stanhope was not the last person she would kill after all.

"Oddly enough," she said, the smile now gone, "that's one of the few neighborhoods I never saw. We were on the west side, not far from Century City. I was just a kid, I don't even remember the name of where we lived."

"Have you gone back?" Kyle asked.

"No, I've never had the interest," she said, and Kyle could see a sadness come over her. She suddenly struck him as very old, and very tired, a woman coming to the end of her journey, whatever that journey might be.

"Does anybody care that Happy's gone?" Elzbetta said, coming up to their table carrying plates with their breakfast. "It doesn't seem to me anybody gives a shit."

"Who's Happy?" Bo asked. "What happened?"

While Elzbetta gave a quick rundown on who Happy was and that he'd been found dead in a creek the night before, Kyle looked over to see Dylan signaling him, nodding toward the kitchen.

"Excuse me," Kyle said, standing and putting his napkin on his chair. "I need to wash my hands."

Kyle left the table and headed toward the restrooms. When he got to the hallway that led back to them, he veered left into the kitchen and saw Dylan standing there with an apron on.

"Cece called in sick. She's our morning cook," he said. "When you run a place like this you have to know how to do everything."

Dylan wiped his hands on his apron and began to pace. "Happy's dead, before Teddy, from what they said on the news. Do you think Teddy knew?"

"I think Teddy knew too many things," Kyle said. "That's why I need to get into his room."

"Do you think he did it?" Dylan asked.

"What, kill Happy?"

"No!"

And with that Kyle knew he meant Sid. It struck him how quickly Dylan had allowed himself to believe Sid could be a thief, and now a murderer.

"I wouldn't read too much into the timing of this," Kyle said, trying to calm the situation. "Happy left days ago."

"Yes, and he didn't say anything to anyone about it, and he turned up dead in a creek. Before or after Teddy died at the bottom of the pool, we won't know until they announce it. Maybe Happy died last night, maybe he died the day he disappeared! Can you imagine being dead in the woods for three days? Oh my God, the animals. Unless his body was moved!"

"Listen, Dylan," Kyle said, "I need to get into Teddy's room. It's not sealed off. There isn't any crime scene at this point, as far as the police are concerned. You can be there with me, I'll be very respectful, but I have to have something solid to show the detective. So far it's all just crazy imaginings, however un-crazy they are to you and me."

"I want to wait until Sid's not around," Dylan said, nodding. "He'll know something's up if we go into Teddy's room."

"Just tell him I want something to remember Teddy by."

"He's a very smart man, he'll know better. No, let's wait."

Kyle would normally not go looking through someone's belongings, let alone a dead man's, but he was convinced a significant piece of the puzzle might well be in Teddy's room.

"Sid's going into New Hope this afternoon," Dylan said. "For more party supplies. We'll have plenty of locals coming tonight, we always run out of something. That's the time for this, when he's safely away for a few hours."

"Perfect," Kyle said. "Text me when it's time, we'll be in the cabin. And now I think I'll get back out there. You wait a minute so it's not too obvious we're having an affair."

Dylan smiled for the first time that day and watched as Kyle went back to the table.

CHAPTER 23

A LATE START

Detective Linda Sikorsky. Even after fifteen years on the force, six of them as the only active homicide detective in New Hope (a job she performed for other towns in the area when needed, so seldom did murders occur in this bucolic stretch of Pennsylvania), Linda still felt uncomfortable with the title. As if she'd come to it by accident, or been given the position when someone else had displayed more merit for it. But there was no one else, and she had worked long and hard to get where she was. It just seemed like such a dream come true, regardless of how few people dream of being homicide detectives. It wasn't the sort of thing you'd hear from little girls asked what they wanted to be when they grew up. A nurse, maybe, or a teacher, or a pop star, but not someone whose job it was to investigate the killing of one human being by another. Still, it had been her dream ever since she'd been a child in Cincinnati and her father, a cop on the Cincinnati Police Department, was gunned down in the most absurd way: as a bystander when shots broke out during a fight outside a grocery store. A grocery store! Not a bar, not a craps game he was breaking up, not anything that said "hero" when the papers covered the story the next day. Oh, they called him a hero. Every person in uniform was instantly transformed into a hero when they died, even if it was from a heart attack in a church parking lot. But try as she did, she was never able to think of her father's death as the death of a hero. It was a cruel, capricious, meaningless death, when he had stopped at the store to pick up a short list of groceries her mother had given him over the phone, and as he was walking to his car in the parking lot, two thugs started shouting at each other outside the main entrance as a nearby police cruiser screeched to a halt. By the time Peter Sikorsky was even aware that trouble was happening, a bullet had entered his neck on the right side, leaving a hole on its exit from which he quickly bled to death.

It had never made sense to her, and she had long ago stopped trying to make it. Ideas like "closure" and making sense of random tragedy were for people more desperate to believe everything happened for a reason. She knew better. She knew people were felled by stray bullets and children were raped and very few people were heroes. But while she would not humor others by calling her father's death anything but senseless, she would honor him by becoming a police officer and seeking out a career he had been deprived of. That was thirty-five years ago, in a world and life so removed from the one she now lived that she only believed it had ever happened because it had happened to her. Her mother, Estelle Sikorsky, had met another man two years after her father's death, and the three of them had moved to Philadelphia. Her stepfather, too, had died, but from a stroke, something less dramatic but no less sudden or pointless, and her mother now lived alone six blocks from Independence Hall. She recently retired from her job teaching fifth and sixth graders, and Linda visited her once a month, making the hour's drive to sit and talk about this and that, never anything too deep, including the men who had died on Estelle and left her sitting alone in her kitchen on Sunday afternoons.

That they never spoke of anything too sensitive was a big reason Linda had never told her mother, or anyone else, that she was—all things being considered—a lesbian. Linda didn't like calling herself anything. And, at the same time, she was very honest and always had been. Someone who could not kid herself about the brutal and meaningless nature of her father's death could not kid herself about her own nature. She had known she was attracted to women long before she was one herself. Back when she was a child, in middle school, probably earlier. But she had chosen, for reasons she still did not fully understand, to never label it, to never call herself anything other than Linda. She had chosen as well not to act on it. Not because she was ashamed, or wanted to be something other than who she was, but because she feared the loss it could bring. That, she had finally come to realize, was the real reason: not any perceived hostility, not some sad self-rejection, but because a bullet had taken away the one man she had loved in her life, and she feared, in a way words could not express and consciousness could not quite define, that acting on her desires would open the door to love, and love would open the door to loss.

Even last night, when she had asked Bo out and they'd had coffee at the diner, she felt herself as much repelled as attracted, as if something were in front of her that she both wanted and feared. Something that simultaneously promised pleasure and threatened pain—comfort with a caveat. It had been her way of testing waters whose shore she had stood gazing from for twenty years. It had not been a particular attraction to Bo Sweetzer, but a way of finally saying, yes, this is me, this is who I am and who I want to be. She was grateful to have made this initial foray into her truest identity with someone as nice, patient and free from expectation as the woman from St. Paul. That this woman, Linda now knew, was not who she pretended to be complicated things but did not take away the simple joy she'd had the night before, sitting in a diner with another woman, for all to see (most of whom, she knew, had assumed she was gay all this time anyway). It had given her a sense of freedom she had always hoped was available but was never really sure, until then, until that moment when she went from questioning to certainty. That was hers to keep, despite what came of the things she'd learned after going home and, instead of sleeping, doing what an obsessive detective does: investigating. Bo Sweetzer, jewelry maker, website, history, dead end. And if there was one thing Linda Sikorksy did not like, it was a dead end. There were already too many at Pride Lodge for comfort.

In this day of social networks, data mining and seemingly endless public access to anyone who has ever typed their name online, it's a major accomplishment to have nothing about yourself available to anyone with a keyboard. The jewelry site was easy enough to find, its whole purpose was to sell jewelry and Bo gave the URL to everyone she met. But when Linda tried to dig a little deeper, find a college record, a past, it stopped. Bo Sweetzer had told her in their initial interview she was from St. Paul. Apparently that was truer than Linda could imagine: there was no Bo Sweetzer before St. Paul. Bo had managed to emerge fully formed from the world's womb, if not her mother's. And while it wasn't all that miraculous for her to remain off Facebook and Twitter and the other hubs of virtual friendship, followers and fanatics, it was nearly astonishing to simply arrive online as a twenty year old.

Linda had not spent the entire night trying to solve a puzzle she had created for herself. She was too tired, and, to be honest, not that concerned with what she had found—or not found—about a woman she would never see again after this weekend. But she made a note to herself to ask Bo about this at the Halloween party that night. She had decided to go, even though it meant pulling together some kind of costume at the last minute. All the years she'd been in New Hope and she had never spent an hour at Pride Lodge. Maybe she'd been avoiding it, maybe it offered answers to questions she had not been fully prepared to ask until last night. But here she was, planning to spend yet more of her weekend there. And not all for fun . . . the questions had changed, and the answers could be fatal. She would need to be prepared.

CHAPTER 24

ON THE ROPES

Sid didn't know what was happening, only that something terrible was coming his way and leaving dead men in its tracks. First Frank and Sam, then Teddy, and now Happy. It was a trail, he had no doubt about that, and it led to him. Time was not on his side; he would need to make his escape soon. The Halloween party that night seemed like a perfect opportunity, when everyone was distracted, having a good time, drinking too much. No one would notice him driving away, and if they did, they would never dream he would not be back.

At first he'd thought what everyone else did, that Teddy had fallen into the pool. He had claimed to be sober for several months, but Sid had known a drunk or two in his life and as lovable as they may be, they could not be trusted to tell the truth when it came to their drinking. So he had assumed Teddy had relapsed, "slipped" they called it, and had somehow fallen into the empty pool. But the martini glass was odd. Sid had always seen Teddy with a tumbler of whiskey, never something so sophisticated as a martini. But he also knew that an alcoholic wasn't generally choosy, and it may have been that Teddy took whatever was at hand. Or at least that's what Sid had believed until Happy turned up in the creek bed. Too many deaths in too short a time, with the real possibility his own would be next.

Sid had spent the last twenty-four hours trying to put the pieces together and only getting more confused with each attempt. If the Bo woman was behind this, which seemed a conclusion impossible not to draw, why would she kill Teddy? Why Happy? She would have had to be here days ago, staying somewhere else. Or, as he had begun to fear, was more than one person involved, perhaps even conspiring to pull the noose ever tighter around his neck? Had Teddy found out that Sid Stanhope had been in the Lapinsky house that night thirty years ago? Was he planning to go to the police? That would certainly throw a wrench into the killer's plans; taking down the last of them would be impossible if Sid was behind bars. It seemed ever more likely that Teddy had unknowingly put himself in harm's way, directly in the path of someone who had no hesitation leaving dead bodies behind her. But why Happy? And why now?

The *now* of it was as mysterious as anything to Sid, maybe the most mysterious. They'd gotten away with it for three decades. They had all moved on, two of them leaving Los Angeles, with nothing to tie them together . . . except a watch. Sid had told himself all these years that he was innocent in the scheme of things. He had never hurt anyone, had never even carried a gun. He was expecting the same thing they'd experienced at all the other houses: a quick in and out, no one home, no harm done, but then the Lapinksys had been there, and Frank, oh Frank . . .

Sid felt his eyes watering and immediately took control of his emotions. He would have to leave Dylan, and do it without saying why. No one could know what became of him or why he disappeared. He loved Dylan and had counted on spending his last years with him, years that would require companionship as his body found itself more and more worn down. Their age difference would put Dylan in the position of taking care of Sid, but they both knew that and Dylan even joked about it from time to time. It was not, he had said over and over, something he would consider a burden, but an honor, a continued demonstration of his love for Sid. And for this he would be betrayed, abandoned, left wondering for the rest of his life what had happened.

It was for Dylan's own good, Sid told himself. Anyone who would murder someone as hapless and accidental as Teddy Pembroke would not hesitate to turn their sights on Dylan if he was seen to be a threat. The sooner and cleaner Sid made his break, the better for them all.

He got up from his computer where he'd been looking at maps and reading about places where a man could disappear easily enough; not all of them were big cities, either. There are many small towns, not much more than bumps in the road, where there are few people to ask questions and vast spaces into which a man can disappear. He erased his search history and tried to focus on a plan. He was heading soon into New Hope for more supplies for that night. He would fill up the gas tank when he was there and buy some supplies of a more personal nature, food stuffs and water, packing for a long journey whose end he would only know when he got there. And then, sometime that night, when everyone was having a good time and looking the other way, Sid Stanhope would simply go away.

CHAPTER 25

CABIN 6

Kyle was sitting cross-legged on the bed, the laptop open in front of him. Next to the laptop was his camera, with a USB cable running from it to the laptop: Kyle had downloaded all the photographs he'd taken since they arrived. He had come to believe over the years of taking pictures that people experience the world in images, one instant after another in a series that stretched from birth to death, and that, without intending it, answers could be found among the many accidental photographs he took. It was why he wore the Nikon around his neck nearly everywhere he went. He seldom knew what he would shoot, or, looking back over the forty or fifty pictures he might take in a day, what he would find.

"What are you looking for this time?" Danny asked. He was wearing beige shorts and a sweatshirt, settling in to rest until dinner and the party. The weather hadn't turned especially bad, but the sky had filled with clouds and a chilly rain looked likely. He had no desire to go sightseeing or make a trip into town. For Danny, the weekends at Pride Lodge were about resting, about not looking at seating charts (even though he did peek), about lying in bed reading a newspaper with the television turned low in the background. He knew Kyle was looking for answers in his photographs, but that was his process for making order of chaos, of connecting dots that otherwise formed no pattern.

"I don't know, you know that. That's the point. I'll know what I'm looking for when I see it."

"Are you calling Imogene back?" Danny asked. Kyle's boss had been trying to reach him since early that morning, but Kyle had successfully ignored her voicemails and texts. Danny wondered if he had finally convinced Kyle that he was not on call for Imogene twenty-four hours a day.

"It's just withdrawals," Kyle said absently, peering intently at his laptop screen. "She has to go cold turkey. Forty-eight hours from now and I'll be back, handing her a cheese Danish and a cup of coffee from Cecil's and it'll be like I was never away."

Cecil's was a diner on 38th Street near the studios where Japan TV3 rented space for their programming. Kyle happened upon it the first day they were working there and had presented Imogene with of cup of their rich, distinctive coffee most mornings since then.

"You're making progress on ignoring Imogene," Danny said.

"You forget there's been a murder," Kyle replied. "There are a few things in life more important than meeting her needs."

The luck of the lens did not appear to be with him this time. Nothing in the dozens of photographs he had taken since they arrived told him anything. He didn't even know what he was looking for, some image that would tell him what words could not. It had been a picture of the woman on the cruise ship kissing her paramour by the hanging lifeboats, taken accidentally when Kyle was aiming for a shot of the walkway, that gave him the evidence he needed in the cruise ship murder. But so far this weekend at Pride Lodge . . . nothing.

"A picture wasn't worth any words this time, apparently," Kyle said, resigned. He closed the laptop and decided he was finished with the camera. He needed to be present now, to stay alert and pay close attention to his surroundings and the people in it. Sometimes the camera was a way of hiding, of giving himself to distraction. He would put it in the drawer and let his eyes be the camera from here on in. Whatever he'd been looking for in the photographs he had probably missed because of them. The time had come to watch everything closely and commit what he saw to memory.

Kyle's phone vibrated just then and he picked it up. A text had come from Dylan: "Sid leaving, come up in 10."

Kyle got up from the table and put his camera in the dresser.

"Where are you going?" Danny asked, wishing for once that Kyle had answered Imogene's calls instead, that he'd given in to her needs and not pursued something that would certainly lead to trouble.

"I'm meeting Dylan."

"Stay out of this, Kyle. What's Dylan involvement?"

"Nothing, but he can let me into Teddy's room. Hopefully that's where I'll find what I'm looking for."

Kyle slipped on his shoes and grabbed his jacket. "I'll be back, hopefully soon," he said, and opened the cabin door to leave.

"But you don't know what you're looking for!" Danny said too late, as the door closed. Within a minute of Kyle leaving, Danny's worry got the best of him and he began searching for the business card that Detective Linda Sikorsky had given to everyone she had interviewed. Kyle may think he needs to wait, but Danny feared waiting was precisely the wrong thing to do.

CHAPTER 26

TEDDY'S ROOM

Dylan watched from the empty restaurant window as Sid drove off in their Highlander toward town. No sooner was the car out of sight than Kyle came walking up from the cabins. The two men waved at each other, Dylan looking anxious and forlorn in the window.

Kyle had never been upstairs at the Lodge. There had not been any reason to go there, since he and Danny always stayed in the cabin. When he entered the main room, he saw several people he did not know sitting around chatting and drinking coffee, and there in his recliner perch sat Jeremy Johnson, wearing the same clothes he'd been in the night before. Maybe they were duplicates, like someone who dresses only in black. Maybe it's all Jeremy wore.

"Don't tell me you've been here all this time," Kyle said, closing the outside door behind him.

"No," said Jeremy, "I'm still capable of making it up the stairs. And I wasn't here earlier when you came for lunch."

"I didn't notice."

"But I noticed you," Jeremy said, winking.

Kyle was struck again by how enigmatic Jeremy was: the guest who'd been coming the longest, whose presence everyone was aware of, but who blended in so well he might be said to be invisible; and he clearly enjoyed his status as a fly on the wall. Kyle knew there couldn't be much that went unnoticed by the old sentinel.

"Speaking of upstairs," Kyle said, nodding at the staircase. "I've never been up there and thought, why not take a look."

"I'm sure Dylan can show you around," Jeremy said, winking again before turning and reaching for his cup of tea, the string dangling over the side.

Kyle suddenly had the idea that Jeremy thought he was having some kind of affair with Dylan. It was unnerving enough to have himself so astutely observed, but that wink when he mentioned Dylan, as if something was going on between them, was a step too far. He made a mental note to set Jeremy straight before the day was over. He would not have anyone, however imaginative, thinking he was cheating on Danny. That was untrue, unfair, and just the kind of innuendo that could spread through Pride Lodge like a brushfire.

He turned then and headed for the stairs, leaving the others to their lively conversation and old Jeremy to his fantasies.

Bo saw him coming up the stairs just as she was about to head out and she quickly backtracked into her room, closing the door until only an inch was open, just enough for her to peer through. She didn't need to know Kyle had never been upstairs to know something was different. The old man in the chair wasn't the only one skilled at watching, and if there was one thing Bo could spot in human behavior, it was the clandestine. It was the way he climbed the stairs, as if he didn't want to make any noise, didn't want anyone to see him. And then easing his way down the hall, glancing at each door, still moving carefully so he would not alert anyone to his presence. Only a man up to something acted this way. It wasn't even conscious, she knew, but the body's way of accommodating a guilty mind, a mind that feared it might be caught. And when she thought that, she, too, wondered if Kyle Callahan was meeting someone up here, someone with whom he was being unfaithful. Or maybe faith had nothing to do with it. Maybe Kyle and Danny had an arrangement. Bo knew such relationships existed. "Open marriages," they were called. But if that was the case, why the stealth?

And then the door to room 208 opened and Dylan waved at Kyle, equally careful to be quick and quiet. (Her great luck had been to get a room so close, having never been here before, but finding the room assignment exceedingly favorable to her plans.) Her first thought was that this was the man Kyle was having his affair with, but when she saw Dylan hurry Kyle into the dead man's room, glance back out into the hallway to make sure no one had seen, and close the door, she suddenly had a different thought, an uncomfortable suspicion: what if this wasn't about sex at all, but about looking for something with Sid gone? She, too, had watched him drive away, and not more than ten minutes later Kyle Callahan came skulking up the stairs. If the two men were meeting for lust, they could have used any empty room, or met somewhere on the grounds away from prying eyes. It would be macabre in the extreme to meet in a dead man's room for any reason other than to search it. (She knew room 208 was Teddy Pembroke's room because the police had gone through it, but not sealed it off; they were probably looking for a suicide note, just in case Pembroke had decided to end his life in grand fashion by flinging himself to the bottom of an empty swimming pool, martini glass in hand.)

Once Kyle was in the room and the door closed, Bo quietly slipped out, made sure the door was locked, and headed downstairs. Things may be moving more quickly than she'd wanted.

Dylan thought he saw the door to Bo Sweetzer's room opened a crack, then close as Kyle walked by. He gave it only a moment's thought, his mind on more important things, and quietly welcomed Kyle into Teddy's room.

Kyle was taken aback at the thought of anyone living in a single room. He and Danny had always taken Cabin 6 and he never stopped to wonder how small a room seemed without a bathroom. There was only a bed, a dresser, a flat screen TV mounted on a wall, a makeshift kitchen Teddy had set up on a bookcase, with a hotplate, some dishes and cups, and essential items for making coffee. He had eaten all his meals in the restaurant or in town, and he didn't seem to own many clothes. The small closet wasn't even full.

Kyle was able to get the complete tour by simply standing in the middle of the room and turning around.

"Did he have a computer?" he asked. It was unusual these days for someone not to at least have a cheap laptop or a low-end tablet, and he'd emailed Teddy enough times to know he had access to one.

"Teddy wasn't very computer literate," Dylan said. He had slumped down onto the corner of Teddy's bed, his shoulders hunched, clearly not wanting to be in the room. "He would use the guest laptop if he needed to go online. Sometimes he would use ours."

Yes, Kyle thought, he used yours and it got him killed.

"I don't know what you're expecting to find," Dylan said. "Teddy was a simple man in most ways. You can see he didn't own much."

Well, of course not, Kyle thought, there's no place to put anything!

"I just want to look around. You're right, there's probably nothing here, but humor me a moment."

And then he saw it: the "Big Book" of Alcoholics Anonymous. On the shelf underneath the coffee pot and hotplate. It was their bible of sorts, the text they used to turn their lives around. Kyle only knew what he'd learned about "the program," as it was called by people in it, from friends and acquaintances he had known. He had never even held their book, and when he took it from Teddy's shelf he had the odd sensation he was holding some sort of holy manuscript.

He started slipping slowly through the pages and saw that Teddy had underlined dozens of passages. As he looked at the book he was more convinced than ever that Teddy was sober when he died, that he had changed his life and would never knowingly end it with the appearance of a drunkard's death. And then, toward the back, he came upon Page 417, so often quoted by Teddy Pembroke. Acceptance. It was a passage on this page that Teddy repeated over and over, like a nun reciting her rosary. Kyle opened the pages and there, slipped between them, was a piece of paper. He took it out and opened it: an email.

"What's that?" Dylan asked, getting up from the bed. He walked over, staring at the sheaf of paper as Kyle read it over:

From: "Sam Tatum" <s.tatum@zipmail.com:>
To: "Sid_Stanhope323@inboxx.com>
Wednesday, September 12

Sid—Lucky we even stayed in touch, surprised you would, but maybe not. Maybe I was the canary in the mine for you. Frank was for me, that's for damn sure. I can't say God rest his soul. That's a man who's soul won't ever rest and shouldn't. Stone cold killer, Frank was, and look at what it cost us. Someone's coming, I don't know who. Frank was killed in Detroit and I know it wasn't random, they came for him. I only know because he owed me money and some lawyer called to say he was paying me back, from the grave. Landlord found him with a bullet in the head and an empty watch box. Watch box, think about it. Two months later and still no suspects. It's only a matter of time for you and me, you should know, that's why I wrote. You gotta keep a look out, check in sometimes, make sure I'm still alive. Kidding. Not really. I'm not counting on being around too much longer. I'm too old and tired to run. I think instead I'll just get some more nose candy and a pretty young man to share it with. Yes, I haven't changed. No, I don't care what anyone thinks. This is some serious shit. I thought we'd made it, but some things you just can't escape.—Sam

"The 23rd is when we met," Dylan said, sounding fanciful.

"What?"

"His email name, Sid Stanhope323. Our anniversary is March 23rd. That's sweet."

Kyle thought it was an odd time to be sentimental. He'd just read an email that implicated Sid in something terrible, something that would make someone want to kill three men, and he was sure he knew what it was.

"Where does Sid come from?" Kyle asked.

Dylan looked at him as if it was the strangest question he'd ever been asked. "What do you mean?"

"When you met him, where did he say he was from?"

"Jersey, always. He was born in Elizabeth and grew up in Newark. His family moved to Atlantic City when he was in high school. What difference does it make?"

"None, for now," Kyle said. "I need to take this, or a copy."

"Take it," Dylan said, exasperated. "I wish I'd never seen it. This is a horrible situation, Kyle. Something's going on, something awful, and Sid's involved. The guy in the email said as much."

The guy in the email may well be dead, Kyle thought, not saying it. If his warning was right, someone had killed one of the three already, and since they'd now moved on to Sid, it seemed likely that Sam Tatum's next communication, if there was any, would be from beyond the grave.

Dylan's mood had darkened still further and he spoke softly, almost in a whisper. "Do you think this has anything to do with the money?"

"What money?" Kyle asked, folding the email and slipping it into his shirt pocket.

"The money Sid used to buy the Lodge!" Dylan said sharply, as if Kyle had not been paying attention when he should.

"I don't know what the connection is, or if there even is one. I'm going to give this to Detective Sikorksy and see what she makes of it. Whoever's in on this game isn't going to stop now, and if they've killed several times already, they're dangerous indeed."

"'They,'" Dylan said. "You make it sound like there's more than one."

"If you mean more than one killer, I'm afraid so."

Dylan visibly shivered, rubbing his hands on his upper arms as if a sudden chill had slipped into the room. "What do I do?"

"Wait, just a little while longer," Kyle said. "I think by tonight we'll have all the answers we need."

"None of them answers we want," Dylan said sadly. "None of them."

Kyle nodded, aware that as the threads came together it would weave a very different life from the one Dylan had been living, had dreamed himself living. Hopefully no more lives would be lost, but everything, for Dylan and the Lodge, would be changed.

CHAPTER 27

CABIN 6

Kyle had not stopped pacing since returning from Teddy's room two hours earlier. He had shown Danny the email, providing the evidence he had insisted he needed to take to Detective Sikorsky. On learning that Danny had already reached her and that she was coming that evening, he had decided not to add fuel to the fire for now. He would wait patiently and give her the email when he saw her. After that, he expected things to move rapidly.

"Why don't you call Imogene back?" Danny said, having watching Kyle try to sit still and repeatedly fail. It was the last thing he thought he would ever suggest, but he wanted something to distract Kyle from the escalating events at the Lodge. "It'll take your mind off this."

"I don't want to take my mind off this. Focus, Danny, it's time for me to focus."

"Wearing a hole in the carpet is not focusing. She's going to start calling the hospitals, you know."

"Who?" Kyle said, turning on his heel toward Danny. "The detective? Whatever for?"

"Noooo! Imogene. You never ignore her completely like this, unless we're in the middle of the ocean and there's no cell phone reception. I know you sneak texts to her when you think I'm not looking, it's okay."

Kyle sighed and sat at the table, channeling his restless energy into his shaking foot. "She doesn't even know where we are. I mean she does and she doesn't. Manhattan is her universe, get her outside the City and she doesn't know east from south. All she knows is we're in the countryside somewhere, which to her is the entire continent, with the possible exceptions of Los Angeles and Chicago."

Kyle took the email from Teddy's room out of his shirt pocket, flattened it on the table and read it over again.

"It hasn't changed since the last time you read it," Danny said. He was doing his best not to get caught up in Kyle's anxiety. "You act like it's going to disintegrate if you don't keep handling it."

Kyle didn't respond for a moment, choosing to lose himself in thought instead. "It seemed a little easy, " he said.

"What did?"

"Finding this! I can't be the only one Teddy was always quoting that passage from the AA book to. It was his mantra, 'Page 417, 'Acceptance is the answer to all of my problems today.' He'd repeat it two or three times in a conversation. It's almost as if someone wanted me to find it."

"He did!" Danny said, exasperated. "Teddy wanted you to find it! He was afraid something might happen to him."

Kyle wasn't fully convinced and let his imagination take over, trying to make connections of events that seemed random. Teddy's death, Happy's body found in the creek. Sid was a killer, or at least a bystander to murder. He'd been there in the Lapinsky home when it happened. And so had Bo Sweetzer, then young Emily. And now the collision course they'd been on was coming to a head.

"Imogene will survive," Kyle said absently, trying again to regain his composure, and the mention of his boss gave him a most unexpected idea. "Maybe she can turn what's going on here into something for Tokyo Pulse."

"Oh, great," Danny said. "Never miss an opportunity when there's news to be made. She really has you trained."

"That's not what I mean. But there's a story here. They're looking to beef up their general news and she wants off the finance beat, she doesn't have the head for it."

"She has a head?!" Danny said, trying to bring a little levity to the situation.

Kyle frowned. "She's a very good reporter, Danny. It's not that she can't do this job, it's just that it bores here. You have to admit finance is not very sexy. She might be able to take a story about murder at a country resort and get some attention."

"Don't forget the 'gay' part. Pretty soon we'll be completely assimilated and lose the curiosity factor, better hurry."

Kyle waved him off, not willing to get further into it. It was not that he disrespected his friend Teddy, or the Lapinksy family, or anyone else. But he was a realist as well. For one thing, they were all dead and wouldn't care, and for another, someone should tell their story, it was a hell of a feature, and not some talking head from Philly6, either. The story was going to be reported regardless of how Kyle or Danny or anyone else felt about it. It might as well be Imogene who broke it.

"I'm going to call her back," Kyle said, and he got his phone from the dresser. He dialed Imogene, glancing at his watch as he did: 5:30 p.m. They would need to leave soon for dinner and the party.

"Imogene, it's Kyle," he said into her voicemail as he headed into the bathroom to get ready. "There's a story here you might be interested in. Not Manhattan-local obviously, we're in Pennsylvania, but a seriously meaty story with history and cold cases and more angles than you could shake a microphone at. Maybe Lenny-san would go for it." He was referring to her boss, Leonard Baumstein, who ran the small newsroom and reported up to his bosses in Japan. "Call me when you can."

"I don't know about you, Kyle," Danny said from the living room.

"I don't always know about me, either," Kyle said, "but I'm in the land of the living and Teddy's dead. He's not coming back, he wouldn't care who told the story. Hell, he would've been the first to tell me to call her anyway. He always liked attention, so why not give him that?"

Kyle closed the bathroom door before Danny could say anything else. Danny shook his head, reached for the remote and un-muted the television just in time for the local news. He had the uneasy feeling they would all be part of it the next time he turned it on.

CHAPTER 28
ROOM 202

Bo sat on the bed staring across at the wall. It felt to her almost like a trance state; she would know because she had been in this state before, just before killing Frank Grandy and Sam Tatum. A calm overtook her, and a sadness, too. Especially this night. It brought a finality the others did not. She had to admit that once she'd found Grandy and set off on her mission there was a sense of anticipation, of taking the next step, but after tonight there would be no more steps. Or, rather, she would be stepping finally into oblivion.

She would be fooling herself to think they wouldn't connect her to this murder, and then the others. For all she knew, Linda Sikorksy had already been following her leads and instincts and may be closer to the truth than Bo could guess. She would be driving off from Pride Lodge, going west somewhere, maybe Chicago, where she would stop and plan, stop and re-arrange. She would never see St. Paul again.

She took her father's gun from the velvet cloth she kept it wrapped in and held it in her lap. It felt heavier tonight. It weighed on her in a way it hadn't before. The last time she used in, in Frank Grandy's apartment in Detroit, it had seemed almost weightless, an extension of her hand. She had felt exhilarated, so thrilled to be able at last to silence the cries of her parents' ghosts that she nearly levitated, or at least it felt that way. She had no remorse when she shot Grandy; certainly no more than he had had when he shot first her father, then her mother. Bang, bang. Just like that. Why hadn't she cried out from the closet? Was it fear, or was there an instantaneous determination to survive this, and to survive it for vengeance? Could a ten year old girl in the moment of her life's greatest crisis really be that calculating?

Yes, she thought. Yes, I was. Maybe I'm just cold inside and always have been. Maybe when I saw my father shot I knew then and there I would shoot back someday. Shoot back, or stab back, or strangle back, but the score would be settled, and yes, I knew even then.

She felt foolish in her cat costume. She was not a cat by nature. A serpent, perhaps, patient and deadly, but not a cat. That was part of her thinking, she knew, to obfuscate who she was and why she was here. It distorted the picture anyone might form of her, and distortions served her purpose. Cats did not shoot people, although they did pounce, and the thought of it made her smile. She reached up with her free hand and touched her face, so peculiar did the smile feel. Her smile had never been genuine since the day her parents died. It was a mask, a device, and suddenly the falseness of it startled even her.

She rose slowly, slipping the gun beneath the waistband of her costume. She would go to the party, smile and be a Halloween cat for a time, and she would wait. Once the opportunity came, and it would, she would lure Sid away from the crowd having its party, and she would put an end to him and to it, this lifelong ache and obsession. Within minutes after that, she would be gone. As for luring him, that might not be the right word. Challenge would be more accurate, since he knew who she was. He'd made that clear, and he would be looking for a chance of his own. Who struck first would decide the matter, and she had no doubt about who that would be.

CHAPTER 29

THE MASTER SUITE

Sid knew he should leave now. Maybe his instincts were too rusty after all these years; he hadn't had to act this quickly in many years. And maybe it was sentiment, hesitation from loving the life he had with Dylan. A soft life, despite the demands of running a resort. A life of love and coffee in the mornings and the absolute quiet of the Pennsylvania countryside. He would never see it again, and he wanted to make as slow an exit as he could, providing it did not ensnare him.

Dylan was already downstairs at the party. He had been too nervous to linger in the Suite. He loved this life, too, but he worried much more about the details and the requirements than Sid did. Dylan was a fretter. He'd gone to the basement an hour before anyone else would arrive, determined to have every chair in place, every balloon and paper ghost. The good thing about his being so distracted was that Sid would be able to leave quickly, quietly and unnoticed. He just wanted one more look around, one more deep breath of air he would not breathe again.

He was taking only a suitcase with him. There was no need for more. He had no idea how to go about changing his identity if it came to that. He knew he could learn much from Bo Sweetzer, but she was the last person he ever wanted to see again. She had destroyed his life and it wasn't fair. He had not pulled the trigger. He hadn't even taken anything from the house! Yet she had targeted him and Sam for revenge, as well as the only man who really deserved it. Could he blame her? Yes, he could. He could blame her for saving her rage all these years and aiming it at an old man who had never meant her harm. Her obsession was costing him everything.

There was no plan A, let alone a plan B. His only plan was to get in his car and drive to New York City, or Queens or the Bronx. Somewhere he could melt into the urban landscape and make a plan. He'd have to get rid of the car. Maybe not get another one, cars were too easy to find. In a big city like New York or Boston he could live out his life never driving again. Would he need to change his name? How, exactly, does someone do that?

He was thinking it all through, trying to let it gel into definite, clear actions he could take, when a knock came at the door.

Odd, Sid thought. No one ever came to the Suite. Dylan would just walk in, of course. He sighed, annoyed that one of the guests would take the liberty of bringing some minor problem to his attention here, where he lived, and here was considered off-limits, even if there was no official policy about that. There were boundaries to keep, and someone was crossing them.

Sid left the small suitcase on the bed and went to answer the door. Whoever it was, with whatever needless complaint they had, could be dispatched quickly enough and he could get on with the sad task of saying goodbye without uttering a word.

CHAPTER 30

UNHAPPY HALLOWEEN

After falling off some the last few years that Pucky and Stu owned Pride Lodge, the Halloween party was back to its all time highs. Fifty-six guests, not including staff, and another seventy-five locals that Dylan had counted, all packed into the basement bars that had been turned into one large frightfest. No detail had been spared that day as every hand on deck spun cobwebs, hung spiders and placed cackling witches and howling skulls along the bar and table tops. DJ Slam, a college kid from Princeton, had driven in to make $500 for the night and keep the crowd on its feet.

The space was dark, and as Kyle and Danny ordered drinks at one of the corner tables in Clyde's, Kyle had trouble telling the guests from the locals, and one person from another. He thought he saw Maggie dressed as a firefly, taking pictures on her smartphone, and Eileen not far from her as a mummy ordering beer at the bar.

"What do you think is going to become of the place?" Danny asked, having to raise his voice over a Lady GaGa song being played too loud for his tastes. Danny had never liked loud music, or any music when he was talking, and would even turn the radio news off in the car when they were having a conversation. It all became noise to him, especially when it was competing with him.

"Dylan's still here," Kyle said, sipping his margarita while continuing to scan the crowd.

"You think he'll still want to be here if Sid . . . "

"Go ahead, say it. If Sid goes to prison. I can't imagine Dylan leaving under any circumstances."

"What if the bank takes the property?"

Kyle had thought about that. If Dylan was right and Sid embezzled the money to buy Pride Lodge, the bank was going to want its money back. Kyle had no idea what the laws were about something like that, but he imagined they favored the bank.

"Maybe they'll come to some arrangement. I can't imagine the bank wants an old, sprawling gay lodge on its hands, and selling it's a pain. They'd take a loss, I'm sure. And anyway, it's all conjecture. Wait and see."

Danny was first to spot Detective Sikorsky coming through the door. She'd taken the easy way out, costume-wise, and was wearing just a long black wig, witch's hat and cape, the kind of costume a mother would throw together quickly for a child.

"Good thing she's not in the fashion industry," Kyle said as Sikorsky waved and approached the table.

A sudden gasp of recognition went up in the room. Kyle, Danny, and even Linda mid-stride turned to the door that connected Clyde's with the karaoke room and saw none other than Pucky Green standing in the doorway, smiling at everyone. He had forgone a costume, either not wanting to wear one or, more likely, wanting to make sure everybody recognized him. He hadn't been to Pride Lodge in nearly two years, and even though people had speculated all weekend he would come, there was an assumption that he might not. It was a hard place for Pucky to be, as haunted by his memories and it ever could be by make-believe ghosts and plastic goblins.

"Who's that?" Linda asked, sliding into a seat across from Danny.

"That's Pucky Green," Danny said. "The original owner of Pride Lodge, the visionary."

"Ah, yes," she said. She was aware of the Lodge's history, having looked into it quickly the last thirty-six hours. "He moved to Key West after his partner died. On the steps, no less."

The three of them were silent a moment, watching partygoers make their way to Pucky for a hug or a handshake, several of them trying to get him to sit with them. He seemed to prefer staying near the door, holding court for a time, and deserving to. If Pride Lodge truly belonged to anyone, it was Pucky.

"So," the detective said, turning back in her seat, "what's this evidence you have for me?"

Kyle reached into his jacket pocket for the email. He wasn't sure it constituted evidence, or of what: that Sid had a dark past, that he was possibly involved in a crime? That Bo Sweetzer was connected, and that somehow it had all come together and caused the death of Teddy, and perhaps Happy? Were there others?

"He put it where I would find it," Kyle said, handing the email to her. "In his AA book. He was always quoting a page, and sure enough . . ."

"Convenient," she said, unfolding the email.

"I told you," Kyle said.

"Shh." Danny hushed him as Sikorsky read over the message.

Linda Sikorsky folded the email back up and put it in her blouse pocket. "This isn't much, you know. And anyone could have written it."

"But anyone didn't," Kyle said. It came from that man, Tatum. He's dead, I read about it before dinner. An ice pick in the back of his head."

"And you think Bo Sweetzer had something to do with that?" She felt herself blushing and was glad for the darkness of the bar. She had gone out with Sweetzer, not a date by any stretch, but still a revealing of herself. With a murderer? A criminal? She felt her stomach dropping.

"She's not Bo Sweetzer," Kyle said. "At least she wasn't always. She was Emily Lapinsky, I'm sure of it." And to Danny, "I should have brought that photograph, I could've used the Lodge printer. The resemblance is obvious."

"The timing's not right," Sikorsky said, her mind starting to work out the puzzle. "She was here the night before Teddy Pembroke's death, but what about Happy? And why would she kill Pembroke in the first place?"

"She wouldn't," Danny said. "That's the point."

"It's Sid," said Kyle. "There are two killers at Pride Lodge. That's where this is taking me."

Austin came up to the table carrying a tray of drinks. He was wearing a Frankenstein costume, complete with bolts in his neck. He looked the way the monster would if he'd been a post-Stonewall punk with blond and purple hair. "Courtesy of Mr. Hern," he said, handing each of the three a special drink the bar had come up with just for this party. "Monster Mashes," Austin explained.

"Of course," Kyle said.

Danny peered around the room, trying to locate Linus Hern and his pocket-sized entourage. "Why would Linus Hern buy us drinks?"

"A truce?"

"More likely slow acting poison."

"Do you want them or not?" Austin asked.

"You can just leave them on the table," Danny said. "And please tell Mr. Hern we appreciate the gesture."

Austin set the drinks down and hurried off.

"He's up to something," Danny said, taking the drink and sniffing it. "No faint smell of almonds. Cyanide's out."

"You two really don't like each other, do you?" Linda said.

"It's a hate-hate relationship," Kyle said. "And a long story. I'd even say they respect each other, the way a cobra respects a mongoose."

"Please tell me I'm the mongoose," Danny said.

Pucky had been making his way around the room, choosing not to sit anywhere. He was enjoying the attention, the glad-handing and congratulations, although he wasn't sure why anyone would congratulate him. For still being alive? For surviving Stu's death? He had arrived that evening and the "welcome backs" had not stopped since. He walked up to the trio's table just as Danny was hoping to be the mongoose.

"I see you more as a cobra," Pucky said to Danny, extending his hand. "Patient and wise."

Danny would have none of the hand shaking and quickly stood instead, putting his arms around the old man. "You're looking great," he said.

Pucky was dressed like someone who lived in Key West, with lime green pants, a beige sweater and what looked like dock shoes, the kind you see people wearing on a cruise ship. Or a beach.

"I've gained a few," Pucky said. He turned to hug Kyle, who'd also stood, as had the detective. It just seemed the right thing to do, paying deference to a Pride Lodge legend.

"Linda Sikorsky," she said, extending her hand. Pucky took it in both of his and welcomed her to the Lodge, just as he would have when he ran it.

"Sit, sit," Danny said, and to their surprise Pucky agreed. Apparently he was weary of walking slowly around the room hugging and shaking, shaking and hugging.

"Ah," Pucky said, seeing the drinks. "You're enjoying the Monster Mashes. I have no idea what's in them. Creme de Menthe from the look of it."

"Please," Danny said, "have mine."

Pucky thought about it a moment, then agreed, taking the green drink and sipping. He made a face as if to say the Monster Mash was monstrous, and put the drink back on the table.

The conversation veered away then from emails, murders and criminals. Pucky told them about his life in Key West, and how his only regret is that he didn't go there more often with Stu. He talked about life on the island and his neighbors, and the near-perfect climate. Kyle could tell by the tone of his voice and the sadness that kept coming into his eyes that life in the Keys, while no doubt as enjoyable as Pucky said it was, was still life without Stu and that hole would never be filled.

"You could always come back here," Danny said. "Maybe in the summers."

"No," Pucky said. "My time has passed here. I'm sure they'd have me, and maybe even put me to work! But we have to let go eventually. Of everything, and everyone."

"The timing was certainly perfect," Kyle said. "You wanted to go, and Sid and Dylan were there. I can't imagine what would have happened to this place if Sid hadn't had the money."

Pucky looked at him. "Sid?" he said. "Oh, Sid didn't have the money. Jeremy did."

Kyle stared at him. "Jeremy?" he said. "Old Jeremy who sits in the chair for hours and stays up till two in the morning?"

"What other Jeremy is there? He lent them the money, I know that for a fact."

The significance of this information was lost on Danny and Detective Sikorsky. They both waited for Kyle to speak, not sure where he was going with this.

"Pucky, it's great to see you again," Kyle said, as he stood up quickly from the table. "You'll have to excuse us."

Kyle turned to Linda. "We've been played," he said. "We need to go upstairs, now. Have you seen Sid or Dylan?"

"Come to think of it, no" she said.

"Now!" Kyle said again, and he lead the way as the three of them hurried out of the bar.

"Where are we going?" Danny asked as they headed up the stairs.

"To stop a murder," Kyle replied, taking the stairs two at a time now. "I hope."

CHAPTER 31

AND THE WINNER IS . . .

Dylan was standing in the doorway to the Suite, his face frozen in shock. He was babbling under his breath as Kyle, Danny and Detective Sikorsky hurried down the hallway toward him.

"She killed him," he said, holding out his bloody hands. "She killed Sid."

Sikorsky eased Dylan to the side as the three of them filed into the living room. The scene was horrific. Sid was at his desk, the X-Acto knife from the pumpkin carving sticking grotesquely from his throat. And there, next to his computer keyboard, was the Cinderella pumpkin Bo Sweetzer had carved.

"I tried to save him," Dylan said, still dazed. "I should have taken the knife out . . . I didn't know . . . why would she do that?"

Linda Sikorsky had been to her share of murder scenes, more than one might guess for a place like New Hope, but this one ranked among the worst. Sid Stanhope was now a corpse in a chair, with a considerable amount of his blood drained from his neck onto his shirt, his pants, his shoes, the floor. No one, she knew, could lose that much blood and survive. The knife had been buried fully half its length into his neck. She did not immediately reach for her phone; calling the paramedics now was pointless. Sid was as dead as Sam Tatum had been when a mother and daughter came upon his lifeless body.

"What am I going to do?" Dylan sobbed. He buried his face in his hands.

"You can start by telling the truth," Kyle said. There was no compassion in his voice.

Everyone turned to Kyle, startled by what he'd said.

"My husband's dead!" Dylan shrieked. "That maniac killed him!"

"I doubt she would make it so obvious after killing two other men quite efficiently," Kyle said coldly, staring at Dylan. "This is more the work of someone local. Someone very close to Sid. About six feet away, as a matter of fact."

Dylan suddenly seemed not quite so shocked, not quite so shaken by the death of his partner, as he began to quickly appraise the situation. Kyle could see it in his eyes, the instant calculation.

"The police are already here," Dylan said, and to Linda, "Arrest her! She can't be far, you have to find her! Do something!"

Detective Linda Sikorsky thought she'd seen it all, but this was rattling her. The only clear victim in the room was dead in a chair. But who was the killer? Who should she be arresting?

Kyle glanced out the window then and saw a pair of taillights disappearing down the road. "I think she's gone by now," he said, turning back to them. "Probably hours ago."

"But Sid stole the money," Dylan cried, desperate to cast the blame on anyone but himself. "And he did something terrible, years ago, it was in that email. Someone wanted him dead."

"They did indeed," Kyle said. "There was no embezzlement. Sid was a criminal, there's no doubt about that, but he didn't steal a dime from the bank. The money came from old Jeremy. Dylan only wanted us to think Sid was a thief."

"Why in hell would I want that?" Dylan demanded, now a very different man from the one who'd been standing in the doorway when they came up the stairs.

"Because it's all yours now," Kyle replied. "Or it would have been, had Pucky not shown up. Not a bad plan, Dylan. Not a flawless one, but you could have gotten away with it. Sid gone, the Lodge and inheritance, whatever there was, yours free and clear with just a sizable loan to repay. Bo Sweetzer—or should I say Emily Lapinsky—blamed for the murders. Who would believe her if she denied it? And Jeremy bankrolling the whole thing, unaware of what you've done. He is unaware, isn't he? I just can't see him as a partner in crime."

"You're out of your mind. She killed him. I have no idea why she was careless. For the same reason she brought the pumpkin, so everyone would know it was her!"

"You mean so everyone would *think* it was her."

Linda Sikosrky stepped toward Dylan. "You're under arrest, Mr. Tremblay."

"Arrest? Me?! For what?!" Dylan shouted.

"For finishing the job Bo Sweetzer started," Kyle said. "For Teddy, for poor Happy, just a kid who couldn't keep his mouth shut. Is that what happened, he told you what Teddy told him, what Teddy found out, and the wheels were set in motion? You're a monster, Dylan. And as bad a man as Sid was, I wish he'd lived to know it."

Dylan thought about running, dashing out of the room and through the Lodge front door, but he knew there was nowhere to go. How far could he get? Everything he owned was here. Better to try and talk his way out of this later. What proof was there? He'd been careful every step of the way. He would find a way out of this, he believed that, he had to believe it. In the meanwhile it was time to be silent, to give them nothing that could and would be used against him, and to think.

Detective Sikorsky finally pulled out her phone and started making calls. The coroner's office for a dead man, back up to help her get Dylan Tremblay to the station house. It was going to be a very long night.

CHAPTER 32

IN THE REARVIEW MIRROR

S he'd had the chance to do it, then and there, and yet she had refrained. Hesitated. Was it the influence of her evening with the woman she would never see again, the beguiling detective from New Hope? Or had vengeance run long enough through her veins?

She'd left her room and headed downstairs when she was suddenly, strangely, compelled to see this man face-to-face again. She had thought her reasoning was to tell him the end was near. So near, in fact, it was *here*, right then and there, and she would shoot him in his doorway. But when he had answered her knock—her hand sliding to her waist where the gun could be slipped out quickly—she had stopped hating, just for an instant, just long enough for the two of them to stare silently at one another.

Finally, she said to the man she had been waiting thirty years to kill, "Why did you do that to me?"

Sid thought a long moment, even as he expected to die any second, and said, "You weren't supposed to be there."

"Well," Bo said to him, "I was. And now, I'm here. I'll be downstairs, waiting. I know you'll come. There's no way around this. You know that as well as I do. "

Sid nodded. She was right. He could run, but she would find him. She was that determined. He had closed the door then and gone back to his desk to sit and think. Maybe the best thing to do was call the police, to give himself up, to be done with it once and for all. He was trying to decide his course of action when the door opened and Dylan came in, carrying a pumpkin.

Bo knew they would probably catch up with her eventually. When she saw the three of them rush out of the bar—Kyle, Danny and the detective—she knew it was time to go. At first she'd thought Sid might have killed himself, but whatever had happened, an alarm had been sounded and her plans had changed in the instant. She had been at this long enough to know something big had happened, and the time for an escape was now or never.

They had not seen her. She had been alone in the crowd, watching and waiting. She had planned to give Sid another hour to show up, then she would go looking for him. He would be waiting, too, she knew that. Waiting to die, or to kill her instead. And now, just like that, everything had changed.

She drove away from Pride Lodge with nothing but her purse and a gun that would soon be rusting at the bottom of the Delaware River. She could not have gone back to her room, and she knew she was leaving everything behind her, including Bo Sweetzer. She'd glanced in the rearview mirror as she drove down the hill, wondering what name she would take next, when she swore she saw Kyle Callahan in an upstairs window. But of course he had no way of knowing it was her car, if he'd seen it at all.

She drove carefully along to the highway, thought of making a left turn, then made a right instead, and disappeared into the night.

CHAPTER 33

CHECK OUT TIME IS 11:00 A.M.

Seventeen messages. That's how many times Imogene had tried to reach Kyle, once he added up voicemail, texts and two tweets. He'd tried to tell her that, while he had a Twitter account for his photoblog feed that would send out new posts with photos when he put them up, he never actually tweeted. Not with his phone, not with his thumbs, not in any way. So trying to reach him @AsKyleSeesIt was like people who tried to communicate with him through Facebook messages. He seldom ever looked to see what was there.

It didn't matter anyway. He had seen Imogene's car drive past ten minutes earlier. There weren't many like it, a vintage, pink 1968 Mustang that only Imogene Landis would be seen driving. He knew she was at the Lodge now, already asking questions, and he regretted having called her in the first place. Danny was right: it was unseemly, and it appeared, however much Kyle told himself the appearance was deceiving, to be taking advantage of a particularly bad situation. Three people were dead, not counting the men in Los Angeles and Detroit. Having a mouthy livewire like Imogene show up with a microphone, reporter's notebook and handlheld HD camera made it all seem so . . . *DeathWatchNewHope.*

"You can't hide forever," Danny said, putting the last of his clothes in his suitcase. "She's at the desk now, pestering poor Ricki for details. Ricki and anyone else unlucky enough to show up this early."

"I never should have called her," Kyle said. He was packing up his camera, wondering if he'd taken any good pictures at all, then feeling guilty for caring.

"It's not so much that you called her, Sweetie," Danny said. "But that you never called her again!"

"We were a little busy," Kyle reminded him. "We spent what, two hours at the police station giving statements? I didn't get to sleep until three a.m. this morning, and that was fitful."

"Murder doesn't care. Hell, we're lucky that's all the time we were there. At least we get to leave! Dylan Tremblay won't be seeing the outside of a jail cell for a very long time."

"Nor should he," Kyle said, with a little too much righteousness.

"Nor should he," Danny agreed.

The two then fell silent as they continued packing for their exit from Pride Lodge. Finally, Danny said, "Do you think they'll find her?"

"It would only be right," Kyle said, not looking at him. He knew it was highly unlikely that the taillights he'd seen from the upstairs window were those of Bo Sweetzer. They hadn't even known she'd fled until later, when the police who came to support Linda Sikorsky found no trace of her except the clothes and pocket watch she'd left in her room. And even if they had been her taillights, what was he supposed to have done? Cried out for someone to chase her? He knew he was simply feeling guilty for having wanted her to get away.

"She's a murderer, after all," Kyle said, closing his suitcase. "It would only be right."

When they got to the check out desk Kyle glanced around nervously and asked Ricki in a hushed voice, "Where's Imogene?"

"You mean Genie? The reporter lady?"

Ricki was unusually alert and seemed more than a little excited. Kyle knew it meant he must have already been interviewed, however quickly. An interview with Imogene meant flattery, a wink if the person she was talking to was a straight man, and letting a desk clerk at a countryside gay resort call her "Genie." That really was the giveaway. No one called Imogene Landis

"Genie" and lived to tell about it. Except Ricki. Kyle could see it now, the not-too-sophisticated man who'd never lived in a place with more than a few thousand people in it calling the diminutive newswoman "Genie," the way a waitress in a roadside diner calls everyone "Sweetheart," and Imogene saying, "You can call me Genie, everyone does." Anything for the story.

"Yes, her," Danny interjected.

"Oh, she's out by the pool talking to the twins. They're on set-up today."

"She'll love that," Kyle said. "What murder in the woods is complete without a set of identical twins? But it gives us a chance to get out of here. I'll just say I didn't see her, didn't know she'd come. Give me ten minutes down the road and I'll call."

"As long as you tell her we're just about into the Lincoln Tunnel. No turning around! You know she'll ask."

It was then Kyle realized that the Lodge had gone on, even with Sid dead and Dylan in jail. He and Danny had missed the coroner's van coming to take Sid's body away. They'd missed the other cops helping to handcuff and incarcerate Dylan. They'd wanted to be away from it as quickly as possible and had headed to the police station in their own car as soon as backup for Detective Sikorsky arrived.

"What happened?" Kyle asked quietly.

"Oh, she asked a few questions, took some footage," Ricki said.

Footage, Kyle thought. Of course Ricki would consider a few minutes on a digital video camera footage, as if he were going to see his name in the final credits at an Imax.

"No," he said. "I mean last night, after . . . you know."

"If you mean, did the band play on? Yes, it did. They put yellow tape up outside the Master Suite, but most of the people downstairs never knew what went on. The cops weren't interested in them, and the staff wasn't about to empty the place. It's our best weekend!"

That thought struck Kyle and Danny both. Dancers danced on, drinkers drank on. Halloween weekend at Pride Lodge celebrated and partied unfazed as the lives of the very people who provided it were destroyed.

"I told them to stay the course," a voice said from behind them. "They weren't being greedy, if that's what you're thinking."

Kyle and Danny turned to see Jeremy standing just a few feet away, leaning slightly on a cane in his left hand. He was doing just fine without the walker today. He seemed much sturdier this way, not like the frail old man everyone imagined him to be. Kyle wondered if that had been what he wanted them all to think. He was a cagey sort, an observer and listener, for whatever his purposes.

"Pucky told me you were the silent partner here," Kyle said. "That's how I knew, how the pieces fell together. Dylan wanted me, Sikorsky, everyone, to think Sid had stolen all that money."

"They weren't a happy couple," Jeremy said. "At least not Dylan. Sid, probably, he was older, his options more limited, by time if nothing else. But Dylan wanted his freedom, as long as it came with the property."

"If you knew all this, why didn't you say anything?" Danny asked.

"Say anything about what? I never imagined Dylan Tremblay would kill people to get what he wanted. I thought he'd stick it out, maybe try for something in a divorce. Honestly, I thought he would even just wait it out. Sid was in poor health, he'd probably die at least twenty years before Dylan. The whole thing is conjecture anyway."

"Correction, Jeremy," Kyle said. "Teddy dead at the bottom of the pool is not conjecture. Happy dead in a creek is not conjecture. And Sid dead upstairs with a knife sticking out of his neck is not conjecture."

Jeremy had defended himself as much as he intended to. " I can't help it that my imagination is not as vivid as yours, Kyle," he said with a shrug. "We're going to need new innkeepers here. I don't suppose I could get the two of you . . . "

"Not on your life," Danny said. "Pride Lodge is a great place to visit, and I'm sure we'll be back, but running a resort is the last thing I would ever want."

"True, true," the old man said. "I expect you'll be running Margaret's Passion soon enough. No one lives forever, it's just the way life goes. But have it your way. For now I've got Ricki, the twins, Cowboy Dave, everyone really, except the owners! Oh wait, that's me."

"So the place is yours?" Kyle asked.

"It is now," Jeremy said. "Sid and Dylan made monthly payments to me, with Pride Lodge itself as collateral. If for any reason the loan was not paid off, which I imagine it won't be now, the Lodge becomes mine. Had I died first that wouldn't be the case. Apparently Dylan didn't think of everything or I'd be the one dead at the bottom of a pool. I'm not the old fool people take me for, you know."

Kyle smiled at him. "I never thought you were. But that's what you want people to think. Camouflage. Pretty impressive, too. It probably saved your life."

Jeremy stuck out his right hand. "So, boys, onward and downward."

Kyle and Danny each shook his hand. They knew he hadn't omitted anything out of malice, and that he really had no idea what lengths Dylan was going to to secure a fantasy future for himself.

A sound of laughter floated up from outside. Imogene, "Genie" to Ricki the desk clerk, was working her charm. And she was charming, to anyone who didn't know her as more than an acquaintance or a brief encounter. To her loyal assistant Kyle Callahan she was a terror, but a lovable terror. He was in no mood to have that love tested this morning.

"Quickly," Kyle said to Ricki. "Just the bill. We have appointments with destiny in, oh, about ten minutes."

"Five," Danny said, hurrying them along. "A laugh means she's just about through with them."

"Whoever she is," Jeremy said, "I like the sound of her."

Kyle turned to him. "Yes, I think you would. I think the two of you are going to hit it off very well. You might want to get back in your chair. She's as much a sucker for frail old men as the rest of us. "

"Call her," Danny said, signing the credit card slip. "Ten minutes down the road."

"Lincoln Tunnel," Kyle finished. "Got it, now let's go."

They each grabbed the handle of a suitcase and hurried out of the Lodge. They took the steps two at a time as they turned right into the main parking lot. Moments later Danny was pulling out of the drive just as Kyle saw Imogene hurrying down the hillside, waving at them.

"Look the other way!" Kyle said. "Drive! I'll call her back eventually."

"You're going to hear about this for days, Kyle. She may even threaten to replace you."

"Again?!" Kyle said, and the two of them shared a laugh for the first time in nearly two days.

Danny watched Pride Lodge recede in the rearview mirror. "Do you think we'll ever come back?"

"Sure," Kyle said. "It's become an old friend by now, and one thing about old friends is that you want to know what happens to them. We'll be back."

Danny nodded; they would indeed. He turned the first corner and took one last glance in the mirror to see Imogene standing in the road behind them, hands on her hips, wagging her finger at them. She wasn't fooled. And she would never replace Kyle. Love was love.

PRIDE AND PERILOUS

Book II

CHAPTER 1

Bluejacket, Oklahoma - 1978

The summer had been particularly hot, even for Oklahoma. Corn had withered and died on the stalk, acres of land had choked and killed many crops, leaving others so feeble the farmers who subsisted on them had been forced to charity. Predictions were made from pulpits across the state that if ever there were clear signs of the End Times, this fever baking the landscape was surely among them.

The four Stipling children could only pray for cooling rain and fan themselves with paper fans their mother brought home from the Baptist church they attended. Clement Stipling, their father, considered the use of electricity to power fans an extravagance and a waste of money. Air conditioning was for rich people, and the Stiplings would never be rich. Clement had even refused to donate to the church's special collection two years ago for a new ceiling fan. Paper on sticks worked just fine for him, and it would work for his family.

The Stiplings were poor but proud. Clement worked as a handyman sometimes, other times as a farm hand, and every now and then as a carpenter, bringing in enough to pay rent on their small house and put food on the table most days. His tall, wiry frame, his natural agility and his unusually large hands made him well suited for physical labor. He'd never learned a trade, nor studied anything at the knee of his no-account father. He had left home at fourteen and never looked back, which made for thirty years of staring straight ahead, taking whatever next step there was to take. Those steps had gotten him a wife, Pearl, and four children, ages two to thirteen. He was about to be a father for the fifth time, if Pearl made it through, which was looking less likely with each passing minute.

Pearl Stipling was an obedient woman. That was probably the most descriptive thing to say about her, and the virtue, as she saw it, of which she would be most proud, were pride not a sin. Humility, perseverance, and obedience. If Pearl knew what a mantra was, those three words would be it. She had humbly submitted to her life as Clement Stipling's wife, even though she was pretty enough to have found several alternatives – or so she'd been told. Middling height, with a kind face and just enough plump to her to attract men looking to raise children, Pearl had been a prize in her youth, and marrying Clement had been seen by her parents as a waste of that prize. Running off with him to elope in Tulsa was the only significant act of disobedience in her entire life, and one she had been forgiven for once the grandchildren began to arrive.

She had persevered for thirty-two years of her own difficult journey. She had been obedient, foremost to the Lord, and secondly to her husband. She loved her little ones, even though Jeffey was officially a teenager now and would not kiss her anymore except on the cheek. Doreen was ten, Emiline eight, Jessica two, and now, God willing, they would finally have another son, whom they had decided to name Kieran, after Pearl's late grandfather. Pearl, in her innermost thoughts she shared with no one and hoped God could not hear, wanted no more children after this. If Clement insisted, of course she would bear them, and if God saw fit to keep her pregnant, she would obediently stay that way, but she sure hoped the fifth time was the charm and that a second son would be the end of her child-bearing.

The way the delivery was going, it might well be the end of Pearl. She had gone into labor three weeks early. It had caught them both off guard and unprepared to get her to the hospital. Clement Stipling did not own a car, which he considered even more of an extravagance than an electric fan. He walked everywhere he needed to be, and if that place was too far he hitched a ride. There was always someone willing to take him; they knew Clement Stipling wouldn't distract them with useless talk, since he was a man of few words and the ones he spoke were seldom entertaining. So it was that on an extremely hot Thursday morning while Pearl was making breakfast, her water broke and she plunged into the hardest, most painful, most prayer-inducing labor she had ever experienced. None of the others had been like this, and two hours into it, as she lay in their bed sweating through the sheets, she knew something was wrong. She knew this would certainly be her last, as there would be nothing left of her when it was finished.

Clement Stipling had not delivered any of his children. He had done repair work and house painting to pay off Doctor Simonson for bringing his other four into the world, but to be in his own bedroom, in his own home, desperate to have this child come out already and stop this terrible experience, was something from a dream worse than any he'd ever had. He sent Jeffey off to the neighbors to call the hospital (since telephones were a waste of time and money), only to be told the doctor was in surgery. Pearl was bedridden by then, and it was just her and Clement, trying to free her body from the baby who wanted to rip her apart and at the same time stay safely inside her.

Mrs. Jansen, the neighbor woman, arrived a half hour into it. She was helping Pearl, or trying to, while Clement paced back and forth by the closed door. It was bad enough that his children could hear Pearl's screams, he didn't want them seeing any of this. Back and forth, back and forth, while Mrs. Jansen just kept telling Pearl to push. Something was terribly wrong. Well, yes, Clement thought, that's pretty obvious. Terribly wrong.

And just about the time Kieran was willing to let go and exit his mother, Pearl saw the sky open up, in the ceiling! It was the strangest thing she'd ever seen, but not frightening at all. Like a very bright skylight, like a window in the plaster, and it slid open, and there was Jesus. Smiling at her and waving. She knew then her belief had not been in vain, her faith not wasted. She knew, too, there would be no more children, no more hardship, and no more Clement.

"What is she looking at?" Clement said, standing at the foot of the bed as Mrs. Jansen midwifed Kieran Stipling into the world. She ignored him, too busy with the birth. "What are you looking at?" he said to Pearl. She ignored him, too, immersed in the joy of her own liberation as she reached up as far as she could, took the hand of Jesus, to whom she had been most obedient all her life, and walked away into the clouds.

The baby did not cry, even when Mrs. Jansen slapped him to get him breathing.

"She's dead," Clement said, staring at the frozen rapture on his wife's face. His voice was cold, flat and fierce. Within those two words were accusation, statement, and promise: he promised then and there never to love this child, never to give it warmth, never to forgive it. Not *him*; it. It was a thing, a murderous thing that had taken from Clement Stipling the only treasure his trying life had ever known.

Clement was not the drinking sort, or he would have slipped into a bottomless bottle then and there. Instead he slipped into himself. By day's end he was a widower, alone with five children, one of whom he would just as soon be rid of. The child had taken Pearl from him, and he never felt the slightest obligation to repay the theft with love. He didn't love little Kieran and never would.

That was how Kieran Stipling grew up, knowing he had killed his mother and that no prison term would ever be as harsh as the sentence his father handed down. He was hated by the man, ignored, berated and belittled. Clement never raised a hand to him, but the looks were cold enough to freeze the deepest recesses of space, the words sharp enough to bleed a man out on the spot. Kieran would never amount to anything, his father told him. He was no good, bad blood, and a gott-damned cripple to boot! The sooner he was grown and gone, the better. At the age of fifteen, Kieran granted his father's only wish for him and left home; like his father, he never glanced back.

Time passed, the road hardened, his father's prediction – his curse? – came true as nothing became of his son, his *it*, losing job after job, hustling to survive with the assistance (for it could not be called kindness) of strange men. And now, twenty years later, at the age of thirty-five, the boy who would be no one, stained at birth and declared a failure from his first breath, was about to make his mark.

CHAPTER 2

A RAINY NIGHT IN BROOKLYN

It had been five years at least since Devin had worried about being followed. That's how long he had been living as Devin 24/7. Denise Ellerton had ceased to exist – officially, legally, physically, psychologically, and every other way in which each person functions in the world. For Devin, she had ceased existing long before that, when he had realized as a teenager that he was not like other girls; that the simple reality of pronouns was different for him, as he thought of himself as "he" while everyone else insisted on calling him "she." Tom-boyish Denise, odd Denise, rough-and-tumble Denise. He had wanted to correct them then, and even younger, as early as the third grade. "I'm not a girl," he had wanted to say, but it wasn't until he was in college that he fully understood what was going on with him, and when he finally had the distance from his family to do something about it.

The sensation of being shadowed down a dark street was one of those things that belonged to Denise, to women. Devin had long been aware of the differences in experiences men had from women; to suggest there were no differences was to choose denial over reality. There were experiences unique to men, and experiences unique to women, as well as experiences unique to those who did not fit readily into either. Devin had become a man in every way possible. The transition had been made, the journey completed, and not since before it had he worried about being followed down his own Brooklyn street, late on a rainy Friday night. There was something different about this, too. It wasn't random, as if he'd crossed paths with the wrong person in an accident of fate, as so many people did who found themselves the victims of crimes of opportunity. Devin had the very distinct and unsettling feeling that the man coming up slowly behind him had been there for awhile, had followed him off the R train, along the platform, up the stairs, and now, six blocks later, nearly to his apartment on Prospect Avenue.

Devin was tall at five-eight, and worked out religiously at the local New York Athletic Club. He'd had a trainer for two years and always believed he could handle himself in a tight situation. Not that it happened often: he didn't drink, didn't stay out late unless he had a showing of his artwork or was attending one of a friend's exhibits; he hadn't dated in three years, and he was a night person, meaning he worked at night in his studio apartment and made every effort to be home by 7:00 pm, when he would start his routine of coffee-fueled creativity, putting together his latest collage or designing a multi-medium piece that he would then spend the next two or three weeks bringing to life.

He was an attractive man, too, or so he'd been told enough times to believe. His natural height was complimented by a thin frame, short black hair he gelled back, a high, wide, forehead, moist brown eyes that had never been bothered by glasses, a thin but ready smile, and a nose that had once been broken in a fall, although he told everyone it had been a boxing match. It was the one lie he allowed himself. He just liked the idea of having a nose broken by a fist in a boxing glove. And it made the person who had once been Denise all but unrecognizable.

He'd stayed out later then usual tonight and had been cursing his lapse in discipline when he first realized someone was behind him. This stretch of Prospect Avenue, unlike nearly all streets in neighboring Manhattan, was sparsely populated at night and the presence of other people was noticeable, especially other people who were shadowing you. He'd become aware of the man behind him not long after coming up the subway stairs but had thought nothing of it at the time. Then, a block later, he could hear the footsteps, as if he were in some B-movie thriller and a stalker was shortening the distance between then. Now, four blocks from the subway and just one from his apartment building, he became convinced he was the object of the man's attention. Had it not been so worrying it would have been interesting: why would a strange man be following a reclusive artist down a deserted Brooklyn street on a rainy Friday night? He decided to ask the question directly. He adjusted his umbrella, with its caved-in side to his back, letting rain trickle down and soak his jacket, and he turned around to get a look at the man he now knew was his pursuer.

As Devin turned to face him, the stranger stopped. He was only about thirty feet away now. Devin saw that he did not have an umbrella, but his face was hidden by a hoodie pulled down over it. In late April the air was still chilly at night and most people wore jackets, sweaters, other clothes that kept them warm in the cool darkness. Hoodies were especially popular, but also had the disconcerting effect of hiding the person's face. It was only human nature to want to know who was beneath the hood, and why he was covering his face.

The man made no attempt to pretend he was not following Devin. He didn't keep walking with a turn this way or that; he didn't cross the street and continue; he didn't even keep coming, as someone would who really was just walking along the same street at the same time. He stopped. In the rain.

"Who are you?" Devin shouted, tilting his umbrella back to show himself and improve his line of sight.

The man just stood and, Devin assumed, stared. It was dark out and raining, and neither could see the other with any great clarity.

Then the man began to walk toward him.

Decision time. Devin could run for his apartment, which was only a block away; he could call for help, someone would throw open a window and call 911 – or would they? – or he could do what he decided to do and stand his ground. He was tough, he trained two hours, three days a week; he was quick and fit and thin, and above all he was not Denise, not anymore. He had not endured the challenges of his life, the demands of simply being and becoming who he was, to flee in front of some punk on a Brooklyn street. He eased his shoulders back, loosened his grip on the umbrella to free his hands, and prepared for a fight.

The closer the man got, the more familiar he looked. He was wearing jeans, red sneakers and the green hoodie, and although his face was hidden, something about his overall presence rang a bell. There was also the limp, if that was the right word, a way of walking that made it appear one leg was shorter than the other, but housed more in the pelvis, a sort of up and down motion, like a piston misfiring every time the man took a step. Devin noticed the emblem on his sweatshirt, a rainbow flag with wording underneath it he couldn't read. He relaxed; it must be a neighbor after all, or someone coming to visit a neighbor. At the very least the stranger was gay and, by inference, non-threatening.

But still he had not responded to Devin's asking him who he was. And he had stopped, then kept coming. He was only about ten feet away now, and Devin put it all together: the walk, the sweatshirt, and finally, as the man drew close and eased his hood back – the face.

"You!" Devin said, startled.

"Yes, me," the man replied, now face-to-face in the rain.

"Why are you following me?" Devin said, still trying to piece this puzzle together in his mind. He knew the man, but not really, not in any but a passing way.

"I'm following you, Devin," the man replied, "because I heard the whispers."

"The whispers? What whispers?"

The man said nothing as he stepped forward and quickly slipped his hand out from the sweatshirt's front pouch.

Devin had no time to wonder what the glint of metal was, where it belonged in this picture, this rainy night in Brooklyn, before the knife blade entered between his ribs. Once, twice, a final total of sixteen times as the man he knew but didn't know reached his free hand around Devin and pulled him close, stabbing and stabbing.

Anyone watching would think two men were hugging each other goodbye, a familiar sight just about anywhere in New York City. But no one was watching. No one saw the man ease Devin, now unconscious and quickly bleeding to death, down to the sidewalk and carefully drape him there, then turn as easily as he'd come and walk away.

"So much for art," the man mumbled to himself, clutching the knife in his shirt pouch. He turned and began heading slowly back the way he'd come. He would not take the train, but instead walk, walk all night if he had to, over the Brooklyn Bridge and back into the darkness of Manhattan, pulling the night ever more tightly around himself as he thought about the next one.

CHAPTER 3

WEDDING BELL BLUES

Kyle had been fretting about the wedding for two months, ever since the sudden decision had been made for the two of them to marry. It wasn't unexpected; they'd been talking about it for the past year, but now that it was upon them he hoped they'd made the right decision, that it would be, as every cultural assumption about wedded bliss predicted, the happiest day of their lives – a day to remember, not a day to regret.

He and Danny had rented tuxedos since neither of them could fit into the ones they owned. Kyle had never worn one until he met Danny, but once they began going on cruises together it was a must-have for the formal dinners: at least once on every cruise the diners would dress to the nines, giving the evening the odd feel of a doomed celebration (Kyle always imagined the ship jerking suddenly as it hit an iceberg, the diners pretending not to notice and carrying on with their fancy meal).

"I'm feeling especially confined in this," Kyle said, as Danny adjusted his bowtie. Danny was a good six inches shorter than Kyle, who was not a particularly tall man, and he had to lean up on the toes of his spit-shined shoes to get a direct look.

"Well you can't blame weight gain," Danny replied. "We just rented these yesterday." He stepped back and nodded with satisfaction at the tie adjustment.

"In a hurry, at that," Kyle said. "If I'd gotten it last week like I meant to, I'd know it was too tight. Jesus."

"Just relax. It's nerves, Kyle, that's what has you feeling trapped, not the penguin suit."

Danny stepped back and examined his partner. Not bad. Kyle Callahan was still as handsome as ever to Danny, though both would admit it was a plain-handsome. Kyle still had a full head of hair, and, like most men his age, he wore glasses. He had a slightly high forehead, and he wore his hair brushed back with just a touch of pomade, opening up a soft, inviting, and distinctly intelligent face. Standing in front of his "perpetual fiancé" as he now called Danny, he suddenly had a flash at what they might look like at their own wedding when it came.

"I know this is hard for you," Danny said quietly.

"It's not hard. I'm very happy for David. Elliot's a great guy, and being the best man …"

"At the wedding of your first love, yes, I'm sure you have no mixed feelings."

Kyle had moved to New York City from Chicago nearly thirty-three years ago with his then-boyfriend David Grogan. David wanted to be a journalist and insisted he must go to Columbia – all serious journalism students went there, or to another of a select few schools that turned out the true stars of the profession. And while he never became a journalist, let alone a star, the young, ambitious David packed his things and drove the 800 miles to upper Manhattan, with Kyle Callahan following behind in his used Gremlin. Both their cars were soon sold, given the complete lack of a need for automobiles in the city, and upper Manhattan was immediately traded for Brooklyn, where rents were halved from anything livable on the island. The two love birds managed to nest for just three months before David announced that he was too young for this kind of commitment; and while Kyle knew it meant there were too many other men David wanted to sleep with, he took it in stride, as devoted first-loves sometimes do. He moved out, letting David live his life as he needed to, make the mistakes he had to make, and suffer the losses. There were some devastating losses over those thirty years, too. David's partner Tom, who died from AIDS-related lymphoma in 1992. David's mother Patricia, who passed away on David's fiftieth birthday. Jobs, moves, over a decade of being single for both of them, and now … Kyle the best man in David's wedding. Life was nothing if not surprising, when you just gave it time.

They both turned toward the door when they heard Joshua start singing "Bridge Over Troubled Water" by Simon and Garfunkel. Joshua was Elliot's twenty-two year old son, soon to be David's stepson. From what David had told him, Joshua and his sister Clarice, eighteen and heading for UCLA in the fall, had accepted their father's gayness with more of a yawn than a shock and he, David, was quite excited at the prospect of becoming a stepfather at fifty-four, especially since having children wasn't something he'd ever allowed himself to imagine. Babies were a must-have accessory with same-sex couples these days, but men like David, Elliot, Kyle and Danny were from a generation just across the border, when having kids was still an anomaly in the gay community. Now, it seemed, they were everywhere, and David was delighted to come into stepfather-hood when the kids were all grown up.

"He has a lovely voice," Danny said, feeling some nerves himself. He knew David well enough, but he hadn't been in a wedding party since his sister Jennifer married her husband Henry twenty years ago.

"Is this not weird?" Kyle said, glad they were alone in the choir room. The other men of honor, friends of David's and Elliot's Kyle did not know, had already gone into the sanctuary at Manhattan's Blessed Redeemer Church and he and Danny were the last of the wedding party still straggling behind. Maybe Danny was right. Maybe he was sad about David getting married, and he was dragging his wingtips to the last minute, postponing the inevitable.

"Is what not weird?" Danny said, aware they needed to join the others.

"The whole thing. It's so … normal. We used to be outlaws."

Danny smiled. "I doubt you were ever an outlaw, Kyle Callahan. But you can be my Butch Cassidy any time."

"And you my Sundance Kid," Kyle said, leaning down and kissing Danny gently just before leading him out to join the happiest day of the happy couple's lives.

Kyle Callahan and Danny Durban had been together for six years this coming November. They'd met by accident at the Katherine Pride Gallery on Little 12th Street in Manhattan's Meatpacking District. The show that time was photography; Kyle had gone to support the photographer, a friend of his, and Danny had gone to keep things oiled with Katherine Pride, the gallery owner and a new customer at Margaret's Passion, the Gramercy Park restaurant where Danny was the day manager. Margaret had turned eighty last October and used to make these homages herself. It was good business, good relations, and good publicity: a satisfied customer was a returning customer, and one who told others.

Danny had come around a corner with a glass of white wine in his hand and walked right into Kyle, spilling both their drinks. After an initial glare, their eyes softened, their smiles spread, and four months later they were living together in Danny's apartment at 25th Street and Lexington Avenue, kept company by their cats, Smelly and Leonard.

Kyle was the assistant to Imogene Landis, a down-on-her-luck television reporter who would never admit to being anywhere but at the top of her game, while Danny managed Margaret's, still a hot ticket after thirty years in business. Margaret Bowman lived in an apartment above the restaurant and had all but adopted Danny as her only child, having been widowed for fifteen years with no children of her own. Danny had been with her for ten of those years and, next to his mother, held no woman in more esteem. He had taken lately to fretting over her health – eighty struck him as a mile marker toward the end of the road. There was nothing he could do about the passing of time, and he shook off his worries as he searched for Kyle at the wedding reception. The guests had moved from the church to a trendy new hotel named Heaven that had opened in Hell's Kitchen. Danny wondered if the name was some kind of wordplay, given the neighborhood, and he worked his way through the crowd in the hotel's ballroom.

Kyle saw Danny looking for him and waved him over. He was standing at one of two bars the ballroom boasted, sipping on a vodka and cranberry, marveling how the crowd had managed to balloon since coming over from the church. He was thinking it might be wedding crashers, or hotel guests who felt entitled to a party when they saw one. Behind the bartender, mounted on the wall, was a flat-screen television with the sound muted. Kyle was using the straw in his drink to play with the ice when an item on the news caught his eye. A photograph of an artist he knew had been pinned to the corner while the reporter talked into his microphone.

"Excuse me," Kyle said to the bartender, a pleasant enough man who made his living as much on his looks as on his skills (or maybe not, Kyle thought, depending on what those skills were). His nametag identified him as Todd. He looked like most of the guests in a tuxedo, but he was clearly uncomfortable in it; this was a man who belonged in faded blue jeans and a vest with no shirt.

"Yes, Sir?" Todd said, sliding a drink across the bar to a guest and moving over toward Kyle.

"Could you turn the volume up on that? Just a little. I know the person they're talking about."

Todd shrugged, sure, and turned the volume up enough to be heard without disturbing the revelry.

"Hey," Danny said, walking up to Kyle at the bar. "There you are, I was looking all over for you."

"Shhh," Kyle said, putting his finger to his lips. "I want to hear this." He leaned across the bar as much as he could, trying to get every word from the television reporter.

" … Devin – no last name – lived just three buildings from where he was attacked," the reporter said. "The victim was stabbed multiple times. Police say robbery does not appear to be a motive and so far no witnesses have come forward."

Kyle recognized the reporter as having started on NYNow and moved on to a network. It happened with quite of few of the local reporters, cutting their teeth on the popular local station and then heading to one of the Big Three affiliates. The segment was live, and Carlos Espinoza, the reporter, had been doing these updates all morning.

"What's this about?" Danny asked.

"I know this guy who was killed. Devin. From the Katherine Pride Gallery, multimedium, transman."

"A multi-medium transman?" Danny said, surprised.

"Shhh!"

"Much of what evidence there might have been was washed away in the last night's heavy rains," Carlos said, as the camera panned from him to the empty sidewalk and up the street, showing apartment buildings, brownstones and yellow crime tape stretching across the sidewalk. "If you have any information at all on this brutal murder, please contact your local police precinct. All calls are kept strictly confidential."

Kyle turned to Danny, his brow furrowed as he thought about the news he'd just heard. "They're two separate things," he said. "Devin was a transgender man, and a multi-medium artist. That's how I knew him. Through the gallery."

"Oh, I'm sorry," Danny said.

"I didn't really know him," Kyle said. "Not in more than a very conversational way. He had a show at the gallery in January, part of the New Year New Visions exhibit Kate does every year."

"The one she wanted your photography in."

"Yes, well …" Kyle had been encouraged by Kate Pride to finally show his photos, but he'd thought it was too soon. He was also discovering he had an ego, and being part of the New Visions exhibit meant sharing the spotlight. So he had passed, and instead was preparing to have his own show a week from now. His first show. The one, depending on the public's reaction, that would determine if there would ever be a second.

"I should call Kate."

"We're at a wedding reception!" Danny said. "Celebrating the marriage of your oldest, dearest friend aside from me. This is a happy time, let's keep it light."

"He was stabbed to death!" Kyle said. "That's not exactly light. And there's something there … something I'm not recalling just now, but a connection."

"The only connection for us to be concerned with today is making sure David and Elliot have the time of their lives. Hopefully this wedding will be the last for both of them."

Kyle nodded, Danny was right. What happened to Devin was terrible, but he was dead; there was nothing Kyle could do about it at the moment. The police were on it. Someone would most certainly come forward with information, or an eyewitness account. Whatever connection was nagging at the back of Kyle's mind could wait. It was just about time for a toast to the happy couple.

CHAPTER 4

HOTEL EXETER, HELL'S KITCHEN

As Kyle and Danny toasted the blessed event of their friend's marriage, Kieran Stipling balanced on the edge of his bed in a sleazy hotel room and toasted himself from a half-pint of bourbon. He'd had to spend more of his dwindling cash to buy it, but what the hell, he thought, watching with an irrepressible smile as some hack reporter standing not ten feet from where Kieran had been last night told the city there were no suspects in the brutal murder in Brooklyn. Of course there weren't. Kieran had developed an ability to remain invisible when it suited him. He had been invisible in Buenos Aires, invisible on an uptown Manhattan subway platform, and completely invisible on that Brooklyn street where the reporter kept repeating himself every half hour. He took another swig from the bottle and wiped his chin with the back of his hand. Staying in a dump like this was no hardship; it was part of the plan, part of the way he remained unseen.

In the sanitized oasis of wealth New York City had become under successive mayors determined to fumigate it, to rid it of crime and, as many believed, a soul, there were still pockets of degeneration, islands of poverty and decay that had not been whitewashed. Among those throwbacks to a time few people missed was the Hotel Exeter, located in the aptly named Hell's Kitchen neighborhood. The Exeter was a fleabag hotel, a flophouse, where rooms could be rented for $45 a day – a sum that for many who found themselves there might as well be a million dollars.

Hell's Kitchen had become fashionable again in the 1990s, as the city found itself scrubbed clean and the hookers, drug addicts and street-level criminals pushed ever further uptown. For awhile the neighborhood called itself Clinton, but once the yuppies and the Gen-Xers felt safe on the surrounding streets they decided it was cooler to be Hell's Kitchen again. They enjoyed the thrill of living in a place with one of the meanest reputations in the history of New York City, but now without the mean. Mean can't afford the rents here, and the survival of the Hotel Exeter was a fluke of zoning and location. Sitting on a corner of 36th Street, the hotel overlooked the Lincoln Tunnel entrance and exit, which would not be exchanged any time soon for the smiling faces of Mickey Mouse and Snow White. So for the time being the hotel stood, as grimy as it had been forty years ago, a beacon to the likes of the man who congratulated himself from the edge of a bed and who had been staying there for the past three weeks. Soon he would have no money left, and that was okay with him; he only had a few more things to do, a couple of loose ends to secure. All he would need then was enough for a bus ticket far away, to some border town where he could practice his Spanish and disappear into the woodwork. For a man with the power of invisibility, it would be especially easy. His dreams, dark and bloody as they were, will have come true, and things like hotel rooms and paying for them would no longer matter.

Kieran smiled as he stared down at the cars coming off the highway, driving into the heart of the city, merging and mingling with traffic from the Lincoln Tunnel. He had long believed the people in New York were all in a mad rush to nowhere. He had lived here for five years, having arrived an innocent in many ways, believing in the power to reinvent his life. He was proof that dreams were still shattered here, and that no amount of prettifying and industrial cosmetic surgery would ever rid the Big Apple of its rotten core. That is where he had found himself, the dark heart of a city putrefied beneath the shine and glitter, and where he was now. Living in a hotel room barely large enough to turn around in, sharing it with hundreds of roaches that did not have to come up with $45 a day to stay there. The three dresser drawers were empty, except for his two changes of clothes, minus his favorite sweatshirt he'd had to throw away because of the blood. Sixteen times were simply too many to stab someone without making a mess. The room's television had never been converted to hi-def; just as well, since the cable was out and the best he could do were the local channels barely grasped by a rusted antenna. But it was enough to watch the news, enough to make him smile as he finished off his bourbon, wondering if he should spend ten dollars to buy more. He would be making a trip soon, a side journey of utmost importance and ultimate delight. He muted the TV and reached for his wallet. He deserved to celebrate a little more, and by the time he got back from the liquor store they would be running the news clip again. Murder in Brooklyn, no suspects, no witnesses. Reality television at its best.

CHAPTER 5

THE KATHERINE PRIDE GALLERY

Much like Hell's Kitchen, the Meatpacking District had a very Old City sound to it while having little Old City about it except a few stray cobblestone streets. The area was originally the home of Fort Gansevoort, also known as the "Great White Fort" for its many coats of whitewash. The name was Dutch, appropriate given the original settlers of the island, whose presence could still be felt in place names around the boroughs. Following the Civil War, the area became home to butchers and meat packers serving the thriving, crowded city, and these slaughterhouses gave it the name its current residents still used, even though the only meat to be found there now was on high-priced dinner plates at high-end restaurants.

Another feature of the new Meatpacking District was its shops and galleries. Nothing said Old World quite like a Stella McCartney dress shop next to an art gallery whose least expensive item was for sale at $75,000. In some ways it was an odd location choice for Katherine Pride, since she valued new artists, up-and-comers, artists whose work might go for the average week's salary of a local secretary. She showcased more established artists and photographers from time to time, but her real pleasure was in introducing someone new to the art world, and, more importantly, to the public. And if an artist went on to fame and fortune and happened to remember the break Katherine gave them, well, great, she could sell their work and make ends meet on the East Village condo she shared with her husband Stuart.

Katherine Pride had been Katherine O'Connor before her marriage twenty years ago to Stuart Pride. She'd planned to keep her own name if she married, but the chance at having such a unique and bold last name was too good to pass up. Even then, when she was working behind the ticket booth at the Metropolitan Museum of Art, she knew a branding opportunity when she saw one. She'd had no specific idea of what her place in the art world would be, but could see the name Katherine Pride emblazoned on a business even then, at twenty-three. All these years later she was still married to the doting Stuart Pride, a successful real estate broker, and the Katherine Pride Gallery was an established, well-respected gallery among her peers and in the neighborhood.

Katherine was what people often called statuesque, standing just over six feet in heels, thin and possessed of a strong posture. Her late mother had instilled in a young Kate (as most people called her) the sense that posture was destiny: anyone who wanted to go places in this world needed to see where they were going, and you don't do that by hanging your head or slouching. Stand up straight! Stand up tall! Head back! Kate and her brother Justin had heard these commands many times, and when their father died in a freak boating accident, the calls to be straight and tall only grew more frequent and more insistent. Pamela O'Connor became a widow and a single mother on the same day, when Kate was only twelve and Justin nine, and she brooked no nonsense in a world that afforded her none. That was in Louisville, where her mother managed to survive and raise two successful children, until she, too, lost her life. Breast cancer made Kate and Justin O'Connor orphans much too young.

Kate quickly made her way to New York City after college. She didn't know then what she wanted to do, but she knew exactly where she wanted to live. New York City was the epicenter of art, fashion, literature and finance. Somewhere in there was her future, and not long after she began working at the Met she knew which one it would be: art, for art's sake and for profit, for better and for worse in a fickle world that loved you one minute and pawned you the next. She was a gallery owner who kept her distance from the sharks and the scene, a wife who loved spending evenings with her goofy, lanky, adoring husband more than attending another cocktail party for another shining star. Still, she loved the gallery and what it could offer people like Kyle Callahan, the photographer she'd befriended after meeting his partner, Danny Durban. Kate and Stuart had enjoyed lunch at Margaret's Passion some years ago, their first time there, and who should show up at a gallery exhibit two days later but Danny Durban. She knew it was marketing, making sure a customer came back, but she had liked Danny straight off, and she took great pleasure in having been the catalyst for his relationship with Kyle. They had met at that exhibit and were still madly in love. Or at least in love enough to be sharing their lives together forever and ever, Amen.

Kate had been encouraging Kyle to show his photographs to the public. He was a bit shy, but with a definite gift for images. She would never have known this if Danny hadn't told her, and even once she had seen Kyle's pictures it had taken a few years of nudging to finally get him to accept that he should have his own show, which was now only four days away.

Kyle was waiting with two cups of coffee when she got to the gallery at 10:00 a.m. Monday morning. One thing about businesses in New York City: they may stay open until midnight, but finding much besides diners and drugstores open before mid-morning was a challenge. Even the Katherine Pride Gallery didn't open until 11:00, but Kate had wanted to go over the details and exhibit photos with Kyle before the final installation.

"You're alone today," Kate said, fishing a key ring from her oversized brown leather purse. Danny usually came with Kyle on these visits and would head from there to Margaret's Passion.

"Danny's on vet duty. Smelly has some kind of nasal infection," Kyle said, referring to one of their two cats. Smelly had been with Kyle when they met, and Danny had been spending his life alone with Leonard, Smelly's senior by three years. Smelly was a she, and Kyle had found her as a kitten outside his apartment in Brooklyn, digging through trash that had seeped onto her coat, giving her the name. He'd thought about changing it to something else, Gloria, or Smittens, but Smelly had stuck and he never gave it a second thought now.

"She's sneezing a lot. And he's getting her weight checked again."

"She's diabetic, yes?"

"Pre," Kyle replied. "But she's been pre-diabetic since she was two years old. She's just an ample girl, I think."

Kate slid open the iron gate that protected the front glass, unlocked the door and led them into the gallery. "I see you brought me coffee from Breadwinner's. Very thoughtful."

"I'm used to getting Imogene's on the way to work," Kyle said, following her into the reception area and setting the coffee cups down on the front desk.

"How is she, by the way?" Kate asked. "She moved up or something, you said, after those murders in New Jersey."

"Pennsylvania. Pride Lodge. Yes, they were quite the hit in Japan. She's on the general news beat now."

Kyle had been the personal assistant to Imogene Landis for the past five years. A diminutive woman whose height was overshadowed by her personality, she was once a successful TV reporter in New York, but had a habit of telling her bosses and anyone else what she thought of them, their competence, and at least once, their toupee. She subsequently found herself on the downslope of a career that could have kept rising, had she been more politically savvy. Now she worked as an English language reporter for Tokyo Pulse, a cable TV show that aired in Japan three hours before sunup and was produced by Japan TV3, who had their New York studio on 46th Street. Kyle met her there most days with two cups of coffee from their local spot, Cecil's. Kyle had tipped Imogene to the murders at Pride Lodge last Halloween. The story caused a cult sensation in post-midnight Japan and got her off the financial beat. She was back into the city she loved, covering everything from City Council meetings to bathtub decapitations. She couldn't be happier.

"You're good to her, Kyle, I hope she appreciates it. Danny, too."

"Oh, I'm sure they do. I didn't even have to coerce Danny into the vet visit this morning, and that's something he always wiggles out of. He hates doctors' offices, even when they're for the cats."

The Katherine Pride Gallery looked like most galleries. It's all about wall space and lighting. A dividing wall here, some pedestals there, and you have your basic art gallery.

Kate had gone into business on her own eight years ago. Before that she was an assistant to the late, great Hildegarde "Hildy" Bingham, the woman who had single-handedly discovered most of the top geniuses of the New York art world in the 1970s. She was already old and well past legend status when she hired Kate as her personal assistant. Kate had studied at the feet of an art world icon, spending many evenings on the floor in Hildy's Upper West Side penthouse, taking notes for the autobiography that was still unpublished nearly a decade after her death.

"When's Corky come in?" Kyle asked, referring to the young man who worked the front desk at the gallery. Corky was somewhere in his mid-twenties and loved – absolutely loooooooved – working at an art gallery, for Katherine Pride, in the Meatpacking District, a neighborhood he only knew in its sanitized state. Corky very much wanted to get married, but he didn't have a boyfriend and had reminded Kyle more than once that he was on the market, should Kyle or Danny know anyone with a suitable income.

"I gave him the day off," she said, setting her purse on the front desk chair. "He had a wisdom tooth removed Friday and he's still mending. Funny thing to call it, the boy doesn't have a lick of sense in his head."

"Wisdom comes with age. Sometimes not even then."

"So," Kate announced, waving her left hand toward the walls as she flipped the track lighting switch with her right.

Kyle turned and marveled at his own photographs on the walls. He'd seen them when they entered, of course, but having them lit now, a penlight aimed at each individual photograph, sent an unexpected charge through him. He saw himself as a shutterbug, just a guy with a camera who liked taking pictures. A couple years ago he took the next step and started putting them on a Tumblr photoblog, AsKyleSeesIt, with no intention of ever presenting them in any professional sense, and none of charging money for what he loved to do.

Frowning suddenly, Kyle said, "What if they hate them?"

"Who's 'they', Kyle? You mean the critics?"

"Never having displayed my pictures before means never having read a review of them. So yes, the critics."

"You know as well as anyone we do these things for love. Your photographs, Stuart being a real estate agent in a city stuffed with them, me running an art gallery. It's all because we love doing it, and sometimes we make some money. What other people think of what we do really doesn't matter." She sipped her coffee. "And if the guy from the New York Times calls you an amateur, well … you are!"

Kyle looked at her, horrified, just as she winked to let him know she was joking.

"Now let's take a slow tour through the rooms and see what all the fuss is about with this Kyle-Somebody."

They started with the first photograph, left wall as people would enter the gallery. It was among his favorites, but also an emotional reminder. "Lonely Blue Pool" was the picture he had taken of the empty swimming pool at Pride Lodge, the pool where his friend Teddy Pembroke had been found dead just last Halloween, his neck broken from a shove into the cold, waterless pool.

"I still can't believe it's not a painting," Kate said, staring at the photograph. It was what everyone said when whey saw it: an expanse of blue, with just a white ladder running down it and a gathering of brown leaves at the bottom, near the drain. So simple, and so beautiful.

Kate and Kyle were watched from across the street as they made their way further into the gallery along the wall. Kieran thought he would feel excited to be this close to his prey, this close to winning a game only he knew he was playing. Devin knew, of course, but Devin was dead. He'd recognized

Kieran just as the knife was coming out, and the puzzled look on his face was immediately replaced by fear and terror.

What whispers?

The ones I heard when you thought I wasn't listening.

What whispers?

The ones that sealed your fate.

"You want a refill on that?"

He jumped, startled by the young barista at Breadwinner's who had stopped by his table while he stared across the street, lost in his thoughts. They didn't have waiters at coffee shops like this, but she was wiping down the tables and happened to notice his empty cup. He turned and saw how pretty she was, her long curly hair held back with a purple ribbon, her brown eyes liquid and trusting. If he'd been into women he would put her at the top of his list, but he wasn't, and the only list he was keeping was getting shorter and shorter as he killed the people on it.

"No, thank you" he said. "But I appreciate your asking. It's a rare courtesy these days. Nobody gives a shit anymore. You give a shit, it's very touching."

She wasn't sure how to take this man and there was something disturbing about him, not least the way he was speaking to a stranger who had only thought to ask him if he wanted more coffee. She smiled nervously and headed back behind the safety of the cash register.

He turned back to the window and saw that Kate Pride and the Callahan guy were gone, having turned at a dividing walling into the next room. He would get to her soon and hoped it wasn't a situation where Callahan was with her when the time came. He didn't want to kill an innocent man – as far as anyone can really be innocent in this life – but he would if he had to.

Kyle was happy with the layout. He and Kate had chosen the photographs carefully over the last two weeks. He'd been sure to include one of Danny's favorites and one of his mother's favorites. The other thirteen, for a total of fifteen of his best pictures, were lined along the walls in a way that reflected not so much a progression of any style, but a small set of subjects. Two from his shoe series, in which he took shots of people's shoes as he went about his daily life in New York City. Three from his "blur period" as he called it, when he was fascinated by blurred photographs, a few of his seasonal photos, and the best of his interiors – rooms, hotel lobbies, office buildings, and two cathedrals. It was a fair and solid representation of Kyle Callahan, Amateur Photographer, and as much as Kate wanted to believe she'd found another rising star, Kyle wasn't invested in the outcome. He just loved taking pictures.

"I have to head to the studio," he said, letting out a deep sigh.

"I thought you loved your job," said Kate, misreading the sound.

"Oh, the sigh, no, that was for the show. The people. The nakedness of it all. My mother's coming from Chicago, Danny's parents from Queens, our friend Detective Linda from New Hope, it's too much."

"You'll be fine. And trust me, you'll want more. The limelight can be intoxicating. Just don't become addicted."

Kyle hugged his friend and mentor, for Kate Pride had become both, with her encouragement and her insistence that Kyle take himself seriously as an artist. He was thinking how lucky he was to have Danny, his mother, Kate, so many supportive people in his life, when he noticed a man across the street in front of Breadwinner's, staring at them. "Who's that?"

But as quickly as Kate released the hug and turned to the window, the man was gone. "Who's who?" she said.

"Nobody, really. Just someone I thought I recognized." He tried to think of where he would have seen the man, but nothing clicked and he let it go. "Speaking of recognizing someone, it's terrible about Devin, I saw it on the news."

Kate's smile fell. "Yes," she said. "Horrible. No one would want to hurt Devin intentionally, he was a sweetheart. All that rough and tumble, it was just attitude. The guy was a creampuff. It had to be the wrong place at the wrong time."

"I'm not so sure," Kyle said.

"Why's that?"

"Something keeps nagging at me, another death, but I can't remember it. We'll talk about it later, maybe you can help me jog it loose. I have to be at the office ten minutes ago. Imogene's one virtue is punctuality."

They hugged a last time, and Kyle wondered, as he breathed in Kate's subtle perfume, if anyone was ever truly in the wrong place at the wrong time.

CHAPTER 6

MARGARET'S PASSION

Margaret's Passion had been at 21st Street and 3rd Avenue in the Gramercy Park neighborhood for thirty years. The park itself was only a block away, occupying a private, gated rectangle that was one of the most historic and famous in a city filled with landmarks. The area was once a swamp, and a developer named Samuel Ruggles proposed the idea to drain it and turn it into a park. "Gramercy Square," as it was first called, is now held in common as one of the city's two privately owned parks, which the general public must enjoy by gazing at it through wrought iron bars.

Margaret's restaurant had been a number of businesses over the hundred years the building had stood. Some of its previous incarnations included a pub, a bookstore, and a haberdashery. Margaret and her husband, Gerard, first leased the space, while living in one of the twelve apartments on the three floors above it – theirs being directly over the main dining area and accessible by a staircase they had built in the rear of the kitchen. After ten years of success, the Bowmans bought the building, which became a curse as well as a blessing. Neither of them had any experience as landlords and they finally hired an agent to manage that unwanted part of the business, which left only the restaurant for Margaret to deal with after Gerard died.

The death of Gerard Bowman was a greater blow to Margaret than she had anticipated. The man she had spent nearly fifty years of her life with, first meeting him when they were both still teenagers, had been a lifelong smoker. She was able to get him to stop smoking in their apartment, which led in a way to his untimely death. It was while smoking on the side of the building that he was run over by an impatient livery driver. It had been raining, and he had walked to the curb to stamp out his cigarette butt. Just as he was doing that, a black sedan came flying through the light, determined not to have to wait for the next one. The driver lost control somehow and plowed into Gerard. He died instantly from a head trauma, the one mercy the Bowmans were given from that terrible day.

Margaret wasn't the same after her husband's death. Already short and thin, she all but stopped eating, and reached a critical point when her doctor threatened to have her hospitalized. Her hair, naturally graying, became all white, and while she kept it long and tied back with ribbons most of the time, it began to fall out. She was determined to keep Margaret's Passion open and thriving, but it was something she now forced herself to do. A year after Gerard's death, Margaret was at a crucial juncture. She was just about to walk way from it all, including New York City, when a man come into her restaurant for lunch. His name was Danny Durban, and Margaret happened to be down in the restaurant that day. He was very cheerful, and the two of them struck up a conversation. He invited her to join him, and she did – something she had refrained from as a business policy all these years. It was one thing to sit for a moment with a dining couple or a family (never alone with a man), but eating with them in your own establishment was simply not done.

She didn't tell Danny Durban much that day. It was not her style to pour her heart out to anyone but the man who had died outside their restaurant. But he was kind, and inviting, and amusing, and experienced in the very same business. Danny was then working as the day manager at a restaurant on the Upper East Side that was struggling to survive and likely would not. As it turned out, Margaret was looking for a day manager herself: Pierre, the one she'd had for twenty-five years, had retired six months earlier and the new man, Salvatore, was not working out. She had decided to let him go but needed someone to bring in as his replacement. Meeting Danny Durban was a long-needed moment of serendipity.

Two weeks later Danny was working for Margaret, and a relationship that would shape both of their lives was born.

It was less than a ten minute walk from Danny and Kyle's apartment to Margaret's and the weather couldn't be better. While Danny enjoyed California and points west, he couldn't imagine living without the distinct change of seasons that people east of the Mississippi enjoyed. The East Coast was particularly nice. It didn't have the kinds of harsh winters you found in Chicago or Minneapolis, yet there was never any question which season you were in; and of the four, only summer made Danny wish he were somewhere else. The heat and smell of summers in Manhattan could be nasty.

Margaret's Passion had the feel of a restaurant that had been running successfully for three decades. That comfortable, settled feeling was part of its attraction. Like a number of other well-known eateries in Manhattan, it valued its place in the neighborhood, as if it were an old friend who, along with the residents, had weathered good times and bad and managed to survive. There was a large bay window looking out onto 21st Street, through which passersby could see people dining, conversing, and eating some of the best food in the city. The entry was narrow, reminiscent of its pub days, and just inside was the lectern where the maître d' greeted guests. It was dark wood, matching the rest of the wood in the restaurant's interior, and – so Margaret claimed – had belonged to the church in Poughkeepsie where her parents' married hastily just before her father went off to combat in World War I.

Chloe was on duty today when Danny got there late after taking Smelly home from the vet. She was the senior day waitress and a real pro, making each diner feel as if they were the center of her attention, and for it pocketing tips that kept her living in style.

Danny waved good morning to Trebor, the bartender, who was behind the long oak bar serving a few early customers. Trebor was the youngest of the people working in the restaurant, aside from some of the kitchen staff, and had been with Margaret's for four years now. Danny had poached him from one of Linus Hern's restaurants. Linus was Danny's nemesis, and the restaurateurs' version of a vulture capitalist: he got restaurants off the ground, then sold them for a profit and quickly vanished, leaving nearly all of the buyers bankrupt a year later with "Closed for Renovations" signs in their windows, which meant they were never coming back. Danny knew the future did not look good for Trebor and offered him a job, telling him as discreetly as possible that the restaurant he was working in, having been sold by Hern, was in all probability doomed. It was only after Trebor started at Margaret's Passion that Danny discovered it was Robert spelled backward. Clever boy.

Chloe made a cup of coffee for Danny, a routine she had that he had not discouraged, and set it on the table closest to the kitchen. That was where the two of them would usually have coffee and go over details for the day. The menu didn't change, but there was a checklist Danny adhered to faithfully. It was also their time for some casual conversation before the lunch crowd showed up.

Chloe took a seat, stirring cream into her coffee. "He was back this morning," she said. "Her new lawyer. And he wasn't alone."

Margaret's longtime lawyer, a man named Evan Evans who had been with her since she and Gerard opened the restaurant, had passed away nine months ago at the age of eighty-six. The old gentleman, whom Danny had always found to be as mischievous as he was gracious, had been a weekly figure there for many years. He would come in for lunch every Thursday, eat alone, then head upstairs to visit with Margaret. He was as much a companion for a woman whose companions had nearly all died as he was an attorney. At that age the wise tend to make preparations, and he had suggested Margaret hire a young lawyer named Claude Petrie – the man who, Chloe had just explained, had come in again to see Margaret, this time with two other men.

Claude bothered Danny, though he couldn't say why. He was not much taller than Danny, but considerably heavier. He could always be found in a suit and tie, with a briefcase in his hand, although Danny had the feeling it was for effect and probably empty. Claude seemed to need people to think he was very busy, and of late that might be true: he had been to see Margaret several times the last month, never for very long. Unlike the man who had recommended him, Claude did not dally, did not sit for a leisurely lunch on the house, and spoke little to anyone, including Danny.

"Something's up," Danny said to Chloe. She nodded, having concluded the same thing.

"Estate stuff?" she said. Margaret was now an octogenarian and likely sensing her own mortality these days.

"I'll find a way to ask her," Danny said, a dark mood starting to descend. He couldn't imagine life without Margaret, and the thought of it reminded him his own parents were getting old. Once they were gone, he and Kyle were next in line. That's the way it went in the human carnival.

Fortunately customers began to arrive, pushing thoughts of funerals and grieving periods out of his mind as he rose to greet them with a smile. Ever pleasant, ever present. Just another lunch Margaret's Passion.

CHAPTER 7

HOTEL EXETER, HELL'S KITCHEN

The reporters had moved onto another story by Monday afternoon. New York City had been cleaned up over the last twenty years, but it was still the nation's largest city, with plenty of crime stories to shock its jaded citizens. Kieran didn't care; he had watched the same reports of the murder he had committed enough times to be bored by them. Brutally stabbed, sixteen times, no leads, call this hotline, blah blah blah. He was just waiting for them to say a reward had been posted, contingent on his capture and conviction, and they could check off all their little murder story boxes and move on.

Kieran wasn't interested in watching television, anyway. He was interested in the man in Philadelphia who had answered his ManCatch ad. He had used one of the computers at the internet café on 9th Avenue, which was really just another overpriced, pretentious coffee shop with mouse turds in the muffins and a couple bolted-down laptops customers could use for .50 cents a minute if they didn't bring their own.

ManCatch.com was a symptom of a society gone digitally wrong, where no one really had to meet anyone unless there was an exchange to their mutual benefit, usually of bodily fluids, and where everyone could pretend to be someone else. That's what he'd done, placing an ad on the Philly page of the website, posing as exactly the kind of young man Richard Morninglight would notice immediately: barely legal, with an aw-shucks tone in his message they both knew was a put-on. Roles, games, players. For thirty or so words he had played the part of a young college student trying to pay the bills, for which he would gladly be an escort, no harm in that, and if anything untoward happened, well, he was a willing student of experience. He knew this is what Morninglight enjoyed, and sure enough, not long after the artist arrived in Philadelphia for a show that would take his career several steps up the ladder, he responded to Kieran in New York, not knowing where he was. Among the Internet's dubious advantages was that you could be anyone, and anywhere. *Hi, Kevin*, Morninglight wrote. *I'm at the Hamilton Inn the next few nights for a convention* (of course he wouldn't tell the truth) *and would love to help out with the cost of those college books! Email me back and let's see what we can do.*

What they could do, it turned out, was arrange for Kieran, posing as Kevin the college student, to arrive at Richard Morninglight's hotel that night. As soon as Morninglight knew he was downstairs, he would leave his door unlocked, slip naked into his bed as if he were sleeping, and wait with every cell of his body tingling in anticipation.

He probably won't even open his eyes, Kieran thought as he gathered his Latex gloves, the guitar strings he'd bought that morning, and a change of clothes in case things got messy. Morninglight will think the man climbing into bed on top of him is there at his pleasure, just another pretend college student making ends meet. But no, Richard, he thought. The pleasure will all be mine.

He zipped up the gym bag, grabbed his brand new hoodie from the bed, the one with "I Love NY" stenciled on it that he picked up next to the liquor store, took one last look around a room he would soon be checking out of forever, and headed to the bus terminal for the ride to Philly.

CHAPTER 8

APARTMENT 5G

"**S**top staring at me," Danny said. "You should know after all these years the sad-eyes routine won't work with me. And judging from the size of you, neither does this diet cat food."

He was standing at the kitchen sink having just given Smelly, their rotund six-year-old tiger, her evening ration of dietetic cat food that was costing them $2 a can from the vet. Smelly no longer smelled badly but she was eighteen pounds heavier and nothing they had tried seemed to slim her down. Danny often described her as a bowling ball with legs, a barb she ignored. She sat staring up at him, her pleading eyes calculated to get at least a small cup of the dry food her feline housemate Leonard enjoyed, fed separately behind a closed door in the bathroom. Leonard indulged his status as the alpha cat and could often be seen throwing a smug glance back at Smelly as he was put in the bathroom with a tasty dish of calorie-rich dry food for only him to savor.

"I really don't have time for this," Danny said, as Smelly did her usual approach-and-retreat to her food bowl before hunger finally made the decision for her. She caved, walked over to the food bowl and began eating. She would only tolerate this treatment for so long before she would find a way out of this place, this prison of veterinary design, and live freely once again among the trash bags. They may think it an idle threat, as she had many times dashed into the hallway when the front door opened, only to panic at the great unknown and come slinking back in. But she meant it, damnit, and if they insisted on feeding her this awful, tasteless mud, she would make it to the stairwell next time, through the door, down the stairs and out, and who would be sorry then?

"What are you doing in there?" Danny shouted. Kyle had been in their second bedroom, one they used as an office except for the rare occasions when company came. One of those occasions was upon them; Kyle's mother, Sally Callahan, was arriving Friday from Chicago to be at the opening of his photo exhibit and they still needed to get the room in order. Absent a guest, it tended to get sloppy, dusty, and generally used.

"A photograph, what else would I be looking for in here?"

"A book maybe," Danny said, wiping his hands on a dishtowel and heading into the room. "Papers of some kind."

They had turned the second bedroom into an office shortly after Kyle moved in. He had been the one to give up most of his furniture and belongings, since there was simply not enough room for two full apartments in one, but he had insisted on a working space of his own. He needed a room with a door he could close while he spent hours working on his photographs, cataloging his photographs, archiving his photographs. He was rarely without a camera around his neck or in his backpack, and had long been in the habit of shooting hundreds of pictures to get a few good ones. Images were like that: so many flashed by in the course a day that you had to grab as many as you could and hope for a diamond or two. Even the same image might need to be shot ten times, from ten different angles, to find its essence.

His share of the room consisted of a file cabinet and his father's large maple desk. It was the only thing of his father's he requested; he wanted it for its history, the stains in the wood, the burns from when his father smoked, and not at all for the fact his father died with his face pressed against the desktop. An aneurism had felled Bert Callahan in a matter of seconds and Sally had come home to find him slumped over his papers, cold and departed. She was glad Kyle had wanted anything at all by which to remember his father, given the chill of their relationship from the time Kyle was a boy, and she was happy to be rid of another reminder of her loss.

The back wall that divided their respective office spaces, Kyle's to the left, Danny's to the right, with a window between them, was taken up with bookshelves. Both men were bibliophiles, Kyle more so, and it was probably his books more than anything that gave him a sense of continuity. Some of the books he'd had as a child, and he could let his eyes wander slowly up and down the shelves remembering periods of his life by reading the book spines.

Kyle was at his computer scanning photographs. He would pick one out of a dozen, enlarge it and peer at the people in it. He had learned early that the eye doesn't always know what it is seeing. In this case he was looking at people who had come to the opening night of the New Year New Visions show. He could name some of them: Devin, Richard Morninglight, Kate and Stuart Pride, others among the crowd he knew from the gallery. He was hoping to recognize the man from across the street that morning, without being sure why he thought this is where he'd seen him.

"What are you looking for?" Danny asked, resting his hand on Kyle's shoulder.

"Not 'what,' but 'whom,'" Kyle replied. "A man I saw outside Breadwinner's this morning, staring at the gallery. He looked so familiar, but it was one of those things, you see somebody and you swear you know them …"

"Happens to me all the time. Hundreds of people come into the restaurant in a week, I remember a fraction of their names."

"Not his name, so much, just where I saw him. The New Visions show, it's stuck in my mind for some reason but I don't see him in any of the photos."

"The invisible man," Danny said, as he moved away from Kyle, looking around the room. "We should get someone in to clean." He slid his finger along a bookshelf and examined the dust that came off it.

"I can clean."

"Before Friday? Your mother's coming."

Kyle sighed. Yes, his mother was coming. She stayed in this room on the sofa bed and it needed to be dusted at least. The reminder of his mother's impending arrival got him thinking of it again.

"I'm worried," Kyle said, swiveling around in his chair.

"It's not cancer," Danny said. He knew where this was going. Sally had told her son she had something to talk about. Kyle, being prone to imagine the worst, assumed she was going to tell him she was seriously ill. He was already imagining a leave of absence from Tokyo Pulse, flying to Chicago to spend a month with his ailing mother. Danny was looking forward to Sally coming out with whatever it was and putting and end to the morbid speculation.

"I never said it was cancer," Kyle replied. "But something. She doesn't keep secrets from me. Even less so since my father died."

Kyle spoke to his mother at least twice a week and always on Saturday. He had worried about her after Bert died just shy of their forty-seventh wedding anniversary. To his surprise, she had adapted well and quickly, but she was still a seventy-five year old woman living alone in Chicago and he considered it his duty as her only child to fret over her.

"She's probably moving to Florida, or San Miguel. Lots of ex-pats down there in Mexico, you can live very well, very cheaply."

"How do you know these things?"

"I listen to my customers, talking is what they're there for. Talk, food, and sometimes a chat with Margaret. Speaking of which, I think your mother is not the only one with a secret."

"Really?"

"Yes," Danny said. "Something's going on with Margaret. She's had that new lawyer of hers —"

"The rodent."

Danny smiled. He had referred to Claude Petrie as a rodent when he first told Kyle about him. "That's the one. He's been to see her several times, and today Chloe told me he was in with two other men."

"Smells like investment."

"Possibly. But in what? Chloe thinks it's her estate, that she's getting things in order. Why the two men, though? Claude could easily do a will, which I'm sure she had done a long time ago with old man Evans"

"You have to just wait and ask her."

"Exactly," Danny said. "Same with your mother. You have to wait and ask her what this big secret is. Life is change, Kyle, that's the nature of it. It's not by design."

Kyle froze suddenly, struck by Danny's words. "Exactly!" he shouted.

"Is there an echo in here?"

"No, no," Kyle said, excited. He got up and crossed to a bookshelf. "I remember now the other death, the one I couldn't think of when we were watching the news."

He skimmed along the bottom shelf and found what he was looking for. It was the catalog for that year's New Year New Visions show at the gallery. Devin was one of the artists, but it wasn't Devin he was looking for. He opened the front cover and read the credits.

"There," he said, holding the catalog up so Danny could see as he pointed to a name: Shiree Leone.

"Who's that?"

"She was the graphic designer for the catalog. Designer. *Design*, you just said it. I couldn't remember her name, or what the connection was. It was just a fly buzzing around in my head after we saw the news on Devin."

"What about her?" Danny asked.

"She's dead!"

Great, Danny thought. Here we go again. The murders at Pride Lodge were a fading memory, but a memory still new enough, and he feared Kyle would go off on another chase at precisely the worst time, with his mother coming and his show opening on Friday.

"Murdered, I suppose," Danny said.

"No. Yes. They don't know. That's what I remember. She fell in front of a subway train."

"Coincidences happen, Kyle, no matter what people say."

"But nobody saw it! There was no one else on the platform, I remember that. They were asking for any witnesses, just like Devin's murder the other night. They assumed she fell or had a seizure or something."

"But you know better."

"She could have been pushed."

"There was no one there, you said so yourself."

"No one *saw*," Kyle said. "That's not the same thing. Maybe there was someone there. An invisible man."

"I was joking. There is no such thing as an invisible man."

"Devin might beg to differ with you. And Shiree."

"Please don't say you have to find out."

"What choice do I have? This could be connected to the Katherine Pride Gallery. There could be more already dead … and more to come. I can't just wait and see what happens, can I?"

Danny did not respond. He knew anything he said to Kyle to dissuade him would fall on deaf ears. This is what Kyle did, along with photography and being a personal assistant: he solved murders. Stopping him would be tantamount to taking a thought from his head and putting it outside, go away, thought, you're not wanted here. They were Kyle's thoughts, in Kyle's mind, and nothing Danny could do or say would chase them away. Even if Kyle said he would drop the subject, Danny knew he wouldn't.

"When does Detective Linda get here?" Danny asked, referring to Linda Sikorsky, the homicide detective from New Hope, Pennsylvania, they had befriended after the Pride Lodge murders. She had since come fully out as gay and was making a trip to the city for Kyle's show.

"Tomorrow. We're having lunch."

"Good. Tell her whatever theories you have flapping around in your brain. If you're going to go running after killers, at least have back up."

"I'm not going to get hurt," Kyle said. He stepped to Danny and put his arms around him. "Don't worry about me."

"And you don't worry about your mother, and I won't worry about Margaret, and nobody will ever worry about anyone again."

Kyle took Danny by the hand. "Come with me," he said, leading them out of the office and toward the bedroom.

"Are you asking me or telling me?"

"Just start with the top button and we'll see."

Danny smiled as they walked down the hallway. It had been two weeks since they last had sex. That seemed pretty much the norm in relationships that lasted more than a few years, and they were men in their fifties, whatever part that played. It was good to know they could still cut loose when the opportunity and the desire came upon them. For the next hour he would not be concerned with anything else, including a killer whose trail Kyle had picked up in an art gallery catalog. He knew Kyle would go where it led, and the best he could do was hope he made it back safely.

CHAPTER 9

A CORNER TABLE AT OSAKA

Linus Hern didn't care for sushi, but the restaurateur knew his two investors were very fond of it, and it was their money he would be using in his most recent and most anticipated venture: to buy Margaret's Passion, with neither Margaret nor her flying monkey, Danny Durban, knowing it. As far as Hern was aware, Danny didn't even know the old lady was selling, and if all went well he wouldn't find out until it was too late. By then Linus could step out from behind the curtain and tell Durban his services were no longer needed. It would be a costly vindication, but one he'd imagined for years, ever since the two men first met and knew it was disdain at first sight.

Linus had made a career of starting restaurants, and in some cases taking them over, getting them ready for their big debut, which would be covered by absolutely anyone worth being called press, launching them into the nightlife stratosphere, and getting out with his investment doubled. What happened to the restaurants after that was not his concern, and most had not lasted more than a year, by which time Linus Hern was long gone, his bank account that much fatter, convincing the next investors to ride his coattails to the New York Times Food Section. He was a venture capitalist, a man of industry. He knew how to open with a bang and close without leaving a trace. A master, if he said so himself.

He was tall, even seated at a corner table. He was wearing a blood-red velvet sport coat, something as uncommon as it was distinctive, with spotless white leather jeans. His high forehead masked a receding hairline and at the same time favored his face, highlighting sharp blue eyes that just last year had undergone Lasik surgery. At fifty-six, Linus refused to wear glasses; he didn't care how fashionable they were, or which top names were designing them. Linus Hern was determined to appear a superman, a specimen of the highest order. Glasses would be a blemish in an otherwise flawless presentation.

He motioned to the waiter for another Scotch. One was normally his limit, but his venture partners were late and he needed something to sip. Late was a mortal sin to Linus Hern, but considering the amount of money they were putting into this, he would make an exception.

Osaka was the latest in Japanese fusion, whatever the hell that was. Anytime someone added a new ingredient it became "fusion." Some Thai farmer adds carrots to the pot for the first time and it's "Thai fusion." Hern disdained such labels, knowing them as a marketing ploy and only really meaningful to lower-tier food critics and the floods of trendy young diners lining up to get a table at the latest "fusion" restaurant.

He got a table, of course, probably one that had been reserved for lesser people who would be told upon arrival that there had been a mix up, so sorry, that table is taken. "That table" being the best one in the place, nineteen stories up in Midtown, southwest corner overlooking the nighttime Manhattan skyline. The City was Linus Hern's only true love; that and making money. Men were treats, tasty bonbons he enjoyed and discarded as quickly as a caramel nugget might melt in his mouth. What was the last one's name? The one he'd taken for that regrettable weekend at Pride Lodge. Carlos, was it? What a mess that whole business turned out to be. The Lodge was still standing but Linus had no idea who ran it now, and no plans to go back. Murder had a way of making a place less attractive.

He looked over and saw his partners arrive, a full fifteen minutes past due. Had they not already given him a hefty retainer with much more on the way he would have left them greeting an empty table. But he was shrewd, a winner, and rather than even glance at his watch to tell them they were late, he smiled, stood, and offered a warm hand.

"Victor," he said to the taller of the two, a man near his own height whose air of stupidity was underscored by a scar running from his left eye to his chin. The result of a car crash in his twenties, but a very effective visual when someone needed to be intimidated. (Margaret Bowman had not been among them, and took pity on the man whose face had been disfigured at such a young age.)

"Linus," Victor said, shaking his hand and taking a seat in the booth to Linus's right.

The second man was downright jolly, more than balancing any discomfort people might feel in Victor's presence. Jay Tierney was a financier, a venture capitalist like Hern, only his specialty was in demolition: tearing down the old, the decrepit, and putting up the new. Tierney was robust, affable, his hair cropped short and his face round and pink. He smiled easily and often, and had mastered the art of including that smile in his eyes, something most predators simply could not do. It was impossible to tell with Jay Tierney if his smile was fake or not, only that it was meant just for you, and you might find yourself being swallowed by it if you weren't careful.

Jay Tierney and Victor Gossett had been business partners for twenty years, with dealings that stretched from Manhattan's Lower East Side to San Francisco's waterfront. They could buy a building like Margaret Bowman's with the change rattling around in their pockets. The plan being presented to the old woman was to save her restaurant and secure her final years by buying the building and everything in it. She would have enough money to live comfortably anywhere she chose, and the restaurant would pass to Danny when she died. What only the three men at Osaka knew was that it was all a lie: Margaret's Passion would be permanently closed for renovations, and the building that had stood there for over a century would be replaced by something shiny, new, and very costly to inhabit.

It helped that her old lawyer had passed on. Evan Evans had been smart and worldly, and this particular sleight of hand would never have gotten past him. But the young one, Claude Petrie, that had been a stroke of luck. He still lived in the old man's shadow and pressured himself to make his own mark, establish his own credentials. Finding new owners for Margaret's building had been the best timing of his life. He had been on the verge of disappearing and had started looking into exactly how some-one does that, when Hern showed up in his office with a proposition.

Linus had come up with the plan when he first heard rumors of the old woman's troubles. There may be 20,000 restaurants in New York City, but the world of the best is a small one. When something happened at The Greenery, or Casa Pueblo, it was known by all the others in hours. When Margaret Bowman had her young new lawyer put out feelers for a buyer, Linus Hern was among the very first to hear it. He had quickly contacted his fellow predators Victor and Jay, and in amazingly short order the three of them had formulated a plan. A plan so slick, with a truth behind it so carefully guarded, that Margaret Bowman and her sidekick Danny Durban, a man Linus could not wait to fire, wouldn't know what hit them until it was too late.

Linus again waved his hand, summoning their table server.

"I'm still waiting for my Scotch," he said to the young Asian looking woman, wondering if she was some kind of fusion, too. "Not a good sign."

"In so sorry, Mr. Hern," she said, even bowing a bit to emphasize her embarrassment. "Right away. And the gentlemen? What may I bring you?"

That was better, Linus thought, as the other two placed their drink or-ders. He wasn't listening. He was drifting away for a moment, daydreaming of the sweetness he would feel when he'd accomplished his greatest coup. Margaret's Passion would be no more.

CHAPTER 10

The Hamilton Inn, Philadelphia

The Hamilton Inn was located in the heart of Philadelphia's gay neighborhood, an area of Philly's Center City district that ran from Market Street on the north to Spruce on the south, and from 11th Street on its west edge to Juniper on the east. It was among the nation's most well known and well liked concentrations of LGBT urban life that were once called gay ghettos. But unlike many such enclaves, Philly's had not fallen on hard times; it had seen itself prosper, becoming and remaining one of the city's most vital attractions.

Two of those attractions were the Gilliam Museum of Modern Perspective, and the Hamilton Inn, a storied old hotel that had remained gay-owned and mostly gay-populated for forty years. The late Marcus Gilliam founded his museum, which was really more of a midway point between a high-end gallery and a true fine art institution, in the 1980s during the height of the AIDS crisis. His longtime lover died from complications of the disease and left Gilliam with two dozen specimens of art so modern it wasn't worth anything at the time. Gilliam had two objectives in launching his museum: to effectively erect a monument to Jonathan, his lover and partner, and to demonstrate his remarkable eye for an investment. Considering how much the art was now worth, his prescience could not be disputed. He had specialized in finding new artists, much like his peer Kate Pride in Manhattan, whom he had known for several years before his own death from prostate cancer in 2009. Since then a foundation had run the Gilliam, but it had not compromised his vision. The museum still featured a mix of established artists and those well on their way. It was just such a show that brought Richard Morninglight to Philadelphia that weekend; and where else would a gay painter on the verge of art world stardom stay in Philadelphia but the Hamilton?

The Hamilton Inn had been around since the 1920s. Its premiere suite, while no longer called Presidential, had seen its share of American Presidents resting their heads on its pillows. Just five stories high, the Inn had fallen on hard times in the 1970s and was very close to being demolished, when an entrepreneur and friend of the very same Marcus Gilliam who opened his hybrid gallery/museum decided to recreate the Hamilton as a specialty gay hotel. Back then "gay hotel" was something one could say, before the arrival of the acronym LGBT and before there were many people now called allies. The hotel no longer advertised itself as gay, and it made every marketing effort to welcome all visitors to the fine city of Philadelphia and this amazing neighborhood. But it was still gay-owned and operated, and rare was a visit from a guest who didn't know it.

Richard Morninglight had checked into room 306 Friday night, just about the time a fellow artist named Devin was having his life stolen at the end of a knife blade. Richard's last name was not Morninglight, but once he had decided on a career as an artist, long before he was anywhere near achieving it, he concluded that his last name Smith simply would not do. Even adding a middle initial, which remained popular among artists and writers for reasons he didn't understand, would not make the name Richard Smith any more arresting. Ah, but he painted in the morning light; he studied effects of the morning light on canvas and the objects he painted; he had a vision one sunrise in the morning light, and that was that: Richard Morninglight was born.

Richard had few real friends. He'd been ambitious all his life, even as a child, and he had known instinctively that ambition was an all-consuming master. Given the choice between achieving his aims and having friends who wanted this or that part of him, let alone a lover who wanted it all, he had chosen achievement. He'd found soon enough that there seemed to be a ratio of friends to success (one increases with the other), and as for lovers, they came cheaply enough. Ads in local papers, profiles online. Why get into the mess of a relationship when all he really wanted was his needs attended to?

He wasn't an unattractive man, and at thirty-two he was still young. He'd gained too much weight since the checks began coming in for his paintings, but not one young man had complained about the extra twenty pounds. He was middling height, with a pronounced nose, what might be called Roman, and brown eyes that were just the slightest bit crossed, something he'd had to deal with as a child wearing corrective glasses. He wore his thinning black hair long and in a ponytail – it just seemed to go with his name – and he'd gotten his first tattoo to commemorate the show at the Katherine Pride Gallery just a few months ago that had launched him into semi-fame.

Success had not come easy, but adjusting to it had. Richard had imagined the finer things for years; becoming accustomed to them felt natural, as if he had always been entitled to the best life had to offer. His artwork had been selling since he was in his early twenties, but the Pride show had taken it to another level, exposed him to people like the Gilliam's curator, in town to see what was on the art horizon. While several of the artists for the show had gained attention, Richard was one of the two real breakout stars, along with Javier Velasco. Velasco was somewhere in South America these days, maybe Argentina, wowing whomever constituted the art world there, and here Richard was in Philadelphia, a nice enough town for a stepping stone. Now that he'd made it to the Gilliam, MOMA couldn't be far behind.

He sipped his red wine and slipped off his robe. He'd had several emails back and forth with Kevin, the young hustler who called himself an escort and who must be on his way right about now. He had already laid out the scenario with him. Richard would be naked, face down on the bed, pretending to be sleeping. Kevin would let himself in through the unlocked door – how careless of me! – and Richard would be startled, feigning panic just as Kevin scrambled onto the bed and held him down. So helpless. So exciting. He eased down onto the bedspread, slipped his hands under the pillows, and waited for the sound of the door opening.

Kieran never cared much for Philadelphia. History was its only real selling point. If you didn't care where the Constitution was signed or who the hell signed it, Philly was just another big city with funny accents and greasy food. He admitted to enjoying its skyline, though. He had a fondness for skylines; they represented for him a far away place he had almost arrived at, a destination of soaring towers and deep, shadowed canyons. For some it was as if they were going into a land of light, neon and fluorescence; for him it was a descent into night. He felt safest then, when no one could see him. His power of invisibility was strongest in the darkness, when onlookers strained to see and he became a shadow among shadows.

He arrived at the bus station just as the sun was setting. All bus stations seemed the same to him. On the upside, they tended to be seedy. Someone with a limp and a filthy backpack, unshaved and gaunt, was just another Joe coming off the bus. One among hundreds.

He made his way to the Hamilton Inn and stood outside looking up at its lush green awning. There was only a tasteful, polished brass plaque on the building to announce its presence in the neighborhood. Pretense, he thought, as he walked quietly and quickly along the side of the building to where he knew there was a service entrance. Once upon a time this is where the dark-skinned dishwashers and laundresses, the hotel maids and the chauffeurs, made their way to the hotel basement from where they would fan out on their duties, always around and always unseen until needed. He knew about the entrance from a reconnaissance trip two weeks ago. He knew as much about the people on his list as he needed to, which was much more than they would ever know about him. He knew where they went, when they went, and how often. He knew Richard Morninglight stayed at the Hamilton, and that he enjoyed the company of unfamiliar young men when he did. It had been easy; too easy, and he felt a certain disappointment that there wasn't more effort needed. He would have to take his satisfaction in the killing itself and leave the challenge to the last one, the one who would see him in broad daylight. Unlike the fool Morninglight or the hapless Devin, startled by recognition into thinking he'd come as a friend and not an executioner.

There would be no description from the desk clerk because he did not stop at the desk. He pulled his hood over his head and made his way through the side entrance, down the cellar stairs and up in the freight elevator. He doubted anyone at the desk even noticed the elevator was moving, if they bothered to monitor it at all.

He got off on the third floor and walked quietly to room 306. As he stood in front of the door, he slipped his backpack off and reached inside for the set of six guitar strings. He carefully took out the thinnest of them, a slim, deadly piece of silver wire, held it in his left hand and walked into the room.

Richard heard the door open. He was on the bed, naked, as arranged, with his head turned toward the wall and his eyes closed. He could feel his heart race as he pretended to sleep, anticipating the "attack" they'd agreed on. The only person he'd ever told about these get-togethers had said it was dangerous, but he assured them, no, the men came by the desk, there were video recorders everywhere, nothing was going to go wrong.

Kieran stood over Richard, cocking his head and examining the artist's body. It wasn't much to look at, he decided. He wondered if Richard tipped the young men who played this game with him. He could use some extra cash and might have to take a gratuity whether it was offered or not. He gently laid his backpack on the floor and stretched the guitar string between his hands.

Something felt off to Richard. He'd expected a giggle, a word of hesitation. He feigned waking up and raised his head, turning to see someone he vaguely recognized, and it was not a beautiful young man come to play.

"What the fuck are you doing here?"

Kieran may be lame but he was fast and lean. Before any real resistance could be mounted, he jumped on the bed and straddled Morninglight, who was trying to turn over. It all happened so fast. In seconds he was firmly on top of the artist and he'd looped the guitar string over his head. All he had to do then was pull.

"You can't talk now, can you?" he said to the frantic man trying desperately to throw him off. "No more whispers. No more looks. Who's looking now? I am!"

Richard Morninglight flailed as best he could, but his attention was divided: his body was trying to buck the man on his back, while his hands were clawing at the metal string around his neck digging deeper and deeper. Nothing more was said; it was all done in a strangely silent tableau, with only the bouncing of the bed to make any noise. Soon it was over, and Kieran hopped off Morninglight just as blood from his nearly severed head began to soak through the sheets and mattress. For a moment he thought of taking the head as a trophy, but it would create problems and complicate what should be a swift, silent exit.

He left the guitar string embedded deep into Morninglight's neck. He went through the artist's wallet and took the $263 dollars he found there. And then, just as easily as he had come for the kill, he vanished. Paying no mind to the camera on the hallway ceiling, he was beyond that now. Back down the freight elevator, out the side door, and into the cool Philadelphia night.

CHAPTER 11

A View of the Cloisters

Kyle hadn't been this far uptown in years, not since he was looking around at apartments to buy just before he left his job at TriCore. It had been a whim, really; he knew he would have to take on a stifling mortgage to afford a co-op in Manhattan. He also knew he might not last much longer at the company he'd been with for six years, the last two of them miserable as he went from working for a man he cared about and who treated him well, to working for a group of mid-level managers when his boss was let go who considered him just another pool assistant. The kind of character you'd see in movies from the 1950s, women at typewriters churning out letters for a half dozen bosses who only knew them as outboxes. When Harry was let go, Kyle wanted to go with him, but the man he'd supported with the same kind of devotion he now showed Imogene Landis didn't land anywhere. A bar stool, Kyle guessed, cursing his bad luck to get old in a workforce that discarded people over fifty. Harry had been a decade older than that, and despite getting a sizable severance package and reassurances he would do just fine, Kyle doubted his boss had what it took to claw his way back in a recession. He never knew, because Harry never told him. As close as they were from 9 to 5, they did not have an off-work relationship. He knew, too, that Harry was a proud man and chose not to keep Kyle informed of his fate. Maybe things had turned out all right, but maybe they hadn't.

Kyle left the company before he could pursue buying an apartment. It was just as well; he'd called Brooklyn home since moving to New York and he was perfectly happy to stay there. Then he met Danny, and here he was – living near Gramercy Park, in a two-bedroom apartment with a partner and two cats.

This morning Kyle was riding the A train all the way to Inwood, to visit a woman he had never met who might have information for him, but who just as likely might slam the door in his face. Her wife had died recently in a most horrible way, falling from an empty subway platform beneath the wheels of an oncoming train. It had been very late at night and no one had seen what happened. Shiree Leone died as alone as anyone can, her last emotion stark terror as a monstrous train tried to stop, its wheels screeching like some demon from Hell's basement, drowning out the sound of her screams. Alone, without a single witness, dead with no one to tell her goodbye.

The intercom in front of Shiree's building didn't work, so Kyle lingered out front in the small courtyard until someone came out. The woman looked at him with mild suspicion, either pegging him as another harmless middle-aged gay man, or simply not caring enough to ask him why he didn't have a key. She was bundled up more than was needed on a cool late April morning; she clutched her oversized purse to her side, and even held the door behind her just long enough for Kyle to enter the building with a quick, "Thank you."

The building was what New Yorkers called pre-war, meaning it was constructed before World War II. These buildings were strong, and often had the kind of detail and ornamentation not found in more recent buildings. Kyle was among the many who loved buildings like this: enormous lobby, high windows, most comprised of dozens of small panes, wide marble stairs for anyone not using the small, creaky elevator, and a fire escape at every landing. He stopped between floors and looked out to see the Cloisters not far away. He stared at the strange and magnificent museum. Built with an endowment from John D. Rockefeller to house his art collection, the Cloisters were designed to resemble a medieval European abbey.

Many visitors who happened upon them and didn't know what they were, assumed they had once been a monastery.

It was a breathtaking view, and Kyle forgot for a moment why he was here. He pulled himself from his thoughts and continued up the stairs to apartment 4J.

He knocked lightly and waited for an answer. When none came, he knocked again, more forcefully.

"Who is it?" he heard a woman's voice call from inside.

"My name's Kyle Callahan," he said. "I'm with the Katherine Pride Gallery."

He was telling the truth, sort of. He had a show coming up at the gallery and was friends with Kate.

"I don't believe you," the woman's voice said. "You're a reporter. I don't fall for this kind of thing. I have nothing more to say."

Kyle thought for a moment. If she assumed he was a reporter, then he wasn't the only person who'd been around asking about Shiree Leone's death.

"I'm really not a reporter," he said, his face close to the door. "I'm … a friend of a friend of Shiree's."

The deadbolt sounded and the door opened a crack, held in place by a chain as a dark-skinned woman with short red hair and piercing brown eyes took measure of this man at her door.

"A friend of a friend," she said. "So that means you knew Shiree exceedingly well, does it?"

"Well, no. I didn't know her at all. But I care about how she died. And I am involved with the gallery. She did their last catalog."

"I know that."

"I have a show coming up there, and an artist who was part of the last one was killed over the weekend. Stabbed, in Brooklyn. I think it's not a coincidence. Shiree dying in the subway, I mean."

"I know what you mean," the woman said. "But let me point something out to you, Mr. Friend of a Friend. You want me to speak to you about something that has been a profound tragedy for me, yet you've not even asked my name."

Kyle blushed and looked down, as embarrassed as he could remember being. "Yes, you're right. I'm so sorry. Are you Olive? Olive Washburn?" He had read her name in the news reports.

"Olivette. Please don't use the diminutive. But I won't hold it against you. And I could use company for a cup of coffee. That's as much time as I'll give you."

"And that's as much time as I'll ask for," Kyle said, as Olivette Washburn slid the chain back and welcomed this curious, gay, white, intrusive man into her home.

The apartment was cavernous, with high ceilings and arched doorways. Olivette led Kyle into the living room and offered him a seat on the couch. He glanced at a hallway leading back into the apartment and guessed there was at least one bedroom there.

A large black cat sauntered up to Kyle just as Olivette said, "Excuse me," and headed into the kitchen.

"I'm Kyle," Kyle said to the animal as it sniffed his hand. Its response told him it would not be remembering his name. The cat turned away, uninterested in the intruder, and hopped up on a brown leather recliner, curled into a ball and eased its head down on its paws.

"That's Hector," Olivette called from the kitchen. "Don't pay him any mind. He won't pay you any."

Kyle was looking around at the room, curious at how sparse it was: one maple bookshelf with three shelves given to books, the other two to photographs and knick-knacks. The cat's recliner and the couch Kyle was sitting on, which felt like a sofa bed. A plaid armchair opposite the recliner, with a coffee table between them. A few framed posters that appeared to be Shiree Leon's artwork, and a cathode-ray television that looked not to have been used for several years.

Olivette came back in carrying two cups of coffee. Kyle quickly took stock of her again, taken by how lovely she was: short red hair, a flattish face, ebony skin, black hands with nearly pink palms, and eyes that knew she was being examined, knew the difference between a fool and a friend, and that Kyle was neither. She was wearing a red sweater and black jeans, with house slippers in the shape of tigers. She smiled slightly, setting Kyle's coffee on the narrow coffee table in front of him, then taking her own to the recliner. She shooed the cat away and sat down.

"I've told the police everything I know," she said. "But you're not the police. So what is it you were wondering?"

"Well," Kyle said, trying to gather his thoughts. "Do you think it was an accident?"

"They said she jumped, that's the last I read about my wife's death."

"So you were married?"

"No," she said, smiling again. "We always called ourselves married. One for the revolution, so to speak. I don't need the state to validate my relationship. Do you? Assuming you have one."

"I do, I do," Kyle said. "My partner's name is Danny. Sometimes I call him my husband ..."

"But you think it's not real until you go to City Hall and get a license. How did we make it the last few thousand years, with our fake relationships? Makes you wonder. Anyway, I'm just being contrary. What were you saying?"

"I got to thinking ..."

"After Devin's death."

Kyle looked at her, surprised.

"I read the news, too. I don't watch it. That TV's a piece of crap and I won't pay for cable. Shiree only kept it because she said it was an art installation. She was like that."

Kyle could see the sadness in her eyes, even as she smiled at the thought of her beloved, gone forever.

"I didn't think anything of it at the time, except how terrible it was," she said. "But I read the news online and it did seem kind of strange. The whole three-deaths thing."

"When two celebrities die, a third's not far behind."

"Crazy, I know, but I thought if Shiree was one, and this Devin was a second, maybe there would be a third. So I watched for it. But it's only been two days, there's still time." She chuckled at the absurdity of it, then grew serious again. "He was a nice guy, Devin. He and Shiree weren't close, but she got to know him when she did the catalog for the Pride Gallery show."

"Well, that's the connection," Kyle said. "If there is one, I really don't know at this point. But if there is, I think the killer may not be finished. You said Shiree and Devin were friends?"

"Not friends, unless you're someone who thinks a few hundred people on Facebook are your friends when only about three of them really care what happens to you. Friendship used to be meaningful. There I go again … no, they were not friends. They formed a little group, a little bond, while the show was going. Shiree was a shy girl, and it helped her to have someone to talk to at these events. She also had to work with the artists to do the catalog. It was a short-time thing. Show closed, everyone moved on."

"Not everyone, clearly. If that show is what connects them."

"Do you think you might be next? Is that what you're afraid of? I read you're having an exhibit yourself there this week."

"It's not me I'm worried about. I wasn't involved with the January show, and I don't have any connection to the Katherine Pride Gallery, aside from being friends with Kate."

She stared at him, waiting a moment for him to realize what he had just said.

"What?" he asked, then, "Oh my God. Friends with Kate. Is that his list? But she has so many friends, dozens of friends. He can't be after them all."

"If it's about Kate Pride and the gallery, that narrows things down a bit."

"It is and it's not," Kyle said, suddenly sure. "It's about *that show*."

"New Visions."

"Yes, the New Visions show. Something about that show and the people involved."

Olivette took a moment to weigh her words, caressing her coffee cup. "How well do you know Katherine Pride?" she asked.

Kyle was surprised by the question. "Not terribly well. She's a friend, and a mentor, of sorts."

"Yes, a mentor. That she is. She likes to encourage people."

"Is there something wrong with that?"

Olivette shrugged. "Not if you're the person she's encouraging."

Not if you're the person she's encouraging. It was an enigmatic statement, and one Kyle decided not to question for now. It could have several meanings and he preferred to ponder it rather than pursue it and appear hostile.

"Was there anything different the last few days of Shiree's life?" he asked. "Anything out of place that either of you noticed?"

"Like the man she said was following her?"

Kyle stared at her.

"She couldn't prove it. She couldn't even describe him. It was more a *presence* she felt, the last two, three days before … the fall. The slip. The push. The shove. Take your pick."

"Did you tell the police?"

"Of course I told the police. But this guy was a phantom. She said he looked familiar, but she couldn't say how. He wore a hoodie, she couldn't see his face. It was the way he walked."

"The way he walked?"

"Like a rooster, she said. Cocky like, but wrong, like he was off balance."

"Was she close to other people involved with the January show?"

"Nah," Olivette said, finishing her coffee. "Shiree was a freelancer and a loner, except for me. She did a job and moved on. She got friendly with a circle at the Gallery while it lasted. Devin. This cat named Richard Morninglight, whose real name was probably Jones. These artists can be so full of shit."

"So you're not an artist?" Kyle asked.

"No, no. I'm MTA. Transit Authority. I'm a bus driver."

Kyle suddenly realized how much of our perceptions of others are built from assumptions. He would never have thought Olivette Washburn was a bus driver. He didn't like making assumptions. Deductions, yes. Intuitive guesses, certainly. But assumptions were not only unfair, but could get you killed.

"I'm going to leave you now," Kyle said, having gotten what information he could from Olivette.

"You're on the right track," she said.

"And what track is that?" Kyle asked, as he slowly stood from the couch.

"That Gallery. That show. Maybe even that woman."

Maybe even that woman. Did she have something against Kate Pride, or had Kate Pride wronged her somehow? And if she had, had she wronged a killer as well?

Olivette walked Kyle to the door. The moment she was out of the chair, Hector traded places, hopping up on her chair and curling into a ball on the warm cushion.

As Kyle was about to leave, he pulled a business card from his wallet and handed it to her.

"Japan TV3," she said, reading the card. "Personal Assistant to Imogene Landis."

Kyle cringed. He had never liked having that title on his card, but Imogene insisted.

"I dig that chick," Olivette said. "Saw her on TV at my mother's house. Did a story about some murders at a gay hotel."

"A lodge. In Pennsylvania."

"Well, I'll be. She's a piece of work, that one. You can just tell."

"Yes, you certainly can."

Olivette held the door open for him.

"If you think of anything else," Kyle said.

"I try not to, to be honest. But if I do, I'll call Imogene's assistant, don't you doubt it."

Kyle saw a gleam in her eye, a hint of mischief, and it came as a relief. Olivette Washburn would survive. He suddenly wished they'd met under different circumstances, that the coffee they shared could have been over a very different conversation.

"Thank you again," he said, as she nodded and closed the door behind him.

CHAPTER 12

PENN STATION

Detective Linda Sikorsky had not been to New York City in thirty-five years. Her last visit was with her parents, to see a production of "A Christmas Carol" and tour the light-strewn city in mid-December. It was the most magical time to be in Manhattan, with giant toy soldiers guarding street crossings and reindeer flying over Fifth Avenue. It was also three months before her father was gunned down in an act of random violence outside a grocery store in their hometown of Cincinnati. They'd flown to New York for the occasion, Linda, her father, Peter, and her mother, Estelle. It had been planned for a year, and the anticipation had built through September, October, November, until finally Linda burst off the airplane in Queens and never stopped talking about all the things she saw on the taxi ride into Manhattan. So magical had it been, and in such horrible contrast to the death of her father the following March, that Linda had never come back.

Pete Sikorsky had been a Cincinnati cop for fifteen years when he was shot outside a corner grocery, off-duty, an innocent bystander killed in a senseless act of violence. It was a nightmarish bookend to the time they'd had in New York, and Linda had never wanted to see the city again. Not when she lived in Ohio, not when her mother remarried and moved them to Philadelphia, and not when she became an officer on the New Hope, Pennsylvania, police force. A mere two hours away by car, less by train. It was as if she could look out her kitchen window and see, far in the distance, the city that had put a divider in her life between the good and the evil, the before and the after. For her New York City would always be a perfect memory followed by a perfect loss, and the fragility of it had kept her away, until she met Kyle and Danny.

All these years later she was living a life she would never have imagined that glorious Christmas thirty-five years ago, followed so soon by the defining tragedy of her father's death, and it was time to chase away the ghosts. She put her misgivings aside and took the train from Trenton to spend four days in Manhattan, to think about her new relationship, and to see Kyle and Danny, whom she had befriended during the Pride Lodge Murders – as they'd come to be known. In part because of Kyle's boss, the overbearing television reporter who managed to revive her career with a story about the killings, and in part because it was an easy thing to call them. "The Murders at Pride Lodge." She admitted it had a ring to it, and had even toyed with writing a book about it. Maybe she would do that when she left the New Hope police force, something she'd been discussing with Kirsten, and something she wanted to talk to Kyle about.

Kirsten. The other thing she wanted to talk about. The woman she met at a New Year's Eve party four months ago, and who was now Linda Sikorsky's first official girlfriend. Linda had wanted her to come along, but Kirsten wasn't quite ready to meet "the family," and both of them felt there would be plenty of time for it. Linda believed Kirsten would also be the only girlfriend she would ever have; she knew the odds were not in their favor, given the survival rate of relationships in general. But their ages – Linda at 43 and Kirsten at 47 – played into her thinking as well. They were not school girls in the throes of a crush. She had known she was lesbian pretty much all her life, but she had never acted on it. Not out of any doubt or self-loathing, but because she had lost someone she loved so completely – her father – at such a young age, that she associated love with pain. To love someone was to accept that you would eventually lose them, or they would lose you; it was as inevitable as death itself, and while Linda knew that might be a morbid way to look at it, it was her truth. Until

Kirsten. Until she became aware that some pain down the line was worth the joy that could be found living in the present.

Linda was a tall woman, six feet in her stockings. She had let her blonde hair grow out since last October and wondered what Kyle would make of it. She'd become a bit more feminine, if that's the word, influenced by Kirsten's sense of style and ease with a makeup case. She was still what was her mother called a big-boned gal, but she had trimmed down a bit. Having a woman like Kirsten McLellan by her side made her want to look her best. Kirsten turned heads, with her ramrod bearing, her svelte physique, startling green eyes sprinkled with flecks of yellow, and her style. Kirsten was a real estate broker whose presence spoke high-end: she sold only the best, to only the most demanding. Kyle had even mentioned it as another connection between them all: Kate Pride's husband was a real estate broker, too. Kyle was always looking for connections, as if he saw the world in dots, or pixilated patterns that could be brought into focus by staring at them long enough. Oh look, your girlfriend sells real estate, and the husband of the gallery owner who's showing my photos sells real estate, it must mean something! To Linda it simply meant the world was smaller than most people think, and nearly all roads cross if you just stay on them long enough.

Kirsten was successful and demanding, yet her heart was as true and generous as any Linda had ever encountered. Kirsten McLellan knew how to win, that's all, and when she was alone with Linda she turned that sense of competition off. The two women had nothing to prove to one another, and everything to enjoy. It was Kirsten who encouraged Linda to consider leaving the police force. Linda had long imagined opening a store in New Hope and spending her days talking to shoppers, selling them vintage finds she'd bought at auctions and flea markets. Not antiques, God no; Linda didn't know an antique from an old piece of furniture. But she loved perusing aisles and bins, sifting through drawers and racks of gently worn clothes. She even had a name for the place: *For Pete's Sake*. Named after her father, naturally. She would add some kind of sub-title, maybe *Vintage Everything*, something to tell people when they saw the store sign exactly what they were walking into. It was her dream, her fantasy, and until Kirsten came along she'd always kept it locked away. Maybe not much longer.

Her train pulled into Penn Station just as Kyle was getting back on the subway in the northernmost reaches of Manhattan, having learned enough from Olivette Washburn to know he was onto something. They had arranged to meet for lunch at a diner called the Stopwatch, a block from the station. She was early enough to have time to check into the hotel – she had paid for early arrival – and maybe even a short nap before heading to the restaurant. She had a lot to think through and already her nerves were on edge. She had wanted Kirsten to come with her, but there would be plenty of time and opportunity for them all to meet. They could come back in the summer, or get Danny and Kyle to visit New Hope again. They could even stay at Pride Lodge. It had changed managers since the killings, but the old man Jeremy who had been the silent partner in the whole affair still owned it.

"They'll love you, Kirsten" Linda whispered to herself, hoping it to be true. How could it not be? Linda Sikorsky was level headed. Linda Sikorsky was an excellent judge of character. Love was not blind this time.

She eased up from her train seat and reached for her luggage in the overhead rack. All would be well. Kirsten was everything she'd fantasized in a partner. She was back in New York City and excited to see how it had changed, considering how little she remembered of it from her childhood. She was going to her friend Kyle's first photography exhibit. Renewal and happiness were in the wind.

CHAPTER 13

HOTEL EXETER, HELL'S KITCHEN

Kieran watched the people on 36th Street six floors below hurrying for the sake of hurrying, as was the case with nearly everyone in Manhattan. He had noticed when he first moved here that everyone was in a mad dash to nowhere, thinking themselves terribly important with terribly important things to do. People didn't so much walk on the streets of this city as maneuver, quickly circling around and through one another to get to the same destination five seconds faster. The first rule of life in New York was to *seem* to matter. To give the impression to anyone who might be looking, while assuming everyone was, that you had something to do right this minute. You were one of the busy people. There were only three stages of being here: up-and-coming, already arrived, or dead. He had never been the first two, and hoped the third was a long way off, but he had observed it around him since the moment he first arrived as a man without a home. Oklahoma was no place to go back to, and New York City was no place to stay. Between the two he had lived – drifted, really – from Salt Lake City to Seattle to New Orleans, never staying long enough to leave much trace of himself. Wherever he ended up, he would be on the run, and that was okay with him. He had been running all his life.

He hadn't slept since returning from Philadelphia at one o'clock that morning. He'd thought he might, given how tiring it was to strangle someone. The only people who seem to know that are the people doing it.

Everyone else experiences murder in the abstract, as part of a movie or a television show. But to actually straddle a man and nearly decapitate him with a guitar string, now that will exhaust you. He padded naked from the window into the bathroom for a third cup of instant coffee, made with hot tap water. He couldn't afford real coffee, the kind that tasted good and didn't make you feel like it was corroding your stomach. The kind that didn't make you puke. He had been throwing up more lately and wasn't sure if it was from the wretched instant coffee or from the excitement of killing people he'd been planning to for the past two months.

He caught a glimpse of himself in the full-length mirror mounted to the back of the bathroom door. The mirror was cracked and covered with stains; the maid service at the Exeter left as much to be desired as everything else about it. He set his cup down on the toilet lid and examined himself: not bad, he thought, thinner than he'd ever been, pale, in need of a haircut, but still a catch at thirty-five. He'd fallen far, there was no denying it, but he would rise again. He would put on a few pounds easily enough, get firmly back on his feet and face the day with a smile. It had been so long since he smiled.

He pushed the door in against the wall, tired of looking at himself and the things it made him think. He was too busy for idle thoughts. He had a plan to carry out and only four days left. The big opening at the art gallery was Friday night and here it was already Tuesday morning. All those fancy people coming to the opening of The Next Big Thing, the next *artiste* destined for fame. Some shutterbug, another photo-auteur, as if the world wasn't overrun with people taking pictures on iPhones and calling them art. The picture he had in mind for them, the centerpiece, would not be an image at all but the real thing. Three-dimensional, sensory stimulation at its most unimaginable. Performance art they would be talking about for the rest of their lives. He'd bought a digital camera just for the occasion, the kind that makes video recordings, too. The internet was flooded with stupid videos from stupid people who thought dancing kittens were the best thing ever, or their stupid babies laughing at nothing while they recorded them and put them online, hoping to end up on some idiotic morning show. The next must-see, the next YouTube sensation! Boy, did he have something for them to watch ... very soon. It had taken most of his meager cash to buy, but once it was finished, once he had released it into the world, he would be complete and not in need of anything.

He finished making his coffee with the lukewarm water from the sink, stirred it with his finger, and walked back into the hotel room to work out his itinerary. His planning had been meticulous so far, and now more than ever he must focus, focus, focus.

CHAPTER 14

TOKYO PULSE

Kyle hurried across Ninth Avenue at 46ᵗʰ Street, carrying a bag filled with two medium coffees, a toasted bagel for himself, and a croissant for Imogene. He glanced to his left and saw the Hotel Exeter sign, visible from ten blocks away by virtue of an unobstructed view. He'd never been to the Exeter, or even known anyone who had, but the big red letters extending up above its rooftop provided a signpost, a way of orienting oneself in a city that can be very disorienting to the uninitiated.

He'd picked up the coffee at Cecil's, a bagel shop he'd been stopping at every morning since he first started working at Japan TV3 as Imogene Landis's personal assistant. Imogene was diminutive in body only: short, thin, with a brunette bob she somehow made fashionable, and an outsize personality that surprised many people coming from such a small woman. Tiny would be an apt description. But once she opened her mouth most people took cover, and the ones who didn't tended to be thick-skinned, since Imogene's language was more like pepper spray. She'd lost more than one job because of it, and had been on the verge of leaving this one just when the murders in Pennsylvania made her a hit on late-night TV in Tokyo. The show was called Tokyo Pulse, produced by Japan TV3, whose English-language correspondents were in New York – all three of them – and whose bosses in Tokyo knew a novelty act when they saw one. She'd been their financial correspondent, interviewing C-level economists and talking about financial matters she knew nothing about, nor cared to. And then, death in the countryside. A gay resort. Murder, mayhem, and ratings that shot up like a rocket. Now Imogene Landis was as close to a star as someone on television at 3:00 a.m. in Tokyo can be. She'd even learned to speak enough Japanese to sound ridiculous in the occasional asides she did to camera. But mostly it was business, as she now covered the city in a segment called Straight Up New York. Crime, politics, some culture when she got lucky. But a headliner in any event. Imogene-san was a hit.

Japan TV3 was located on the third floor of CityScape Studios, which were really just a large office building converted to television studios in the 1980s. They were big, and they weren't much to brag about, but they generated considerable revenue for the building's owners. They were also home to some of the best bad television shows no one has ever heard of. The YouTube of shoestring budget broadcasting. It was saying something that JapanTV3 could have an entire half-floor to itself. This is where you'll find Kelly Gerson, national political reporter who only went from her apartment in Flushing to the studios and back and had never been to Washington, Michael W. Podesto (the middle initial was in his contract), who had taken over the financial beat when Imogene moved up and who was quite good at it, their boss Leonard "Lenny-san" Baumstein, who reported directly to the high-ups in Tokyo, Lenny-san's icy assistant Gretchen, and, of course, Imogene and Kyle. The operation was supported by a dozen quasi-producers and assistants, and felt most days almost like a real TV show. There was even a deal in the works to expand beyond the single Japanese cable channel where New Yorkers could see the program. Someday soon, they all hoped, viewers would be able to enjoy Tokyo Pulse in every major American market. Imogene believed when that happened she would be able to write her own ticket, after thirty years in the business.

The elevator opened and Kyle hurried to his cubicle. The train back from Inwood had been delayed in two separate stations, once for traffic and another for a sick passenger, and he was almost an hour late. He managed to slip his jacket nearly off when Imogene saw him. She had her own cubicle – the days of an office were long gone – and was reading over a script when she looked up at the sound of the elevator.

"The withdrawals have already started, Kyle," she said, referring to the coffee he brought her every morning.

"I'm sorry, I got stuck on a train."

Kyle handed her coffee to her and set the croissant on her desk, at the same time draping his jacket over the back of his chair. Even though they sat back to back, in identical cubes, there was no mistaking the two spaces: Kyle's little fabric square was decorated only with a few photos of himself with Danny, their two cats, Danny's parents and Kyle's mother. Imogene, meanwhile, had given her cube the royal treatment, a sort of presidential suite of office cubicles. There were framed photographs her of her smiling next to New York City politicians, some whose names Kyle did not know (any Councilman would do), as well as a signed letter of thanks from Former President Bill Clinton, an invitation to some official state dinner that she probably picked up at a flea market, and a photograph of an Emmy. Imogene Landis had never won an Emmy, but anyone stopping by her cubicle would not know that. One of her favorite truisms, true mostly to Imogene, was that "Appearances matter." She could be heard saying it at least once a week. It was lost on her that an over-decorated 5 x 5 foot cubicle spoke more of desperation than success.

"You're coming to the opening, yes?" Kyle asked. He'd been counting on Imogene to attend his exhibit at the Pride Gallery. While she wouldn't cover it for Tokyo Pulse (she had pitched it to Lenny-san but he deemed it not interesting to a middle-of-the-night Tokyo audience), she promised as Kyle's long time boss and friend she would be there.

"I've made dinner reservations a block from there, of course I'm coming!" she said. "Lenny-san is my date."

"Lenny's coming?" Kyle was shocked. Their boss was a sixty-ish, squat, barrel-chested, balding Jewish man everyone knew was gay but who had never come out. He had lived alone with his aging father until the old man passed away two years ago, after which Lenny moved from Staten Island to Chelsea, expecting no one to notice.

"I may yet get him to let me do a short piece," she said, referring to the opening. "A sort of 'Tokyo Pulse' reporter makes good' thing."

"I'm not a reporter."

"They don't know that. It's three o'clock in the morning there, for fuck sake!" She sipped her coffee and sniffed her croissant – an odd habit she had of smelling her food. "If you want to be successful – "

"Appear successful," Kyle finished.

"Absolutely. Appearances matter. Like this morning, it appeared you had either quit or just didn't care enough to be here on time."

Kyle sighed. She was ribbing him, but he still didn't like it.

"I had to talk to someone in Inwood."

Imogene set her script down. "Inwood? Above Harlem, that Inwood? What the fuck's in Inwood?"

Kyle frowned at her. She'd been asked several times by Lenny-san to watch her language. A few people in the office had complained.

"The wife of a woman who died a month ago, fell in front of a train.

Imogene's eyes lit up just a bit. "Or was pushed? Is that what you're thinking? There's a story in being pushed in front of a train. And 'wife of a woman' means gay, I like that."

"Oh my God."

"No disrespect, Kyle, but gay has been good to me. Pride Lodge sent my ratings through the roof in Tokyo. I'm just being realistic. It adds to the story."

"At this point there is no story. Just thinking. Connections."

"I can use some, it's been very dry here the last few weeks."

"What are you reading?" Kyle asked, looking at the script on her desk.

"Bor-ing. Lenny-san wants me at one of Councilman Danhill's town-hall meetings on the Upper East. Have you ever been to one of those? It's all old people. Not that I have anything against them, I hope to be one myself someday and get a lifetime achievement award. But we're talking zoning shit, wheelchair accessibility shit, kill me now shit. How he thinks this kind of thing won't tank us is beyond me."

Kyle booted up his computer, hoping Imogene would head out to the field soon with her producer Caren. In an operation this small, producers were also camera operators, script writers, editors, and sometimes office supply buyers, although that generally fell to Kyle. (Gretchen had been an executive assistant for one senior manager or another for nearly forty years and did not order office supplies.)

"Now, a juicy strangulation in a hotel room, with a guitar string, no less, *that*'s a story," she said. "But it's a Philly story, and we're not in Philly, are we?"

Kyle was barely listening, trying to think how the murders of Devin and Shiree could be connected. The Gallery was the most obvious answer, but how, and why?

" … this guy Richard Morninglight, did you read about that?" Imogene said, continuing to chatter while Kyle barely paid attention. The name got through to him and made him sit up, turn to Imogene, and ask her what she had just said.

"I said it has all the elements of a great story. Gay hotel in Philadelphia, artist on the edge of fame, a hustler nobody saw come in our out, and having his head nearly taken off with a wire."

"A wire."

"A guitar string. You really have to pay attention, Kyle, or get your hearing checked."

"Richard Morninglight?" Kyle was staring at her now.

"You know him?"

"No. Well, I met him, once, at the New Visions show."

Imogene waited for him to explain.

"It's the New Year show Kate Pride has every January, to showcase talent she thinks is on the verge. The show last January had a half dozen artists. Devin was one of them."

"Who's Devin?" Imogene asked.

Kyle waved her off, wanting to complete his thought. "Devin was one of them … Richard Morninglight was another … and Shiree Leone did the catalog. That's it! The New Year New Visions show. The Pride Gallery."

"I want an exclusive on this," Imogene said, having no idea what 'this' could turn out to be, only that she wanted the rights to tell it first.

"There may not be any story here. Maybe it's a coincidence. I mean, Brooklyn, Inwood, Philadelphia? I don't want to see something that isn't there. Where did you read about Richard Morninglight?"

"Where did I read about him?" Imogene said, as if Kyle had missed the assassination of the President. "Online, where the hell else? It was front page news."

By front page, Kyle knew she meant what had once been called "above the fold" when newspapers were still in wide circulation. Now that nearly everyone got their information from the Internet, it meant stories that were seen before the reader had to start scrolling down.

"Let me read about this," Kyle said, turning back to his monitor. "When's your townhall?"

"Half an hour from now. I'm just waiting for Caren, then we'll take the van. You wanna ride along?"

"I'll skip it, thanks. The excitement might kill me."

"Fine, I'm sure you have work to get caught up on, considering you were an hour late. But if there's any 'there' there in this New York-Philly killing spree …"

"It's not a killing spree! Not yet. Maybe never. Just let me think it through."

"So think, Kyle, and if it's not a coincidence, if there really is a story here, I take it to Lenny-san while everyone else is still in the dark. Deal?"

"Of course," Kyle said.

Imogene began to quietly read her script, memorizing her introduction to the townhall segment.

Kyle turned back to his computer and immediately did a search for Richard Morninglight. He pulled up the first story he saw and began to read the sordid details of a murder in a hotel room ninety-five miles away.

CHAPTER 15

MARGARET'S PASSION

Danny found himself in a quandary. For the decade he had worked for Margaret Bowman the two of them shared a trust few people have with another. Best friends. Couples. Occasionally a boss and her assistant. A mother and son. That had always been a sensitive matter for them both, since Danny's mother, Eleanor, was alive and well in Astoria, Queens. She was retired these past fifteen years, living comfortably in a row house on 28th Street with her husband, Big Bob Durban, also retired. Danny and Kyle had Sunday dinner with them almost every week. Eleanor, *Ellie*, was a strong willed woman, a good mother, but possessed of a certain jealousy when it came to her son. She didn't like having to share him with anyone, including Kyle, and Danny had been careful all this time not to speak too much of Margaret in front of her.

He'd kept his relationship with his two mothers distinct. There were things he told Ellie, and things he told Margaret, and each of them told him everything. So it was strange for Danny to be fidgeting at work Tuesday morning wondering what Margaret was withholding from him, and how to go about asking her. He had never had to pry information from her before, and as far as he knew she had never kept a secret from him.

Something had been going on for the past several weeks. Margaret's new lawyer Claude Petrie, while having been referred by the old gentleman he replaced, struck Danny as an odd duck. Maybe it was the way he avoided looking directly at you, or the perspiration that seemed always present on his upper lip. *Shifty* came to mind. And now he was bringing in two strangers to speak with Margaret. He had been mulling it over for days, not wanting to question her judgment, yet worried something might be wrong. She might be ill, or preparing in some other way to leave. He wanted her to know he and Kyle were there for her. If she needed care, there was always the spare room, though he doubted someone as proud as Margaret Bowman would submit to being looked after. He had to know what was going on.

Danny slowly climbed the staircase Margaret and Gerard had built behind the kitchen. There were only twelve apartments in the entire building, six on each of the two upper stories, including the Bowmans', with the restaurant taking up the entire first floor. The restaurant had been their one true love, aside from each other, and they had wanted to be able to come and go easily, at any time of the day or night, without having to go outside. The staircase was no secret, except to the city, from whom they had never sought or received the proper coding to build a staircase. At this point nobody cared.

Normally Danny would call up and tell Margaret he was visiting, but he wanted an element of surprise. He knew she would be there – she was always there, and when she went out, she used the staircase and left through the restaurant when it was open. He told Trebor he'd be back and to please seat any guests who came in. Patricia, one of three day servers, was already stocking. Lunch was still an hour away, there was no reason to think he'd be needed for the next twenty minutes, so he climbed the stairs and gently knocked.

He was startled when the door opened before his knuckles hit the door a third time.

"Come in," Margaret said, opening the door. She was wearing a powder blue dress with a white sweater, looking much as she would were she heading to dinner with someone. She was always dressed as if company might be coming – except for the house slippers.

"No call, Danny?" she said, referring to his habit of letting her know he was coming.

"I wanted to talk to you," he said. He followed her wave and sat at the kitchen table. A kettle, anachronistic in this age of coffee machines and iPhones, was just on the verge of whistling above a stove flame.

"Tea?" she said, shuffling in her slippers to the stove.

"Yes, please."

Margaret set about pouring boiling water into two cups and dropping in tea bags. Neither of them said anything until she'd brought the cups to the table and taken a seat herself.

Danny looked around the kitchen. He'd seen it a thousand times, and it always reminded him of his grandmother's kitchen. There was a permanently outdated feel to it. Not old, but out of time, as if from another era.

"Chloe tells me Claude was here again yesterday, with two men," Danny said finally. Unlike Claude, he looked directly at Margaret. She was no-nonsense, and would not expect anything but directness.

"Investors," she said. Just like that. "Money men. I quite liked them."

Danny didn't know what to make of it. Was this simply about her investments? Were they financial advisors? Why the secrecy?

"Do they handle your … estate?" he said, uncomfortable with talking about things that might bring up her death, her will, or the fact she was now in her eighties.

"No, nothing like that." Now Margaret was the one who looked away. She was hesitant, embarrassed. Finally she turned back to him and said as plainly as possible, "I'm in trouble, Danny. I'm broke."

He was stunned. Margaret's Passion was a very successful restaurant in its fourth decade, in a city where restaurants came and went like tourists. He knew the numbers, he did the budget and the ordering. While his position was day manager, he really was the overall manager. He saw the receipts. The idea that Margaret was broke was like finding out someone who appeared perfectly healthy had a month to live.

"I don't understand."

"Of course you don't," she said. "You remember all the news last year about Rebecca Effron?"

"The Ponzi scheme lady? 'Bride of Madoff' or whatever they called her?"

"Yes, always clever, these news people. Well, she was very successful at making people believe she was successful. I was one of those people, Danny."

He knew where she was going with this and his heart sank.

"Just over a million dollars," she said. There was no other way to put it. She had given a thief her life savings and now it was gone.

"I see."

"I don't think you do, Danny. It was everything I had."

"But the restaurant …"

"It does well, yes. The tenants are reliable for the most part. But I'm eighty years old! The margins."

He knew she meant the profit margins, on the restaurant and the tenants. There was very little for either. The tenants essentially paid for the taxes and upkeep, with some left over, and the restaurant provided Margaret's regular income. What she was telling Danny also let him know that it had taken Margaret and Gerard nearly fifty years to save up that money she had lost in a bad bet, probably the only bad bet she had ever made.

"I'm not a greedy woman," Margaret said, her voice now thick with sadness. "Not even much of a needy woman. But I'm old. I may want to go somewhere warm soon, while I still can, and that takes money. And even if I stay here … well, I may not be able to keep living on my own, you understand."

Danny felt his throat tighten. The last thing he wanted to do was cry, and he held it in check as best he could.

"The point is I'm going to need help sooner rather than later. The management company does well enough with the building," she said, referring to the small company that collected rent and took care of the day-to-day maintenance of her property, "but I'm hardly a fit landlord anymore."

"You don't need to be," he said, quickly trying to think of alternatives.

"Messieurs Tierney and Gossett, the two investors, are interested in buying the building."

"What about the restaurant?"

"Well, Danny, the restaurant is *in* the building. But they've made me a most generous offer: the restaurant stays, and I stay, until I pass."

There it was again, Old Man Time coming for them all.

"I don't like it."

"I didn't expect you would, which is why I was waiting to tell you."

"How can you trust them?" Danny asked.

"It's called a contract."

Danny stood up. He began pacing the small kitchen, from the table to the stove and back. "I don't know, Margaret, it just feels wrong."

"You're letting your emotions make that determination for you. You'll be safe as long as I am."

"I don't care about being safe! I don't want to be safe. It's not about that. It's about your legacy. Gerard's legacy."

She sighed and put her teacup down. "Dead people do not care about their legacies."

"What if I had a counter offer?" he said, stopping in front of her.

"What does that mean?"

"Exactly what it sounds like, Margaret. What if I came up with a counter offer? I can't promise a million dollars, but maybe half that, for the restaurant. You keep the building."

She thought a moment. "I pay you well, Danny, but I don't pay you that well."

"It doesn't matter. You're not the only one who can find investors."

"I didn't find them. They found me."

"What?" Danny said, struck by that bit of information.

"They came to me, through Claude."

I see, Danny thought. Young, new lawyer Claude knows Margaret has lost all her savings, and just happens to know two characters looking for a building to buy. Danny began to notice an unpleasant smell.

"Just don't make any decisions," he said. "Not until I do some research. You've trusted me for ten years, don't stop now."

Margaret sat staring into her tea a long moment. Finally, she said, "Okay, Danny Durban. I have trusted you since the day I met you. I don't even remember where you were working ..."

"The Lamb Rack, East 63rd Street."

"Yes, dreadful place, it didn't last long."

"Which you saw coming, and you offered me a job."

"Oh, yes, you're right. But I really offered it to you because I was impressed. You know that, don't make me flatter you again."

He blushed. "I won't. But I will ask you to please give me till the end of this week."

"That's when Kyle's show is. Aren't you busy enough with all that?"

"I'm never too busy for Margaret Bowman," he said. "Now, speaking of busy, it's lunch hour and I imagine people are arriving right about now."

Danny leaned down and kissed her cheek. He had several things to think about, important things. Who were these men? Who were these men *really*? And how was he going to save his beloved Margaret from her own mistakes without making too many of his own?

"I'll let myself out," Danny said, and he headed back downstairs, quietly pulling the door closed behind him.

CHAPTER 16

LUNCH AT THE STOPWATCH DINER

You can't miss the Stopwatch Diner, with its colorful neon "Stopwatch Diner" sign, complete with a stopwatch in the middle, and its throw-back design that lets you know this is a diner, not some high-end, overpriced Midtown Manhattan eatery. It's also directly across from the Seventh Avenue entrance to Penn Station and just a half block from Macy's, which is where Linda Sikorsky was shopping and why she was late.

Kyle had been punctual, arriving at the diner's entrance at precisely 12:30. He'd walked from the Japan TV3 studio, a short stroll on a sunny April day. Spring was in bloom and it always rekindled Kyle's love for New York City. Once the summer heat kicked in with its humidity and its smells he would again think there were a number of places he'd rather live, but spring and fall reminded him what he loved about this place.

The restaurant was packed, as it always was for lunch. Kyle was led through the crowd to a booth and handed a menu by a hostess who seemed distracted, eyeing the customers, looking for the next empty table. No sooner had he sat down and started looking at the overstuffed menu than Linda arrived. He saw her. The two of them waved at each other and were soon hugging before Linda slid into the booth. They hadn't been together since the Pride Lodge murders. They spoke on the phone every few weeks, and emailed every other day, but no amount of virtual communication can take the place of being physically near those with whom we share our lives.

"I like the hair," he said, noticing immediately she'd let it grow out. He also noticed a touch of makeup, something Detective Linda had done without until recently. He made no comment on it, unsure if she would take his notice as compliment or criticism.

"It was Kirsten's idea," she said. "The makeup, too. Or maybe her influence. 'Idea' isn't accurate."

"I wish she would have come."

"Me, too," she said, holding out her hand to show Kyle the small but sparkling diamond on her finger. "It's a friendship ring, not quite at the engaged stage. It's one of the things I wanted to talk to you about."

Kyle smiled. He and Danny had worn rings since their first anniversary. Back then they couldn't marry in their home state of New York, but it had been important to both men to wear rings as a way of telling themselves, and the world, they were a couple. Kyle did not consider them engagement rings at this point, they were well past that, but he briefly wondered if they would get new rings when the time for a ceremony came, or just slip the ones they already had onto each other's fingers.

"I have things to talk to you about, too," Kyle said.

The waiter came over, in the harried way waiters in busy diners do, and held pen to pad for their order. Kyle told him they needed a few more minutes, and off he went for a more decisive table.

"Please don't tell me it's about murder."

"Yes, and no."

"I'm on vacation."

"Death doesn't take a holiday."

"No, but Linda Sikorsky does. And it is Linda Sikorsky, by the way. 'Detective Linda' will be no more in a few months."

"That's impossible," he said. "You'll always be Detective Linda, even if you're working in a car wash. Now what's this about?"

"I'm tired of police work," she said. "I want to do something different. Something I'm doing because I care about it, not because my father was gunned down by some thug when I was eight years old."

Kyle listened patiently. He wondered how much of this was Linda's decision, and how much had been suggested, subtly or overtly, by the new woman in her life.

"I became a cop because my dad was a cop. You know that, we've had that conversation before."

Indeed they had, that conversation and many more. Kyle was the first person Linda told about the real estate agent she'd met at a New Year's Eve party, a party just four months ago. But what could he say about moving too quickly? Kyle had essentially moved in with Danny sooner than that.

"You're not listening to me," Linda said, seeing the look on his face.

"Yes, yes, I am. You want to do something else, fair enough."

"I've wanted to own my own business for years," Linda went on. "A vintage store, like this one in Doylestown I love. They have everything there, just everything, and it's a very successful place. Jenny, the woman who owns it, has already agreed to be my mentor. And I have a name: *For Pete's Sake.*"

Kyle knew that Pete was her father's name. He started to comment that this wasn't quite the clean break she thought it was, then stopped himself.

"Wow," he said. "Friendship ring. Retiring from the police force – you are retiring, right? You're not walking away from a pension."

"Retiring. I've got my twenty years in come September."

"Good. Good."

"So okay," Linda said. "I'll give you this. Since I'll always be Detective Linda to you, what's your question."

"My question?"

"Murder. I know that's what you want to talk about."

"Right, well … it's two murders for sure, and one death, the cause of which remains undetermined, except that it was a subway train. How she got in front of it is a mystery."

"Ah, Kyle Callahan loves his mysteries," Linda said.

"I don't love them. I just feel compelled to solve them. I would be perfectly happy if no mystery ever presented itself."

"No, you wouldn't. If dead bodies didn't pop up, you'd go looking for them, and you know it."

The waiter came back, displaying some impatience this time, so they did him the favor of ordering lunch. He paid just enough attention to write the order down and scurried away.

With the waiter gone, Kyle said, "I was hoping I could convince you to do some sight seeing in Brooklyn this afternoon. Imogene's covering a town hall on the east side, then she's heading to Gracie Mansion for the mayor's press conference. She won't miss me."

"I wonder," Linda said. "Might Brooklyn be where one of these murders occurred?"

"I just want to ask around while the memories are still fresh. The news said no witnesses, but that's impossible in a city like this. People just don't always know what they saw. There's a coffee shop and an all-night laundry near where Devin – that's one of the victims – was killed. I scoped it all out online, easy to find, won't take long, and I could show you were I used to live in Carroll Gardens."

"I don't know, Kyle. You have a show opening on Friday, isn't that what you should be focused on?"

"I think stopping a killer is more important. If all these people are connected, there may be more to come. I can't take that chance."

She thought about it a moment. "Fine, it's been thirty-five years since I was in this city and I've never seen Brooklyn."

"Excellent," Kyle said. "Next stop Brooklyn."

With their afternoon plans set, the two of them caught up over lunch. Linda became more animated as she told Kyle about the woman in her life, her mother's reaction, what was different for her now that she had come out to her colleagues on the New Hope police force. It was as if they were continuing their last phone call, but this time with the added pleasure of seeing each other across a small diner table. For the next twenty minutes there was no talk of killers or motives, whys or whens or hows, just two friends cementing a relationship they both knew would last a lifetime.

CHAPTER 17

LUNCH AT THE STOPWATCH DINER (MEANWHILE)

Linus Hern disdained diners, and the Stopwatch was no exception, with its ridiculous watch theme and the cheesy racecar flags on the wall. It may well be at the top of the list, if he'd had any reason to keep a list of pedestrian, crowded, loud, cheap restaurants that barely earned the name. The city's "A" rating on the window was meaningless — falafel stands had them in New York City, *bars* for godsake, and who with any sense eats in bars? The same people who eat in diners, he thought, barely listening to the weasel lawyer sitting across from him. He didn't like Claude Petrie, but he found him useful. It was Linus's overriding criteria in his relations with other human beings: they were either useful to him, or they were not. Some had the potential to become useful; those who would never be had no claim to his attention, and got none.

"She only knows that Jay and Victor are kind-hearted investors with her best interest in mind," Petrie said, referring to the two men who had convinced Margaret Bowman to sell them the building and everything in it, including her restaurant.

"Second only to theirs," Linus said. "She's no fool, so be very careful, we've almost closed this deal. Do not underestimate her ability to see you for who you are, Claude. Don't go around too often, you might spoil the ruse."

Claude was once again fidgeting in the presence of the restaurateur. He knew condescension when it was being heaped upon him, not to mention contempt, but he had been in a tight spot for some time and was in no position to tell Linus Hern to drop dead. *Please, right now, in this tacky diner.*

"You know," Linus said, sipping his coffee, "I'm curious why you've been the Judas in this, why the betrayal."

Claude stared at his fork, keeping his gaze away from the man across the table. "I don't ... it's not really ... we're not friends, Margaret Bowman and I."

"So she doesn't know about your little gambling addiction. The one you'll be able to pay off when this is over, providing you don't just spend your generous fee at a poker table."

Claude's face flushed with embarrassment. The truth of what Linus had just said was painful for him. He'd had a gambling addiction for years and it had cost him dearly: his wife, his co-op on the Upper East Side, the affection of his two teenage daughters who lived with his mother and had been trained to think as poorly of him as she did. The old lawyer Evans, Margaret's attorney for decades, had not been the best judge of character. He had not seen through Claude. It was another source of shame for him, to be taking such egregious advantage of a favor done him by a dead man. But he owed nearly a hundred thousand dollars, much of it to people who would soon be asking for his life if he couldn't give them his money. Money he didn't have. Money Linus Hern was paying him to deceive and defraud the old woman who lived above the restaurant named after her.

"I just ..." Claude half-said, trying to regain his composure.

"Yes?"

"I just wondered, why you're so determined to get her out of that building."

"Oh, its not her," Linus said. "It's her restaurant. Specifically, the man who runs it."

"Danny Durban?"

"Yes, Danny Durban. The one and only."

Claude could see Linus's face darken, the lids of his eyes lower slightly as hatred slid over his face like a veil.

"What did he ever do to you? It must have been terrible."

"It was, Claude, terrible. But that's not your concern, is it?"

Claude had never seen Linus Hern taken by surprise; it was quite a sight, like watching a supremely confident man slip on the sidewalk and land in a puddle.

"Are we about through here?" Hern said briskly. "I think I just felt a cockroach run across my foot. When will she be signing?"

"I'd say another couple days, maybe a week."

"A week?" Linus said, displeased.

"She's asked me to have Tierney and Gossett meet with Durban."

Linus nearly choked, his face reddening in the time it took for Claude to say those names, names that should never have been spoke in the same sentence.

"No, no, no," he said. "That's not going to happen. When did she ask for this?"

"Just before I came here. It seems she told Danny Durban about the sale and she wants them to meet."

Linus was fuming now, in a most dangerous way, his anger tightly controlled. His left eye started to twitch, and he set his coffee cup down to hide the tremble in his hand.

"You've failed me, Claude."

"Excuse me?"

"I am about to, yes. This could ruin everything. I'll have to speak with Jay and Victor. They'll need to be coached, quickly. I don't think all is lost, but things are very much in jeopardy now. Not only is Danny Durban sharp, but he has motives of his own."

"But he loves the old woman."

"Precisely!" Linus hissed. "Love is the greatest, strongest, most driving motive of all. Why do you think I'm so determined to destroy him?"

Claude knew then that Linus had been deeply hurt, somehow, at some time, by Danny Durban. But the two of them, together? Claude couldn't see that in a million years. No, it was more complicated than that, more involved. And complicated could work to his advantage. Linus Hern wasn't the only one with leverage. His hatred of Danny Durban and his mission to harm him could be used very effectively in Claude's defense. All was not lost after all.

It was then, as Linus tried to calm himself and Claude schemed to safeguard his payment, that Kyle Callahan and Detective Linda Sikorsky made their way past them to the exit. Kyle glanced over and did a double-take, wondering why Margaret Bowman's lawyer would be having lunch with Linus Hern, and for that matter why Hern would be eating at a place like the Stopwatch. From everything Danny had told him, Hern would never be caught dead in a tourist trap diner. He made a quick mental note of the sighting and herded his visitor to the exit.

Linus Hern never saw Kyle pass by. He was too busy thinking how to keep his plans on track. His partners would have to meet with Durban, if that's what Margaret Bowman wanted, and they would have to keep the deception going. Just a few more days, it could be done.

"Stay calm," Linus said, wiping his mouth and setting his napkin down. He stood up from the table.

"That's it?" Claude squeaked. He was startled that Hern would simply get up, without any indication the meeting was over.

"Yes, and no, my dear attorney, although you would never be mine. If we succeed, you'll be able to pay your debts and have enough left over to start the entire sordid cycle anew. But if you fail," and he leaned down, speaking inches from Claude's face, "if this mission fails because you tipped our hand, or the sweat on your upper lip gave you away … well, Claude, I know some of the people who want their money back from you. It would be easy enough to tell them they won't be getting it."

Claude felt his throat go dry. Linus Hern did not make idle threats.

"Now, if you'll excuse me," Linus said, "and even if you won't. I've stayed in this rat's nest of a diner long enough. Don't call me again, Claude. I'll call you."

With that, the tall, dark, brooding man named Linus Hern strode out of the restaurant, his heart nearly as heavy as his determination for revenge. He left the check on the table for Claude Petrie to pay.

CHAPTER 18

BROOKLYN BOUND

The N train was among the more sprawling subway lines in New York City, spanning three boroughs from Queens, through Manhattan, and into Brooklyn all the way to Coney Island. It had held a place in Kyle's life since he first moved to New York. He had ridden this train from his longtime home in Carroll Gardens, Brooklyn, transferring from the F, for most of his working life in the City. And then for the last six years with Danny, the two of them rode it the opposite direction, into Astoria most Sundays for dinner with Danny's parents. It was also among the lines that were both underground and overhead, snaking up after a ride beneath the East River to travel along elevated tracks where it finally came to an end at Ditmars Boulevard. You could ride the N for well over an hour, and some people did: homeless men, women and the occasional child; curious tourists, the kind with backpacks and ragged, stained maps; cops, undercover cops, and the opportunistic thieves who could spot them through a crowd. It was one line among many in the spider's web of the New York City subway system, a marvel acknowledged to be among the best in the world. A public transportation miracle that was as easy to love as it was to hate.

Linda had never been in the subway. When she had visited Manhattan with her parents all those years ago they had taken taxis and walked. Her refusal to come to New York City meant she was as new to the subway experience as a child, or as the many people who visited this place with no desire to live here. She was trying to pay attention to Kyle, while marveling at the experience of riding the N train. They were on their way to Brooklyn, where the artist Devin had met his end last Friday night.

"I don't know what I expect to find," Kyle said, and he noticed Linda staring curiously at a street vendor transporting his entire shop rolled up and roped on a hand truck. "Detective Linda? Are you listening?"

"Yes, yes," she said, turning back in her seat to Kyle. "You don't know what you'll find but you're hoping to turn up something."

"Or someone, which would be better. There won't be anything to see but a sidewalk that's been washed clean for days. But there are a *lot* of people around there. There are a lot of people everywhere in New York City. Out in Astoria, where Danny's parents live, you can walk for six blocks and not pass anyone, but there are row houses along all those streets, apartment buildings, and for every one of them, eyes watching from the windows."

"Sixteen million."

"Pardon?"

"If you've got eight million people here, that's sixteen million eyes."

Kyle thought about it a moment. "God, that's creepy," he said, just as the train pulled into the Prospect Avenue station.

The street vendor tilted back his portable warehouse and off they all went, leaving the bowels of the subway for the afternoon sun.

Brooklyn has been around for over 350 years. Now one of New York City's five boroughs, it began as a small Dutch-owned settlement in the 17th century called "Breukelen." By the 19th Century it was a large, full fledged city of its own, and was consolidated into New York City in 1898. Were it still separate it would be the fourth largest city in the United States. As it is, many people who live in Brooklyn consider it a world apart from Manhattan. They live and love in enclaves like Prospect Park, Park Slope, Williamsburg, Brooklyn Heights, and Kyle's home for twenty-six years, Carroll Gardens. People who lived in the outer boroughs did not, by and large, regret living outside Manhattan; by the same token, most people in Manhattan considered it, and it alone, New York City, and places like Queens and the Bronx might as well be Iowa. Some of those attitudes had changed after 9/11, Kyle noticed. Something about having the World Trade Center destroyed, with all those lives falling out of the sky into a pile of rubble and dead souls, united the city in a way it had not been before. New York City now meant *New York City*, with all of its sprawl and mess, and many more people were clueing into the advantages of living "out there," where rents were lower (not cheaper – nothing is cheap here anymore) and entire lives could be lived without ever setting foot on the Island.

Kyle was thinking of how long it had been since he'd taken the train to Brooklyn. Could it really have been since he moved in with Danny five years ago? He wanted to think he would not have so completely abandoned his old home, but it was probably true. There wouldn't be any reason for him to come here.

"What are you thinking?" Linda asked as they walked toward the building Devin had lived in. Kyle wondered if someone was going through the dead man's belongings yet, who had loved him, whose lives would be forever changed because of his murder.

"Nothing, just how long it's been since I've come here."

Kyle stopped them in front of an apartment building. "It must have been here," he said. "Somewhere around here. I found his address, that was easy enough, and the news said he was killed just a few houses down from where he lived, toward the subway. So here, somewhere in here."

Kyle stopped and looked around him: apartment buildings as far as the eye could see. And in those apartments, thousands of eyes. But would any of them have seen the killing, or the killer, and would any of them say so?

Linda glanced across the street and saw the coffee shop Kyle had mentioned. Sacred Grounds had been around for a decade, surviving the Starbucks onslaught with the support of a fiercely loyal neighborhood. "Maybe we should start there," she said, pointing at the shop.

"I think we have to. We can't knock on people's doors. You can't even get to people's doors here, you have to ring buzzers."

They headed across the street to the coffee shop. Linda noticed, two doors from it, the Laundromat Kyle had told her about: Fluffy Foldy's. Did the clever names ever end, she wondered.

Sacred Grounds had needlessly underscored its name with religious icons and paraphernalia on the walls, but clearly done in a post-religion, ironic sort of way: there was nothing overtly religious or spiritual about the place or the people who worked here, but the owner had thought it a good idea to hang replicas of Catholic relics and a dizzying array of saints, gurus, martyrs, and the obligatory photos of Gandhi and Mother Teresa. All to be gazed at while sipping a cinnamon dusted soy cappuccino stirred with a mint biscotti.

There were three disinterested baristas on duty when Kyle and Linda walked in. Kyle walked up to the front counter and was immediately told by a short, acned late-teen with a prematurely shaved head and a look of millennial disdain that, "The line starts there." He pointed at a sign that said exactly that, but there was no one waiting in front of them. The only other customer was planted by the window with a laptop and a headset to eliminate the sound of other life forms.

Kyle was hoping for some information from the child so he obliged him, shuffling backward to the sign, then, upon receiving a smile of approval, walking the few steps back to the counter. Linda did the same thing, staying silent for now.

"I was hoping someone here was on duty last Friday night."

"You mean the night Devin was assassinated?" the barista said.

It was a strange choice of words, Kyle thought. "Yes, that Friday night."

"I told the cops everything I know already, which is nothing. I worked a double that day 'cause Pigpen has 'the flu' again, too much Tequila on Thursday night, and I was stuck here. It's not that busy on a rainy Friday, but busy enough that I didn't see anything, didn't hear anything, just saw it on the news the next day."

Linda leaned in, her hand on the counter. "So why would you say he was assassinated?"

"I have no idea why."

"She means, why would you use that word," Kyle said.

"Because it's Brooklyn, man! There's a government program to assassinate artists here, didn't you know that?"

"This is the first I've heard, thanks for sounding the alarm," Kyle said, wondering how such a delusional young man held down a job. "In the meantime, do you think your friends here saw anything?" He indicated the other two baristas who were multi-tasking with smartphones in one hand.

"Creamy and Soup?" the kid said, leaving Kyle to wonder if he'd spoken in code or those were their names.

"Yes. Creamy and Soup."

"Nah, they don't work nights, they're in school. Out to make something of themselves," he said derisively.

"Well, thanks for the information."

"What information?"

Kyle let it go at that and led Linda out of the coffee shop. Once outside, he said, "The kid's nuts."

"A diversity hire?" Linda said, smiling.

"Maybe. Like you!" and Kyle smiled, too. Linda's making homicide detective had been resisted by some on the New Hope police force who claimed she'd been hired just because she was a woman.

Kyle and Linda walked two doors down, turned in and found themselves at Fluffy Foldy's, the neighborhood Laundromat. Fluffy Foldy's matched its corny name with a corny interior, displaying photos, paintings, and one large mural of clowns. It seemed designed more for children than bored and impatient neighbors trying to get through one of life's most tedious chores.

There were a half dozen people in the place, several women of varying ages, one man Kyle pegged as gay the moment he saw him, and one old man who was sitting in a chair by the bathroom door, looking as if Fluffy Foldy's was his home during its hours of operation.

"So who are we looking for?" Linda asked.

"I don't know exactly. I doubt any of these people were here Friday night. It's too soon to be doing laundry again."

Kyle had begun to wonder what or whom he expected to find when he noticed a petite woman cleaning out a row of dryers. She was wearing the kind of mustard yellow uniform normally seen on hotel housekeepers. She was so short that he almost didn't see her as she bent into one of the large dryers and wiped it out with a cloth.

"Excuse me," Kyle said, heading over to her.

She pulled her upper body out of the massive dryer and turned to them suspiciously. Her hair was salt and pepper, heavy on the salt, and tied back in a long, thick ponytail. Her complexion was olive, Mediterranean, Kyle guessed, and she had intelligent, coal black eyes that he knew immediately missed nothing. She could be anywhere from forty to sixty; she had that kind of ageless look of some women of color who never seem to get older.

"Yes?" she said. "May I help you?"

"I'm hoping so," said Kyle. "What's your name?"

She stared at him with an expression that said her name was none of his business.

"This is Detective Linda Sikorsky," Kyle said, trying another tack. "We're investigating the murder that took place across the street last Friday."

Her eyebrow arched up – another policeman, this one a woman.

"My name is Yolanda," she said reluctantly. "I already gave a statement."

"Yes, yes," Kyle said, "and we are so appreciative of that. But Detective Sikorsky here just arrived from another jurisdiction, and, well, communication with the New York police has been slow. Could you just tell her what you told the other officers?"

Linda was impressed. Kyle had seen an opportunity to bend the truth to his advantage, with her in the middle, and had done it without a moment's thought.

"Just so we get our information in sync," Linda said to the woman. "A quick recap would be fine."

Yolanda thought about it for several long moments, and Kyle began to think she had seen through them. Then, she said, "I saw them. I was here that night. I'm always here. There is no one else."

"Oh, you own this establishment?" Linda asked.

Yolanda looked at her as if that was a preposterous idea. "No, I don't own it, I work here. Just me, and Willy who fixes the machines when they break. But he wasn't here. Just me. There is no one else."

"So what is it you saw, Yolanda?"

"I saw the dead man, he comes here to do his wash, or did, until … He was walking toward the building he lives in – I see everything – and then he stopped and turned around. It was raining, but I could see the other man, the one who hurt him. They spoke, like they knew each other."

Kyle wondered how that would be determined, but he knew this was a woman who had been observing people all her life. Watching how they move, where they go.

"Then the one man takes the hood off his face, but I can't see from here, and he limps up to the dead guy …"

"Limps?" Kyle asked.

"Yes, limps, but not like he was hurt, like he was born that way."

Kyle and Linda looked at each other. This was significant news. There was also something familiar about it to Kyle, but he couldn't think what at the moment. A tiny, faint bell had rung, and just as quickly gone silent.

"I have an aunt," Yolanda said, "She was born with a short leg. She walks like that."

Kyle felt his excitement rising. They had something as close to a description as they might find.

"The bad man goes up close to the dead one and … makes him dead. I was in shock. I called 911 but it was too late."

"Did you try to help him?" Linda asked.

It was the only time Yolanda looked away from them. She had not gone across the street, nor had she told the 911 dispatcher who she was, or that she was calling from the Laundromat.

"It was raining," she offered weakly. "I thought they were, you know, kissing. It happens a lot."

"Yes, of course," Kyle said, leaving her to deal with her guilt another time. "This has been very, very helpful, Yolanda." He pulled a business card out of his wallet and handed it to her.

She read it. "You're with a TV station?" she said, alarmed.

"Japanese," he said quickly. "Nothing local, it has nothing to do with this. Detective Sikorsky can vouch for that. We're just following up on the investigation, and we thank you, Yolanda, we thank you so much."

Kyle took Linda by the hand, something Yolanda noticed and thought odd for policemen, and led them out of the Laundromat. Standing on the sidewalk, with Yolanda staring at them from inside, Kyle said, "Finally something substantial."

"A limp."

"But not just a limp. Something congenital maybe, or an accident of some kind. And it sounds familiar."

"You know this guy?"

"No. Yes. I've seen him somewhere, but I see thousands of people every day! Maybe I saw him in the subway and it stuck in my mind."

He recalled the man watching from across the street at the Katherine Pride Gallery. He hadn't seen him walk, so he couldn't say if he limped, but something told Kyle it was the man they were looking for, and if that was the case, he was getting much closer.

"I want to talk to Kate Pride again," Kyle said as they walked toward the subway. "Olivette Washburn – I'll fill you in on the ride back – said something about Kate being good to know if you were the one she was promoting, something to that effect."

"And you're wondering who it was she did *not* promote."

"Yes. If she chooses who to have at the New Year New Visions show, she must choose who she leaves out."

"A grudge."

"A deadly grudge," Kyle said, as they headed down the platform stairs to the sound of a train pulling into the station.

CHAPTER 19

THE KATHERINE PRIDE GALLERY

Corky Richards was alone at the gallery that afternoon. Kate Pride had been there throughout most of the morning, but had left for a late lunch with her husband, Stuart. It was a treat she allowed herself when she felt that everything was in order, as she did today. Kyle's photos were ready for public viewing, the two rooms where they'd been hung blocked off with velvet rope until the Friday evening opening. That left only the parlor, as it was called, for the other work they were showcasing. It was a small room, although large enough for Corky to have imagined many times how it might look as a studio apartment. Anything much bigger than a shoebox would make a suitable apartment in Manhattan, something of which Corky was painfully aware. He was currently staying in a dump in Coney Island with his cousin Patrick, and the commute itself had him longing for the day when he could find some cozy eighth-floor walkup with a Murphy bed and a hot plate within walking distance of his job.

It was a job he'd only had for two months. Corky Richards was new to the city, having migrated from Las Vegas less than a year earlier. The son of a showgirl and one of her string of boyfriends – she never bothered finding out which one – Corky had hated the desert heat and the garish lights, the vice that permeated everything about Las Vegas. And while it was certainly gay friendly, it was no place for a man like Corky to find a suitable husband, whom he would skillfully balance with a career that headed only upward.

Was working the front desk at the Katherine Pride Gallery that career? No, but it aimed him in the right direction and put him in frequent contact with people he could step gently on as he made his way to the top. Some of the men even enjoyed being footstools.

He looked up at the sound of the bell ringing. Kate had not installed a door buzzer, the kind you have to buzz while waiting for someone to unlock the door. She considered it cold, and although this was an art gallery, nothing here was of great value. That was the whole point of the Katherine Pride Gallery: to launch those she found promising into the art world, where the next gallery would sell their work for much more. She was a talent scout, really, and a gambler. It didn't always pay off; some of the artists she had highlighted over the years had gone no further, while a few others had made good after their deaths from drug overdoses. And now Devin, of course, murdered. His works would immediately triple in value.

The man who entered the gallery did not at first look at Corky, but instead scanned the front room, the parlor, and the rope sectioning off the main gallery.

Corky, normally outgoing to a fault, chipper and always looking to network, remained unusually silent. Something about the man did not invite conversation. Part of it was the way he walked, with a shuffling limp that made Corky think not of a deadened foot but of a broken axle; part of it was his expressionless face, flat, almost reptilian, but very handsome. Corky was perplexed by the incongruity: a man with one leg that appeared to be twisted, walking as if his hips were out of alignment, yet the man himself was fit, good looking, even hot. Corky felt himself flush, and that thought, that annoying thought that flitted into his mind every time he saw a good looking man alone, buzzed into his head: Might this be the one?

"Good morning," Kieran said, walking up to the desk, still looking everywhere but at Corky.

"Good afternoon," Corky replied. He was strangely nervous, and he had the uncomfortable sensation of being exposed, even though the man appeared to deliberately not look at him.

"Yes, it is afternoon, isn't it? I stand corrected."

"I wasn't correcting you, that's not what I meant."

"No, I doubt you were." Kieran gazed at the roped off rooms. "It appears you've got something planned. An opening?"

"The rope, oh, yes. There's an opening Friday night. A photographer."

"A photographer."

"But we still have pieces available," Corky said, motioning toward the parlor. "We're not closed. What are you looking for?"

Kieran sighed, thinking a long moment. Finally he turned and looked at Corky. "Do you have anything by Devin? I think that's his name. Or Morninglight? Richard Morninglight?"

"Morninglight," Corky said, and he suddenly believed he knew the man's game. Obviously he was a buyer who read about the murders and was hoping to snap up something before the prices soared. What artist has ever been worth more alive than dead?

"We don't currently have anything of Devin's. We may never, actually. It's not like we're the executor of his estate."

"Oh," Kieran said, frowning. "Is he dead?"

Corky was confused, but only for a moment. He now thought the man was toying with him for some reason. You don't live to be a twenty-seven year old gay man, grown up in Las Vegas and now living in Coney Island, without knowing the games people play.

"Listen …"

"How about something by Katherine Pride?" Kieran said. "Or isn't she dead yet?"

Corky felt the hairs on his neck rise. Something was wrong here, very wrong. "Kate's not an artist," he said.

"Does she have to be?"

Corky quickly rose from his chair. "I'm about to close up for lunch."

"So late? You must be starving."

"Yeah, well, I lose track sometimes."

"I'm sure you do. We all do."

"If there's nothing else …"

"Oh, but there is, there is," Kieran said, smiling again. The smile made Corky nearly crumple. He wanted to be away from this man as soon as possible.

"I was hoping to speak with Katherine."

"Kate."

"If she prefers. Kate. Will she be here anytime soon?"

"Um, no, I'm sorry, she's out with … the police, she's having lunch with some friends from the police force, they come here all the time. They keep an eye on the place."

Kieran turned and looked out the windows. "So they might be watching us right now?"

"I'm sure of it. By the way, I didn't get your name."

"That's okay," Kieran said, and he began to walk toward the door. "I'll give it to Kate myself."

Please, please let him leave, Corky thought, in as close to a prayer as he ever came.

Kieran turned back just as he reached the door. "We'll see you at the opening," he said. "You will the there, won't you?"

"Maybe. Listen, I have a boyfriend," Corky lied.

"As well you should, Corky. A young man as sharp as you, as fearless, really, I'd say the sky's the limit."

With that he turned back and left the gallery.

It took a moment after the door closed for Corky to feel himself relax. He hurried to the door and locked it, flipping around the hanging sign that said, "Back in 30 minutes!" He sat back down behind the desk and let his breathing slowly return to normal. It was only when he felt like himself again, a good five minutes after the man had left, that he realized he had addressed him by name. *"As well you should, Corky."* But Corky had never offered his name.

The chill returned, and Corky sat for a long while rubbing his arms, trying to get the warmth back. What was that old nonsense his mother always said when he felt a chill? "Someone just walked over your grave." For the first time in his life he believed her.

CHAPTER 20

APARTMENT 5G

Kyle was in the kitchen preparing dinner for the three of them. Linda was staying in a hotel, which was fine with Kyle since it meant he wouldn't have anyone in the spare room until his mother arrived on Friday. Sally Callahan was usually the only guest they had during the year, but when anyone used the room Kyle would have to forego his morning ritual of working on his photography and scanning the Internet so as not to disturb them.

Linda was in the living room, talking on their landline to her new love, Kirsten. Kyle could hear her chattering away about her visit so far, their lunch at the Stopwatch, and the plans for the big opening night that Friday. She had not offered to have Kyle or Danny speak to Kirsten just yet, but Kyle suspected they would meet soon, and he wanted to. He would never dissuade Linda from being in a relationship, and he trusted her judgment, but he wanted to meet Kirsten as soon as possible, given she would become part of their extended family. Perhaps he and Danny would make a trip to New Hope in the summer, though not likely staying at Pride Lodge. As much as he wished them continued success, he would always associate the Lodge with the murder of his friend, Teddy Pembroke.

"You ready for the big night?" Danny asked.

Kyle jumped, sending speckles of spaghetti sauce across the stovetop. He'd been lost in his thoughts and hadn't heard Danny come into the kitchen.

"Well … yes and no," Kyle said, quickly recovering. "I didn't want all this attention, you know."

"Of course you did. You take great photographs, Kyle. You wanted people to see them."

"They're on the Internet, anyone can see them!"

"I mean professionally. Artistically. The Katherine Pride Gallery is a big deal, and Kate would never be doing this if she didn't believe in you."

"Speaking of the gallery," Kyle said, about to bring up the dots he'd been connecting since his trip to Brooklyn.

"There's something I wanted to discuss," Danny said, interrupting him.

Kyle felt his heart sink. Danny did not often have things to discuss, and they were usually of a serious nature. Otherwise, they simply talked about things. "Discussing" them was on a deeper level, something reserved for grownups who needed to be very mature for the next few minutes. His immediate assumption was that something was wrong with Smelly. The vet would have called that day with the results of whatever tests they always insisted on doing. Was she sick? Terminally ill? He put the spoon down in a dish on the counter and turned to Danny. They could hear Linda on the phone in the living room, as alive as anyone newly in love.

"It's Margaret's," Danny said.

Kyle thought he said "Margaret" and that he was about to hear terrible news for the old woman they both loved.

"Is she alright?"

"She's fine," Danny said, realizing Kyle's misunderstanding. "Not 'Margaret.' Margaret's Passion, the restaurant." He took a deep breath. "I want to buy it."

Kyle didn't quite get what Danny was saying. He leaned back against the counter and waited for more explanation.

"She's in financial trouble. It's a very long story, but she lost all her money with that swindler who's been in the news."

"The Effron woman?"

"Yes, yes, Bride of Madoff and all that."

"Margaret Bowman lost her money? But she's so smart!"

"Smart has nothing to do with it," Danny said. "And it's beside the point. She lost her money, that's that. She's about to sell the building to these men, I've never met them but she's asked to arrange it. They're connected to Claude Petrie somehow."

"Claude?" Kyle remembered having seen him at the Stopwatch that afternoon.

"Listen to me, Kyle, there will be plenty of time for questions later. I just can't let this happen. Now I know we can't buy the building, but we could buy the restaurant. It would be enough to get her through, she's in her eighties for godsake."

"How much?"

"Do you love me?" Danny said. He slid up next to Kyle and put his arm around him.

"How much, Danny?"

"Five hundred thousand."

Kyle would have choked if he'd had anything to choke on. He heard the sauce bubbling on the stove, turned away from Danny and lowered the heat. He needed that moment to think of a response.

"We don't have that kind of money," he said quietly, knowing this is not what Danny wanted to hear.

"We can come up with half, I know that."

"That's our retirement money!"

"That we'll still have," Danny said. "It just won't be sitting in IRAs and 401(k)s. We'll see what it looks like, invested in one of the most reliable, loved, successful restaurants south of Central Park."

"Yeah, well," Kyle said, not convinced. "Where is the other half coming from?"

"Excuse me?" Danny said, having heard him perfectly well.

"The other half, Danny, where is it coming from?"

Danny grew quiet, weighing his words. "We have a visitor coming this Friday …"

"You want to go into business with my mother! Are you out of your mind?"

"Not go into business," Danny said quickly.

"Everything all right in there?" Linda shouted, having heard the surprise in Kyle's voice.

"Fine," Danny shouted back, "We're fine. Tell Kirsten she can't let you come alone next time."

Kyle lowered the heat on the sauce and kept stirring, gazing into the pot.

"It's a loan," Danny said. "A silent partnership."

"Margaret won't let us borrow money from my mother to save her."

"Margaret doesn't have to know."

Kyle thought about it, stirring and stirring. Finally he turned the flame off. "We can ask her," he said, both resigned to it and dreading the prospect. He already knew she would say yes, but being indebted to his mother was not something Kyle ever imagined happening at fifty-five, and anyone who thought she would be a silent partner didn't know Sally Callahan. The only time she had ever been silent was the last few weeks when she refused to tell Kyle what it was she wanted to talk about. Now they would both have news.

"You might want to contact Claude if this deal is something you need to stop," Kyle said.

"I'll call him first thing in the morning. Margaret already reached out to him. She hasn't signed anything yet."

"Speaking of which, I ran into him at the diner. Not really ran into him, he didn't see us, but we passed his table. He was having lunch with Linus Hern."

Danny, who had relaxed after getting the hard part over with, was suddenly suspicious. "Linus?" he said. "I wouldn't have thought they even knew each other."

"They seemed to know each other well enough."

Danny filed the information away in the back of his mind, where he could turn it around over and over through the night: Linus Hern having lunch with Claude Petrie. Claude being Margaret's new attorney. What did Margaret know about him, really? Only what her trusted attorney Evan

Evans had told her, and even someone as world-wise as Evans could be fooled.

Just then Linda called them from the living room. "Kyle, Danny! Come, come, I want you to say hello to Kirsten."

Kyle turned the burners off and the two of them headed to the couch, where Linda was holding out the phone.

"Who wants to be first?" she said.

Kyle and Danny exchanged looks, then Kyle shrugged and took the phone.

"Kirsten," he said, "We meet at last."

Kyle glanced at the digital clock on the nightstand: 11:30 p.m. He and Danny had engaged in one of their infrequent but luxurious rounds of sex, beginning with mutual massages. Neither of them had ever been highly sexed, and the comfortable sexual routine that many couples settle into after being together for years was workable for them. It made their sex life something to be savored, an expression of intimacy rather than frenzy.

Despite their weeknight sex, sleep had not come easily for either of them. Danny had been disturbed by the news of Claude Petrie having lunch with Linus Hern. It made no sense, yet the more he thought about it, the more it made perfect sense. He had wondered where these men came from, only a signature away from owning Margaret's building. He knew altruism was never a motive in business, and whatever promises they made could be broken with the right sleight of hand. And now, a connection to Linus. But for what? Was Linus Hern the man behind the curtain? There were many questions to pose, and Danny had every intention of getting answers to them. He managed to fall asleep thinking of a visit he would make to Claude Petrie in the morning.

Kyle stared at the digital clock and sighed, wondering if he would be able to drift off as well. He had his own obsessions, his own puzzle. He kept turning the pieces round and round in his mind: two dead artists and a dead graphic designer. Two clear murders and a third likely one. All of them connected to the Katherine Pride Gallery. And the man with the limp, who was he? It kept flitting about in his head. A glimpse of someone, a conversation overheard. He knew it centered on the New Visions show. He and Danny had gone to the opening. It was during the show that Kate Pride had begun to pressure Kyle to have an exhibit of his own. Something small, she'd said. Just his work, not like New Visions, which highlighted a half dozen up-and-comers. The deaths were of people who had all been involved in that show. Were they being targeted? Were there deaths Kyle didn't know about? A list?

Feeling like he was onto something, Kyle quietly swung his feet off the bed, careful not to wake up Danny. Leonard, who slept between them, quickly uncurled and leapt to the floor, thinking Kyle was going to feed him, while Smelly just raised her head from the floor pillow she kept as a throne, glanced his way, and went back to sleep.

He'd put the show catalog back with the other books in the spare room. Flipping the light on, he hurried to the shelf. He'd been thinking too narrowly, only trying to identify Shiree Leone, the catalog designer. Now he realized the 20-page booklet contained the answers for it all: each death was connected to this particular show at the Katherine Pride Gallery. There had been six artists shown. Two of them were dead. Could this killer have them all in his sights? And was he one of the names left off, feeling his dreams thwarted by an arrogant art gallery owner who couldn't see his brilliance?

Kyle sat at his desk and flipped open the catalog. Leonard was at his feet, demanding tribute. Kyle absent-mindedly reached across his desk with his free hand, grabbed a few kitty snacks and dropped them on the floor. He ignored Leonard's pounce as he ran down the biographies of the artists: Devin, Richard Morninglight, Suzanne DePris, Javier Velasco, and a graffiti artist duo named Little Bit and Winter. He could check off Devin and Morninglight, they were dead. He'd have to quickly find out the status of the others. If they were alive, he could warn them. If they weren't, then his thesis would prove correct.

He needed help. With his job, and the show opening in a few days, his mother coming to town, he couldn't possibly accomplish everything by himself. He was going to call Detective Linda Sikorsky as soon as the hour was reasonable. She would have the rest of her life to run a vintage second-hand store and be happily married in New Hope. Right now there was a killer in Manhattan who was getting closer and closer, and the Katherine Pride Gallery was his bulls-eye.

CHAPTER 21

HOTEL EXETER, HELL'S KITCHEN

Kieran could see the massive, collective light of the city reflected in the clouds as he lay on the mattress staring out the grimy hotel window. Sleep was beyond him, a memory of something that had once been pleasant but had turned on him the last few months. Sleep was now dreaded almost as much as the dreams that came with it.

He stared up into the dark haze that hovered permanently over Manhattan once the sun had fled. New York City produced so much whiteness in the night sky he doubted anyone here had seen a star in years. The billions of tiny fires in the heavens could not hope to compete with the overpowering glare of neon, streetlight and a million apartments rising floor upon floor, their combined incandescence smothering the shine of God Himself. He knew how God must feel, too, overshadowed and forgotten. They were two of a kind, he and God. The difference, he supposed, was that he had no intention of slinking away to hide his impotence behind mystery. Kieran would not content himself with unanswered prayers from the vain and selfish. He would instead exact revenge and leave his name engraved with the great ones. All of New York City, and soon all the nation, would know his name. What the whisperers would make of him then wouldn't matter. They would be dead.

He listened as muffled sounds of violence echoed through the old hotel. In the month he had been living here he had witnessed little, but heard much. Groans of sex, shouts of rage, the occasional thud he assumed was a falling body. The police did not seem to care much what happened at the Exeter. They only showed up when someone was dead on arrival – or departure, as the case may be – otherwise leaving the denizens of the place to fend for, and devour, themselves. Junkies, drunkards, prostitutes and pimps, all roamed the halls here like living ghosts. They looked right through him, just as he considered them no more meaningful than the roaches he ignored crawling across his floor. The roaches would outlive them all and deserved more respect.

He would be glad to leave this place soon. Its decrepitude had begun to seep into his bones. He was used to the smells in his clothes, in the walls, in the people shuffling up and down the stairs when the elevator was broken, which was often, but there was another smell beneath them, the smell of failure, that he did not want clinging to him much longer. He had not failed; he had in fact succeeded most spectacularly. But if you stand in shit long enough, you will smell like it, and he wanted to be finished and gone before it could not be washed off.

Kieran watched in silence another hour as the sun began to come back, slowly pushing out the darkness. He liked the sun. Sometimes he believed he was the sun, so brightly did he shine. He and the sun together would chase the blackness from the sky and from his mind. Only his heart was out there beyond the edges of the void, broken and scattered and beyond healing. This suited him fine. He needed to be heartless now. Thinking on it, he rolled over, away from the window, and closed his eyes. The day had arrived and it was time to plan.

CHAPTER 22

SUNRISE ON 8ᵀᴴ AVENUE

Kyle and Linda met for breakfast at the Sunrise Café in Chelsea, tucked between one of the ubiquitous nail salons that peppered the city and a neighborhood pet shop called Animal Nation that had weathered the neighborhood's changes for forty years. Chelsea had been known for half that time as a gay enclave, like San Francisco's Castro or Chicago's Boystown. It came about because the place had once been cheap, and bohemian types who could not afford Greenwich Village moved uptown just a few blocks to the once-industrialized Chelsea.

Chelsea took its name from the estate and house of retired British Major Thomas Clarke, who obtained the property in 1750. In time, factories arose in Chelsea, and the neighborhood still bears its working class roots; many of the buildings now housing million-dollar condos and impossibly high-end co-ops were once textile factories and 19th century sweat shops. By the 1970s the area had fallen on hard times ... and along came gay people to begin its gentrification. As is the case with changing tides, they were being overrun and priced out by young couples with children, and Chelsea was now a mix with a decidedly healthy dose of gay, but a mix nonetheless.

The Sunrise was one of Kyle's favorite restaurants. It had only been in existence for nine months. Judging from the empty booths it may not make it another nine, but he loved the interior, with its exposed brick walls, the two old hutches they used to hold dishes, the slowly rotating ceiling fans. It had a rustic feel to it, as did the staff: older, with a whiff of country about them that made them seem out of place, yet very much at home, in the heart of one of Manhattan's most trendy districts. One of the waitresses, a buxom woman in her sixties wearing a white apron around her waist, had just taken their breakfast order and left with the menus.

Kyle had brought the catalog from the New Visions show with him and was running his fingers over the cover. "It's in here," he said. "The answers."

Linda had not complained about having her first visit to New York in thirty-five years turned into a hunt for a killer. She'd admitted to herself the first day that she didn't know what she wanted to see here, and had done nothing to prepare – no maps, no itinerary, no places of interest. Kirsten had encouraged her to lay it all out, or at least make a short list of sights to see, but Linda had told her no, she wanted to explore, to see it all before her as if she'd stepped into a wonderland and would decide to go left or right once the road was in front of her. But here she was in a café with Kyle Callahan, the two of them puzzling over a series of murders. Kyle and Detective Linda, an unlikely pair. She knew this is what she would rather be doing. She was not a sightseer, a shopper, a *tourist*. Maybe that would change when she and Kirsten went places, as they surely would. Paris had always been on her mind, and she'd never been west of the Mississippi. So many places to see, all the more reason not to think she had to spend her few days here running from building to building, must-see to must-see. She lived only two hours from here; those places could wait.

"What are you thinking?" she said, sipping the especially rich coffee the Sunrise served up.

"I'm thinking it's someone we won't find in this book."

She looked at him, puzzled.

"Someone who wanted to be," he explained, "but who was left out. Someone who missed the train to fame they think this is."

"And it's not?"

"For some, yes, but for just as many, no. To tell you the truth, Detective Linda, I don't aspire to be more than an amateur photographer. The show

Friday is great, don't get me wrong, but it's not going to make me famous, and I don't want it to. But a lot of these artists" – and he tapped the catalog again – "this is how they measure their success, their value. It's who they are, and being left out, being rejected, is probably as life-changing as being in the show."

The waitress returned with their breakfast, each of them having three-egg omelets, toast and potatoes, set it in front of them and quickly left, realizing they were mid-conversation.

"I have to go to a luncheon with Imogene," Kyle said, as he slid his plate away and opened the catalog. "I need you to do two things. You're in on this with me, yes?"

Linda nodded, trying to look reluctant but knowing from the first words Kyle mentioned of a killer she'd be hooked.

"Good. I emailed Kate already and she's expecting you at the gallery. Two things: one, what became of the other artists in the show. Their names are here." Kyle quickly pointed out the names of the graffiti duo, the woman Suzanne DePris, and Javier Velasco. "And two ..."

"Whose names are *not* there."

"Exactly."

"Notice the plural, Kyle. 'Names.' What if we're looking at several people here? What if Kate Pride turned down a dozen?"

"We'll worry about that if it's true," Kyle said, closing the catalog.

Kyle looked at his watch and began to eat. He was running late again, but he knew Imogene wouldn't notice today. She was being honored at a luncheon at the Carlton Suites Hotel, a big deal for someone whose career had been on the wane just six months ago. She'd be consumed with how she looked and what she would say, should she find herself at a podium.

"Have you thought about women?" Linda asked, setting her toast aside.

"Not since ... ever, really," Kyle replied.

"Not like that, silly! I mean for the killer. Isn't it a little misogynistic to assume a man is doing this?"

"I don't think Richard Morninglight would make a sex date with a woman."

"What if he didn't know?"

Kyle was intrigued, but not convinced. The murders were too brutal, too personal. They had all the hallmarks of a very angry man. "One step at time. Let's narrow down the possibilities and see what's left."

Linda nodded. Her visit to New York City was turning out to be more than she'd imagined. It also reminded her of the things she loved most. Did she really want to walk away from the police force? Or could she do both? Could she run a store named after her father, *and* be Detective Linda? And what would Kirsten make of all this when she told her? So many thoughts turning around in her mind. She would have to shut them off and focus. Twenty minutes from now she'd be at the Katherine Pride Gallery, looking for answers and needing to think clearly.

"When do we get the police involved?" she said at last.

"They already are," Kyle said. "They bark up their tree, we bark up ours."

He winked at her then, not something that came naturally. His father had been a winker, and Kyle had no idea why he'd done it. Maybe his mother, and whatever she had to tell him – mercifully forgotten in the chase – had made him think of his father.

Kyle waved at the waitress for the check. "You finish," he said, seeing that Linda was barely halfway through her breakfast. "I'll get breakfast, you get yourself to the Katherine Pride Gallery. We'll meet after the luncheon. I'll text you the address."

Before she could say anything, Kyle took the check and hurried out. It wasn't being late he dreaded, but the list of things he knew Imogene would already be asking for. Timing was everything, and the timing right now could not be worse.

CHAPTER 23

CLAUDE PETRIE, ESQ.

Claude Petrie's office was at the very top of the stairs in a fifth floor walkup on 41st Street a half block from the Port Authority bus terminal. The entire building smelled like exhaust from buses rolling in from the Lincoln Tunnel, endless lines of them that never seemed to stop. And if you stood on the fire escape, craned your neck out and looked south, you could see the Hotel Exeter. You could also fall to your death, as one burglar did two years ago when she slipped on the ice that had built up on the landing. Her body had gone unnoticed for two weeks; that's how long it took for the smell of decomposition to be stronger than the small of bus fumes.

To the right of Petrie's door, which had *Claude Petrie, Esq.* stenciled on it in chipped black letters, was a dentist who catered to Guatemalans and, to the left, an escort service whose escorts were sometimes seen but rarely heard. Young men for whom wages had remained flat over the last decade and whose appearance reflected the decreasing standards of the service that employed them. Claude had been careful, when under the tutelage of Evan Evans, never to meet here, lest they encounter one of the "models" or overhear an argument about compensation. His relationship with the old gentleman had begun as a favor to Claude's late father, who, like Margaret Bowmen, had retained Evans for many years. Noah Petrie had no idea his son moved in such seedy circles, and Claude had made sure it stayed that way until Noah's death, and Evans's three years later. It wasn't that

Claude would not prefer an office on Central Park South or somewhere in TriBeCa, but this is what he could afford, and most of his clients were quite at home in this environment.

Danny stood outside the door wondering how long ago Petrie's name had been painted on it and if he would ever have it refreshed. He'd seen a short man who looked to be of Central American stock leaving the dentist's office with an ice pack held to his face, listening while an older woman hectored him as they walked down the stairs. Danny checked the business card Margaret had given him. While he was obviously in the right place, it just didn't seem like somewhere old Evan Evans would have spent time. Danny assumed Claude Petrie did the visiting.

After pressing the door buzzer and waiting several seconds, Danny was greeted by Claude himself. There was no receptionist, no receptionist's desk, and no one else in the office, which proved to be one room. A desk was in one corner by a window that hadn't been washed in thirty years. Behind it, a swivel chair that looked to be among the first manufactured. On the desk were stacks of manila folders, pieces of paper, two staplers, a phone, and a coffee cup being used to hold pens and pencils. Two guest chairs were in front of the desk; Claude motioned to them as he welcomed Danny in.

"Mr. Durban," Claude said, shaking Danny's hand. "I would have been happy to meet you at the restaurant."

"I enjoyed the walk," Danny said, in way of an indirect reply. "Gramercy Park to here, it's a good half hour in foot traffic."

"Indeed, indeed. Please, have a seat."

Danny sat in front of the desk and waited for Claude to take his place behind it. A long, awkward moment ensued as Claude leaned forward, his elbows on the desk, his hands clasped together, waiting for Danny to speak.

"I'm going to buy Margaret's Passion," Danny said finally and in a tone that did not make it a suggestion.

Claude looked at him a moment, then smiled. "I'm sorry, Mr. Durban, but that's already been arranged with Mrs. Bowman. I just have to take her the papers."

"She won't be signing them."

"I don't understand."

"It's not complicated." Danny leaned forward, close enough to make Claude uncomfortable. He pulled back from Danny, nearly sliding backward in his chair.

"I know who your investors are," Danny continued. "At least the one who matters, the one I'm sure is calling the shots. The one you're going to arrange a meeting with, for me, as a surprise. Linus Hern doesn't like surprises, this should be fun."

Claude had gone pale. He slumped in his chair, and even though the office was cool from the spring air coming in its one window, he had begun to perspire.

"I don't know where you're getting your information," he said, "but my investors' names are – "

"It doesn't matter who they are," Danny interrupted. "It matters who they're working for. We both know it's Hern, so we can stop this little game of cat and mouse, Claude. May I call you Claude? I'm the cat here, make no mistake about it. Margaret doesn't yet know what you've done or who you've done it with. I'd rather not tell her, it could do serious damage to your career, such as it is."

Claude had slipped into full panic mode. Margaret Bowman was very well known in this town, and very well liked. She could most certainly make his life more difficult than it already was. He flashed on himself being smeared in the daily papers.

"What is it you want?" he asked Danny.

"I want you to arrange a meeting with Linus, without telling him he'll be meeting me. This afternoon is fine, say … one o'clock? I can get Chloe to cover while I take my leave from the restaurant early. You know Chloe. She certainly knows you. Just tell Linus you have very important news about the deal with Margaret's Passion and you'll meet him at the Stopwatch for lunch."

Claude's eyes widened. How could this man know about the Stopwatch?

"He doesn't like it there," Claude stammered.

Danny smiled. "I'm sure he doesn't. So one o'clock it is. And the second thing, Claude, is that you'll be telling Margaret Bowman in a letter you won't be able to continue as her attorney. Very sorry and all that, but your workload has gotten just too much. An abundance of riches."

Claude almost laughed at the barb. He wasn't about to tell Danny Durban about his gambling debts or the shambles he'd made of his life. He knew that Linus Hern, too, could make things worse for him. He suddenly started thinking of places to go, destinations on a train route where he could stop anywhere and simply vanish. It was coming to that.

Danny stood up. "Don't worry about the contract with Margaret. My partner Kyle, his mother and I will be seeing another solicitor about that, but we appreciate the offer."

They hadn't yet spoken to Sally Callahan about investing in the restaurant, but Claude didn't know that, and Danny hoped by saying it he could make it so. He stood from the guest chair, declining to shake hands a second time.

"Good day now, Claude. I'll expect to see Linus at one o'clock this afternoon. I know he's very punctual. Not from experience, just from his character. Evil is always on time."

Danny knew he would never see Claude Petrie again and was glad of it. He showed himself out of the office, leaving Claude to wipe at the sweat running down his forehead. Much in both their lives had just changed.

CHAPTER 24

TOKYO PULSE

"**I haven't been** in the top fifty in five years," Imogene said. "I'll take forty-seven. This is progress."

Imogene, Kyle and Lenny-san were gathered around Imogene's desk while she fretted over the luncheon she and Kyle were attending. It was an annual event recognizing the best of New York women in media. There had been a time in her career when she would have been in the top ten, seated near the lectern and busy signing autographs outside the banquet room, but those days were long gone. She hadn't even attended the luncheon for the past three years. She'd grown tired of being asked who she was and if she could please provide identification.

"Who's forty-six?" Lenny-san asked. "Probably that cow from Wander Women, what's her name?"

"Corrine," Kyle said, naming the woman who had managed to start a successful YouTube channel featuring New York women's travel stories. "Corrine Bradlaw."

Imogene started to say she remembered Corrine when she was just an intern at the local ABC affiliate where Imogene sat at the weekend anchor desk, then she realized it would date her and left it unsaid.

"It doesn't matter who's number forty-six, forty-eight, or number one, really, we're all in this together. Is that what you're wearing?"

Kyle looked down at himself, sitting in his chair. He'd worn his usual work clothes: khaki slacks, a button-down shirt with the sleeves rolled up above his wrists. "No," he said. "I have a suit in the closet for these things."

"Thank God. You're my assistant, Kyle, appearances matter."

Lenny-san nodded, knowing all too well the truth of it. At sixty, he appeared to be what he was: the manager for an obscure, often cheesy, Japanese cable show that prided itself on including segments from America, produced as cheaply as possible. He also appeared to be forty pounds over-weight, short of breath after walking across a room, and in need of a good teeth whitener. Leonard Baumstein had been in the business even longer than Imogene Landis. Their paths crossed often over the years but he had never expected to be her boss, which in this case meant joining her near the bottom of the media barrel. He considered himself a short timer now, with only two more years until he could start collecting social security to supplement his various 401(k)s. Then he could take a cruise every summer and spend his days reading autobiographies. Life at the bottom could be good, or at least good enough for Leonard Baumstein.

"I gotta make some calls," Lenny-san said. "You look great, Imogene. And congratulations. You get, what, a plaque or something?"

"A certificate. Without a frame. These bitches are cheap."

"Well, if anyone deserves a certificate without a frame, it's you," he said, and he turned and headed into his tiny office.

"I might have a story for you after all," Kyle said when Lenny-san was gone. His tip on the Pride Lodge murders had resurrected her career and gotten her off a financial beat she hated. It was the story that all late-night Tokyo had talked about for a month, and was entirely responsible for her making her number forty-seven out of fifty named in today's event program.

"More murders I hope," she said. Then, realizing the insensitivity of it, "As long as no one gets hurt, of course!"

"Of course. No one gets hurt, just killed. Don't worry, dead people don't care what you say about them. But I get it. It goes with this business.

I've run into that with my photography, finding myself in the position to taking a photo of something I think I shouldn't."

"Like that guy who got a shot of the man on the subway tracks, just before the train hit him. Gruesome. But great front page."

"Yes, like that. It's a fine line sometimes. I felt bad about poor Teddy dead at Pride Lodge, but he was gone and someone was going to tell the story."

"So what's the big mystery this time?" She swiveled around in her chair to face him.

"I'm not sure yet, but several people connected to the Katherine Pride Gallery have been killed, and more may be on the way. Which reminds me, I need to make a call."

He took his cell phone and stood up. He had a landline but making personal calls in an office cubicle always made him self-conscious. Everyone pretended not to be listening when they were.

"I'm looking forward to your opening Friday," Imogene said. "Lenny-san caved, I'm doing it as a gritty art world after dark piece. The Tokyo audience won't know there's nothing gritty about New York anymore."

Kyle felt his stomach lurch. He had hoped Imogene would abandon the idea of covering his exhibit. It wasn't news, and the Tokyo kids who so enjoyed laughing at Imogene (something she had never been told but that Kyle knew was among the show's main attractions) would probably find it pointless. But he loved Imogene and Imogene loved him, and she had dogged their boss to do a short piece about the gallery show. Now she thought it might tie into some murders and get her another salary bump, maybe even a better offer.

Kyle excused himself and walked into the station's kitchen. It was barely large enough to hold a table with six chairs, a microwave, and the Keurig machine Kyle had bought with his own money. He was a K-cup fanatic and even traveled with their least expensive model. The kitchen was usually empty mid-morning. He walked over to the window where he could look west toward the Hudson and called the familiar number on his speed dial.

"Linda here," the voice said, answering on the second ring. "You need to unblock your phone, Kyle. You're one of only two people I know who still has a blocked phone. It might as well read 'Kyle Callahan' when you call."

"I'll get around to it," he said. "In the meantime …"

"In the meantime I'm waiting, Kate's running late, it's just me and the desk guy."

He heard Corky correct her in the background.

"Corky," she said, "more than a desk guy, very available for the right suitor. Does anyone say 'suitor' anymore?"

Kyle could imagine her rolling her eyes as she said it. "Listen," he said, "I just thought of something else."

"The limp."

"Yes! How did you know? And please don't say 'elementary.'"

"It just makes sense. Maybe she turned down a dozen people for the show, but I'd bet only one of them walked funny."

Kyle heard more chatter from Corky.

"Oh, sorry. I'm told I shouldn't say 'walked funny.' People who walk funny might be offended."

Kyle smiled. He knew there were things about living in a culturally sensitive world Linda needed to learn, or that, being Detective Linda, she might reject out of hand, like fretting about language when lives were at stake.

"I'll remember to ask about the man who walks differently," she said, "and soon. Kate just pulled up in a taxi."

"I'll let you go then. No phone calls until the lunch is over, but text me, I'll keep it on vibrate. Meet me outside the Carlton Suites at 2:00. If it's not over by then I'll leave anyway."

Kyle clicked off, wishing he could be there with her. The last place he wanted to be was a luncheon listening to Imogene whisper criticisms of the forty-six women ahead of her.

CHAPTER 25

THE KATHERINE PRIDE GALLERY

Corky pegged the woman as lesbian the minute she entered the gallery. Kate Pride had not told him to expect a Detective Linda Sikorsky, so when she walked through the door as if she had something terribly important to discuss with Kate, he switched to full screening mode. Filtering was part of the job; Katherine Pride was well known in the art world, especially its cutting edge, and plenty of artists tried to get their portfolios to her through improper channels. Pretending they were there for some other reason was a favorite and transparent ruse. It was like impersonating a doorman to give Taylor Swift a CD of your material as she stepped out of a limo. Corky was not easily fooled, and would have none of this "I have to see Kate Pride right away" business. Besides, information was power, and screening people who insisted they had booked time with Kate was one of his best ways of staying informed. To be informed was to have leverage, New York City's most valuable currency.

Linda was patient by nature. It was a necessary trait in homicide investigation; you often had to wait for evidence to present itself, or wait for test results, or simply wait for someone you were questioning to stop crying and give you an answer. But even someone as calm as Detective Linda could lose it when faced with an obstacle like Corky. He didn't seem to hear her when she said she needed to speak with Kate Pride right away. He began asking her where she was from and with whom she had made this alleged appointment. She told him she was a friend of Kyle Callahan's, the photographer whose photos were on the walls, for godsake, and that the matter was urgent. He stalled some more, and Linda realized he was pumping her for information. Finally she pulled out her badge, something she refrained from doing outside her job unless it was absolutely necessary.

"I'm a homicide detective," she said, holding out her shield. "New Hope Police Force."

Corky's eyes widened. This was definitely prime information. He felt his Twitter finger twitching already.

"Is this about Devin?" Corky asked, staring up at her.

"I'm not at liberty to say."

"Where's New Hope? Isn't that California?"

Linda sighed heavily, wishing someone had told this young man she was coming.

"Listen," Corky said. "I don't know if it's related, but there was this guy in here yesterday, really creepy. We never met but he knew my name, weird, huh?"

Before Linda could respond the phone rang. She saw it was Kyle and had a quick conversation with him that Corky interrupted to tell her he was not "the desk guy" and to poo-pooh her use of the words "walked funny." She was about to slip into the parlor to escape the presumptuous young man when she saw Kate Pride pull up in a taxi and ended the call.

Moments later the door opened and Kate Pride came in, an oversized leather purse hanging from her left shoulder. She had a binder in her right hand that she handed to Corky when she got to the desk.

Corky took the binder without a word and said nothing more. Kate was the boss, and as much as she liked Corky, she had no patience for his prying. He was a very young man with a lot to learn; she was happy to teach him what she could, but on her terms and in her time. This was not one of those times.

Linda shook hands with Kate. "Linda Sikorksy."

"Kate Pride."

"Is there somewhere we can talk privately?" Linda said, glancing at Corky.

"Yes, certainly, I have a small office in the back."

Kate led Linda to the back of the gallery. "Can we get you something?" she asked as they left the room. "Coffee? Water?"

"I'm fine, thanks," Linda said, disappointing the eavesdropping Corky. When Kate asked if 'we' could get her something, she meant Corky, and he was hoping for the chance to scurry to Breadwinner's across the street, get some coffee or scones, and insert himself at least one more time into the conversation. Now he had been effectively shut out, and he started brooding. It took Corky all of ten seconds to switch from aloof to brooding, excited to brooding, any mood at all to brooding; if he was born to succeed, as he often insisted, he was equally born to brood.

He turned his attention to the binder. It was filled with photographs for the next exhibit. Kate was always three steps ahead. The photographer Kyle Callahan would have his moment in the sun, and within a few weeks there would be another one. A sculptor this time, Corky could see as he flipped through pictures of the woman's pieces. Women sculptors remained a significant find in a medium still dominated by men. The most famous ones tended to be potters, but this woman, Geraldine Wenzel, did absolute wonders with heavy metal. Corky quickly forgot about the detective from California and the strange limping man and his horrible landlord harassing him for back rent, as he glanced at the amazing sculptures that would soon be placed around the Katherine Pride Gallery. So short was his attention span that he did not notice the same limping man watching him from Breadwinner's as he enjoyed his last meal in New York City. Had the good detective asked for coffee, things might have turned out very differently. Corky would have gone across the street and seen the man he had tried to tell her about. But that is the dark side of serendipity. One man's happy coincidence is another man's misfortune. Bad luck appeared to be on a roll.

CHAPTER 26

THE STOPWATCH DINER

Danny arrived at the Stopwatch twenty minutes early, knowing Linus would not be late. He took a booth facing the front so he would be able to see Linus before Linus saw him. He wanted to observe the look on Linus's face when he realized Claude was not the one waiting for him.

The bad blood between the two men went back a decade. Danny had first met Linus when he began working at Margaret's Passion and Linus had dinner there one evening with several companions. He'd stared at Danny throughout the meal and at first Danny thought it was flirtatious; but then he sensed hostility in the restaurateur's gaze, and finally something close to hatred. A hatred he had never understood, but that had become almost mutual. 'Almost,' because Danny was not the hateful sort, but he had witnessed enough destruction brought about by this venture capitalist to come close to hating him. *Despise* would be a better word. Linus left victims in his wake, starting up restaurants with an investor or two, then selling to some hapless dreamer and making off with a nice profit. More often than not the restaurant failed within a year, and the poor owner and his backers, who were usually family members, were left holding an empty bag while Linus was off to the next start up. That was his specialty: starting up, then leaving. He never stayed for the unhappy endings.

"You want a warm up?" the waiter asked, nodding at Danny's coffee cup. He hadn't seen the man scurry up to him, coffee pot in hand.

"No, I'm fine," Danny said.

He looked over as the waiter disappeared and saw Linus Hern enter the front door. Hern scanned the restaurant for Claude Petrie, and after a few moments of puzzlement – he was not one to be kept waiting and knew Claude would be punctual – his gaze landed on Danny and he froze. He cocked his head, not sure if this was a chance encounter or if Danny was the one he was here to see.

Danny nodded: yes, Linus, I've been waiting for you.

While not exactly going pale, Hern's face fell even further than its natural frown. He brushed past the maître de and walked to Danny's table.

"I'm assuming Claude's not coming," Linus said.

"You would be correct," Danny replied. "Please, Linus, have a seat."

Hern hesitated and considered leaving, then decided the only way out of this situation was through it. Now that his plan had been found out he would have to sit and get it over with. He slid into the booth across from Danny. No sooner had he settled in than the waiter reappeared.

"Go away," Linus said to the man, who'd had his share of rude customers and did not take it personally. He shrugged and shuffled off to another table.

"So. Danny Durban. I never anticipated this, if anticipation is the right word."

"I think it is for you, Linus. The sweet anticipation of deceiving Margaret Bowman. She just turned eighty, but you know that."

"Yes. I remember her birthday luncheon. I wasn't invited."

"Don't worry, you're on the list for her hundredth. Where was I? Oh, yes, tricking an elderly woman into signing over her building, in which both she and her very successful restaurant reside, only to find herself out of a home in a few months and that restaurant closed. Am I right? Did I get the plan down?"

"Close enough. But the eviction part's off. I would never put someone that near the end of her life on the street."

Danny sighed. He was tiring of the man already. "What I don't understand," he said, looking at Hern now as if examining him for his many imperfections, "is why Margaret? Why an old woman who has run a restaurant for thirty years? She's not defenseless, but obviously vulnerable. Her mind's not quite as sharp as it used to be, or she would have seen through your hired guns the moment they walked in the door. I'm sure it was Claude who told you about her financial problems, and there you were, like a snake that had lain patiently in the grass all this time."

Linus thought a long moment, considering his reply. "It's not Margaret," he said, leaning across the table, inserting himself perilously into Danny's personal space. "It's you."

Danny couldn't help himself; he pushed back against the cushion wanting to distance himself from a much too close Linus Hern. Finally Linus eased away, the hint of a smile coming onto his face.

"Me?" Danny said.

"You really didn't know, did you?" Linus said, waving over the waiter. "I'll have that coffee now."

Linus took the time they waited for his coffee to be poured to gather his thoughts. He felt a sudden peace come over him, if peace can relieve a malevolent man. He put creamer into his coffee, stirred it slowly, and carefully set his spoon down on a napkin.

"It's a very short story," Linus said finally. "I was in love once, very much so. He was younger than I, about ten years. Sal was his name. Salvatore Minelli." He looked at Danny, waiting to see any indication the name meant something to him. "No," he said. "I suppose you wouldn't remember him."

Danny had become intensely uncomfortable, regretting the meeting. He should have done it formally, in the company of witnesses, or in a letter, anything that would have given him distance; but it was too late now, Linus was at this table, in this diner, and he had no choice but to hear him out.

"Anyway," Linus continued, "he was the only man I've loved, really. Certainly the only one for whom I've ever let down my guard. I honestly believed we'd be spending the rest of our lives together. Me, a successful restaurateur, Sal the manager of a very popular Gramercy Park restaurant."

Hern watched Danny again, and this time something clicked.

Danny felt his stomach lurch. He did remember the name.

"I have to correct myself," Linus said. "A moment ago I said this was not about Margaret Bowman, but it is. It's about Margaret, her restaurant, you. All of it. You see, Sal was on the fragile side. It's one of the things I loved about him. I was hard, he was soft. I was the storm, he was the calm. And one day he got fired from his job, for reasons that were never clear. It seems the old woman who owned the restaurant had found someone she preferred, someone she favored and has favored ever since."

Danny knew now, he remembered. The blood flowed out of his face and his hands went cold.

"The other weakness Sal had, aside for a foolish trust in people, was drugs. He took the job loss hard. He took it personally. He had trusted the old woman, and she had betrayed him, threw him off for someone more pleasing to her."

"It was just a job," Danny said weakly.

"Oh, wonderful, then you shouldn't mind at all losing yours, or care in the least what happens to Margaret. She's just a woman who gave you … just a job."

Linus let it sink in a moment, sipping his coffee. "Sal was inconsolable. He was hurt and angry, not safe emotions for someone with addictions. He didn't believe he could take his anger out on Margaret, so he took it out on himself. Must I continue or do you remember him now?"

Danny waited, staring at Hern. "Yes," he said. "I remember him. I never knew what happened to him."

"Because you never cared," Linus hissed, sending shivers down the back of Danny's neck. "You never cared, that old woman never cared, no-body cared. He couldn't get clean again, Daniel, and six months later he was found in the Hudson River. It was not an accident. It was not some fun murder for your husband to solve. It was a sad, broken man ending his own life. And for that I vowed to someday destroy Margaret Bowman, her restaurant, and the man she threw Sal away for. Now if you'll excuse me - and even if you won't - I'll be leaving."

Linus slid out of the booth, watching Danny a final moment while Danny's gaze was frozen on the table. A ten dollar bill appeared in his line of sight as Hern threw it down. Danny looked up; he had never seen such hatred in a man's eyes before.

"I'm sorry," Danny said.

"Don't be. It's much too late. And don't think this is the end of it. Consider it a pause, now that you know what this has been about, this animosity between us all these years."

"No one ever told me."

Hern cut him off, leaning down into his space again. "Because it's none of their fucking business," he said slowly. "This is not for some sad gossip page. This is personal, private. And I'll be back. She'll have to sell to someone, and whoever it is will regret the day they got in my way. People who do that don't usually survive."

Danny knew he meant it, and that Linus Hern, now that his reasons were out in the open, would be more dangerous than ever.

"Give Kyle my congratulations on the photo exhibit," Linus said, turning to leave. "And my regrets. I'm previously engaged. I'll have to read the scathing reviews in the New York Times. Don't worry, their critic will be there, I made sure of that."

Linus Hern left him then, striding out of the restaurant with a spring in his step. The air had been cleared between them, but to Danny it felt like the preparing of a battlefield. The clouds had parted, the sun had come out, and beneath them the artillery was now in place. The first shot had been fired long ago; today the war had begun.

Danny motioned for the check. He wanted to be away from here as quickly as possible. Linus Hern had left a chill in his wake and Danny needed to be warm again.

CHAPTER 27

THE KATHERINE PRIDE GALLERY

The back office of the Katherine Pride Gallery had once been a utility closet. Kate had expanded it to twice the size, which made it just large enough for a small metal desk, two folding chairs and a water cooler that held a five-gallon jug. This was where many a hopeful artist first learned she would be stepping into the limelight with the blessing and support of one of Manhattan's most experienced art dealers. Kate Pride had been around long enough to be considered part of the establishment, but not long enough to be irrelevant. She knew the day was coming when she would be seen as entirely Old Guard and she didn't care. She loved sitting in this little office at her small gallery meeting new creative minds, welcoming new talent into the world.

"So," Linda said, sitting in the visitor's chair to the side of Kate's desk. "Here's what we're thinking."

"We? You have a partner?" Kate asked.

She glanced at her phone, noticing the red "message" light was on. Probably a call from her husband; they were set to have lunch again that afternoon.

Linda blushed at the question about a partner. She had several: Kirsten McLellan in New Hope, Bryan Frazier on the force, not technically a partner but the one other cop she'd really bonded with, and Kyle Callahan.

"Kyle," she said.

"Photographer Kyle?"

"Yes, that Kyle, the one who has a show here Friday night."

"He solves murders?"

Kate could tell Linda was becoming frustrated. "Sorry, I just had no idea. What is it you're thinking, you and Kyle?"

Linda reached for her tote bag, the one she'd bought at Grand Central with the subway map stenciled on it, and took out the New Year New Visions catalog. She placed it on the desk. "Someone involved, somehow, with the New Visions show is very unhappy and taking it out on the others." She looked gravely at Kate. "That could include you, Ms. Pride."

"Kate, please."

"Kate. After all, you're the ringmaster, if I may put it that way. I need to know what became of the others, the ones who aren't dead as far as we know, and especially the ones we'll never know at all."

Kate took the catalog and opened to the front. She remembered the artists very well. That year's New Visions show had been one of her most successful, in terms of launching the artists' careers. The show had become quite the hot ticket every January; style pages and art blogs across the city started anticipating the show as early as October, speculating on who might be included and what waves they would send through art circles.

"The graffiti couple are in Paris," Kate said. "I just read about them in Le Monde. That's the French paper. I don't speak it well but I can read fair enough. I'm a Francophile, what can I say. Suzanne DePris is in Seattle last I heard, and Javier Velasco's in Argentina."

"You know this for a fact? That they're all alive and well?"

"I don't know if they're well, that's a very broad term, but it's easy enough to find them and ask them."

"That's my next stop," Linda said. "Back to the hotel for research, then meeting Kyle at an event he went to. I'm very much in need of some answers by then. What about the ones you rejected?"

Kate closed the catalog and handed it back to Linda. "There weren't any," she said. "It doesn't work that way."

Linda put the catalog back in her bag. "How does it work then? I can't imagine you accept everyone who wants to be in the show."

"It's not a matter of acceptance or rejection. I find *them*, you see. Everybody knows about the New Year New Visions show, it's gotten a lot of attention, and people do try to persuade me, mostly agents and dealers. Some of the artists, sure. But my policy is also very well known. No one gets rejected because I do the asking. Submissions are not accepted. The New Year New Visions is an invitation-only show."

Invitation-only. No one gets rejected. The information didn't so much change things as narrow it. Detective Linda now knew she was looking at a smaller field, more limited choices. It had to be someone connected to the artists who had been in the show.

The thought hit her like ice water in the face. *What if it was one of the artists who* was *in the show?* What if success had not come to everyone – and why would it? Maybe one of them had found themselves in the shadows instead of the bright, warm light of fame? She needed to track them down, and quickly.

She thanked Kate for her time, feeling hurried now to narrow the field even more. The smaller the focus got, the closer they would be to an answer. As Kate Pride was showing her out, she stopped just in front of the desk. Corky quickly pretended to be looking at his computer, all the while listening for any scraps of data-power he could collect.

"Did any of them limp?" Linda asked.

"Limp?" said Kate.

Corky suddenly looked up.

"Yes, limp. Walk ... differently."

"Oh my god," Corky said. "I tried to tell you! He was here. The guy with the limp."

Kate and Linda turned to him. Kate had no idea what the significance of the limping man was, while Linda knew very well and Corky, to his horror, guessed.

"You think he's the one doing this?" he said. "To Devin and Richard Morninglight? The man who was standing right where you are yesterday? Oh my god."

Kate remembered Kyle insisting someone had been watching them from across the street that Monday morning. Could it have been this man? And is he the one she remembered from the New Visions show, standing off to himself, peering at the opening night crowd from a corner?

"There was someone with a limp," Kate said, taking Linda gently by the arm and leading her away. Corky could be overly dramatic and she didn't want to fuel that fire. "But he wasn't one of the artists ..."

Kate Pride walked out of the gallery with Linda, telling her what little she knew about the strange man. There wasn't much to tell, mostly whispers she had overheard.

She had no way of knowing he had heard them, too.

CHAPTER 28

HOTEL EXETER – CHECKOUT TIME

Kieran Stipling should have known better than to believe his troubled life had changed with the chance meeting of someone who claimed to see his inner beauty. He was a good looking man, that was true; he had always been attractive, handsome they said, and he had compensated for his misshapen hips by making sure that every other inch of him was superb. He'd begun working out as a kid, not yet a teenager, lifting and squatting and curling and pressing. By the time he was fourteen he had the physique of a young man who worked in a rock quarry or who had set his eyes on competition. He'd almost gone that route, too, into competition, where he would be able to show them all, but he had feared he would be seen as the exception, not the rule, the loser who managed to slip into a room of winners and deceive them just until his mask fell. Beneath the mask was a lonely child, molded more by his isolation and troubled emotions than he ever would be by his body. That was what Javier had told him, two years ago this coming June, and what he had believed until the truth came out. He had taken Javier's kisses for a guarantee they would always be together. He had opened the gates of his body and his heart, allowing this man in, this *other* whom he would have run from all his life before, and for his trust he had been betrayed. Abandoned. Turned out. Or so Javier thought. The amazing Javier Velasco. The shining new star that had shone so brightly even the lights of New York City could not obscure him. And once he knew it, once Javier

Velasco saw himself the way all those fawning sycophants saw him, there was no room for something so flawed as his broken lover. Kieran and his crooked walk would draw the focus; people would whisper. Little had Javier known their whispers would be overheard and give rise to the shouts of Kieran's rage.

Katherine Pride and her wretched gallery were at the center of his pain. Until that show, until Javier had seen what could be his, had been told what could be his by that tight little circle of traitors, Kieran had believed they were inseparable. He had been happy in their studio apartment in Washington Heights, living among the Puerto Ricans, Dominicans, and the influx of the young with their big dreams in the big city. Kieran and Javier were just another couple in the neighborhood. The men who ran the corner bodega knew them. The old Korean woman at the Laundromat knew them. It had been a perfect life ... until that show. Until critics came around with their ten-dollar words and their blessings. Oh, how that had changed things. Javier Velasco was one to be watched. Javier Velasco was tomorrow's news. Javier Velasco was halfway up the mountain already, so talented, so gorgeous. Too bad he had that gimp tagging along. He could do so much better.

Javier believed them easily enough because he wanted to. He pretended nothing had change, for a month or two. They traveled. They went to San Francisco and Buenos Aires for Javier to be toasted by the town's art royalty; and the whispers had grown louder, the looks more cruel. Finally, Javier had said he had to go, Kieran with his sad eyes and his bad hips. He would always love Kieran, but they should be good friends, nothing more.

Nothing more.

The words echoed, bouncing off one side of Kieran's skull, careening to the other and back, as he stared up at the gray afternoon sky. *It's never really dark here*, he thought. Not the kind of dark you find on a country road. Two things you cannot see in New York City: stars and the absolute, final, blackness of the universe. He intended to soon see them both. Once he was finished. He would take a bus and ride west, into the desert. Somewhere on the road to Las Vegas he would step off, never to be seen again. He would lie on his back and gaze up into an infinity wrapped in stars and blackness. And sometime, many years from now or maybe just a week, he would take his last breath attempting to count a billion flickering lights. Now it was afternoon and dreary, an appropriate landscape for the painting he had in mind.

Kieran felt a strange sadness as he prepared to leave the hotel room, the last place in New York City he would call home. It had been fitting: to go from living alone in a tiny basement apartment on the Lower East Side, to life with Javier in the upper reaches of Manhattan as their star – *their star* – was in its ascendency, to the unimaginable fall from grace that left him here in a hotel room that had seen a thousand like him. There were people who actually lived here, but most came and went like shadows moving across the filthy carpet. Some had left stains; he looked at one of them, a dark red oval near the closet, and wondered if it was blood. He would be gone in a moment, and the thousand who had come before him would be followed by a thousand after.

He packed his backpack with the few thing he would need: his one change of clothes, a toothbrush with no toothpaste, a pre-paid cell phone about to run out of minutes, his camera for capturing the finer moments just ahead, the ones that would make up his ultimate still life, and the knife he had used to kill Devin. He had exacted each revenge in a different way, with a different killer's tool. Only the knife would be a repeat performance. He had thought about trying to buy a gun, but he had no idea how one goes about purchasing a firearm on the streets of New York City. He'd bought cocaine once, from an itchy prostitute who walked the corner near his cousin's delicatessen in Flatbush, but that was the extent of his black market experience. He had quickly abandoned the idea of a gun and settled instead on the knife, a guitar string, and his own hands. He was his own weapon of choice, as it should be. He took full responsibility for what he was doing, and full pleasure in doing it. These people had harmed him irreparably; they had crushed his dreams as well as his soul. He had to settle accounts face to face, in as personal a way as possible.

Take it personally, Kate Pride. Take it very personally.

Today he would be closing out the accounts altogether. He had made an appointment to see a condominium in SoHo. The sort of living space he had visited recently as part of Javier's growing entourage, but that he would never, ever, live in. Those doors had been shut to him when he was turned away. But just this once, this one last time, he would stand in an apartment he could not dream of affording, smiling politely at Katherine Pride's husband – yes, yes, lovely closet space, the second bathroom is a bit small, but that view! – and waiting patiently for his wife to arrive. If it meant Stuart Pride took his last breath there, if things went a little wrong and there was collateral damage, so be it. That's what Kieran was, after all, collateral damage. But sometimes, yes, sometimes, the damaged strike back.

He zipped his backpack, slung it over his shoulder, and left the seedy little Hotel Exeter, knowing he would never return.

CHAPTER 29

THE KATHERINE PRIDE GALLERY

Corky was sipping blueberry herbal tea, watching Kate Pride show her husband the exhibit layout. The opening was Friday night and they had 125 registrations already. Fire code limited the number of occupants to 160 and Corky knew there would be a flurry of last minute comers. Shows at the Pride Gallery were a top ticket, not just to see the new artists being exhibited, but to be seen as well. Openings were about hobnobbing, glancing around for the nearest camera, complaining about the same papparazi they had tipped to their presence with a phone call on the way over. It didn't matter that no one had ever heard of the photographer Kyle Callahan. That was part of the experience, coming to see what new fabulous talent Kate Pride had discovered. Corky would be working the event and he looked forward to an evening of networking, moderate drinking of wine and eating of cheese, and possibly finding a new boyfriend. His last one, Phillip, had left a bitter taste in his heart and he was eager to move one. Nothing said 'next!' like a fresh romance.

Kate had shown Stuart the lineup of Kyle's photographs and he was duly impressed. He'd met Kyle and Danny a few times, and the couples had dinner once at Margaret's Passion, but they weren't more than acquaintances to him. Stuart and Kate Pride kept separate lives in many ways: professionally and, when they were not together, personally. Kate had her

New York art world friends, her gallery, and her love of reading biographies; Stuart had his real estate sales, his preference for horror fiction, and his philately: Stuart was a stamp collector. Kate had no interest in stamps beyond how much it cost to do her gallery mailings.

The couple had enough common interests that being without children was of no significance to them. Of their parents, only Kate's mother remained alive, and her gay brother Douglas with his partner and three children provided all the extended family she needed. She could get her kid fix anytime by calling her young nephews and niece. Kate and Stuart had survived this long in a child-centric culture, they might as well go all the way.

Stuart looked at his watch. He'd had a new client call from out of the blue. The man had reached him directly, rather than going through his office. He thought it was odd at the time, since his cell number was private. When he asked the man how he got the number, the man told him Javier Velasco had given it to him. Stuart had shown the artist several one-bedrooms in TriBeCa just a month ago.

"Another showing?" Kate asked, seeing her husband look at the time.

"Yes, and it's a big one. Just came on the market. SoHo, three bedrooms, top floor."

"Anybody I know?"

Stuart smiled at his wife's curiosity. As the owner of a respected art gallery, Kate knew just about everyone there was to know in Manhattan's upper atmosphere, and if she didn't know them, she knew someone who did. Her Rolodex was her networking and in her opinion it still worked better than any social media. Index cards: the first LinkedIn.

"Possibly," he said. "A gentleman from Buenos Aries, says he got my number from Javier Velasco."

Corky looked up at the name. He thought of interrupting but decided it could wait. The Prides were a couple he hoped to emulate with his next boyfriend who would love him as completely and faithfully as Stuart loved Kate, and he didn't want to take a moment away from their time together. He knew their busy lives did enough of that.

"Ah, Javier, yes," Kate said. "Full of himself but talented. Sometimes I regret the egos I unleash on the world. He's in Buenos Aries now, from what I know."

"That's the connection then. Nouveau riche, I suspect."

"Oh, yes, of course. I've read a lot about that. Depressed housing market in the U.S., foreigners buying up all our best views. Be sure to invite him to the opening Friday. We take Argentine pesos, too."

They'd come back into the front of the gallery and were standing by the desk.

"I'll call you after this appointment," Stuart said. "Maybe we can have dinner."

"There's a new bistro on Gansevoort Street, Melissa's, I think it's called."

"Sounds fine to me, we like new places. Everything set for the opening here?"

She frowned. Mentioning the opening reminded her that the Katherine Pride Gallery was not MOMA. Everything here was done on a tight budget.

"I'd love to have passed hors d'oeuvres and hot waiters, or maybe it's passed waiters and hot hors d'oeuvres! But we don't have the funds and I want people looking at the photographs, not the men serving them Vienna sausages."

"You're a shrewd businesswoman, Kate Pride. Frugality is a virtue."

"It's about the art, not the money, right?"

"Right. We can leave the money making to me. Speaking of which, I have to dash."

Stuart Pride, standing a good five inches taller than the woman he had been in love with from the moment he'd met her, leaned down and kissed her, first on the cheek, and then, quite un-customarily in public – for Corky was considered public – he eased his face around and kissed her full-on on the lips. She, too, felt compelled to kiss him, long and deeply. It wasn't something they ever did when they could be seen, not in the gallery's front room, not on a street corner, and they were both taken by this sudden passion, this need.

Corky swiveled his chair around to face the wall, as if there were a spot on the paint he needed to inspect.

Finally, Kate and Stuart separated. She had blushed a bright red, and he kept looking down, embarrassed, but not apologetic.

"Well, that was unexpected," she said.

"Under the circumstances," he agreed, nodding toward Corky.

Kate ran her palms down the sides of her dress, as if they'd done more than kiss. "You'd better hurry," she said. "Cabs can be tricky here."

He kissed her once more on the cheek. "Call you," he said, and he left the gallery.

Kate watched after him. The passion of a moment ago was suddenly replaced by a longing sadness. It was as unexpected as their kiss had been, and she wondered where it came from. Was it age? Were they running out of time? She had the momentary, intense premonition that something terrible was coming their way. But those things were ridiculous, like imagining yourself falling from a subway platform when you never got that close to the edge. She felt strangely close to the edge. She shook it off, just as she'd shaken off the awkwardness of kissing her husband in front of Corky.

"You got a message," Corky said behind her. He'd turned back from the wall. "I didn't want to interrupt when you were talking."

She walked to the desk, expecting a message slip.

"Javier Velasco," Corky continued. "Another of your success stories. But he's not in Buenos Aires."

Kate was surprised to hear from Velasco. He'd quickly moved beyond the Katherine Pride Gallery, and while she didn't begrudge him his success, he was one of the few whose careers she wished she'd left for someone else to launch. Javier Velasco had the kind of self-regard that quickly went from down-and-out to entitled.

Corky saw her waiting for the message. "Oh," he said. "No number, nothing. He said he'd call back and was hoping to see you."

"Hmm," she said. Maybe he'd changed. Maybe some vicious critic in Argentina had taken him down a few pegs, or someone, somehow, had reminded him where he came from.

"Find me if he calls again, please," she said. "I'll be in the office." She wanted to go over the details of Friday's opening with Corky but would review them first, making sure she'd checked off everything she needed to do.

"Can I bring you anything?" Corky asked. "I'm dashing to Breadwinner's."

"I'm fine," she said. Then, as unexpectedly as she had kissed Stuart, she said, "Oh, and Corky, let's start locking this door, can we? I'll get a buzzer."

She looked around the gallery once more, picked up her iPad from the desk and headed to her office for some intimate time with a spreadsheet.

CHAPTER 30

BUENOS AIRES – TWO MONTHS EARLIER

The Hotel Vista was located in the Puerto Madera Waterfront section of Buenos Aires. Situated on a significant slice of the Rio de la Plata riverbank, the area was home to some of the best and most current architecture the capital city had to offer. One of the newest neighborhoods in the city, it boasted theaters, restaurants, shopping for any taste, with an emphasis on the expensive. It was also home to the Hector Guiterrez Galeria del Arte, the top rung on the art ladder in all of the country, some said all of South America.

The Vista was a luxury hotel by definition: 120 rooms, a third of them suites, overlooking the river on one side and the vast city on the other. Attendants were at each guest's beck and call, and often showed up mysteriously and silently just when something was needed. There were two restaurants on the lobby floor, one that faced the street and catered to visitors to the area as well as hotel guests, and one tucked into the hotel with an entrance so discreet many people didn't realize it was there. That was where Javier Velasco had eaten his last meal with Hector Guiterrez on a Wednesday night, expecting to attend the opening of his own show on Thursday. It was where he had enjoyed his fantasy of ever-greater fame and fortune, having moved quickly from the Katherine Pride Gallery to a show in San Francisco, and now this. It was like going from zero to sixty in five seconds, from selling paintings on the sidewalk outside the Metropolitan Museum of Art to having his work shown at the Modern. It was a rise that would have made most men's heads spin, but Javier Velasco was not most men, and he was certainly not most artists.

He had gone to dinner at 7:00 o'clock with the eminent Hector Guiterrez in the hotel's exclusive restaurant. Guiterrez had been attracted to Velasco's paintings from the moment he saw them in San Francisco. And, Kieran believed, the old man had been attracted to Javier as well. Kieran was no fool. He had not made it this far in life with a gimp's walk and the cruel whispers that followed it with contempt; he had not survived the brutality of children when he had been a child himself; he had not walked the gaunt-let of a world bent on keeping him the butt of jokes, an object of ridicule, only to be run through by this "artist," this fraud. He had come to view Javier as a charlatan, a keen observer of what people consider important and great, and a manufacturer of those very things: art designed for the admiration of other artists, critics and gallery owners who could further his career. (Kieran had read once that poets wrote for other poets, which he decided may explain why nobody reads poetry.)

He should have known better than to think he was more than a dis-traction for Javier Velasco. Despite the hip dysplasia, he was in very good shape, and God had given him more than bragging rights in the dick de-partment. It was amazing how many flaws men overlooked at the sight of a cock that made those flaws mere inconveniences. Velasco was no differ-ent. *Correction*, Kieran thought, sitting on the hotel bed, staring at the clock that now read nearly midnight: Velasco had professed his love, and Kieran Stipling had believed him. Stupidly. Blindly. Fatally for one of them.

His Greatness had made several critical mistakes. He had not wanted to be seen with his disabled lover, so he had arranged (with thin excuses to Kieran) to have them meet at the hotel rather than arrive together; nor would Kieran's name be on the registry. As far as the Hotel Vista was concerned, there was no Kieran Stipling, only a man they viewed later on security footage with his face obscured by a hoodie, and who limped as he walked to the room, then left in the middle of the night wheeling a large suitcase. Velasco had asked Kieran to go directly to the room. He had also neither introduced nor mentioned Kieran to anyone. It was as if Kieran Stipling did not exist. He certainly did not exist in the world in which Javier now moved. There was no room for imperfection in this world, and Kieran was quite imperfect. Except, as it turned out, when it came to evening the score: you treat me as a nonentity, I treat you as expendable; you treat me as an embarrassment, I leave you in a state of humiliation; you tell me you love me and then abandon me, I make sure you will never repeat that lie to anyone again.

Javier Velasco returned to the room just after 1:00 a.m. Kieran had been sitting on the bed for four hours. Javier wanted to go to bed, Kieran wanted to talk. More specifically, Kieran wanted to confront. What ensued was quick and brutal. Kieran Stipling knew his presence in the hotel was undetected and would only be discovered when they looked at the security tapes. That was why he had covered his face and kept it turned down. He had known what this would likely come to, and even though he had left room for a change in course, he hadn't expected it and it hadn't happened. What had happened was a fast, quick death. There could be very little argument, and no shouting. It would alert people. So Kieran had pressed his case very directly, accusing Javier of throwing him to the wolves now that he had moved into a world where wolves were plentiful and lambs like Kieran were free for the taking. He accused Velasco of preparing to dump him, to which an exasperated, egotistical and foolish Javier Velascao said yes, you're right, we're finished, now go.

Now go. Two words, served over ice. He was being dismissed, in a foreign country! Once it happened, as he had known it would, snapping Javier Velasco's neck had been, well … a snap. Kieran had sighed and agreed to leave. He had come up behind Javier, who was taller by four inches, and put his arms around him for one last touch, a final embrace. And as Velasco started to pull away, Kieran Stipling pulled him back and down, snaking one arm around Javier's neck, and with his free hand quickly, ferociously, breaking his neck. It had been so easy, and so fast. Kieran hadn't expected it to be over that quickly. He was disappointed. But he was also in a hurry to be gone now. He emptied the large suitcase Velasco had brought with him and managed to just squeeze the artist's body into it. He hoped they would never find the suitcase with the corpse of the great Javier Velasco, but if they did, he would be long gone, back to New York City to deal with the people who had started it all, who had begun the whispers and brought about their own deaths.

Pulling the suitcase down the hall was awkward, and it kept nearly tipping over from the dead weight inside it. But Kieran was a strong man, and determined. An hour later he was on the southwest side of Buenos Aries in a massive and notorious landfill. He left his rental car parked near the landfill's edge and trudged, step by shaky step, into the landfill, where Javier Velasco would be attending the closing of his final show. No critics would rave, no buyers would bid. Only birds would come to pluck and rats to dine. The great artist would be climbing no more, and the cripple would go back into the shadows.

CHAPTER 31

THE CARLTON SUITES

Women in New York Media had been handing out their Women EmpOwering Women (WOW) Awards for the past twenty years. Imogene Landis had been to the luncheon ceremony a dozen times and had given up the idea that they were going to honor her with some kind of special award for effort. She hadn't even made the rather long short list in some time, so it was with humility, shock, and an I-said-I'd-be-back attitude that she went to the ceremony guaranteed a certificate. She knew half the women in the banquet hall of the Carlton Suites Hotel. They knew her, too, and as her career had driven slowly but inexorably into a ditch the last decade, they had begun to look away nervously when she came near. They would start to chatter about something inane, hoping that sad creature Imogene would hurry by and let them get back to real conversation. But not this time, oh no. This time she was number forty-seven out of fifty, and even though only the first ten were recognized from the stage, her name was in the program. Right there, between Sherri Vanguard, the pet reporter from Channel 7, and Elizabeth Darling, God rest her soul.

Kyle hadn't wanted to attend the event at all. He'd been there with Imogene two years ago and had seen how depressed and angry it made her to be treated like the has-been she was at the time. The murders at Pride Lodge had changed all that, and now she was a minor local celebrity at home and a cult favorite in post-midnight Tokyo. The looks they gave her today had been of envy, not pity. It was a lunchtime Imogene clearly enjoyed, but that Kyle had quietly, nervously, endured, while he kept checking his vibrating phone.

Detective Linda had been hard and fast on the job, tracking down the other artists from the New Visions show and she had information she kept feeding him as the luncheon dragged on. They were in the banquet hall for ninety minutes total, by the end of which Kyle was nearly ready to bolt. First had come a text from Linda that the graffiti artists were alive, well, and causing a stir in Paris as conjoined pop icons. Then came word that Suzanne DePris was living in Seattle and working as a florist. Apparently the art bug had bitten her, caused a minor irritation and moved on. And finally a startling text about Javier Velasco, the last of them to locate. "When RU finished?" she texted. "Big news on Velasco."

He had texted her back asking what the news was.

"Tell U in person," she wrote back. "On the way to hotel now."

Kyle looked at his watch. The last of the top ten recipients was at the podium carrying on much too long about her family and the job she would consider her most important forever and ever – that of mom to two precious sons, aged thirty-two and twenty-seven. He was about to lean over and tell Imogene that he had to leave, something urgent had come up, when applause broke out and for reasons he would never know the crowd stood to give the woman an ovation. She may have ended her speech with the announcement she was terminally ill, or given thanks to her stricken mother for setting an example. Something powerful that had them all standing and clapping, including Kyle, who mimicked the rest of them with no idea why.

"Thank God that's over," Imogene said, picking up her program as quickly as Kyle did before the applause had stopped. "They'll mail my certificate to me, let's get the hell out of here."

The two of them made a hasty exit, Imogene holding the hem of her dress up with one hand while she flagged a taxi with the other. One of a half dozen hovering near the hotel like vultures quickly pulled up to the curb.

"I'll be in later," Kyle said, opening the taxi door for Imogene. "I've got a few things to do."

"Of course you do," she said. "Your big opening's on Friday. I can't wait! You must be a nervous wreck. In fact, take the day. I'll see you in the morning."

As the taxi sped off, Kyle looked up and saw Linda walking quickly up the sidewalk toward him.

"They found him," she said, out of breath. She'd taken the subway and had dashed two blocks from the station to the hotel.

"Who?" Kyle asked, confused. "The killer?"

"No! Javier Velasco, the artist. They found him. Or what's left of him."

"Oh my God."

"I don't think God was anywhere in the vicinity when this happened."

She pulled him aside, letting the flow of exiting guests get past them to the curb. More taxis had miraculously arrived, swarming the front of the hotel.

"Some kids playing in a landfill found him, outside Buenos Aires."

Kyle's face fell. He knew what was coming next.

"We're dealing with a very dangerous man here," she said, "Javier Velasco's body was stuffed inside a suitcase. It hit the Argentine news over the weekend."

"I'm surprised we didn't hear about it here."

"That's because they didn't know whose body it was! It was only identified yesterday. And if he's as big a name in the art world as you say …"

"About to be."

"About to be … then we'll see something tonight, tomorrow at the latest. Javier Velasco is dead, and not by natural causes."

Kyle's head was spinning. The connections had been made and were pointing in only one direction.

"There's more," Linda said. "Kate Pride knew the limping man. Not well, she didn't even speak to him, but he was at the New Visions show."

"I looked at the photos …"

"You can't see a limp in a photograph, Kyle."

She was right, of course. He'd been looking for a man he only vaguely recognized from across the street, and only glimpsed for an instant. "So who is he?"

"Javier Velasco's partner. Boyfriend. Lover. All of the above."

"Clearly now an ex. I don't think they'll be getting back together." He took her by the arm and started walking west. "We have to see Kate, immediately."

"Where are we going?" Linda said, glancing back at the dozen taxis and two dozen people trying to get them.

"Seventh Avenue, we'll get a cab faster there. These people coming out of the hotel are ruthless."

The two of them fast-walked along 56th Street, cars passing them in the opposite direction as Kyle hurried toward Seventh. Time was escaping them and none could be spared. If the killer had started with Javier Velsaco, and Richard Morninglight was his most recent kill, he was getting very close, his death spiral tightening. Kate had to be warned ... or saved.

They crossed the sidewalk at Seventh Avenue and Kyle led them into the street, raising his hand frantically. A taxi pulled to the curb and the two of them got in, leaving an irate woman with a suitcase on wheels shrieking at them for stealing her cab. Oh well, Kyle thought, that's Manhattan. You win some, you lose more. He ignored the woman's cries as they veered into traffic heading downtown.

CHAPTER 32

TWELVE FLOORS ABOVE SOHO

F ew sights of urban life are more breathtaking than the New York City skyline, among the most recognizable in the world. It had changed, admit-
tedly, since the loss of the massive Twin Towers on 9/11, once magnificent
bookends to the city's panorama, but it remained a breathtaking vision,
whether seen from across the river in Brooklyn or Queens, from a taxi
driving in from an airport, or from twelve stories up in an apartment overlooking downtown Manhattan. That was the view Stuart Pride was showing off now, to a stranger who had yet to give him any real information
about himself, except to say he'd gotten Stuart's private number from an
artist they both knew.

Stuart Pride was not superstitious or easily spooked, but something
about the man made the hair on his arms stand up; it was an undefined
chill, and he wrote it off to the building's heat being low or the cool April
air.

The apartment was spectacular, there was no doubting that, and Stuart
was counting on its sale to provide his best commission of the year. New
York City, Manhattan specifically, had not suffered nearly as much during
the nation's ruinous housing bust as the rest of the country. And while many
Americans were priced out of a stubbornly high market, there were plenty
of foreigners who saw property here as a steal and a sound investment.
There would be no foreclosure crisis in the nation's biggest city, except for

the unfortunate ones who lost their jobs and should probably never have moved here in the first place.

They were currently twelve floors above Prince Street, in one of Manhattan's most famous neighborhoods, SoHo. Shorthand for "SOuth of HOuston," the area had for decades been a home to art galleries and the trendiest of the trendy, and while it now had competition from areas like the Meatpacking District and galleries like Katherine Pride's, it remained a popular tourist destination and among the most expensive places in the city to live. The apartment Stuart was currently showing had three bedrooms, two and a half baths, a kitchen the size of most studio apartments, and a spectacular terrace overlooking downtown Manhattan. The asking price was a cool $2.5 million, a steal by anyone's reckoning. Something about the client made Stuart wonder if he really had that kind of money. He had already cursed himself for not directing the man to his office where he could be properly screened. The thought of selling his most expensive apartment of the year had clouded his judgment; greed had gotten the best of him, and he made a mental note not to let it happen again.

"What is it you do again, Mr. Stipling?" Stuart asked. He seldom showed apartments to people carrying backpacks, and only when the occasional rock star came his way did they look so much like they would never see two million dollars in their lives. Make that two and a half million.

"Art," Kieran said. He had been standing by the glass doors that opened out onto the terrace, looking up and around, as if he wanted to see how exposed it was to the views of neighbors.

"Ah, yes, art. My wife's in the art business, but you must know that through Mr. Velasco. Kate doesn't really see it as a business. She has the heart of an altruist. What part of the art world do you specialize in, may I ask?"

"Call me an accountant."

Stuart thought it was a strange way to phrase it.

Kieran saw the look on his face and smiled ever so slightly. "I settle accounts, let's put it that way."

"For Javier Velasco?"

"He was one of them, yes."

Was one of them, past tense. Another odd choice of words. Stuart had become very apprehensive and wanted to get the showing over as soon as possible. The spacious apartment with the amazing views was suddenly stifling.

"Let's take a look at the gym," Stuart said. "The building offers quite an impressive one on the second floor. It's free to tenants, of course."

"I'd like to see the terrace," Kieran said, as if he hadn't heard him. Without waiting for a reply, he opened the sliding door and stepped out. He glanced quickly up and around, noticing that no buildings overlooked them: they were effectively hidden from view in a city of eight million people. It was too early for plants, but there were several large planters along the edge, where a black wrought-iron gate encircled the space. In the corner, overlooking Broadway, was a glass table with four chairs, all black iron to match the gate. A large umbrella that would fit into the table's center lay on its side, waiting for warmer weather.

Stuart followed Kieran out. He'd never liked heights and stayed away from ledges, but he had a client to please, and the sooner that was done, the sooner they could leave.

"Oh, look!" Kieran said, leaning slightly over the railing and looking down. "You won't see that anywhere but New York City."

As Stuart crossed the terrace to where he was standing looking down, Kieran's hand slipped unnoticed into his backpack.

Stuart stepped up next to him, leaned carefully over the gate, just enough to see the sidewalk twelve floors below. There was nothing of note to be seen. He was about to ask what Kieran had been looking at when then the thin rope slipped around his neck, looping quickly again in his first startled moments. Kieran pulled him back with it, as if it were a leash or the reins on a horse. Stuart stumbled and fell face down on the terrace floor, gashing his nose. Blood began to flow from a nostril and his eyes watered from the impact. He grabbed blindly at the rope around his neck, desperate to loosen it.

"Don't worry," Kieran said, pushing Stuart back down with a foot on his back. "I'm not going to kill you. Not yet."

Stuart struggled to get up, one hand on the stone terrace trying to push himself up, the other grasping for the iron fence.

Kieran shoved him back down. He reached into Stuart's pocket and dug around until he found his cell phone.

"I'm going to strangle you now," Kieran said. "But don't worry. It's only enough to make you pass out. When you come to again you'll be manageable. These chairs look very uncomfortable, but sturdy. In the meantime, I have a text message to send. What was your wife's number? Oh wait, it's on speed dial. I bet she comes when you call her." Kieran laughed at his own crude joke and began searching for Kate Pride's name in the contact list. "Imagine her surprise when you tell her Javier's here."

Stuart Pride thought desperately of a way out, a means of escape, but his thoughts were cut short as Kieran knelt beside him and tightened the rope. His air gone, his head feeling as if it would explode, Stuart Pride gave himself to the blackness.

CHAPTER 33

THE KATHERINE PRIDE GALLERY

Corky was sitting behind the front desk when Kyle and Linda hurried into the gallery. It was nearly two o'clock and there was only one person there, a woman looking intently at one of the collages in the open showroom as if she were meditating upon it. Customers were sparse even on a busy day, it was just the nature of the beast. The survival of a gallery like Kate Pride's depended on a slow but steady stream of sales, not volume, and certainly not discounts. People who bought the artists on exhibit here were getting the best discount they could hope for, although it came with a gamble: someday, the sooner the better, the artists whose work they purchased would be further up the fame ladder, going from unknown to heard-of to must-have, at which point the painting or the photograph they bought for $1500 would be worth many times that. It didn't always work that way and there were just as many artists whose art depreciated as there were whose works tripled in value, but that's the way it went. No risk, no gain, and Kate Pride had founded her gallery on risk.

Corky looked up, surprised to see Kyle and the lady cop. He put his copy of Architectural Digest on the counter. Fantasizing living in homes he would never set foot in was one of his favorite time killers.

"Is Kate here?" Kyle asked, clearly agitated.

"No, she went out. Isn't it bad luck or something for you to be here before the opening?"

"That's weddings, or something, and no, it's not bad luck. Do you know where she went?"

"She'll be back in an hour," Corky said. One of his boss's rules was to never tell anyone where she was, unless she had an appointment with them. She thought the world had become entirely too invasive, with smartphones tracking you everywhere and Google Maps vans driving around videotaping every street corner. It gave her the creeps, and she didn't want anyone knowing her whereabouts who she hadn't told herself.

"This is important, Corky," Kyle said. He had not made any attempt over the previous weeks to befriend the young man and now regretted it.

"I'm sure it is, but ..."

"It's a police matter," Linda interrupted. She'd noticed earlier the deference Corky paid to authority. "We think she's being followed and there's really no time to waste."

"Let me call her."

"I've been doing that for the last fifteen minutes, Corky." Kyle tried his hardest not to let his irritation show. "She's not answering."

By then Corky had already grabbed his desk phone and dialed Kate's cell number. He held a finger up to tell them to wait just a moment; Kyle imagined bending it backward and breaking it. Corky frowned and held the receiver away from his ear, letting them hear the sound of Kate's recorded voice asking the caller to leave a message.

"She's with Stuart, her husband," Corky said, slapping the phone down. "How much safer could she be?"

Kyle and Linda looked at each other. If she was with Stuart, all should be fine, at least for now. It would buy them precious time.

"He's showing an apartment to one of Javier Velasco's friends."

Kyle stopped cold. "Javier Velasco?"

"Yes. He's in town. She got a text from Stuart just awhile ago, this Velasco guy met them at the condo and Stuart asked her to come by. He probably thinks it will seal the deal, he's all about selling his apartments."

"Where is this condo?" Kyle asked.

"I don't know. She didn't give me an address."

"Call his office and find out," Kyle said. "Please, Corky. Now."

Corky picked the phone up and began to dial Stuart Pride's real estate office.

Linda leaned in, impressing on Corky the urgency of the moment. "And once we have the address, we need you to call the police and have them meet us there."

"Does this have something to do with ..." Corky said, his voice trailing off. "Oh my God."

His hands were shaking as he grabbed a notepad and pen, waiting for an answer at the realtor's office.

"Janet?" he said. "This is Corky at the gallery, I need to know where Stuart is. The condo he's showing. I know it's not on his calendar! Just give me the address, please, this is official police business."

Kyle turned to Linda. "Get us a taxi. Tell him I'll be right out."

Linda hurried out of the gallery as Corky began to write furiously. As soon as the address and apartment number were on the notepad, Kyle reached over, grabbed the top sheet and ran for the door.

CHAPTER 34

TWELVE FLOORS ABOVE SOHO

Kate Pride had lived in New York City for twenty-five years and never feared for her life until this moment. Manhattan had remained for her a place of dreams, the Emerald City far in the distance, but not so far she couldn't get there if she tried hard enough and believed in her own potential. Some would call her life charmed; she had not, upon reflection, experienced much difficulty here, no real obstacles to her ambitions. She'd set the trajectory for her life early and mostly just held on for the ride, picking up Stuart along the way, her years learning from the best in the business, her gallery that had never really struggled, and here it all was coming to a sudden and terrifying end.

Stuart was secured to his chair on the terrace with duct tape Kieran had bought on the way from the Hotel Exeter. Along with a spindle of clothes line rope, the purchase had left him with $75 and change to his name; even a bus wouldn't get him far for that, but he had stopped worrying much about his future plans when he left Javier Velsaco's body in an Argentine landfill. Kieran, too, had led a charmed life, at least the last two months of it. The killings had been easy; he'd not taken great precautions, just covered his face and kept his presence unknown to most but his victims, yet here he was, twelve floors above SoHo, on a terrace with a spectacular view that could not be viewed – in New York City, of all places! – and no authorities were coming. No police hot on his trail. He was as much a phantom as a man can be, come back to haunt the ones who whispered. Call it lucky, call it charmed, everything had finally gone his way, and he felt great.

Kate had arrived thinking she was meeting Stuart, Javier and a friend of his looking to buy an expensive apartment. Roscoe the doorman had let her pass without even calling up. Stuart was one of three real estate agents authorized to sell in the building, and Roscoe had seen him come and go dozens of times; there was no reason to bother using the intercom, so he let Kate breeze by and take the elevator to the twelfth floor. He was calmly going through deliveries from the dry cleaners, logging them into the building's online system, while Kate was being bound to a chair next to her husband.

When she got to the apartment the door was open a crack, and Kate should have hesitated then. Stuart was meticulous about these things and never left apartment doors open, even in buildings as secure as this one. She knocked and called out. "Stuart? Are you there?" At first there was no response, and she checked her text message to make sure she had the right address. Stuart brokered a half dozen buildings in this area, there could be a mix up.

"We're on the terrace," a strange man's voice said. It was her second missed opportunity to back away. Why would a stranger answer when she called out her Stuart's name?

Remaining outside in the hall, she said, "Is Stuart there? Am I at the right apartment?"

Kieran opened the door, startling her. "Yes, yes, you must be Kate Pride. Stuart and Javier are on the terrace, it's an amazing view. Come in, please."

Kate still felt something was off, but the man seemed nice enough, and his voice was gentle, his smile sincere. There was also something familiar about him. She entered the apartment, distracted by the sheer size and comfort of it. Just as Kieran closed the door behind her, she remembered with a sudden shock where she'd met him and who he was. She had tried to describe him just an hour ago to that woman detective, tugging at her memories to remember what he looked like. And now she knew.

By then Kieran had placed himself between Kate and any hope of escape.

"How do you not fear for your life riding taxis in this city?"

Linda was completely sincere in her question. This was the third time in two days she had ridden in a cab and each time had been a thrill of the worst kind. "Please put your seatbelt on," she added. "I haven't known you long enough to lose you to a traffic accident."

Kyle was leaning up against the partition, staring at the street ahead as if he could magically make them go faster. The taxi was already speeding, veering from lane to lane as it barreled toward SoHo. Kyle had offered the driver an extra $20 to get them there in ten minutes.

"Relax," he said. "New York City streets are among the safest in the world. Very few people die in traffic here."

Linda found that hard to believe. She'd observed since arriving that walk lights had no meaning here. People swarmed along this way and that, paying no mind whatsoever to traffic lights. It seemed like orchestrated chaos, with cars hurtling through lights and pedestrians walking between them, somehow gauging the distance available and the time it would take them to cross in front of the cars without being hit. It was almost mystical, but unnerving, and she wanted no part of it. She had dutifully waited for a 'walk' light at every corner she'd been on. As for taxis, the sooner she was out of this one the better, and she planned to familiarize herself with the subway system and buses on any future visits.

Kyle had called and texted Kate twice to no avail since they got into the cab. He had also called Corky to make sure he'd notified the police. Corky assured him they were on the way, but that he'd had a hard time explaining the emergency to them. "Someone could get killed" struck the 911 dispatcher as vague and overly dramatic. Corky spent five minute convincing her it wasn't a prank. The best the dispatcher would do is promise him she would send a cruiser to check it out.

"Here!" Kyle shouted. "First building on the left, that's it."

The taxi swerved to the curb, nearly hitting an elderly woman walking an equally elderly Jack Russell Terrier. Once again Linda was awed by the symphony of anarchy, as the old woman didn't so much as glance at the cab that nearly took her life. She tugged on the dog's leash and walked down the sidewalk.

Kyle grabbed two twenties from his wallet and handed them to the driver, a man of Middle Eastern descent and demeanor who had whispered illegally into a headset all the time he was driving. No acknowledgment had been made of his passengers other than to agree to the extra $20. He had gotten them to their destination with a minute to spare.

Linda and Kyle hurried into the building. Roscoe stepped from behind the front desk to stop them when he saw them rushing in. "Excuse me, are you here to see someone?"

"Kate Pride," Kyle said. "She's here with her husband, showing an apartment."

"I'll have to call up," Roscoe said.

"There's no time."

"I can't let you go. Just a moment, please."

Roscoe walked back behind the desk and picked up the phone. Kyle and Linda could hear it ringing as Roscoe held it out from his ear. "That's odd, there's no answer."

"Please," Kyle said. "There's no time."

"Maybe they're on the terrace," Roscoe continued. "I can try calling back in a few minutes."

Linda pulled out her New Hope detective's badge for the second time. "This is a police matter, we really don't have time."

Roscoe nodded, of course, please, go right ahead.

"We need the keys," Kyle said, knowing every doorman kept keys to the empty apartments. Roscoe hesitated again. It was in his training to be cautious, to not assume anything was as it seemed. The city was too full of scammers and con artists, you had to be vigilant.

"Now!" Linda shouted, shocking the doorman into action. He could lose his job for this, or be a hero. He said a quick prayer and fumbled in the closet for the keys to 12D.

Kate had never imagined her life ending on the terrace of an apartment in SoHo, in full view of anyone who had been able to see them, but no one was. The terrace was on the top floor facing south, and no other building overlooked it, nor were any close enough for people in the windows to see without using binoculars. It was the perfect terrace to kill someone on, and Kieran thanked Stuart for providing such an outstanding location. Stuart only looked at him in terror, his mouth sealed with the same duct tape that bound his hands and feet to the chair. His wife, the love and center of his life, was equally helpless, confined to a chair just a few feet from him. They could only stare at each other, attempting to communicate with their eyes as they wavered between fear and hope, determination to survive and un-speakable grief at the certainty they would not.

Kieran snapped another photograph of the couple with his camera. He'd been waiting to use it, and regretted not thinking to buy it before. He would have loved to make a slideshow of photos from the hotel rooms in Buenos Aires and Philadelphia, the landfill and the rain-soaked sidewalk in Brooklyn. Oh well, he told himself, you can't have everything.

"I know you were one of the whisperers," Kieran said to Kate, leaning in and snapping a close up of her terrified face as she shook her head, deny-ing any part in his crazed ideas. "I even think you started it."

She shook her head again. She knew the man was insane, and she knew he was capable of killing because he already had. She needed to convince him of her innocence.

"Oh, yes, Katherine, you're the queen bee, it's your gallery. I saw you. You and Javier, Richard Morninglight, Devin and that Shiree woman. Talking and whispering, laughing and whispering. I watched you closing night at the restaurant celebrating. I wasn't invited. Did you know that?"

She remembered then: a congratulatory dinner with the people he'd named. The other artists didn't join them. It wasn't planned, just an im-promptu meal at Trattoria Del Amo. They'd walked there the night of the New Visions closing to celebrate their success and toast their futures.

Kieran saw that Kate remembered, and he smiled. "Now it comes back. You and the others. Talking about your triumph. Telling Javier he would be better off without me. I was a stone around his neck. What's the word? 'Albatross.' What a strange thing to wear around your neck, a dead bird. I don't want any albatrosses around my neck, but I'm happy to be one around yours. And I am sorry your husband has to pay this price. At least you'll be on camera together." He showed her the small camera he'd spent too many precious dollars on. "It takes video, too. I'm going to be the next YouTube sensation. Well, you are, anyway. It may be the first snuff film to make the morning news. How's that for high art?"

Kate's mind was turning round and round. She began to twist her wrists, knowing it was futile but hoping to somehow break free. She looked across at Stuart and saw he was doing the same, and had begun to buck in the chair as if he might be able to leap up still fastened to it but furious enough to free them while they still had time.

Kyle and Linda burst from the elevator into the 12th floor hallway.

"Every front desk has a set of keys," Kyle said, explaining why Roscoe had them.

"For most of the apartments, tenants like knowing someone can get in if they have to. And definitely the ones for sale. He has to let the brokers in."

Linda didn't care why they had the keys, only that they did. They rushed to apartment 12D.

Kieran heard them fumbling with the lock, then bursting into the apartment. It was both a surprise, and expected. He had fantasized the final kill, the tableau he'd set over and over in his mind that would play out on computers and televisions around the world, yet he had wondered with each successive murder why he had not been caught. At first he had truly believed he had the power of invisibility, but then he thought he was just very lucky, that God was on his side, the side of right. And yet, he knew the time may come, he may find himself in exactly this situation, having raced so far but unable to make it the last few yards to the finish line.

With no time to think it through, no moment to wonder who was rushing toward the terrace, Kieran stepped around behind Kate Pride and placed his knife at her throat, the same knife he had used to stab Devin sixteen times.

Linda and Kyle ran onto the terrace – and froze.

"Ah," Kieran said, holding Kate's head back with one hand, the knife with the other. "The photographer. I recognize you. I watched you from the coffee shop across the street. No camera today? It's okay, you can have mine."

Kyle wanted to reason with an unreasoning man. Knowing it was about buying time and not doing something that would get Kate Pride's throat cut, he said, "I didn't realize who you were."

Kieran stared at him, his expression growing darker. "You still don't," he said. "No one realized who I was until it was too late. Javier certainly didn't know who I was. He thought I was just another throwaway. And the fuckers who told him that made him sure of it, including the woman you're about to watch die."

"Kate never said anything about you. I was there." Kyle recognized him now from some of the photos he'd taken at the New Visions opening. "You were against the wall. No one understood how important you were."

"You're not serious," Kieran said. "You think this is a movie? You think you can just flatter me or pretend you have the slightest idea who I am and I'll, what, give you the knife? Surrender? Let's hear what Kate thinks about that. I'm going to take the tape off her mouth, and if she so much as breathes too deeply, I'm going to kill her."

Kieran reached down with his free hand and yanked the tape from Kate's mouth. "Tell them," he said.

She tried not to gasp for air, worried it would set him off. "Tell them what?" she managed.

"The same things you told Javier, the same things all of you told him, why he tossed me away like a tissue he'd just cum on, why I left his body in a landfill."

The sirens could be heard then, closing the distance to the building. Kieran cocked his head, listening. Sirens were a common sound in Manhattan, but he knew these were for him.

When Kieran turned his head to listen for the approaching sirens, Linda began to ease down ever so slightly, at the same time lifting her right leg, reaching very carefully for her ankle holster. She had never told Kyle she carried a gun off duty; there was no reason to, but she'd been around guns her entire life. She has seen her father's police service pistol, and many like the one that killed him in front of that Cincinnati grocery store. She cursed herself for not taking it out sooner, but the time for regret was over. She could think it through later, if they all made it out alive.

"I told Javier he was lucky to have you," Kate said. "No one wants to be alone in the world. Javier wanted someone to share his success with, that someone was you."

"You don't even know my name," Kieran hissed. "And you're a very bad liar. You all whispered to him, then you laughed and toasted your own cruelty. I saw you, just like I saw you yesterday. I've been watching you, Katherine Pride, watching and waiting."

The sirens had grown louder, screaming down the street until they stopped in front of the building. It was only a matter of moments now.

Stuart Pride had been watching it all, trying to calm himself. He saw Linda begin to ease down. The two of them exchanged glances as she shook her head almost imperceptibly, telling him not to do anything stupid. He understood what she was doing and nodded, knowing he would ignore her anyway. The window of opportunity had opened just a crack and he had to act before it closed forever. Linda had her hand nearly to her ankle, and with just a minor distraction she would be able to reach it. He took a quick breath through his nose and flung himself to the side, crashing to the terrace floor and smashing his head on the tiles.

Kieran jumped back, and at that very moment Linda squatted down and slid her gun out from its holster. Faster than the eye could see, quicker than the mind could calculate, she had the gun raised and aimed squarely at Kieran Stipling's chest.

"Drop the knife," she said. "I'm a cop, I know how to shoot and I won't hesitate."

Kieran raised his hands, the knife still in his right fist, but he made no move to surrender.

"Do you know my name?" Kieran asked, as he began to step slowly backward.

"Stop," Linda said, knowing what he was thinking.

"Who am I, cop lady? Call me by name."

"You're a man who needs understanding," Linda said. She began to ease toward him, holding her free hand out. "Just give me the knife. We can get help for you."

"You don't even know my fucking name!" Kieran shouted, the rage in his voice echoing off the terrace floor, the apartment door, the rooftops around them, out, out into the sky. A cry of pain and anguish unlike anything any of them had ever heard.

It all happened so fast that afterward each of them told a slightly different version. A neutral observer would say that Kieran, knowing his time had come and there was no way out, no bus he would ever be catching to a back road somewhere to disappear, flung the knife at Linda, catching her off guard just long enough to sidestep to the terrace railing.

"Don't do this," Linda said in a last effort to stop him.

"What are my alternatives?" Kieran replied. He was strangely calm. It was the demeanor of a man who knew he had no options. But Kieran Stipling had always known that. His life was one of decisions made to survive, not to prosper, not to create a life that was anyone's dream come true, least of all his. He had been thrown about by circumstances, and had only once believed things had gone his way. Once, with a man named Javier Velasco, who proved to be as cruel as the rest of them.

So fast. No negotiation, no possibilities. It was breathtaking, how suddenly and easily he went over the railing. Unbelievably fast and easy, so easy that Linda and Kyle kept staring at the space where Kieran had just been. Kate and Stuart Pride couldn't see what happened, and stared up dumbfounded at the shock on their faces. It took Linda several seconds before she ran to the railing, leaning out and looking down.

Roscoe the doorman was already standing over the body. A young couple had nearly been hit by Kieran as he landed on the sidewalk, and the woman began to scream.

CHAPTER 35

OPENING NIGHT

More had happened in one week than in any week of Kyle's life he could remember. Just six days ago his first love had gotten married, bringing Kyle both happiness for David, and sadness at such a clear sign of time passing. They had barely been men when they moved to New York City, and now, thirty-five years later, David had married, Kyle and Danny were in the planning stages of their own wedding, and youth for all of them was the stuff of reminiscence.

Then came the news reports of Devin's murder, the arrival of Detective Linda, and the spiral of events that ended so horribly on a terrace in SoHo – and a sidewalk twelve stories below. Even the murders at Pride Lodge had not been such a jolt. And while all of it unfolded, this was always in the background waiting to happen, his opening night. It had gone on as planned, everyone was here, and yet it all felt surreal to Kyle as he sipped a glass of wine and listened to another compliment from another stranger on his beautiful photographs.

Kyle had been making his photos public for over a year on a Tumblr photoblog. The idea of people seeing his pictures was nothing new. But this was different, this was *official*, not quite professional, but very close to it. Professionals were born of gallery shows like this. Word would spread, but luckily for Kyle he was not a portraitist. He would not be taking calls from people looking for someone to shoot their wedding or their black tie event at the Met. His was a photography of isolation, pictures that featured angles, various forms of natural light, *vision*scapes as much as landscapes. The word approached his lips but he held it back, having been afraid to think it, let alone say it ... *art*. Did he dare call it that? He'd considered himself a shutterbug, nothing more. But to be an *artist*? He was uncomfortable with the term, as afraid to be pretentious as he was to be wrong.

He looked around the gallery. Margaret sat in a one of several chairs that had been provided, holding court with a handful of people. She seemed to know more guests among the crowd than nearly anyone else but Kate Pride herself. Nearly 200 people had shown up, only about a dozen of whom Kyle could address by name. Had it been wrong of them to still have the opening after everything that happened? Kieran Stipling's suicide had been two days ago; it was still news, and Imogene Landis had already begun spinning it into her next big scoop. Kyle had promised her that, and no sooner had he and Danny given statements at the police station, than Imogene began calling to remind him of her exclusivity. Such was the stuff of love-hate relationships. It was horrific, yet seedy; tragic, yet someone must tell the story. Why not Imogene Landis? For all her faults, Kyle loved her.

His mother was another woman he loved, but whose faults were harder to name. Sally Callahan had arrived that afternoon, and rather than tell Kyle and Danny her big secret, she had brought him with her: Farley Carmichael, the man she had been seeing for two months without saying a word about it. No doubt she had wanted to wait until she was sure of her feelings, but it had come as a shock to Kyle. His mother was seventy-six years old and had sworn she would never love any man but Bert Callahan. Showing up with a boyfriend almost ten years younger and beaming non-stop since she arrived was not something Kyle had ever anticipated or even entertained. It wasn't that he thought his mother was betraying his late father, that would be ridiculous. But Sally had been so sure she would live out her years as a single widow. His discomfort with it was only heightened when she told him she and Farley would be staying at the Westin. One room, one bed.

"They look great together," Danny said, startling Kyle out of his thoughts. "And what better time to offer her ownership in a restaurant than now, when her life is so new?"

"Of course she'll say yes," Kyle said. "Be very careful what you wish for in this case, Daniel. She won't be the silent partner you're imagining."

Kyle only called him Daniel when he was being extra serious. Danny knew they'd be continuing this conversation for years to come and he didn't care right now. His beloved Margaret and her equally beloved restaurant would be safe. "Timing is everything," he said, as much to himself as to Kyle.

"Appearances, too," replied Kyle, quoting his boss. "They certainly appear happy."

Sally and Farley were across the room, admiring Kyle's "Lonely Blue Pool" photo. It seemed to catch everyone's attention and he was beginning to think he could sell prints of it. Soon it might show up in every bargain-rate hotel room in the country and Kyle would be set for life.

"Why the secrecy?" Kyle asked. They had both liked Farley well enough on first inspection. Sixty-seven, tall, handsome with pure silver hair, still thick and brushed back; sensible half-frame gold glasses, the hands of a piano player, with long thin fingers, a gray moustache, and a very good dresser who knew how to be formal and casual at the same time. Farley Carmichael was retired, but comfortably so. He'd sold yachts for a living, and clearly made a profit. And then there was the adoration in his eyes as he stayed close to Sally. So affable, so likeable, so perfect for her. Something must be wrong.

"She knew it would be hard for you," Danny said, sipping his Vodka martini. "Your relationship with your dad was a tough one, but he was still your dad. There's a reason you wanted that desk."

Kyle let it go. He'd told himself the desk was a keepsake, but he knew Danny was right. He knew it was more complicated than simply wanting a memento. And he knew his mother's happiness was most important. Whatever misgivings he had, he would deal with later. Even if it meant more time on a therapist's couch.

Kate Pride was working the crowd, truly a professional. Stuart had been too shaken by the events of the past three days and had bowed out. He'd taken time off from work as well and once the opening was over he and Kate were planning an unexpected trip to Paris. It was their favorite city, and Stuart, realizing how precious time is and how suddenly life can take a tragic turn, wanted them to go there again. It had been ten years since their last trip, and every spring they promised to visit, only to have it postponed for one thing or another. No more postponements, Stuart told her that morning. No more waiting for next year to do the things that matter.

Nothing new had been learned about Kieran Stipling since he plunged to his death from the SoHo terrace. It turned out the view wasn't as hidden as he'd thought, and several frantic calls had been placed to 911 from people in distant buildings watching something frightening unfold twelve floors above Manhattan. He was an enigma, this damaged man projecting his suffering onto his victims, blaming them for a life he hated. The trail he left was a jagged one, crisscrossing the country over the course of twenty years, and it would be several months before a clearer picture of him emerged. Now, in the immediate aftermath, he remained a mystery, with a past as opaque as a fog rolling in off the Hudson. A man who had come from the shadows and quickly, instantly, returned to them. An invisible man whose existence was only proved by his body on the sidewalk.

Kyle felt a tap on his shoulder and turned to see who it was. He didn't know Detective Linda had any friends in New York City, and for a moment he wondered where she had been hiding this one as Linda started to introduce him to a woman nearly as tall as she was. Then it hit him before she even spoke: he was looking into the smiling face of Kirsten McClellan.

"Kyle and Danny, meet Kirsten," Linda said. "Kirsten, this is Kyle and Danny."

She was a looker, Kyle saw that immediately. Short brown hair with just hints of gray, lithe in her posture, like a cheetah, he thought, slim and dressed to kill in a navy pantsuit that had to have cost as much as most people paid for a month's rent.

"I had to come," Kirsten said. "After everything that happened."

Detective Linda allowed herself a moment of weakness and slipped her arm around Kirsten's waist. It was a public display she would not have been comfortable with under most circumstances, but it felt right. Here with her new best friends, in a city she had avoided most of her life for the loss it represented, being emotionally and physically supported by the woman she truly hoped would be the love of her life. Kirsten hadn't waited to be asked to come once she knew what had happened. She'd called Linda from her car as she sped to New York City, assuring her she would be there in record time.

Kyle looked around again while Danny chatted with the women. It seemed so incongruous, that everything could end this way, feeling this good. He felt a moment of guilt for enjoying the night, when it had been preceded by danger and death. Survivor's guilt, he supposed, something he knew well from losing so many friends to AIDS when he was himself a young man. He knew it was just part of living, that the lucky ones made it through the years and had to let go of those who did not.

"We made it," Kyle said, talking to himself.

"What?" Danny asked.

Kyle turned to them, realizing he'd spoken his thought out loud. "Nothing," he said. "Where were we?"

"You and Danny, a weekend in New Hope," Linda said. "The Fourth of July sounds about perfect."

"We can watch the fireworks," Kyle said.

Danny caught his eye, nodding slightly toward Linda and Kirsten. "That we can," he said, smiling. "That we can."

Kyle sipped his wine again, glancing around the gallery. Everyone was there. Everything was in place. Everything was as perfect as it could be.

They had made it.

DEATH BY PRIDE

Book III

CHAPTER 1

Killing wasn't as much fun as it used to be. He expected to be a bit rusty after three years, but he had never anticipated this … *dullness*, this sense that, in the words of bluesman B.B. King, the thrill was gone. Maybe he had just been away from it too long; maybe he needed to get up to speed. The man whose body he deposited into the East River just before midnight was, after all, only the first in his current series. There would be two more before the week was out, and maybe the old rush would return with the next one. He had to trust it would, to believe as a child believes that Santa Claus is real and will come shimmying down the chimney every Christmas Eve. Or how Dorothy believed, clicking her slippers in that dreadful movie. That might be a more appropriate comparison, given the occasion. Click, click, click … and he was home.

He did not come all the way back to New York to resume his annual ritual for something as lackluster as this first kill. Had it been the young man himself whose death stirred so little response in him? What was his name? Victor? Victor Someone. Dense and inattentive; he had been too easy, and far too handsome. *Cute*, really. The kind of cute that becomes very sexual in manhood. Innocent smile, calculated shyness. Victor Someone knew exactly what he was doing flirting in the store that afternoon, and he had succeeded, much to his regret.

Unfortunately, Victor wasn't nearly as enjoyable to kill as he was to look at. Too easy, too unchallenging. Like a cat who had no trouble capturing a wingless bird, he had not had fun with this one. He would have to analyze the experience, figure out why it had not been as satisfying as it was before, and what he might need to do to reignite his excitement. Did he need to be more brutal? Did he need to introduce tools into the game, a scalpel, perhaps, or a drill of some kind? He would think hard on it. A decision had to be made quickly; he'd already placed an online ad looking for the next one and the emails were flooding into his special account, the one no one would ever trace no matter how hard they tried. A phantom as elusive as he was deserved a phantom email routed through Chicago, then London and Tokyo, server after server erasing any clue to its origin.

Diedrich Kristof Keller III—D to everyone who knew him well (a thought that made him chuckle, since the only ones who truly knew him died with the knowledge) had only been back in his townhouse since March. His tenants, the ones he rented to when he left for Berlin to take care of his mother, had a lease through February and D had waited patiently for them to leave. A lovely young couple with two small children. He'd never met Susan and Oliver Storch—the rental had been arranged through an agent—but they had taken very good care of the place, he would give them that. And you would never know they had children; no stray toys were left behind, no evidence, really, that anyone had been there at all for the past three years. His kind of people.

He was so glad to be back. He'd hated Berlin, all of Germany for that matter, though he saw very little of it and had no desire to see more. For D being German was as meaningless as someone being Scottish who had never been to Scotland, spoke with no brogue, and was only tied to the land by name and ancestry. His parents were from Germany, but they had moved to Anaheim, California, before D was born. His mother, Marta, returned to Berlin a broken, bitter woman, but that was not his fault. She was a coward. *Cowardess?* he wondered, making a cup of tea at his kitchen counter. It was an island counter, surrounded by a stove and refrigerator large enough to impress and too large to be practical—there was almost nothing in the refrigerator, and he rarely cooked. The entire townhouse was furnished for show—the furniture, the artwork, the paintings and photographs of nonexistent family members and forebears. It had been carefully put together to deceive. Anyone who came into his home would think he was just another wealthy man in New York City with a long lineage, should one wonder where he came from. Men with paintings of their grandfathers above a fireplace surely belonged in Manhattan's upper reaches and had unquestionable pedigree. That was the point, to be unquestioned. By the time anyone got around to questioning him, to wondering about his authenticity, it was too late. He answered their questions with a belt around their necks. The belt he kept especially for them. *You're right, good man, I'm not who I appear to be. Please keep that to yourself.* And they did.

He was tired now. He'd worked out how to get the bodies out of his house unnoticed some years ago, but he was getting older, forty-two this coming September. It wasn't as easy as it used to be. And this one had been heavier than he'd guessed when he chose him.

Note to self: never, ever, pick a customer from the store again. No matter how cute or handsome, no matter how liquid and shining the eyes or seductive the smile. Stay online, stay hidden behind a dozen re-routers, change names each time, do not take this risk ever again.

He'd been away too long, losing his edge in his mother's dreary Berlin apartment, saving himself for his return to the killing ground. He'd have to sharpen quickly; mistakes were something other people made. He'd made one this time—the only time in all his successes—and he would not make another one.

He would look at Victor Someone's driver's license in the morning. Sense memory was a beautiful thing, and nothing brought it back quite like his keepsakes. The license was his souvenir—his thirteenth. Lucky thirteen. The rest of the wallet stayed with the body. He wasn't interested in making identification difficult. It didn't matter if the police knew who had been killed, only that they would never find the man who did the killing.

It had been dark when he parked by the river. The new moon had worked to his favor, a first. No one had been around; he made sure no one saw a man with a heavy, strangely shaped object wrapped in black plastic trudging his way to the river's edge. Then a simple heave and splash, and he was on his way home.

Bedtime at last. But before then, for a few minutes anyway, he wanted to go through those emails. He'd requested photos, knowing many of them would be old and meant to trick him, and that was okay. He was less interested in finding a man who looked exactly like his picture than he was in finding a man who made him want to kill. It was like falling in love with an image: he never knew which one it would be, but knew it when it happened. *This one. Oh yes. This one will be here soon.*

He turned off the kitchen light, took his tea cup with the little chain from the tea ball hanging over the side, and headed to his large master bedroom on the second floor. His laptop was open and waiting for him. He would sift through a dozen or so email responses and see if any of them struck his fancy. But first, the pictures of Victor. Victor Someone. He would enjoy those before sleeping. He always took pictures.

CHAPTER 2

Kyle Callahan loved being married, it was the *getting married* that had been such an ordeal. He'd been with his partner, Danny Durban, for just over seven years when they finally made it official—and legal, in the state of New York, at least. That had been one of the reasons they'd waited: neither of them would marry until they could do it in their home state. And now, with the Federal Government recognizing their marriage, there had been no reason to put it off any longer. So on May 12th, just six weeks ago, he and Danny had gone to City Hall in downtown Manhattan and gotten their license. The following Saturday they stood before seventy-five of their closest friends at Metropolitan Community Church and publicly declared their intention to spend the rest of their lives together. Danny had wanted the 12th as their wedding date, to honor the anniversary of their first meeting at the Katherine Pride Gallery, but it fell on a Tuesday. Nobody gets married on a Tuesday, at least not anyone with a mother-in-law flying in with her boyfriend from Chicago, another set of parents from Queens, siblings, nieces, bosses, and Kyle's best friend Detective Linda Sikorsky from New Jersey, along with her own newly minted wife Kirsten McClellan.

The sheer logistics of a wedding were more than Kyle or Danny had ever anticipated. It starts out simply enough as a vision in which all these friends, relatives and loved ones magically appear to celebrate the happy couple's bliss. In that first fantasy phase there are no hotels to recommend, no invitation list to cull, no feelings to hurt by being excluded from the guest list. And certainly no large pile of cash to drop for an affair that seemed to have $10,000 as its starting price. By the time they headed downtown for their license both men were frayed at the edges, ready to elope and send all these people a nice photograph instead. It was too late by then and the worst was over, so they went through with it and now would not have had it any other way. The cost only set them back three years' worth of prime vacation travel, but that was okay. It had been a huge success and they were finally married.

The inevitable let-down after so much stress, planning and execution had lasted about a week for Kyle, less for Danny who was busy dealing with the imminent departure of his beloved Margaret Bowman. Margaret had started Margaret's Passion, the restaurant Danny now owned with Kyle and Kyle's mother Sally. She'd hired Danny almost twelve years ago, then sold the restaurant to him last year as she crept into her 80s. Now, as he had dreaded, she was preparing to move to Florida to spend her remaining days with her sister Rebecca, leaving Margaret's Passion to Danny to fully make his own. As long as there was a Margaret's Passion there would be a Margaret, if only in photographs on the walls with the many celebrities and politicians she'd served so well and lovingly over the decades. But the thought of her being so far away and likely never to return had left Danny in a funk for months. His wedding, despite the rigors of it, the anxiety and the stress, was a high point and a needed distraction from the loss he faced. There would only be one wedding for both men; there would only be one Margaret Bowman, too, and having her there in the front row with their parents was a memory they would cherish as much as the wedding itself.

Kyle was thinking about it all as he scanned the previous day's mail at their kitchen table. It was his habit to get the mail when he got home in the early evening, but he'd been distracted and had forgotten, instead taking the elevator down to pick it up this morning, along with the New York Times that lay outside their door. In the age of online everything, Kyle still preferred reading the paper the old fashioned way—with pages that turned and ink that came off on his fingers.

The men lived on the edge of Gramercy Park, at Lexington Avenue and 25th Street. Danny could easily walk to Margaret's Passion just six blocks away, and Kyle could get to the Japan TV3 offices, where he worked as the personal assistant to firebrand and borderline has-been TV reporter Imogene Landis, with an easy bus ride and a cross town stroll. Their dear friend Detective Linda (now retired from the New Hope, Pennsylvania, police force) was asleep in the spare room, turning it once again from their shared office into a guest room. She'd come into town the day before for her first Pride weekend and parade and Kyle made plans for them to see the city in much more detail than Linda had been able to on her last visit. That was in late April a year ago, and she and Kyle had been caught up trying to stop the killer Kieran Stipling as he murdered his way through a list of people connected to the Katherine Pride Gallery. Whatever sightseeing Linda had planned that visit was abandoned in the race to end the killing. Kyle intended to make up for it this time.

Danny walked in wearing the plush brown robe Kyle gave him the previous Christmas. The smell of morning coffee always brought him out of the bedroom, trailed moments later by their cats, Smelly and Leonard.

"Linda awake yet?" he asked, heading straight to the coffee pot and taking a cup from the cabinet above it. The cats took up position at his feet, expecting early morning treats.

"I doubt it," Kyle said. "I think she was up late, I heard her talking on the phone just before I fell asleep."

"It's terrible about Kirsten's mother. I wish we could see her again."

"I'm sure Linda wishes it, too. We're at that age, Danny ..."

"I know, I know, let's not talk about it."

Time did not take sides, it only passed in a constant flow, and eventually the people we ride the stream with begin to fall off to the shore. Kyle's father had been gone over fifteen years. Margaret was heading off soon for a few good years in Florida before she, too, slipped from the stream.

It wouldn't be long before their parents were gone and they took their place at the head of the line, saying goodbye to friends one by one—or perhaps saying goodbye themselves. Life makes no guarantees and takes no reservations.

Linda's wife Kirsten was in Phoenix with her dying mother. The women had hastily flown her to New Jersey in March and married in a very small ceremony in Stockton with just Kyle, Danny, and the women's mothers in attendance. It was the kind of wedding Kyle envied after the ordeal of his own. The next day Kirsten flew back with her mother and had been spending weeks at a time travelling back and forth. Her mother, Dot McClellan, had cancer metastasized throughout her body and was not expected to see the end of July. Linda's plan was to enjoy this weekend in the city with Kyle and Danny, then head to Phoenix. It had taken a serious toll on both women, and Kyle noticed how much thinner Linda was when she'd arrived yesterday afternoon.

They'd met Detective Linda Sikorsky a year and a half ago during Halloween weekend at Pride Lodge. The Lodge sat on twenty-five acres near the Delaware River, on the Pennsylvania side. Kyle's friend and lodge handyman, Teddy Pembroke, had been found dead at the bottom of the lodge's empty pool, and Linda was the homicide detective investigating the death, which proved to be deliberate. Murder, it seemed, was their first commonality, but since then they'd found many more. Kyle and Linda spoke every few days, and last fall he and Danny spent a week at her small house in the woods in Hunterdon County, New Jersey. Linda had inherited the house from her aunt Celeste and, with some reluctance, moved from her longtime home in New Hope to take up residence with the deer, rabbits and strange sounds nature makes when it has no competition. The highlights of the visit were supposed to be a week of sightseeing, country living and good food at fine local restaurants; instead, it became a hunt for the killer of Abigail Creek, matriarch of CrossCreek Farm and victim of a vicious hit-and-run. Their time together always seemed to attract murderers—or the other way around—and sometimes

Kyle wondered if they should just maintain a long-distance friendship, in the interest of keeping people alive.

"Did you see Vinnie when you picked up the mail this morning?" Danny asked, stirring creamer into his coffee and taking it to the table. He sat next to Kyle and picked up the mail, flipping through it so see what was his. Leonard stayed in the kitchen, staring up at the coffee pot as if he could not understand there were no treats in it for him. Smelly, the wiser of the two, followed Danny to the table and perched at his feet, knowing he would eventually relent and get the pouch of fish-flavored nuggets for her.

"Come to think of it, no. The relief guy was on duty, what's his name?"

"Dayton."

"Dayton? That's an unusual name."

The building had doormen. It was a perk Kyle had never known before moving from Brooklyn into Danny's apartment. It took a while to get used to, but not too long. Having someone open the door for you and receive packages and visitors was luxurious without being too elitist. Vinnie— Vincent Campagna—had the overnight shift and was among the most reliable doormen the building had ever had. He was in his mid-thirties, and in ten years on the door had not been off more than three or four times. This was the second night he'd called in.

"Is Vinnie sick?" Kyle asked, scanning the paper. The city's new mayor was making changes, many of which were controversial and demanded above-the-fold coverage.

"No, it's some family thing," Danny said. "Something about his brother missing, I'm not sure. There's not that much communication between tenants and the doormen, but I've heard things in the elevator."

Kyle kept reading the paper. The mayor was pushing for some new legislation, the mayor was insisting on a vote his way by the City Council, the U.S. Congress was at a stalemate again. He flipped the paper over to see what news hadn't made it to the top … and he froze. An article just below the fold was headlined, "Man Found in East River Identified, Police Searching for Clues."

Kyle started reading the story.

"You know, I think Smelly's finally losing weight," Danny said, looking down at the cat. She had been pre-diabetic for several years, but every effort at trimming her down had failed. "Maybe it's age."

"Shh!" Kyle said, focused on the article

"What's so interesting that you have to 'shhh' me?"

Kyle ignored him, reading. "What is Vinnie's last name?" he said after a moment.

"Campagna. Vincent Campagna."

"He has a brother."

"Yes."

"A brother who's also a doorman."

"Yes. I think their father was, too. A family tradition I guess, like the military. What are you reading? Is Vinnie in the news?"

"No, he's not," Kyle said, sliding the paper to the side. "But his brother, Victor, is."

"In a good way, I hope," Danny said, reaching for the paper to read about it himself.

"Not at all. In a bad way. A very bad way."

Danny read the article quickly. "Oh my God," he said.

"Oh my God is right. Victor Campagna is the body they found in the river Tuesday morning. You saw the story."

"It was everywhere. But nothing about it being an accident or a murder."

"This is awful."

Smelly began meowing, an escalation of her demands for a treat. Kyle swatted her away with his free hand.

"He's back," Kyle said.

Danny looked up at him. The article hadn't named a suspect. "Who is 'he'?"

"The Pride Killer."

Danny remembered then. Every year for four years at Pride weekend the East River had become a depository for victims of a man—assuming it was a man—who remained uncaught. The media had dubbed him the

Pride Killer, because the murders only happened that weekend in June, stopping once the festivities were over. Then radio silence. No killing, no bodies, nothing for another year, and another.

"Three years," Kyle said, as if he'd read Danny's thoughts. "He stopped three years ago and they couldn't figure out why. Everyone hoped he was dead, or that he'd come to his senses, if madmen have senses."

"But the paper doesn't say who—"

"It's him. The hands and feet bound, the strangulation, the location of the body. Even if it traveled in the current they'll trace it back to the general vicinity of where this guy dumps his bodies."

"Now we know why Vinnie hasn't been to work," Danny said. "He must be devastated."

"It says the body was found two nights ago. Poor Vinnie. And his family, I can't imagine."

The men grew silent. Smelly, sensing something was wrong, stopped her meowing and slinked off into the living room. She would get what she wanted, but later, when moods had returned to normal. Leonard was still staring at the coffee pot.

Finally, Kyle said, "He won't stop."

"How do you know that, if it's even him? He stopped for three years."

"Because this was the first. There will be a second, and a third. That's the way he works."

Danny had a sinking feeling. If timing was everything, it worked against them very well. Detective Linda visiting, a body in the East River; the stars had aligned in a way most displeasing to him as he watched Kyle's face for the telltale glazed expression, the speeding, clicking thoughts. He worried Kyle would not stay out of it, and that sooner or later something terrible would happen to them. They were married now, together forever. What happened to one of them, happened to both of them.

"Listen, Kyle …"

"Don't worry. This is one for the police."

Danny had the feeling he had just been lied to. Not deliberately; Kyle had every intention of staying out of it. But it was his nature to wonder—wonder who this man was taking the lives of other men, where he lived, how he found his victims. Danny knew that as much as Kyle might try to ignore this, it would take root in his mind and grow until he had to do something.

"What's cooking?" Detective Linda said, startling them both. Neither had heard her come out of the bedroom.

A sense of dread came over Danny as he blew across his coffee, cooling it. He knew Linda and Kyle would soon be lost in conversation about serial killers and floating bodies. Why can't his husband just be an amateur photographer and a personal assistant? Why must he take it upon himself to rid the world of bad people? Sooner or later one of those bad people might rid the world of Kyle.

CHAPTER 3

She could hear the men in the living room ... or was it the kitchen? Living room, kitchen, entryway, they all seemed to flow into each other in Manhattan apartments, if Kyle and Danny's was a typical example. Linda Sikorsky had no way of knowing—she had not been in any other apartments in New York City, except for the penthouse she and Kyle had burst into just in time to stop Kieran Stipling from cutting Stuart Pride's throat. That was over a year ago, and still the memory of it gave her chills. She stretched on the sofa bed, letting the unpleasant thoughts evaporate as she reached up with her hands, stretched her arms, and pushed her toes down until they almost went over the end of the mattress.

So much had happened since those awful murders. Kyle and Danny had gotten married, an elaborate event to which Linda and Kirsten were witness along with dozens of other people. The women had stayed in a boutique hotel in Park Slope that catered to lesbians, and only overnight; they wanted the men to have time alone, as if seven years were not enough. And even though Kyle had protested, insisting they should stay a few days, Linda knew he was secretly happy to have them all gone. Weddings were intense affairs and while it had been glorious, Linda was glad she and Kirsten had taken a much more intimate approach. They'd had to; Kirsten's mother was living on borrowed time (or, Linda thought, dying on it), and circumstances demanded they move quickly.

Linda's personal life had experienced significant changes as well. She and Kirsten McClellan were living together now as wife and wife, tucked in the woods in Linda's small house. There'd been a rocky, unsure time, last fall when Kyle and Danny visited, but it had passed and things were as secure and comforting as Linda imagined they could be, back when she'd first said hello at a New Year's Eve party to the woman she now shared her life with. Back then Kirsten was a highly successful real estate agent in New Hope, long established with her own company, and infinitely more experienced with relationships than Linda. While Linda had had several relationships with men over her forty-four years and even once considered marrying in her twenties, she had never dated a woman. Now she was married to one.

Another big change since her last trip to Manhattan was retiring from the police force and opening her vintage-everything store. *For Pete's Sake* was named after her father, a cop whose senseless death when Linda was eight years old had left an indelible stain on her heart. It was why she'd become a police officer, and why she named her business after him. She had put in her twenty years on the force, the last five as a homicide detective, and had given her notice. On the last Friday in September, Detective Linda became just Linda Sikorsky. No more notifying the next of kin, no more days at the precinct, no more nights and weekends hoping her phone wouldn't ring, calling her to a crime scene. She loved being a cop, and making detective had been among her life's true high points. But she had gone into the career in large part because of her father and the time had come to move on and honor him in other ways.

She had known even as a child that her mother Estelle worried every moment Pete was on duty, and most that he was not. Pete Sikorsky was the kind of cop—the kind of man—who stepped in if he saw someone in trouble or if he thought he could stop evil in its many forms. It's what killed him, and why Estelle had been right to fret nearly every waking moment of their lives. Pete had gone to the small corner grocery store just three blocks from their house and, proving fate's capricious nature, walked into a robbery. He hadn't entered the store yet when two men who had just held up the grocer at gun point came bursting out of the door. A police cruiser that had been nearby came gunning up the street. One of the robbers fired, confusion ensued, and five seconds later Peter Sikorsky lay dying on the sidewalk, a stray bullet in his neck.

Several years later Estelle remarried and moved with her new husband and daughter to Philadelphia, where she now lived as a seventy-three-year-old double widow. Linda became a police officer, got a job with the New Hope force, and twenty-plus years later she had turned one of the biggest pages in her life. Her one advantage was knowing what she wanted to do "in retirement." Many people have no idea what to do with themselves when they leave a job they'd been at for over two decades; many a cop ended his life with a gun in his mouth, haunted by what he'd seen, usually divorced a time or two, and so lost he or she saw no way out of the tunnel but the bright light of a gun muzzle. Linda would not be one of them. She had long wanted to open a "vintage everything" store, modeled after her favorite shop in Doylestown, Pennsylvania. She'd even become friends with Suzanne, the store owner, and Suzanne had mentored her since the store's opening last November. The business had done well and Linda had even been able to hire an assistant manager, Mitchell Parsons. Mitch was in his fifties, a devoted gay bachelor and an even more devoted assistant manager who ran the store more efficiently than Linda ever could. He'd been a real find and she was relieved beyond words to have him back in New Hope taking care of the store now. With her mother-in-law dying in Phoenix and the frequent trips she and Kirsten were making there, having Mitch to take care of things was among the great comforts in Linda's life. She made a mental note to call him later this morning and see how things were going—if he didn't call her first to tell her, which was usually the case.

Kyle and Danny were sitting at the kitchen table when Linda joined them, wearing yellow silk pajamas with bright green parrots on them. She had picked them up on a trip to San Francisco with Kirsten for their honeymoon. They accentuated her long dark blonde hair. Linda Sikorsky was a tall woman, "big boned" as her mother always said. At five-nine she stood head to head with Kyle. When she'd been on duty, wearing her navy suit, a holster on her hip and a badge clipped to her breast pocket, she had presented an intimidating presence. Sometimes it worked in her favor, such as when she had to question suspects; other times it kept people from trusting and befriending her. She believed it was one of the reasons she had stayed single and closeted for so many years; not because she didn't accept herself, but because life was just easier, simpler, when you spent it alone. It was a feeling she hoped to never have again.

"What's cooking?" Linda said, shuffling into the kitchen.

"Nothing," Kyle replied. "We're going out for breakfast."

"No, not literally cooking. I wouldn't expect you to make me breakfast. I mean what's up. It's seven o'clock in the morning."

"We're up, obviously," Danny said, standing and heading to the sink. He took a coffee cup from the cabinet above it and handed it to Linda. "Kyle was just going through the mail, reading the paper."

"Anything interesting?"

"In the mail or the paper?"

"Either."

"Oh yes," Kyle said, and he tapped the newspaper with his finger. "Something very interesting indeed."

Linda got her coffee and joined Kyle at the table.

"Why are you so interested in this?" Danny asked. He did not sit back down. He planned to go back to the bedroom and watch the news, joined by Smelly and Leonard, each cat settling in on either side of him.

"Because it's Vinnie's brother."

Linda: "Who's Vinnie? What are you interested in?"

Having their doorman's brother found floating in the East River made it personal for Kyle.

"I didn't know you were friends with Vinnie," Danny said.

"I'm not *unfriendly*. We talk. And think about it, Danny. If this could happen to Vinnie's brother, it could happen to anyone … and will. If this is the first victim, which I'm guessing it is, there are going to be two more.

Two innocent men, right now going about their lives with no idea what's waiting for them."

"And what is that?" asked Linda.

"Not what," Kyle said, "but who."

Kyle began telling Linda about the unsolved murders linked to the Pride Killer, how he had struck every Pride weekend for four years, then vanished, and how now, with the death of their doorman's brother, he had managed to hit very close to home.

Danny left them to their conversation and headed to the bedroom, the cats following behind like large mice on a trail of cheese. He wanted nothing to do with serial killers and dead bodies in the river. He had hoped after the Pride Gallery murders and that terrible business at CrossCreek Farm their lives would stop intersecting with murder, but he knew his hope had been in vain. Trouble had a way of finding them, as if it had been patiently waiting just ahead for them to turn the corner. Then it stepped out from the shadows.

CHAPTER 4

D sat luxuriating in the vastness of his king-sized bed, enjoying the quiet of the morning. The bedroom was in the corner of the townhouse's second floor and he could see the sun rising slowly over the river six blocks away. He had loved rivers all his life and would live on a riverbank if he could. If the rains came and flooded his riverbank home, he would stand in his living room with his legs in the water, marveling at the water's mystery and power, and if it swept him away he would glide along in its current, surrendered to going wherever it took him. He had no idea where this love came from—there had been no river in Anaheim when he was a child, no river near his uncle Leo's apartment in Brooklyn, where he'd gone to live when his mother fled back to Berlin in tatters. And it wasn't a general love of water; he was not fond of oceans or lakes. It was specific to rivers, something about rivers that moved his spirit in ways matched only by killing. He kept meaning to examine the connection between the two—a river's mighty flow as it followed its banks along channels carved in antiquity, and the mighty flow of his blood when he ended men's lives and commended their lifeless bodies to the very river he loved and respected so much. But he had no one with whom to examine this connection, no therapist to talk to, no close friend. So he had put it off and put it off, until he finally accepted he may never analyze or understand it. It just was.

He was careful not to drop crumbs on the sheets as he enjoyed his toasted corn muffin, his laptop open at his side. He had no housekeeper; inviting anyone at all into his home was a risk. He occasionally needed a plumber or an electrician, but he made sure they stayed in whichever part of the house he needed them. And they never, ever, went into the basement. Only invited guests went there, sometimes to see his artificial wine cellar, other times to see his one-of-a-kind gaming room with whatever latest computer equipment he'd read about. Victor Someone was into miniature train sets, of all the ridiculous things, and to his delight he discovered that D was, too! In fact, D had what some considered the most elaborate miniature train setup east of the Mississippi and wouldn't Victor like to see that? Why yes, yes he would. It's right down here, in the basement, please come, I'll show you. D had shown him, and like all the guests invited into D's basement, Victor Someone had not come back alive.

He was bored with Victor already. He'd stared at the idiot's driver's license for part of the morning, trying to relive the excitement of the kill, but there had been so little then or now. It was like trying to remember the marvelous taste of an especially bland meal. He gave up after his first cup of tea and half his muffin, tossed the driver's license aside and focused on the two dozen responses he'd gotten from his ad on ManMate. He'd worded it carefully to hint at his wealth and age without coming right out and presenting himself as a sugar daddy. He preferred ones with some intelligence, not run-of-the-mill hustlers. The more success they had in the world, the more they were able to hold an interesting conversation, the more he enjoyed their company for a short while before inviting them to see whatever he'd determined they wanted to see in his basement. He extracted just enough information from them to fantasize something down there they would want to see, and it always worked. But the dumb ones, the hustlers and the rent boys? They were only there for one thing, quick and easy. D was not interested in killing men no one would miss. He wanted worthy prey, so he placed his ads to attract it:

Single older man seeks friendship and possible traveling companion. Enjoy fine dining, theater, quality wine and quality time. Not looking for hookups or one-night stands. You should be intelligent, engaging, fully self-supporting and interested in seeing the city and possibly the world with your new best friend. Must be over 30 and easy on the eyes. Photo with all replies please.

It was broad yet specific enough to get at least some responses from the types of men he was looking for. Victor had been an anomaly, a customer he'd never seen before but whose amazing blue eyes and easy smile had tripped him up, caught him off guard. He did not make mistakes, and would not make one again. He'd paid for it in a lackluster kill that left him unsatisfied. He planned to make up for it with the next one.

There were sixteen responses to his ad. Eight of them he immediately deleted; four he pondered, scanning their photographs with his eyes to see if what initially caught his fancy lasted more then a few moments. It didn't, so he deleted those as well. That left four more. One was African-American and quite handsome. He'd sent a photograph of himself in dress military uniform. D had no idea what branch of service it was, but clearly this man was a serious candidate. D minimized the photograph and moved to the next one. This gentleman—for someone clearly in his 50s ought to be called a gentleman—was also very handsome and well-groomed, salt-and-pepper buzz cut, no glasses, although D suspected he wore them, at least for reading. He was a keeper, so D saved his email and photo. The last two were younger, one Asian, one white. D did not consider himself a racist or especially biased (not to be confused with discerning, which he most certainly was), but Asians were never really his cup of tea. As attractive as the man was, in a suit and tie, no less, he didn't fit the bill. D deleted him, leaving him with three choices.

Decisions, decisions. The fourth and final applicant was very good looking indeed. Dressed casually, "Kevin," as he called himself, listed his age as 32 and his occupation as branch manager for one of the largest bank chains in the city. Kevin lived in Staten Island—a very long way to travel to meet someone from an online ad, but that could be advantageous for D. The further away from home his victim came, the farther afield the police would have to search (futilely, he might add). Kevin had a disarming smile, sparkling brown eyes, longish sandy hair and a button-down shirt, the sort a bank manager might wear on his off-time.

In the end D said goodbye to the military man. He was truly appealing, but also too great a risk. Someone who had served his country might be very quick in a struggle. D had to consider his own strength and age. He could not take a chance at losing the upper hand; and while he drugged his victims first, it was just enough to make them woozy. The kill was a disappointment if they were incapacitated. He'd learned that early on when he first started. An unconscious man was no more interesting than a dead one. No, he would have to pass on Mr. Military, musing on how lucky the man was without ever knowing it.

That left Kevin the bank manager and Scott the well-preserved 50-something. Scott gave no indication what he did for a living or where he lived. If D wanted to know more he would have to respond. Did he want to know more? He peered closely at Scott's picture. Damn, he was a nice looking man. Not too tall, either. D didn't like taller men.

Suddenly D found himself in a unique situation. He had always been able to narrow it down to one. On occasion that one proved to be a poor choice and he'd had to start over, but it had always been one at a time. Now he could not decide.

He took another bite of his muffin and felt his frustration rise—and his curiosity. What was going on with him? His first kill had been uninspiring, even uneventful. And now he could not make a decision! Was it because the two remaining candidates were so different—one older than D, one younger? One vague in his email, saying little about himself, the other an eager bank branch manager whose email, short at it was, seemed written to let D know he was "fully self-supporting" and mature for his age?

Damn, D thought, sliding his plate to the side. *Damn, damn, damn.* This was not like him. This was indecisive. This was … thrilling in its way. Maybe he needed to switch things up. Yes, maybe that was the lesson of Victor Someone. It wasn't that he'd been away from it too long, wasting three years in a dreary German city, unable to speak the language well at first and tending to his pathetic mother out of a sense of obligation that had surprised him after all these years. It wasn't that he'd lost his passion. It was simply that he needed some spice, some new twists. Meeting two men instead of one would certainly be that. He always met them first. In his initial meetings he said nothing of who he was or where he worked, the men's clothing store he owned or where he lived. He was simply a well-heeled, well-mannered man from a city teeming with them, and they were unsuspecting prey.

He would do it! He would respond to each of them and set a time with Kevin for a casual coffee at the Arlington, perhaps meet Scott in a discreet bar. He hated chain coffee shops; nothing could be more banal than meeting in a Starbucks. But the Arlington served coffee and tea in their lobby. The landmark hotel had changed a great deal. The ghosts of celebrities from the 1930s and 40s had been chased away by tourists from Idaho and South Dakota. But the place still had atmosphere and the illusion of something once grand. It was one of his meeting places, but not the only one. He had to be careful; hotel clerks, servers and baristas had memories and could give descriptions. There were cameras absolutely everywhere, too. Most times D would meet them in a park—Bryant Park, or even the majestic Central Park—but not always. Sometimes a public meeting with witnesses added a touch of danger. He felt like being dangerous. He would not have the second one be as boring as the first.

He took a deep breath and felt an involuntary smile spread across his face. He placed his fingers over the laptop keyboard, then began thinking of his reply to each man. Wording was key. He would meet them each, one late morning and one in the afternoon. Jarrod would mind the store. He'd minded it for three years and done a very commendable job. It's why D had hired him; he knew a quality man when he saw one. And now he was looking at two!

He began to type.

CHAPTER 5

Kyle was determined their visit with Detective Linda would be different this time. On her last trip they'd been consumed by their search for the killer Kieran Stipling—whose name and motive they didn't know until they'd stopped his killing spree on a SoHo rooftop. There had been no time to see the city, no time to stroll or stop at one of the coffee shops on every other corner; no time to visit Grand Central terminal and gaze in awe at the ceiling with its constellations or marvel at the human river flowing in, out and around the magnificent train station every day. This time Kyle would show her the city he'd loved since moving here fresh out of college with his then-boyfriend David. He realized, as they walked west on 23rd Street, that it had been over thirty years since then. The city had changed. He had changed. The world itself was a very different place.

"Welcome to Chelsea," Kyle said as they crossed Sixth Avenue. "Once a gay mecca, now more a blend of strollers and gays and yuppies—does anyone still say 'yuppie'?"

Linda was taking it all in. Her memories of New York City were not the best: she'd stayed away from the city for many years, not wanting to taint the memory of her trip here as a child just months before her father was killed in Cincinnati; then, when she finally returned last year, she was pursuing a murderer not long after stepping off a train at Penn Station. Kyle's photography exhibit opening at the Katherine Pride Gallery had been wonderful, but the next day she was gone again. She could not yet say what she thought of the city, not really.

"Why do they call it Chelsea?" she asked. The only other Chelsea she knew of was in London. She also knew it was the kind of information Kyle would have; he was a sponge for just this sort of trivia.

It was warm out, but not yet humid. Kyle hated the humidity that came with summers in Manhattan. It was the only season he didn't like, and he knew come July he would have his annual impulse to move to Seattle or San Francisco, places he'd never been but that he imagined remained in the cool 70s all year round. He wouldn't move, of course, but he would want to.

"Funny you should ask," Kyle said. "It was originally an estate of a British major, who called it Chelsea in honor of Sir Thomas Moore's estate in London. Land was added to it over the years and it became the Chelsea we're walking in. Which, by the way, mysteriously expanded since I moved here."

"Really?"

"Yes. Chelsea twenty years ago ran from 14th Street to 23rd. They extended it to 34th Street when the neighborhood gentrified so they could attract renters. Funny how that works. North of 34th it's Hell's Kitchen, which was called Clinton for awhile, but now that there's nothing the least bit seedy or dangerous about it everybody calls it Hell's Kitchen again. It gives the residents someplace interesting to say they live."

They were both wearing shorts today, a rarity for Kyle who preferred his legs covered in public, and he was thankful Linda would have perfect weather for her brief visit with them. She was leaving for Phoenix on Monday and he wanted her to have a good time, something to take her mind off the situation with her terminally ill mother-in-law.

"I'm sorry about Kirsten's mother," he said.

"Dot. That's what everybody calls her, she'd tell you to call her that, too."

"Dot."

"I like that name. Dorothy's nice, but there's something unique about Dot. I don't know any other Dots, do you?"

"I can't say I do," Kyle said.

"It's hard. But Kirsten's holding up through it. She has to. I can't tell you how much it meant to her for Dot to make it one last time to New Jersey for our wedding. And how much it meant to me that you and Danny were there."

They were nearing Eighth Avenue now and Linda noticed several couples holding hands. Men with men, and at least one young lesbian couple who seemed happy and in love as they stopped to look at puppies in a pet shop window. A sadness came over her as she thought of all the years she'd missed, all the years she had kept her truest self a secret. At the same time, she was thrilled to live in a changing world, a world in which she could walk down the street—at least some streets, in some cities—holding Kirsten's hand without succumbing to the impulse to hide.

"Where are we going?" Linda asked. Kyle had told her he wanted to take a walk, but not where they were walking to. Danny had gone to his restaurant to meet with Chloe the day manager, and to plan for what would be both a celebration and the saddest event of his life: saying goodbye to old Margaret Bowman as she prepared to move to Florida. Danny was the party planner, as he had been for every party at Margaret's Passion the last eleven years. Kyle had suggested Danny let someone else arrange this one, that it would be too difficult, but Danny would have none of it. It was his restaurant, purchased from Margaret, and she was his second mother. No, he'd said, this was something he had to do.

"I want you to meet Imogene," Kyle said as they kept walking west. Once they reached Ninth Avenue they would turn right and head toward 38th Street. It was a good long walk, and he planned to stop for coffee and bagels as he always did, taking one of each for his boss, Imogene Landis. He wondered briefly if she, too, would be moving on soon. It was not a welcome thought and he waved it aside.

"Bugs?" Linda said, seeing Kyle wave his hand in the air.

"No, just something I don't want to think about."

Imogene Landis was a television reporter who'd slid very near the bottom of her profession until events gave her career a second wind. When

Kyle started working as her assistant six years ago she'd been reduced to a position as the English language financial reporter for a show called Tokyo Pulse. The show was put out by Japan TV3, whose studios they were walking toward. The 3:00 a.m. Tokyo crowd got a good laugh out of Imogene; she knew nothing about financial reporting, and her attempts to include a few words in Japanese had them howling on their living rooms floors. Then, a year and a half ago, she'd covered the murders at Pride Lodge—the same murders that brought Kyle and Linda together, and the next thing she knew, she was a star. A minor star, to be sure, but bright enough for her bosses in Tokyo and the New York station manager, Leonard Baumstein ("Lenny-san"), to promote her to city reporter. Since then she'd been back in the thick of things, covering politics, art, even the occasional noteworthy homicide. She was a celebrity of sorts now, and she'd caught the eye of several TV stations across the country. Kyle believed it was only a matter of time before one of them made her an offer she would accept.

They reached Ninth Avenue and turned, walking north. Most of New York City was a grid, something Kyle appreciated. It was both easy to find your way here, and harder to get lost. He'd walked this way a thousand times and wondered if he would keep walking this way if there was no Imogene waiting. He supposed he would, as a matter of habit, at least for awhile.

"I haven't wanted to bring this up ..." he said

Linda knew he was talking about the news he'd read that morning.

"There's nothing you can do, Kyle. Maybe it's not who you think it is, this Pride Killer. Maybe your doorman's brother drowned in the river. People drink too much, sometimes they stumble."

"No, this wasn't an accident. It's him. I know it is."

"So leave it to the police."

"You *are* the police!"

"Retired, Kyle. And I was on the New Hope force, a long way and a world of difference from New York City. I have a bad feeling about this one, I think we should stay out of it."

"And wait to read about two more? He kills in threes. No, this time he struck close to home. This time it's personal. I want to talk to Vinnie."

"Your doorman?"

"Yes, when the time's right." Kyle didn't know when Vincent Campagna would return to work but when he did, Kyle wanted to have a very delicate conversation with him.

"Well," said Linda, "if this is the Pride Killer and he claims his victims every Pride weekend –"

"Minus the last two."

"Minus the last two … I'd say time isn't something we have much of."

She was right. Kyle sighed, knowing he ought to stay out of it, but what if this killer got away with it again? He'd done his dirty work for years before stopping, and now that he was back he would probably do it for years again. Something had to be done, but not this moment. For now Kyle was taking them to meet his beloved, infuriating, demanding boss, and that was where his mind should be.

"Cecil's is just up ahead," Kyle said. Cecil's was the bagel shop where he always bought coffee and a breakfast treat of some kind for himself and Imogene. He was comforted that Cecil's had been around as long as it had—at least as long as Kyle had worked for Imogene. Some things needed to stay the same, he thought, even if it's just a bagel shop. Otherwise the impermanence of life would be too much to bear.

"I could use another cup of coffee," Linda said.

They walked on, approaching the back of the Port Authority bus terminal. Some parts of New York City were breathtaking, and other parts were permanently ugly. But this is New York City, all of it, and Kyle wanted Linda to see as much of it as she could in the next four days. He put the thought of killers and floating bodies out of his mind for now. It was a glorious day at one of the most festive times of year, at least for the hundreds of thousands who would flood Fifth Avenue for the parade Sunday, and he wanted no rain, no sadness, no death. This morning he would have none of them.

CHAPTER 6

Keller and Whitman was not the most well known men's clothing store in Manhattan, but it was certainly considered among the best. D's uncle, Leo Whitman, had eschewed growth, turning his nose up at the bigger stores and having disdain for chain operations. He was interested in quality, not quantity, and he had educated D slowly and steadily in the ways of the discerning man. *You succeeded very well, Uncle,* D thought as he entered the store that bore his name. *Not only are my customers discerning, but I'm quite the connoisseur myself. Take Kevin, for instance …*

He was in especially good spirits this morning. The letdown of his first kill had eased and he attributed it to being out of practice. His time in Berlin had numbed his senses, like eating too much bad food for too long, then suddenly tasting something exquisite. His palate had not been ready for it, but it would be the next time. He was back in form.

"Good morning, Mr. K," Jarrod said when he saw D come through the front door.

Jarrod Sperling was a good man and an even better store manager. His efficiency and way with customers, each of whom he made to feel as if they were the only truly valuable customer in the world, were what had saved him from becoming D's third victim nearly seven years ago. Had it not been for these qualities D spotted in him when they met for a drink, Jarrod would be a forgotten headline now. But he'd impressed D with his manners and his knowledge of the garment business, and instead of killing him D hired him to help with the store. In very quick order Jarrod proved himself capable of keeping things going on his own, and he'd run the business very well when D was in Berlin. For that D must find a way to thank him. Perhaps a ridiculously large Christmas bonus.

"Good morning, Jarrod. I trust you're well."

"Very, Mr. K. And I have good news."

I have even better news, D thought, *but I'll never be able to tell you.*

"What might that be?"

"You know Michael Marzen ..."

"I know *of* Michael Marzen, yes. He's on the cover of everything these days."

Michael Marzen was a software billionaire who had decided to gift most of his fortune to charity. Charities, of course, had lined up for a piece of the action, and Marzen had been giving interviews on the virtues of philanthropy.

"Well," said Jarrod, in a deliberately self-effacing way, bowing his head just so as if to say he was a humble man, with humble tidings, "He wants a new wardrobe, and he wants it from Keller and Whitman."

This was indeed good news. A man of Marzen's means could provide the store with enough income to show a profit for the year. Keller and Whitman always showed a profit, but this would be exceptional.

"Good man," D said.

Jarrod blushed and smiled, not quite a puppy who'd been patted on the head, but almost.

"Now how about a cup of tea from the bakery? And get a scone for yourself, something to tide you over. I'll be taking lunch out today. I have a prospective client to meet. Not nearly as wealthy or famous as Michael Marzen, but a true catch ... if I'm able to catch him."

"Oh my," Jarrod said. "You haven't lost your touch, Mr. K."

"No, I haven't."

Jarrod then did as he was told and left the store, walking briskly across Lexington Avenue to the small bakery that had served the Upper East Side neighborhood for twenty years. They were top notch, with a reputation that needed no preceding, and had been satisfying the tastes of fickle customers since they first opened their doors. D would skip the scones. He never ate before an interview.

Diedrich Kristof Keller III moved to New York City—Brooklyn, to be precise—when his mother went crawling back to Germany in defeat. He was only sixteen at the time, living in the wasteland that was Anaheim, California. It had Disneyland, but that only served to make the point. Even as a teenager, D saw humanity as a vast sea of half-awake people stumbling through their lives from one event to the next, with the in-between filled by boredom. Anaheim was utterly boring. He hated it, and wondered why his parents ever moved there.

His father, also Diedrich, amounted to little and was so unimaginative that he'd thought a large, dull swath of land in Southern California was the place to be. He took his then-pregnant wife and moved from Germany to America, imagining himself an adventurer. But he was not; the most adventurous thing he ever did was also the thing that made D hate him so much—he left his wife and son when D was twelve. Not only did he leave them to fend for themselves in a land both of them despised (D's mother never did like this strange country with its over-inflated sense of itself), but he left them for a man! D's father, it turned out, was running not just from a life he found lacking, but to a life he fantasized silently about until one day he announced at breakfast that he was leaving. He did not say where he was going, or whom he planned to meet there, but D and his mother knew. Samuel was the man's name. He met D's father at the Boeing factory in Anaheim where both men worked assembling aircraft. For a year the two men spent all their spare time together and Marta Keller, while pretending there was nothing amiss as Samuel became a fourth member of their family, knew better. Her husband had changed. He had become happy. He had never been happy with her, and he always treated his son as a peculiar child he wanted nothing to do with but felt obligated to raise.

That sense of obligation vanished one Saturday morning. D was eating pancakes at their small kitchen table. Marta was making a second stack for her husband, with several sausages in a small skillet next to the pancakes, when D's father walked into the room carrying a duffel bag. He announced he was moving to San Francisco with Samuel, picked a sausage from the skillet, bit half and tossed the rest back with the others, and left. Just like that. D never spoke to the man again.

Marta Keller tried to hang on. She got an office job at the same Boeing factory where her traitorous husband met the man of his dreams and her nightmares. She worked there for four years, slowly descending into the neurotic depressed woman she would spend the rest of her life being. Finally, as abruptly as Diedrich Keller had left his family, she told D they were moving back to Germany. As much as he hated Anaheim, he knew nothing of Berlin. He didn't speak the language, and imagined Germany to be a cold wet country cloaked in guilt and regret for its crimes against humanity. He resisted. He was sixteen by then and all but self-sufficient. Marta at last gave him an option (though running away had become his first choice, had things not taken a turn for the better): he could go to Berlin with her, or he could move to Brooklyn and live with his uncle Leo. Leo Whitman was her older brother and had moved to the United States a decade before the Kellers moved to California. Leo was also a successful tailor, unmarried, and willing to take his nephew in. D had only met the man once, when Leo came to visit during Christmas. D was ten years old. The Kellers never went to Brooklyn and D had no idea what it was like, but he believed it must be more interesting than where he was. Any place would be. He jumped at the chance, acted as if it were a difficult choice, and said goodbye to his mother one rainy September. By the evening of that day he was living in Brooklyn, set on a path that changed his life completely, and his mother was on an overnight flight to Berlin.

It was D's idea to open a store on the Upper East Side, D's cajoling and flattering that got his uncle Leo to believe he could be more than a very fine tailor for a very fine clientele. It was also D's money, earned and saved from a series of side jobs while he helped his uncle grow his business, that got them started. Hence the name Keller and Whitman. D played his cards carefully and never suggested he was more than an eager apprentice learning at the knee of a master, but when it came time to open the store he insisted, in the nicest way one can insist, that his name come first. Leo Whitman had no objections, and when D was twenty-two he became a businessman. Ten years later he was a *very successful* businessman, clothier to celebrities and politicians. A year after that he bought his townhouse, thanked his uncle for everything he'd made possible for D, then shoved him down the stairs of the five-flight walkup they shared. D told the police it was a tragedy waiting to happen. Leo was in frail health, he said, and D had tried to convince him for years to move to an elevator building. Leo would have none of it, and one day D came home from work to find his uncle with a broken neck at the bottom of the stairs. It had all been terribly sad. He'd cried and cried but carried on in his uncle's memory. Marta Keller did not come for the funeral. D inherited everything.

D enjoyed his tea while Jarrod nibbled at his blueberry scone in the back office. Food was not allowed in the store, and only D was allowed to have a beverage in front. He kept it below the cash register where he could quickly conceal it if a customer came in. It was just eleven o'clock and only two men had come to the store, one a regular client and the other looking for a suit for a funeral. D had attended to them both and already made two sales for the day.

Jarrod came back in, having carefully wiped his hands and any stray crumbs from his sport coat. Jarrod had just turned fifty-three and was, to D's knowledge, eternally single. His fastidiousness might be the cause, D thought, but it made Jarrod a very good store manager.

"I'm leaving now, Jarrod," D said, finishing his tea and handing his trusted manager the cup.

"Anyone I might know?" Jarrod asked. He rarely asked questions, but there had always been a nosiness to him when it came to clients. Even a man who had checked the inseams of some of New York City's most powerful and influential players could still be star struck.

"No one I might know of, either!" D said, with a short practiced laugh. "No, just someone who was referred to me and is staying at the Arlington. I've arranged to meet him for coffee.

D was just about to leave the store when Jarrod said, "Did you see the news this morning?"

D stopped halfway to the door. He knew he'd made a mistake giving into his impulse with Victor, but he knew, too, that Jarrod would never connect his boss with what happened.

"I'm afraid I did not," D said.

"A young man was found dead in the East River early Tuesday morning."

"Really?"

"Yes, and there was something very familiar about him. They showed his picture on the news. I'd swear he was here the other day."

D, his back to Jarrod, said, "He may have been. We get so much traffic some days, Jarrod, I can't remember everyone who walks in the door."

Jarrod thought a moment, trying to remember. "Victor, they said. That was his name. Victor something."

"Victor something." D's voice was flat and emotionless. "That's quite an unusual name. Now I really must be going. I leave the store in your capable hands, as always."

"As always!"

The compliment worked, distracting Jarrod's attention away from the news and a man he vaguely remembered seeing in the store.

"Memory plays tricks on us all, Jarrod. I'd think nothing of it."

"No, Sir, I won't. Good luck with the new client."

"Luck has nothing to do with it." D glanced at his reflection in the store window and walked out onto Lexington Avenue. June had brought the first real warmth of the season. For a moment he held his face up to the sky, appreciating the sun and the clearness of the day, then he began walking west.

CHAPTER 7

The television studio for Japan TV3 was originally a garment factory, an outlier in what was once a thriving industry in New York City. Fifty years ago, and for many preceding decades, fabrics were central to Manhattan's industrial machine. Long contained in an area called the garment district that stretches from Sixth to Ninth Avenues east-to-west and between 34th and 40th Streets south-to-north, it still serves as a center of fashion, with some of the world's leading designers maintaining factories, but the days of clothing the world are long gone. Shirts, dresses and all other kinds of clothes are now made for a few dollars by people earning pennies in places like Indonesia, Thailand and Bangladesh. But when "Made in America" was the norm, the factory that now housed a Japanese-owned television studio and its offices was humming with the sounds of sewing machines and the silence of an army of workers whose job was to sew, not talk.

Kyle explained all this to Linda as they walked the last few blocks along Ninth Avenue and turned left at 38th, heading west another long block. Linda was impressed if not quite dazzled by the sheer number of people in this city. She also noticed, as Kyle had when he first moved here, the tendency people had to move quickly for no apparent reason. They seemed to maneuver more than walk, each wanting an advantage over the rest in terms of how quickly they got where they were going.

"Why's everyone in such a hurry?" Linda asked as they reached the studio.

"Because they think they have to be," Kyle said. "You can sense it the moment you get back into Manhattan from anywhere, this rush everyone's in."

"And they do it all without seeing where they're going!" She was referring to the omnipresence of smartphones, headsets and ear buds. Almost everyone had one, their eyes fixed on tiny screens in their hands, their ears plugged and deadened by music, their thumbs twitching out text messages and emails. They had all this in rural New Jersey, too, but it was decidedly slower there. Even New Hope, which was as big-city as it got around the area where Linda lived, wasn't nearly as visibly distracted and manic as this.

Kyle held the door for Linda and followed her into the studio. It was like many buildings in this part of the city, architecturally interesting on the outside, with its century-old brickwork and large windows, but basically a series of boxes on the inside. The exception was the second floor studio, which had been divided into three units where programs were made for a mostly-Tokyo audience. The offices where Kyle worked were on the third floor, with the first floor given to nondescript and unidentified rooms.

"What's on the first floor?" Linda asked.

"I have no idea," Kyle replied. "You can spend years in a building here and not know who your neighbors are." He waved at Franklin, the security guard by the front door who had never been required to secure anything and whose waking state only appeared different from his sleeping state because his eyes were open.

Kyle led them past the elevator to the stairs and opened the stairwell door.

"Aren't we taking the elevator?" Linda asked.

"It's broken."

"For how long?"

"Oh, about six months. Don't worry, you won't be winded. It's only two flights up."

Kyle walked up the stairs carrying a bag with coffee and a bagel for Imogene, and a cup of fruit for their station manager, Lenny-san. He was

Jewish but everyone called him that because the bosses in Tokyo did. Kyle, however, had never been Kyle-san.

They reached the third floor and Kyle opened the door, ushering Linda onto a brightly lit floor that looked like a million others in offices everywhere. It was an open seating plan, with a maze of cubicles. Only Lenny-san had an office. Linda followed along as Kyle headed down one row of cubes, turned left at the far wall and walked down another row identical to the one they'd just passed. Finally, in the southwest corner, he reached the cubicle he'd spent his workdays in for the last six years. Next to it, unmistakably, was Imogene Landis's. She had installed tall plants at the entrance to her cube and strung a row of blinking lights. Had she not been one of the stars of the operation none of this would be tolerated and Imogene would surely have left, even if it meant stringing her lights and watering her plants at home while she collected unemployment.

"Oh! My! God!" Imogene shouted when she saw him. "You're on vacation, Kyle, what the fuck are you doing here?" Imogene was known for her loudness and her inappropriate language. "Don't tell me you came here to bring me coffee and a bagel!"

Linda noticed that Imogene tended to exclaim everything.

"Oh, wait, of course!" Imogene said, jumping up out of her chair. "You came to introduce me to … to …"

"Detective Linda," Kyle said. Linda was retired but had stopped correcting him months ago.

"Detective Linda," Imogene said, putting her hand out. "*The* Detective Linda. You solved the Pride Lodge murders."

Linda demurred. "Well, yes and no. I investigated them."

"That's right, that's right. The killer got away."

"One of them," Kyle said. "But we're not here to talk about that. I wanted to show Linda where I worked, and to introduce you."

Imogene Landis was diminutive and thin, a pixie of a woman with an outsized voice and an even bigger personality. She was wearing red cat-eyes glasses attached to a black necklace around her neck. When she was in front of the camera or out in public—anywhere but the office and at home—the glasses came off. She would prefer to see the world through blurred vision than have the world know she needed corrective lenses.

"Where's Lenny-san?" Kyle asked, looking at the empty office with its lights off. "I brought him some fruit."

Lenny-san had been on a diet for several years, the length of it extended because he would have his fruit and top it off with a chocolate croissant he'd snuck in in his briefcase.

"I can't say," Imogene said. "He doesn't tell me when he's coming in late. He'll be here. Just leave the fruit with me, unless you plan on staying awhile."

"No," said Kyle. "Just a few minutes. It is my vacation day and I'd rather not get roped into anything."

"I'd love to get roped into something," Imogene said. She was always looking out for the next big story. The Pride Lodge murders were fading into memory and she needed something explosive. "What have you heard?"

"Nothing," Kyle said. He was concerned about being waylaid and was already thinking they shouldn't have come. He was a loyal assistant, but that came with a cost. Imogene emailed him and called him at all hours, and as often as she'd promised not to, she still did it out of habit.

"There was a news item this morning," Linda said.

Kyle shot her a glance and Linda realized her mistake.

"What news item was that?" Imogene took her coffee and bagel from Kyle and set it on her desk.

"Nothing."

She looked at him like a cat eyeing a toy. "Come on, Kyle, you know something."

"I don't know anything. It was just a body found in the river."

"Oooooh, I like that."

Imogene was not heartless, she was simply driven. She knew dead bodies did not get their feelings hurt, so she kept it honest. Dead bodies in rivers were interesting, depending on how they got there.

"Fine," Kyle said. "But it's your story to run with. I'm not working on it with you, I'm not calling sources, I wasn't even here this morning. You're imagining me."

"Deal. Just some details, that's all, I'll take it from there."

"Well," Kyle said, "I don't know if you remember the Pride Killer."

"Of course I do. He killed people every Gay Weekend or something."

"Pride weekend. It's not called 'Gay Weekend.'"

"Am I not supposed to say 'gay' anymore? I can't keep up with the language, it all becomes offensive to someone so quickly."

Kyle sighed. Imogene was hopeless in some ways, amazing in others. He looked at Linda, who had decided to lean against the outer cubicle wall and watch it all with amusement.

"The Pride Killer did his killing for three or four years in June every year, coinciding with the Pride festivities. Yes, they're gay. They're a lot of other things too, including the time of year he terrorized the gay community. Then, three years ago, he stopped. He was never caught, obviously. The police never even had any suspects, unless they kept that to themselves. We thought he'd died or gone to prison for something else, or simply moved away. But a body was found in the East River early Tuesday morning and I'm convinced he's back."

"Good, good," Imogene said. She had grabbed a reporter's notebook and pen and was quickly jotting things down in her own indecipherable scribble. "Not good that someone's dead, of course, but the good start to a story. What else do you know?"

"Nothing."

"You're lying."

Goddamn her, Kyle thought. Maybe getting this close to anyone was a mistake. Only Danny could read him that easily and quickly.

"Okay," Kyle said. "So the young man he killed was the brother of our doorman."

"Can you get me an interview?"

"No! You're out of your mind. For one thing, he's been on leave the past two nights, for obvious reasons. For another ... no ... you can't interview him. At least not through me."

"So give me a name."

Kyle thought about it a moment. Imogene was a relentless newshound and would put it together soon enough once she read the item in that day's New York Times.

"Vincent Campagna," he said. "He's our overnight doorman. His brother was Victor."

"The dead guy."

"The victim," Kyle reminded her. "Don't forget that. And if you follow up on this, you can say nothing about where you got this information. You read it in the paper, you spoke to the police. I had nothing to do with it."

"Fine," Imogene said. "It's nothing I can't find out from other sources, but it expedites things."

Kyle realized that Linda had been standing there saying nothing for ten minutes. He'd intended for the two women to have more of an introduction, but after spilling the beans to Imogene he decided it was best to leave.

"We're heading to breakfast," Kyle said. He wanted out of the office and food was always a good excuse.

"It was so nice to meet you," Imogene said to Linda. They'd met at Kyle's photography exhibit but had only spoken for a moment. Imogene was there covering it for Tokyo Pulse, a gift to Kyle he had neither asked for nor wanted.

"Likewise," Linda said. She'd taken what measure she could of Kyle's boss and would think it through later. She sensed she and Imogene would either be friends or, just as likely, not like each other beyond a certain civility. Imogene was New York City in a five-foot-one frame and Linda wasn't sure she could take the woman for more than a few minutes.

As they were about to leave, Kyle said, "One thing, Imogene …"

"Yes?"

He spoke with all seriousness. "This one's truly nasty."

Imogene smiled. "I wasn't planning on interviewing the killer, unless he's in a jail cell."

"I'm serious. He's cold and cruel and not someone you should go anywhere near. If you happen to get any ideas about his identity, call the cops.

He's gotten away with a dozen murders and he won't hesitate to make you one more."

"I can handle myself," she said.

"I imagine that's what all the men he's killed thought, too. Now good-bye. I'll see you Monday. After 'Gay Weekend.'"

"Get outta here! And take this wonderful Amazonian with you. So nice to meet you!"

"You're repeating yourself," Kyle said. "I'll see you next week. And put Lenny-san's fruit cup in the refrigerator before it ferments."

Kyle waved a last time and led Linda back along the cubicles the way they'd come. As they walked down the stairs, he thought of the warning he'd given Imogene and how he and Detective Linda ought to heed it themselves. This killer was different. This killer was meticulous—he had to be to get away with it for so long. This killer did not make mistakes, or so the man thought. Everyone makes mistakes, and as Kyle and Linda exited back onto 38th Street, Kyle knew it was the mistakes he had to look for—very, very carefully.

CHAPTER 8

Danny arrived at Margaret's Passion ten minutes after leaving the apartment. It was one of the perks of working there—he had been able to walk to work and home for over a decade. And while he loved being so close to the restaurant he now called his, he had also been close to Margaret Bowman all this time, and that very long chapter in his life was coming to a close. Margaret, as strong and determined as she had been for eighty-two years, was about to move to Florida. Danny had known for several years this was inevitable but he'd kept putting it out of his mind, just as Margaret had kept putting off her decision to move. The time had finally come; the arrangements had been made, and now all that was left was to celebrate Margaret's life and achievements and say goodbye. He did not know if he would see her again. He knew if he did, it would mean taking a trip to Florida—she was not coming back to New York City. Danny had never been to Florida and believed he would die having never enjoyed its stifling humidity, vast flatness, and throngs of the elderly. But for Margaret he would go. At her age, in her health, it meant a trip that wouldn't be put off too long, either.

Margaret's Passion had been in business for over thirty years. It started as a dream Margaret had when she worked for her parents' small Italian restaurant in what was then Little Italy. It was still called that, but there was almost nothing Italian left about it. Chinatown had muscled in long ago, and the Italians had moved on, mostly out of Manhattan to the outer boroughs (as had just about everyone who wasn't wealthy enough to live on the millionaire's row the City had become). Now it was a figment of the tourist imagination. Margaret had been prescient, and also not interested in labeling her restaurant with a specific ethnicity. She and her husband Gerard, so young then, started their restaurant near Gramercy Park, and there it remained. They eventually bought the building the restaurant was in; it occupied the first floor, with three floors of tenants above it. The Bowmans themselves lived on the second floor, with a connecting staircase they'd installed (without city permits, but no one's telling) that ran down into the kitchen of the restaurant. It was how they came up and down without leaving the building.

Margaret had been taking those stairs to visit her guests for three decades—and she meant it sincerely, knowing them by name, knowing their children's birthdays and the major events in their lives; this was no "Next guest!" you hear now being shouted by drug store clerks who couldn't care less if you were a guest or a corpse. Margaret loved and was beloved.

Time took its toll, and eventually Margaret stopped coming down to the restaurant. Then, as things came full circle, Danny made the trip up the stairs to see her. Her Danny, her adopted son. She and Gerard had no children. Then Gerard was struck and killed by a taxi not ten feet from the building. Danny never met Gerard Bowman, but he knew Margaret loved the man with whom she had done it all. He knew she loved *him*, too. She was Danny's second mother, something he did not say out loud to his own mother in Astoria. But everybody knew how much they meant to each other, and how hard this was going to be.

It had fallen on Danny to arrange the going away party for Margaret. The planning had gone on for several months now. Danny worked closely with Chloe, the new day manager. That had been Danny's job until he bought the restaurant with Kyle and Kyle's mother. (If it had been Kyle's mother's *money* he would be much happier, but Sally Callahan insisted on being part of the package.) Danny had been planning the restaurant's events for a long time. Several private parties a year were held there, by the types of people who arrived in motorcades and were sometimes preceded by security details. Among the most star-studded events he'd organized was Margaret Bowman's eighty-first birthday a little over a year ago. He wondered if it had been some kind of signal for Margaret, telling her the time to leave was getting near; or a dress rehearsal for what he was planning now. So many big-name politicians, entertainment figures and philanthropists had shown up that Danny had made the decision to hold a separate, private birthday party with the staff and a few true intimates, including himself. He had worked the main party but had not taken up one of the highly valued sixty seats the restaurant was limited to. Margaret wasn't happy about it, either, but she knew they could not risk excluding someone whose name was on a Broadway marquee or a ballot in the next election. She wanted them all to keep coming there when she was gone, so she had acquiesced; in the end she had a much better time with just her staff, Danny, Kyle, and a half dozen people who could say they truly knew her.

This event was different. It was the last Margaret would attend, and it was her going away celebration. Danny had even wondered if they should have it somewhere else with twice the seating capacity. But that would be wrong and everyone there would know it. This was a party to say goodbye to Margaret, and it could only be held in her restaurant. Memories could not be packed up and transported to another location.

Chloe was waiting for him when he got there. The restaurant didn't open until 11:30 a.m. (only lunch and dinner were served at Margaret's Passion), but there was always a lot of preparation, and Chloe had proved to be as meticulous in her job as Danny had been when it was his. She had been with the restaurant for five years, working as a lunch server, bar back, you-name-it. Chloe was Danny's right hand, and he was glad to offer her his job when he became the owner. No one else had even been considered.

"You really should have taken some days off," Chloe said when Danny arrived. He knew she'd already been there for at least an hour, doing Chloe things, which often extended to jobs well below her pay grade. Nothing was beneath Chloe, and that's one of the things Danny liked about her.

Chloe was tall and thin and sometimes mistaken for a man. She had very short hair and a flat chest she was neither proud nor ashamed of. Her mother was in a nursing home with early-onset Alzheimer's (Chloe was only thirty-six). That was all Danny knew of her personal life. He didn't even know if she was straight, gay, bi, trans, or none of the above. She was a phenomenal asset to the restaurant, a good person who loved the old woman who lived upstairs almost as much as Danny did, and that was all he wanted to know.

"I can't take time off right now, Chloe," Danny said. "Too much to do."

"But your detective friend is here, that seems important."

Danny thought of telling her that Linda was really Kyle's friend. He considered her his friend, too, but not in the best-friends-forever category. He also sometimes felt like a third wheel when they were together, and he was content letting Kyle take Linda around the City. Besides, he had a party to plan—the saddest, least-wanted party he would ever throw, and it was time to get down to business.

"Come," Danny said, sitting at a table and waving Chloe over. "We have names to cross out."

As with Margaret's birthday party, this one involved starting with a list almost twice the size of its final draft, then eliminating names after painstakingly discussing who should not be on it, and whom they could afford to offend. Luckily, the new mayor was scheduled to be out of town (Margaret didn't much care for the man's politics). The previous mayor, on the other hand, would have to be accommodated.

Danny sighed. Dealing with egos was part of his job and it had only gotten harder since he was now the owner. Favors were expected, and although Margaret had always maintained a strict egalitarian approach to seating (reservations were a must, and could not be bought at the expense of a customer who already had a table), but some people still wanted the best table, with the highest visibility, which was never by the window. Common people could see through the glass and that was not the audience these people played for. They played for each other.

"What about Irene?" Chloe asked, scanning the list. "She won the Tony last year, best lead in a musical."

"That was *last* year," Danny said. "She didn't win this year."

He crossed her name off the list and the work began. By the time they opened the doors for lunch a third of the names would be crossed out. Another third would have to go after discussing each one—the pros and cons, their relative importance in Margaret's orbit, and any damage they might do if they knew they'd been excluded. The first draft of the invitation list was highly confidential, a top secret document that had never fallen into the wrong hands and never would.

"Let's keep going," Danny said. He had to get invitations out by the end of the week for a party just a month away. He knew he should have started sooner, but he'd put it off. Saying goodbye to Margaret, then watching her go, was something he would prefer to put off forever, so he steeled himself, took a deep breath, and moved on to the next name.

CHAPTER 9

The Arlington Hotel was a New York City landmark. First built in 1927, the hotel immediately became the preferred place to stay for anyone whose name was recognized by fans, voters, or readers of newspapers in wide circulation. It was also the place for those who aspired to be known, regardless of the slim odds. Hemingway had stayed here, as had the Governor of New York and, on several occasions, presidents of the United States.

New York City was unrecognizable now from what it had been in the Arlington's heyday. Times Square had become sanitized, and the New York Times, for which the Square was named, has moved several blocks over. The Gray Lady, as it had been called for a century, was not gray anymore and the building that housed the paper has been converted into high priced condominiums. Most of Manhattan, it seemed, has been transformed into a playground for the rich and famous. That was fine with D; he fancied himself among them, even though he wasn't that wealthy and planned to never be famous for what he was best at. He was content for his select clientele to know him as the proprietor of a men's clothing store that catered to the crème de la crème. They would never know he was much more well known—albeit in a completely anonymous way—as the Pride Killer. The police thought he was dead, or that he'd vanished or simply given up his one true passion. At least that's what they had thought until Tuesday morning, when his first victim in three years was found floating past the United Nations.

D had never stayed at the Arlington. There was no reason for someone who lived in New York City to stay there, let alone someone who owned a townhouse within a long walk's distance from the hotel. It was true he'd met a few clients in the hotel's restaurant, mostly older men who thought a $2,000 suit was on the low end. He'd shied away from the nouveau riche, the rappers and the winners of television singing competitions. He wanted to keep his profile low; he was known for being discerning and discreet, and many of the newly wealthy were anything but.

He was sitting in the lobby of the Arlington enjoying a decaf cappuccino. He normally did not drink coffee, preferring a small variety of teas, but he would treat himself to something decaffeinated on special occasions, and this morning was one of them: he was waiting to meet one of two (count them, two!) prospective candidates for his next killing. And the candidate was late. D chalked it up to youth. Kevin (if that was his real name) was barely thirty and today was his day off. D checked his watch: ten minutes past eleven. Kevin was supposed to be there promptly on the hour. D realized, of course, that Kevin might not show up at all— it happened. But he would give the young man another ten minutes, then leave. He had his second interview that afternoon. He'd scheduled the killing for Thursday evening. It was possible that Kevin would not be free that night, which would factor into his decision. He was on a timetable. Fortunately, he had two very different men to choose from and there was a high probability one of them would be available. D was an expert at enticement. He would listen carefully as he chatted with each of the men, and if there was anything in what they said—a new movie out they wanted to see, or a favorite artist in a musical genre—he would be sure to let them know he was interested in that very thing. What a coincidence! He has a signed album of Patsy Cline's at home, or he'd gotten his hands on a pre-release DVD of the movie that was opening that very night. These were the perks of being a man who catered to men of the highest order. He would demure—it's nothing, really—and at the very least invite them over to his home that evening. They would ask for the address and he would insist on meeting for a drink first. He never gave his address to his victims. They might tell someone where they were going, or leave a note on the apartment desk they would never see again. Aside from his store manager Jarrod, the only people who knew where he lived did not survive to tell anyone.

D was getting impatient now. He glanced at his watch: 11:17 a.m. Three more minutes and he would have to leave. He was disappointed and was just about to write off Kevin as a fake or a no-show when a young man entered the lobby, harried and moving as if he was late for something, which he was.

"Leo?" he said, walking up to D.

D included his dead uncle's name among his aliases. He changed them up in the event someone overheard them talking. One day he was Leo, the next he might be Edward.

"That would be me," D said, standing and extending his hand. He'd told Kevin where he would be sitting but had not included a photograph of himself. He did not want any pictures floating around. Untraceable email accounts were one thing, photographs quite another. Instead he played shy with them, insisting he had no recent photos but guaranteeing them they would not be displeased, which they never were. He was in shape, average height, with graying brown hair he kept cut every week. He had bright blue eyes and a disarming smile (disarming them was of high importance). And when he smiled, whether for a client at the store or a candidate for his basement, he always made sure to include his eyes. A smile that does not extend to the eyes was a smile to be distrusted.

"I'm so sorry I'm late," Kevin said. "There was a sick passenger on the subway and we were in the station forever."

"Don't worry," D said. "These things happen. Please, have a seat."

Kevin sat down across from D. It was a small low table with two chairs, not for dining but for enjoying a beverage and conversation.

D looked at the man, quite pleased. Kevin was young, shorter than D would have liked, but with an open face and well-groomed. He struck D as neither noticeably masculine nor feminine, a balance he found in many men.

"Coffee?" D said. Kevin nodded and D waved at the waiter who served people in the lobby. There weren't many places like the Arlington left where gentlemen could sit and talk in a relaxing atmosphere.

"Staten Island is a long commute," said D. "It must take up a good part of your day going back and forth."

"I'm used to it," Kevin said. "I've never really wanted to live in Manhattan. It's too ..."

"Hectic."

"Yeah, hectic. I get enough of the city's energy just working at the bank. What was it you said you do?"

"Real estate. If you ever decide to move into the city, I'm your man."

Kevin gave his coffee order to the waiter, then took a moment for a good look at D.

"You're very nice looking," Kevin said.

"I try."

"This isn't something I normally do, meet men online."

"Nor I. But a friend has been encouraging me ever since my wife died."

"Oh, you had a wife."

"To whom I was faithful until she died three years ago. Then I decided it was time to be true to myself. I'd always known, you see, but never acted on it."

D liked to present himself as somewhat of a novice. He also knew that some men were turned on by sleeping with married men—or in this case widowed.

They talked for another twenty minutes. Kevin told D much about his life, how he'd grown up on Staten Island and taken his job at the bank three years ago. Working at a bank wasn't his dream but it was a job, and jobs these days were more important than ambitions. Besides, he'd worked his way up quickly from teller to branch manager, and it could be a career if he wanted it to be.

D told him all about his fictitious life as a Manhattan real estate broker, the pressures of selling multi-million dollar apartments, and the stresses of living in an Upper East Side penthouse.

"Those are some stresses I might like to have," Kevin said.

D watched as the young man's interest in him grew the more he told him about his wealth, position and prestige. Ah, youth, he thought, so easily lured.

Kevin was proving to be a prime candidate. D did not think of them as targets, but as interviewees for the most important position they would ever hold: provider of D's greatest pleasure in life. The pleasure itself only lasted for an evening, but gave D a lifetime of precious memories.

D was leaning heavily toward Kevin and was considering canceling his drink date with Scott that afternoon when Kevin's phone buzzed. He'd had the courtesy to turn the ringer off but he'd left it on vibrate.

"Sorry," Kevin said, taking his phone out of his shirt pocket.

"No problem," D replied, but it was a problem. He waited to see what Kevin said to whoever had called him. If he gave a location or any information that might lead to D, things would change quickly.

"Hi, Mom," Kevin said. He held up a finger to say, "Just a minute," to D and walked over to a corner to speak to his mother.

This was not a good turn of events. D had no way of knowing what Kevin was saying to his mother. Worse, *he was talking to his mother.* What grown man speaks to his mother while he's meeting another man for sex? It was the kind of call you would let go to voicemail, unless you mother's place in your life was overly prominent.

Kevin ended the call and came back, saying, "My apologies, really. My mom's alone now. My dad passed away five years ago from leukemia. I don't have any siblings, so I'm all she's got. I kind of have to take her calls."

Normally this sort of story would not effect D. Life was full of minor tragedies and heartache. But something about a young man as the only living family for a widow who was probably not much older than D himself troubled him. He never gave any thought to the survivors; sentimentality was not an asset in the serial killer business. But something just felt wrong this time.

"Where does your mother live?" D asked as Kevin sat back down.

"With me."

"With you?"

"Well, to be honest, I live with her. It's my parents' house."

D waited a moment. "You live at home?"

"Yeah, it saves a lot of money and it helps my mom. Is that a problem?"

"Not at all," D said, having decided it was. For all his youthful charm and attraction, Kevin was not the one for him. He hid his disappointment, as he hid all his emotions. (People mistakenly think sociopaths don't have emotions, but of course they do. Excitement, exhilaration, joy at the kill and sadness when it was over until the next time—were these not emotions?)

Kevin could sense things had taken a bad turn. "Listen," he said, "I really like you, Leo …"

"And I like you, Kevin, very much. I just have some other business to attend to today. How about if I send you an email this evening and we see where it goes?"

"Oh, okay, sure." Kevin had been blown off before, he knew what was happening.

D waved for the check. Kevin dug in his pocket for his wallet and D said, "This one's on me."

"Fine," said Kevin. "I'll get the next one."

He knew there would not be a next one. What he did not know was that his life had just been spared.

They parted ways with a handshake in front of the Arlington. D waited while poor, forlorn, rejected Kevin made his way up the block. He did not want Kevin seeing which direction he took. He glanced at his watch. He was not scheduled to meet Scott until five-thirty.

It was going to be a long afternoon.

CHAPTER 10

D did not know when he became a killer, only when he began to kill. It was as if the impulse had always been with him but never satisfied until he shoved his uncle down the stairs and the sight of him with his neck broken, his head twisted strangely perpendicular to his body, that he realized the full pleasure of what he had only fantasized until then. He had not tortured animals as a child; he had not set fires. He had been a fairly obedient boy, doing as he was told by his parents. Then his father left them and his mother sank into an acidic bitterness that corroded their lives. By the time D was fifteen he'd had enough—enough of his mother's toxicity, enough of her complaining about the world. He also knew very well she had little attachment to her son. He reminded her in too many ways of the man who'd walked out on her for another man. He had the same name, the same basic physical features, the same eyes.

"It's not my fault," she would say, for no apparent reason and out of context to anything they had been discussing. He knew it came from her deep belief of the opposite: that if she had been enough, if she had been a better wife, if she had done some crucial *something* differently her husband would have stayed and they would have had the ideal life he'd promised her in America. He knew, too, that she blamed him somehow, as if having a child had set them on the course to ruin—at least the ruin of her life.

D was startled when his mother announced she was going back to Berlin and gave him the options of going with her or moving to Brooklyn to live with his uncle. None of this had been discussed with him, and by the way she presented it he could tell which choice she preferred. D was part of the life she'd come to hate. D was unwelcome. D reminded her too much of the source of her anger.

"He has a nice apartment and a spare room. You could live in New York City, imagine how exciting that will be."

Not "would be," but "will be," as if the decision had been made for him.

D was relieved. He did not want to move to Germany, and the thought of being free from his mother's stifling emotions and her increasingly erratic behavior made him think escape was in sight. So on that rainy September morning he said goodbye to the woman he'd taken to calling Marta and boarded a plane for New York.

D's father began sending him letters a year after he moved to Brooklyn. He wanted to make amends, he said. He wanted to reconnect. He was living happily in San Francisco with Samuel and they had started a card shop together. A card shop! Rainbow Spirit was the name of the store. D hated it immediately. He also hated that the letters arrived in a variety of custom cards that Samuel made and sold at their store. It was quite a change from working in a Boeing factory.

His uncle Leo would hand him the cards using just his thumb and index finger, as if the cards might carry something nasty on their envelopes. Leo was on his sister Marta's side, even if he would never, ever, consider moving back to Germany. He was an American now, with citizenship and a thriving tailor business. D found out that Leo had offered to take them both in, but Marta had refused. She said America was a cruel and lonely place for cruel and lonely people. D came to believe her, at least about the cruelty.

D's father also had the temerity to include photos. There was his father and Samuel at the wharf. There was his father and Samuel in front of the card shop. There was his father, Samuel and a half dozen friends at a Pride parade. *A Pride parade?* What, D wondered, was there to be proud of in leaving your wife and young son in a wasteland? What was there to be proud of in opening a pitiful card shop with rainbows, triangles and pink shit all over the place? Pink shit. Pride shit. Rainbow shit. It was all shit to D, and the more he stared at the photos of his father and Samuel, the more he wanted to kill them both. *You did this to me*, he thought. *I'm living with an old man in Brooklyn, sewing suits for men who would wipe us from the bottoms of their shoes if they found a better tailor, a better clothier. I have no friends.* The only thing good to come out of it for D was that he loved New York City. He loved the vastness of it, its famed anonymity. He loved the tides of people swelling its streets. He loved the variety, the diversity, and, as time passed, its great opportunity. You could kill someone here and, depending on who it was, they would never be missed. You could set up shop with the most select customers imaginable and when the bodies were found no one would ever come around asking questions. That is, if you were cunning, careful and meticulous. If you were D himself.

He became aware of his sexuality in high school. He'd known much younger that other boys caught his eye, but at first he experienced it as a fascination rather than an attraction. He was fascinated by all things male. He liked the shape of men, the sound of men, the smell of men. By the time he was thirteen he was not interested in anyone his own age. He preferred to spend time at the barbershop, and he would purposely go when it was busiest, at lunch time or at the end of the work day. He would get in the back of the line and sit, pretending to read a newspaper, just so he could prolong his stay. He would sit and breathe the men in, the smell of the aftershave and many times their sweat.

He continued his visits to barber shops after he moved to Brooklyn. Some people liked libraries, some people liked restaurants. D liked the barber shop. By the time he was eighteen he was aware that some of the men looked at him with more than passing glances. He was a handsome teenager and looked a few years older than he was. Ripe, he thought. Ripe for the picking. But in his private thoughts (aren't all thoughts private?), he knew they were the ripe ones and he would someday do the picking.

He did not consider himself gay. Gay to D was an identity, and it was not his. He was instead same-sex attracted. That is how he had always defined it for himself. His father was gay. Samuel was gay. Parades and card shops and mannerisms and magazines were gay. D had no use for any of those things ... yet.

Then, when he was thirty-two years old, he killed his uncle. It wasn't very gratifying. His uncle was a good man. His uncle had been kind and offered D a place to live. His uncle had taught him the business and opened a store with both their names on it. But his uncle was in the way. He'd also begun asking D why there were no women in his life. *Because I'm not interested in killing women,* he'd wanted to say. Instead he offered the well-worn excuse that he hadn't met the right woman. He did not want to end up in a bad relationship or, worse, divorced like his parents. And besides, Uncle, we have too much work to do, too many things to accomplish together. Then the stairs and the broken neck, and he could finally set about making the life he wanted.

Becoming the Pride Killer was an accident of timing, really. He hadn't planned or anticipated making himself one of the most successful serial killers in New York City history at the same time all the gay people were celebrating. It had just been an auspicious day. He'd met the man named Oscar at a bar that catered to older gentlemen who liked younger ones. D was the younger one in the crowd that night, and within a few hours he had convinced the man to go home with him. His apartment was just a few blocks way. They could have another drink there in privacy. Sure, said Oscar, and fifteen minutes later they were in the townhouse D had purchased with his uncle's life insurance. It had given him enough for a down payment at a time before real estate reached the stratosphere. It was a fixer-upper, and D had fixed it up nicely, especially the basement.

He invited Oscar in and quickly offered him a cocktail. Oscar, having already consumed several drinks, gladly acquiesced. And then, finally, it was a trip to the basement to show Oscar his wine collection. Such a refined man to have a wine collection, and so young! Oscar was impressed and followed him down the stairs. He came back up in a large duffel bag.

The next day D realized, as he waited for news of the floater in the East River, that it was Pride weekend. Talk about perfect timing! He quickly formulated his plan and by the time of the festivities that always followed the parade he was known as the Pride Killer. Some clever reporter at the New York Herald had deemed him that. He thought it was appropriately tawdry, given his low opinion of all things Pride. He might have thought of a better name for himself but it stuck and he'd become fond of it. It was also when he decided on killing in threes.

He'd had to move quickly after Oscar. He found another victim on Thursday night, and a final on Saturday. No more from the bars. The internet made risks much easier to take, provided you had the sense to cover your tracks—and D had always been a man of uncommon sense.

That was seven years ago. He had not been caught, not even close. Some of his success he attributed to having been older when he started, in his mid-thirties. He was not youthfully impulsive. He planned carefully and executed (pun intended) his plan to the T. Or to the D, depending on how you look at it.

He was as professional at killing as he was at providing top-flight suits to top-flight men who had no idea the tailor measuring their inseams could kill them in sixty seconds. He had taken three years off to watch his mother disintegrate in a dreary Berlin apartment, two Pride weekends without their namesake's killer, and now he was back. His mother was dead. His father still sent him letters he left unanswered and immediately shredded— though both the card shop and Samuel were gone. He had a thriving men's store, a townhouse, and above all a career as the Pride Killer. He'd thought of retiring, especially since he had not been caught and wanted it to stay that way. But not yet. Maybe next year, or the year after that. For now he had two more victims to select and set free into oblivion. He saw himself as doing them a favor. Life was grief, anger and tears, for those weak enough to cry. D had never cried in his life.

CHAPTER 11

The Stopwatch Diner was a Manhattan landmark specific to the area of Penn Station, where it had been in business since the mid-1940s. A gaudy neon stopwatch graced the front entrance, forever frozen at the ten-second mark above the front door. Inside it was much like a thousand other diners across America, but done in a racing motif: checkered flags on the walls, giant framed photos of famous race car drivers spewing champagne into the air.

Linda and Kyle had eaten here before, on her last trip to the city to see Kyle's photography exhibit. It was also where Danny had confronted his nemesis, Linus Hern, the restaurateur who'd hated him for years and who had conspired to secretly buy, through intermediaries, Margaret Bowman's building and the restaurant that bore her name. Danny had thwarted that scheme, found himself owning Margaret's Passion, and finally discovered why Linus was set on revenge: Danny had been hired by Margaret to re-place Hern's young boyfriend ten years earlier. Sal was his name, and he took the loss of his position hard. He'd slipped back into addiction and finally gotten sober with a plunge off the 59th Street Bridge. Linus Hern blamed Danny, who'd had no part in it or knowledge of it, and set his sights on vengeance he almost achieved.

"Whatever happened to Linus Hern?" Linda asked as she and Kyle settled into a booth. The diner was full to capacity—it always was. A steady stream of customers came through the doors fresh off their trains, joining tourists who read about the Stopwatch on travel websites, and not a few locals who liked the moderate prices and the atmosphere.

"I don't know," said Kyle. "After the situation with Margaret's Passion he vanished. The last I heard he'd moved to Philadelphia."

"Maybe he got it out of his system, that whole business with Danny."

"I don't think Linus ever gets anything out of his system. I think he just moved on. I'd guess there were opportunities in Philly and he headed that way. He could smell an opportunity the way a predator smells blood."

A waiter came over to them to take their order. They'd been handed menus by the maître d' when she seated them. It was lunch time and both ordered club sandwiches, Linda getting tuna and Kyle the turkey. The waiter nodded and hurried off. Everything moved very quickly at the Stopwatch; meals were served and tables turned over in record time, and Kyle wondered if the staff were all being timed. It was the Stopwatch Diner, after all.

"Your boss is something else," Linda said. "It has to be a challenge working for her."

"It has been, and it's a challenge I'll miss."

"She's leaving?"

"Eventually. And I can't blame her. She was just about on the career skids when she covered the Pride Lodge murders. That made her a star of sorts. Then the bosses in Tokyo moved her into covering the city, and now she's a B-list reporter in a very niche market. She wants out of the niche before she's too old to make another move."

"What will you do if she leaves New York?"

"Stay," said Kyle, looking down at the checkered placemat. He did not want to talk about his boss's future, which would mean talking about his own. "How's Kirsten's mother?"

Dot McClellan had been hit by her third bout with cancer and this one she was rapidly losing. Linda was amazed that Dot had made it nine months, but neither she, Kirsten, nor Dot's oncologist expected Dot to see August.

"It's been very hard on Kirsten," Linda said. "Sometimes I think it was too much change for one person. She sold her interest in McClellan and Powers, she moved into the house with me, and her mother's dying."

McClellan and Powers Real Estate, the successful Bucks County business Kirsten had established with Madeleine Powers twenty years ago, was now just Powers Real Estate. The house they lived in was Linda's in Kingwood Township, five wooded acres just a mile away from the Delaware River but a world away from New Hope, where Kirsten had owned a condominium. Kirsten had not looked for another profession; she was consumed with her mother's care and her frequent trips to Phoenix, where Linda would be joining them Monday.

"The wedding was lovely," Kyle said, wanting to brighten things if he could. He and Danny had gone to New Jersey for the women's intimate ceremony and met Dot McClellan on the last trip she would ever take.

"Nothing like yours," Linda replied.

"Well … we had more in-laws, and a lot more people locally who had to be invited. If it had been up to me and Danny we would have just gone to City Hall."

"But it was up to you."

"Tell that to our mothers."

The food arrived and they began eating, both of them welcoming a break in the conversation. The topics had been difficult ones, and Kyle was hoping to steer things back to Linda's visit to the city, the things she wanted to see this time and the places Kyle never went to unless they had company.

"We could take the ferry to the Statue of Liberty," Kyle said, picking just a handful of french fries from the plate and separating most of them into a pile he would not eat.

"I hear there's a sex museum," Linda said, smiling.

"Really? You want to see the sex museum?"

"It's a thought."

The waiter returned with a pot of coffee and Kyle placed his hand over his cup—he'd had three cups already today and was feeling jittery. The waiter dashed away to the next table.

"I was thinking …" said Linda.

"Yes?" Kyle knew where this was going and wished they'd stayed on the topic of their weddings, or even Linda's mother-in-law.

"If this Pride Killer strikes every week this time of year …"

"Yes."

"And the first victim was found in the river Tuesday morning …"

"Yes."

"Then there's a second victim coming. Probably one he hasn't killed yet, or maybe not even identified."

Kyle sighed. It was a sigh of surrender. He knew as well as Linda did they had to do something. The police had never caught the Pride Killer and hadn't even had a suspect as far as Kyle knew.

"Where would we start?" he said, not looking up from his plate. His mind was working, trying to map out a strategy.

"He dumps the bodies in the river on the Upper East Side."

"Maybe he owns a car and drives them there from Long Island."

"Too risky."

"So maybe he has an accomplice, and the accomplice drives them there from Long Island."

"You're not keeping it simple," Linda said. "I think he feels invincible. He's gotten away with this for years, from what you told me. I think he stays close to home."

"Well the cops must think it, too, and look what they've come up with! Zero."

"We don't have much time."

Kyle thought another moment. "We have to talk to Vinnie."

"Your doorman? You said he was out on leave."

"I didn't say we had to talk to him at our building."

"You want to go where he lives. Is that information you have?"

"It's information I can get," Kyle said. "I'll just say I want to send a food basket. Joseph will give me his address." Joseph was the day-shift doorman and had been on the job for twenty-five years.

"So let's go," Linda said. "The stopwatch is running."

Kyle waved at the waiter and made the sign of a pencil in the air, the universal gesture of asking for a check.

Two minutes later they'd left the Stopwatch, walking quickly west on 32nd Street. Kyle thought of grabbing a taxi but decided they could use the time to think, plan, and work through the questions they would pose to a grieving, fragile Vincent Campagna. It was a delicate situation. Vinnie's brother had just been found bloated and floating in the East River. They would have to be gentle. At the same time, they needed answers quickly. Victor Campagna was the first of three as far as they knew. They hoped they were right, that Victor had not been the second while the first was still undiscovered somewhere.

CHAPTER 12

The slowing of time is a phenomenon D was familiar with. Just as time can seem to pass ever more quickly, especially with age, it can also seem to drag, slower and slower, when one wants to be where one is not. Coming home from a trip, watching the clock as the workday passes, or waiting to meet someone who promises to fulfill your dreams. D dreamed of his next victim. He dreamed of the dance, the delicate charade as he pretended to be the man everyone thought he was while his true self slowly emerged. A conversation, a drink, a visit to the basement, and all would be revealed.

He had returned to his store after the long walk back from the Arlington. He'd been disappointed—not crushingly so, but enough that he wanted time to think and clear his head. It had happened before over the course of his career and his life. He'd had to wait for years while he grew into manhood, years more for the opportunity to be rid of his uncle. And the worst waiting of all, in a dreadful Berlin, waiting for his mother to surrender her bitterness and her regret and finally free him. He'd had to wait, too, for a replacement victim when his first choice didn't work out, twice that he could remember. But it always fell into place. It always came together, and it would this time, too.

"How did it go?" Jarrod asked. It was a slow afternoon. Keller and Whitman was never overly busy. It wasn't that kind of store and did not cater to that kind of customer. This was not the Gap.

"Pardon?" D asked. He was going through the racks of suits, making sure none were wrinkled, the price tags were pristine.

"With your client."

"Oh. You mean prospective client. Well, Jarrod, we win some and we lose some. He wasn't for us."

Jarrod knew not to question his boss further on the matter. Diedrich Keller did not like losing customers, even ones who never bought anything.

"I suggested he try Men's Warehouse." That said it all. The man had likely balked at the prices at Keller and Whitman. It was not a store for those who could not truly afford it. Sometimes they *thought* they could. They put on airs, they wasted Mr. K's time with meetings at hotels. They'd seen some celebrity wearing a suit from the store and imagined having a closet full of them. Then they realized it would set them back two months' rent or a trip to Disneyworld and they tried to bargain. Mr. K did not bargain.

"Easy come, easy go," Jarrod said.

"Indeed," D said.

He looked at his watch—there was no clock in the store. It was now 2:30 p.m. and he had another three hours before meeting Scott. He'd suggested drinks at a piano bar in the Theater District that was always filled with tourists—just the kind of witnesses he liked if there were any at all. Tourists did not stay around long and were scattered to the wind by the time the police came around asking questions. He'd never been to this bar and would not go again after interviewing Scott. He'd been careful all these years never to be seen in the same establishment twice. Fortunately, Manhattan had enough places to go that this was not a problem.

"I'll be leaving early this evening, Jarrod," he said. Normally he would stay until the store closed at 8:00 p.m. His uncle Leo used to stay open much later, always hoping to catch one more sale for the day, but D thought it made them look cheap. Souvenir shops stayed open till midnight, not fine men's clothing stores.

"Someone special?" Jarrod asked. He was careful to keep his few personal inquiries gender neutral. Mr. K had never spoken of his romantic life, if he had one, and Jarrod knew not to pry. But every now and then he would ask this sort of question. He liked his boss and hoped he would someday meet someone special, whether a man or a woman.

D looked at him and said, "The only special person in my life died in Berlin, Jarrod. I'm still grieving."

"But of course, my apologies for asking."

"No need to apologize, I know you mean well. But no, no one special. I just have plans, Jarrod. Even lonely, single men have plans."

Jarrod blushed. He regretted having asked about it. It was none of his business, none at all.

D glanced at his watch again. Ten minutes had passed since the last time he checked it. Time had slowed to a crawl. He decided to use some of it to practice what he would say to Scott, how he would get him to the townhouse, and what he would do if Scott, too, was not the right one. He doubted that would happen. He needed Scott to be the right one, and he was sure he was. He knew from experience that sometimes you had to settle. He wasn't expecting that, but if it happened, he would take what he could get.

CHAPTER 13

The lunch crowd at Margaret's Passion was thinning. It was never especially busy, given the restaurant's location in Gramercy Park—there were no office buildings to supply a stream of executive assistants and the bosses whose every whim they catered to. There also weren't many tourists, except the ones on walking tours of the area.

Gramercy Park was a historic district that was once a swamp. A developer named Samuel B. Ruggles proposed the idea for a park in the early 1800s, when Manhattan was just beginning to push northward. The property was called "Gramercy Farm" and Ruggles spent the then-vast sum of $180,000 to drain the swamp and landscape it around a square, deeding 66 parcels of land to various owners. Today Gramercy Park is held in common as one of Manhattan's two privately owned parks and the park itself is gated, with keys given to the owners of each of the 39 surrounding structures. The Lexington Avenue subway had even been forced to re-route to Park Avenue so as not to go beneath the park and upset the privileged tenants.

Among the residents of Gramercy Park are The Players and the Gramercy Park Hotel. The Players was founded by Edwin Booth, brother of James Wilkes Booth, best known for assassinating Abraham Lincoln. To walk the streets of Gramercy Park is to travel back in time, to see New York City as it once was. Small groups of tourists listen breathlessly, snapping pictures, as tour guides tell them stories of who lived in which building and what moments in American history were acted out along its streets. It's not the sort of neighborhood where you'll find throngs of gawkers looking for neon signs, cheap souvenirs and Broadway celebrities.

It is where you'll find Margaret's Passion, there on a corner where Margaret Bowman first opened the restaurant in 1983. Like the neighborhood, little has changed about it—and Margaret always knew her customers liked it that way. A Who's Who of New York City society has dined there for three decades—mayors, fashion designers, even the President of the United States on several occasions. But just as importantly, it has served the local residents of Gramercy Park all that time. They like its familiarity and its comfort. They like its elegant, old-looking interior. And they love Margaret Bowman. Danny could not imagine Margaret's Passion without Margaret, and even though she seldom made the trip downstairs from her apartment to visit table to table as she'd done for years, they knew she was around, watching over them. Danny knew once she was gone they would rely on the restaurant staying the same. It was a bone of contention he had with Kyle's mother Sally. She didn't want to completely change the place, but she thought it needed "refreshing," as she put it. He disagreed and was planning to have a long talk with her—soon.

The restaurant closed at 2:00 p.m. and reopened for dinner at 6:00 p.m.. Chloe was getting things ready for the daily transition, changing out the menus and making sure the setup was done meticulously, with the help of Trebor the bartender. Danny had hired them both, and they had repaid his decision with loyalty and professionalism. He was sitting at the bar, having a cup of coffee, watching them. He remembered being new to the restaurant himself, hired by Margaret. Poached, really, from another restaurant, but she'd seen something in him she liked and wanted at Margaret's Passion. She had not been wrong.

"She knows you're coming," Chloe said.

"Of course she does," Danny replied. He made the trip upstairs to visit with her almost every day now. Her decision to move to Florida had been made, but Danny and Margaret had not yet talked about it in more than the abstract. The way people talk around things they would rather not discuss in specifics. Specifics are very real. Specifics say, this is happening, there's no turning back.

Danny finished his coffee and headed into the kitchen where the staircase was leading up to Margaret's apartment. He nodded at Chef Cecily, who'd been brought on to replace Chef Jeff several months ago. Another excellent but hard decision (Jeff had been with the restaurant longer than Danny, but his father was ailing in Denver and he'd left to take care of him). He nodded at the dishwasher and the busboy, whose wives' names he knew and whose children's birthdays he remembered every year with gifts. It had been Margaret's way, and now it was Danny's. He climbed the back stairs, slowly, his eyes on the door at the top, wishing he would never get there.

"Hello, Danny," Margaret said, opening the door before he reached the top step. She always did, and he'd wondered many times how she knew he was coming just then. The stairs didn't creak, he didn't pound his feet. His ascent was silent, yet Margaret always knew he was coming and she always opened the door before he knocked.

"Good afternoon," Danny said.

The stairs led into Margaret's kitchen and she waved Danny in, closing the door behind him. There were two cups on the small kitchen table he'd sat at a thousand times, one with coffee for Danny, one with tea for Margaret. They were silent as Danny took his seat at the table. Silence was not something they shared often, but they both knew what was coming … and who was going.

"I was thinking this morning," Margaret said, "how many times you've greeted me with 'Good afternoon' over the last eleven years."

"It used to be downstairs," Danny said.

Until the last two or three years Margaret had gone down to the restaurant every day, often during the lunch service to say hello to her customers, and always to greet the staff.

"A lot of things used to be, Danny."

She was right and he knew it, and it only made his heart heavier.

"That's what life is." She sipped her tea and smiled at him. "One day you wake up—in my case at eighty-two—and you realize pretty much everything you've experienced in your life 'used to be.'"

Margaret had adopted Danny, not legally but emotionally. She and Gerard never had children, and when she hired Danny she soon discovered he was exactly the kind of man she would like to claim as her son.

Danny took a sip of his coffee and cleared his throat. "I've been working on the list," he said.

"The list?"

"The list for your party a month from now."

Could it really be coming that soon, he wondered. Her life in New York, her years with the restaurant, her decade with him coming up those stairs to talk about menus and waiters and guest lists.

"Be sure to invite your parents," she said. "And Kyle's mother, if she'd like to come. And anyone else you'd like to have there."

He looked at her. "Seating's limited. If I invite the politicians and the celebrities and ..."

She cut him off with a shake of her head. "No, no, no, Danny. This one's for you more than it is for me. I don't care if any of those people are there. Unless you want them to come."

He stared at her. *This one's for you, Danny.* He knew then she understood just how hard this was for him and that she had asked for this going away party to give him the sense of an ending. It wasn't for Margaret. She could easily pack her bags and walk out the door tomorrow, but she wanted Danny to have this chance to say goodbye, and say it in a big way.

"Listen," she said, sliding her hand across the table and placing it over his. "I have something for you. Stay here a moment."

She got up from the table and shuffled into the living room, leaving Danny to look around the kitchen he'd seen so many times. Was there anything he'd missed? Had he ever heard the cuckoo strike time on the wall clock? He couldn't remember. Did he know what her view was through the small window above her sink? Had he ever stood there and looked to see?

Margaret came back in with a manila envelope. She sat down and handed it to him.

"What's this?" he said, afraid to open it. Was it her will? Was it a photograph of some moment in their lives together?

"Open it and see."

Danny pulled the flap back on the envelope and slid out a single piece of paper. It was a deed. He read it quickly, then said, "I don't understand."

"I have the money you gave me to buy the restaurant," she said. "It's more than I'll need to live another few years."

"Don't say that."

"Okay, Danny, maybe ten. Is that long enough?"

"Never is not long enough." He felt his eyes sting.

"I won't tell you not to cry. I don't know why people do that, it's wrong. We all need to cry."

He wiped his eyes with the back of his hand and looked at the paper again. She was giving him the building.

"I don't want the building," he said. "You have tenants. I'm not a landlord."

"And neither were we. Gerard had no idea how to be a landlord. So we hired a management company. You can do the same. Or you can sell it and do something else with the proceeds."

"I would never sell Margaret's Passion."

"But you might have to, if someone else owned the building. You see? This way that can't happen."

"I should talk to Kyle."

"So talk to Kyle. But the deed is done." She laughed at the pun. "And just think, my dear Danny, you'll be able to afford to buy out Sally Callahan soon."

Margaret knew Danny did not like being in business with his mother-in-law. If he owned the building, with the rent and even a line of credit against the equity, he could pay Sally back and have her return to being just Kyle's mother.

"I still don't understand."

"There's nothing to understand. I can't take the building with me, you know! And I don't need some albatross hung around my neck a thousand miles away."

"Is that how far Florida is?"

"Something like that."

"I've never been there."

"Well, now you'll have a reason to come."

And he would. Margaret was leaving in high summer and already Danny had imagined spending Christmas in Boca Raton. He and Kyle would be learning more about Florida with Margaret moving there than he'd ever wanted to know.

"Now let's go over this guest list," Margaret said.

"I didn't bring it with me."

"That's okay. We'll start a new one, and no one we once felt obligated to invite will be on it. This one's for us."

Margaret went to the kitchen counter, opened a drawer and took out a small writing pad and a pen she kept there for making grocery lists. She came back to the table and sat down.

"Danny, Kyle," she said, scribbling their names. "What about that sweet detective friend of yours? Would you like her there?"

"Yes," Danny said. "Linda Sikorsky. And she has a wife now, Kirsten."

"Oh does she? How lovely."

They began going over names then, Danny listing people he truly wanted at Margaret's going away party, and Margaret adding her own as she wrote the names down.

The weight of it began to lift slightly for him. He wanted the afternoon to stretch out endlessly, to spend every second he could sitting at Margaret Bowman's kitchen table, watching her elderly hand write names in a shaky scrawl. He glanced at the envelope. *Oh, Margaret, what have you gotten me into?* Everything stays the same, he thought, until it all changes.

CHAPTER 14

When most people think of the New York City subway they imagine a vast underground labyrinth. Kyle had been no exception, and for his first year living in the city, some thirty years ago, he'd taken buses rather than descend beneath the earth to barrel through tunnels dug a century before. It had reminded him of Poe's "The Premature Burial." There was something about being alive down there that had frightened him, until he realized it was a much faster and more efficient way to travel, especially from his then-home in Brooklyn to the various jobs he held in Manhattan.

Not all the trains that snake around the boroughs are subterranean. The N train, on which Kyle and Linda rode to Astoria, glides under the river past its last stop in Manhattan and emerges in Queens to continue along elevated tracks. Once upon a time you could look out from the train windows and see the World Trade Center before it came tumbling down in a morning of terror. Kyle remembered the days immediately following, when a plume of smoke rose from the hole in the ground that had been the Twin Towers. He couldn't believe nearly thirteen years had passed since then.

Kyle and Danny went to Astoria almost every weekend to visit Danny's parents in their row house on 28th Street. He knew the neighborhood well. He knew the Kaufman Astoria Studios. He knew the Museum of the Moving Image, housed in the same complex. He knew Steinway Street, named after the world famous piano makers. And he knew the Greek feeling of the area, still populated by Greek families who had lived here for generations and who still gave Astoria its flavor. They were mixed now with Iranians, Pakistanis, pockets of other Middle Eastern immigrants, and not a few gay people. Astoria was once known for being both affordable and quite nice, and as Manhattan became ever more expensive and out of reach for the average person, Astoria became a favorite refuge. You could get a large one-bedroom, maybe even a two-bedroom, for what you would pay for a studio in Chelsea. The migration brought higher prices, and Astoria was no longer the hidden gem it once was, but still a very nice place to live just a stone's throw from Manhattan.

"I love the skyline," Linda said, looking out the window as the train eased along the tracks, turning and running parallel to the East Side.

"Everybody does," Kyle replied. And it was true. No matter how often he'd thought of leaving New York City, he never stopped being thrilled by the sight of it from a distance. "It may not be the greatest city in the world—don't tell New York that—but it's the greatest skyline. It calls to you."

Four stops in they pulled into the Broadway station. Broadway is a main artery in Astoria, running east to west. It's where you'll find grocery stores, shops, restaurants, real Greek diners, and all the other small businesses that make up a neighborhood. It's also three blocks from Vincent Campagna's apartment. Kyle had called and gotten the address from Joseph the doorman. He'd bent the truth and said he wanted to send a food basket to Vinnie (which he would, just not now). Joseph had no reason to suspect anything and had given Kyle the information. He said quite of few of the tenants had been asking. Word spread quickly about the tragedy of Vinnie's brother.

They walked east a block, turned and walked another two blocks south, and found themselves in front of a large brown apartment building with six stories. Astoria was full of them. Row houses and apartment buildings made up most of the dwellings here. And Kyle knew from friends who lived here that the apartments tended to be large. The buildings were what's called "pre-war" and came at a premium price across the river in

Manhattan. It meant they were built before World War II, between 1900 and 1940, when space was plentiful and architecture still had a flare. They were also known for being very sturdy, just in case a hurricane decided to stop by.

"He's in 4C," Kyle said. They were standing in front of a buzzer box with dozens of apartment numbers on it, each with a name and button beside it. He buzzed Vincent's apartment.

"What if he's not home?" Linda asked.

"Joseph told me he was. Apparently he's the only one from the building Vinnie's been talking to."

Kyle waited a moment, pressed again, and they heard the front door buzzer go off, giving then entrance. Kyle quickly pulled the door open and held it for Linda.

The entryway was massive, as they often are in these buildings. It appeared large enough to hold fifty people, but it was completely empty except for the mailboxes along one wall. A wide staircase led up to the floors above them, and an old elevator stood along the back, next to an apartment Kyle guessed was the super's. Almost every apartment building in New York City has a super—the man (for it is inevitably a man), often with his family, who lives in and takes care of the building.

They took the elevator up to the fourth floor. Vinnie had not called down through the intercom to ask who was there and Kyle assumed the building didn't have one, or didn't have one that worked.

They stepped off the elevator and out onto a hallway. Apartment doors lined the walls in both directions. Taking a quick look at the first two, Kyle determined that Vincent Campagna lived three doors down to the right. They walked to the door and knocked.

Kyle was startled at first by Vinnie's appearance. He looked like a man who had not slept for two days, which was the case. He was on the short side, about five-five, with dark, almost black hair that had not been washed recently. He also hadn't shaved, and a thick stubble covered the lower half of his face. He was wearing a t-shirt that said Key West on it, jeans and no shoes or socks.

"Mr. Callahan," he said, surprised to see Kyle.

"Vinnie, please call me Kyle."

Vinnie looked at Linda.

"This is my friend, Detective Linda Sikorsky."

Linda was surprised Kyle introduced her that way and guessed he was doing it for a reason.

"I spoke to the police already," Vinnie said. "A couple times."

"She's not with the New York City police. She's visiting Danny and me from New Jersey. May we come in?"

"Oh, sure, sure." Vinnie stepped aside and waved them in. "Don't mind the mess."

What mess, Kyle wondered, as they entered the apartment. Vinnie Campagna was neat and orderly, among his other traits. The apartment was a studio, with a murphy bed folded up into one wall, a small dining table beneath a window, and a comfortable couch and chair in one corner. A television was on but muted, with a news channel playing.

"I'd offer you something …"

"No, Vinnie, that's fine," said Kyle. "We won't stay long. Linda just wanted to ask you some questions."

I did? Linda thought. She wished Kyle had told her before they got there.

"Yes, well," Linda said, improvising as she sat in the chair with Kyle and Vinnie taking the couch. "I was wondering …"

Kyle saw the hesitation. "She was wondering what you could tell us."

"What I could tell you?"

"About the last time you spoke to Victor."

Vinnie thought about it. He didn't know what difference it would make, since he'd been over these details with the police, but anything that might help find his brother's killer was worth it.

"It was Monday," he said. "I was at home in the afternoon. Vic's on a dayshift at 230 Park" – that was the apartment building Victor worked at – "and he was off Mondays and Tuesdays. He was excited about our niece's christening on Saturday. Ah, Christ, that's been postponed."

"I'm sorry," Kyle said. "But please go on. You spoke Monday?"

"Yeah, for a few minutes. We talked every day. We were very close." He stopped a moment, composing himself. "Vic wanted a new suit for the christening and said he was going to look for something nice."

Linda had taken her phone out and was making notes on one of its applications.

"But he was stopping for a drink first," Vinnie continued. "Said he was meeting a friend at Cargill's."

"What's Cargill's?" Linda asked.

"It's a bar. A gay bar. On East 58th Street."

Kyle knew of the place. It was one of the oldest gay bars on the East Side, and one of the few remaining. Kyle remembered it as a local watering hole that catered to a neighborhood crowd. No go-go dancers, no drag shows. Just booze and companionship.

"Do you know the name of the friend he was meeting?"

"No, sorry. Vic was out of the closet, but very … discreet, I guess you'd say. He had boyfriends from time to time but never brought them around. He wasn't uncomfortable being gay, he just didn't feel like he belonged anywhere. The gay scene, whatever that is, it wasn't for him and he was still looking for his place in the world. Now he'll never find it. But he liked that bar, yeah, something about it."

"Did you hear from him after that?" Linda asked.

"No."

"And what time was your conversation?"

"About three o'clock, sometime in there."

Kyle hesitated. He didn't want to bring up anything that would make Vinnie uncomfortable.

"Do you know if Vic ever met men online?"

Vinnie stared at him. "For hookups, you mean?"

"Or dates. Dinner, a movie, whatever. People meet online all the time."

"Is that how you met Mr. Durban?"

"Danny," Kyle said. "You can call him Danny. You're not on duty, Vinnie. And no, I didn't meet Danny online. We met at an art gallery."

Vinnie nodded. "I don't really know if he met guys online," he said. "Vic was …"

"Discreet," said Linda.

"Yeah, discreet. I'm sure he did meet men that way. But it's not the kind of thing he would tell me."

"So your phone call on Monday was the last."

Vinnie didn't answer and looked about to cry. He glanced away a moment, not wanting to break down in front of these people.

"Yeah," he said at last. "I called him later to make plans for Saturday, we were going together to the christening. But it went to voicemail. Tried texting too but that didn't get a response. He was known to turn his phone off, especially on his days off. He liked to 'unplug' he said, walk around and just look at things, listen to sounds and other people's conversations. He had his head in the clouds sometimes, that kid. He was my little brother, did I say that? Three years younger."

"You didn't mention it, no," Linda said. "We're so sorry, Vinnie."

"Thanks." He took a deep breath. "So I talked to him Monday when he was going to Cargill's, and never again. Never will, either. You think they'll catch the guy who did this?"

Kyle did not answer immediately. He knew the Pride Killer had not been caught for four years before vanishing. "We're going to try," he said. Then, very gently, he asked, "Do you have a photograph of Vic?"

"A picture?"

"Yes," Linda said. "So we can ask around, see if anyone remembers seeing him on Monday."

"Sure, sure." Vinnie got up and crossed to a small bookshelf. He had several framed photographs of his family and friends. He took one of his brother, quickly slipped it out of the frame, and brought it back, handing it to Kyle. "It's a couple years old but this is what he looks like."

Kyle took the photograph, glanced at it and slipped it into his shirt pocket. "Thank you, Vinnie, thank you very much. I'll be sure to get this back to you. We're going to go now, but I really am terribly sorry for your loss."

"My loss? Vic's the one who lost. Lost it all. I just want to find the man who took it."

"We're going to do our best," said Linda.

Kyle and Linda rose and thanked Vinnie again for talking with them. Vinnie followed them to the door.

"He's not the only one, is he?" Vinnie asked as he opened the door for them.

Kyle had not wanted to tell Vinnie what he knew of the killer, his elusiveness and success. But Vinnie had spoken to them at the most difficult time of his life and was owed the truth.

"No, Vinnie, I'm afraid not," Kyle said. "But we're trying to make sure there won't be any more."

"Good luck," Vinnie said as they left the apartment. "You'll let me know, right? If you find him?"

Linda turned back and said, "You'll be the first to know. Then we'll call the morgue."

Kyle was struck by the coldness in her voice, and by the implication in her words. She was prepared to make sure the Pride Killer never claimed another victim. Dead predators can't hunt.

They left Vincent Campagna's building and headed back to the subway. As they climbed the stairs at the station, Linda said, "Where to now?"

"I could use a drink," Kyle said. "And I know just the place."

The train pulled into the station just as they reached the turnstiles. Kyle used his MetroCard to swipe them through, and together they rushed up the stairs. Even the ten minutes it would take for the next train to arrive was time they did not have to waste.

CHAPTER 15

E d Cargill opened Cargill's bar when he was just twenty-five and new to New York City. Back then the Upper East Side was an inexpensive part of the city to live in, which could be said of much of Manhattan in the late 1950s. Ed made his way from Dayton, Ohio, as a young gay man looking for a place to belong. He found it in New York. He also found it in the bar that bore his name, and even though he endured police raids and the pervasive discrimination of a society and its police force that thought homosexuality was a mixture of crime and illness, he loved his patrons and he loved his city.

Cargill's had weathered the storms and the decades, and though Ed had long since passed on to the Great Gay Bar in Heaven, the establishment he founded still served the locals who had come to know it as their bar. They weren't all gay, either. Cargill's was inclusive before inclusivity was in vogue. You can find gay customers there having an after-work cocktail with their straight co-workers, their bisexual co-workers and, increasingly, their transgender co-workers.

The interior remained understated and comfortable. This was no splashy Chelsea bar. There was no loud music. Ed had installed a jukebox that people still loved putting quarters in, playing records by Janis Joplin and Patsy Cline mixed with current music from the bartenders' mix-tapes. Cargill's managed to be a comforting friend without being a throwback. It was run now by Ed's nephew, himself a man in his 60s who'd made his way to New York when he was just out of college and needed a little coming out of his own. Phil Carter didn't work at the bar much and wasn't there when Kyle and Linda arrived, but he'd kept the place in almost exactly the same shape, look and feel his uncle had left it when he took over in 1995.

"So this is a gay bar," Linda said as they walked through the door.

Kyle was surprised. He knew gay life was new to Detective Linda, but he hadn't imagined she had not visited at least one bar since her coming out a year and a half ago. Then he remembered so much had changed with the advent of the internet. Gay bars were becoming an anachronism, and bars like Cargill's almost museum pieces.

"Yes and no," Kyle said. "There are lots of different kinds of gay bars. Not that I know. Danny and I don't go to bars and I was never much of a bar person before I met him. This is more like an old neighborhood bar with a more interesting clientele than most."

There were only a half dozen people there; it was the middle of the afternoon, and the few customers at the bar (with two at a pool table) were the types who either stopped by for a friendly drink or who never left.

A tall man in his 40s was behind the bar washing glasses and nodding to patrons who talked to him whether he listened or not. He was dressed in khakis and a green long-sleeved shirt with the cuffs rolled up to reveal several tattoos on his forearms.

"Afternoon," Kyle said as he and Linda each took a stool.

"Afternoon," said the bartender. He put down a glass and walked over. "What can I get you folks?"

"Diet Coke for me," Linda said and Kyle ordered the same.

When the bartender set their drinks on napkins, Kyle said, "We're looking for some information."

The bartender eyed them, but not suspiciously. He'd had plenty of people—police and others—who came in every now and then looking for information. Most were just tourists wondering how to get to the South Street Seaport or the Empire State Building. Occasionally he'd get a private investigator trying to track down someone's errant spouse.

"I'm Kyle, by the way. And this is Detective Linda Sikorsky."

The bartender came to attention. "Robert," he said. "Robert Jeffries."

"Yes, well, Bob ..."

"Nobody calls me Bob."

"Sorry," said Kyle. "Robert ... we were wondering if you saw this man on Monday afternoon."

Kyle pulled out the photograph of Vic Campagna and handed it to Robert. He took the picture and held it up to the light.

"Vic," he said. "Yeah, I knew Vic. Very fucked up, what happened to him."

"Very," Linda said. "We think he may have met someone here."

The implication was not lost on Robert. He glanced around, as if someone dangerous might be sitting at one of his bar stools.

He handed the picture back. "He was in here to meet his buddy Sam, but Sam's no killer. He never even showed up. I remember Vic waiting about a half hour. Then he said Sam stood him up again and he left."

"Sam stood him up?" asked Kyle. "Were they dating?"

"Dating? Ah, no. Sam's got a husband. They're just friends, as far as I know. They met here a couple years ago, I remember that. And once or twice a month they'd meet for drinks, get caught up I guess. I try not to eavesdrop."

"Does Sam have a last name?" Linda asked.

"Paddington. Fortyish, works at the Met I think. The museum, not the opera."

"Any idea where we might find Sam?"

"The museum," Robert replied dryly.

"Right," said Kyle. "Not the opera. Do you know what he does there?"

"He's a ticket-taker, maybe an usher, I'm not sure." Robert leaned closer. "Listen, you think this is that guy, that Pride Killer? I heard he died or something. I remember when he was doing this before. Very scary."

"No one knows what happened to him," Kyle said. "Only that he's back. If he's back. It could be a different killer. It could be random."

"Word's starting to spread. My customers are getting nervous. Some of them, they knew Vic, they knew he came in here."

"I have a feeling that's not how Vic met his killer. The internet's a much more likely place to meet men who don't want to be found."

"Or seen," Linda added.

"Right, right. Should I put up posters or something? You know, warn people?"

"That's up to you," said Kyle. "But it might start a panic. As long as people know to use their instincts and common sense."

"I never meet guys on the internet, and I don't hookup. It's crazy. I'm like, control your impulses already, you could get killed doing this. And now they got apps on phones, you can find some guy in the coffee shop sitting next to you."

Kyle had read about these things but knew nothing of them and didn't want to know. The only man he ever wanted to find was Danny, and that was easy enough.

"Listen, Robert, you've been very helpful," Kyle said. He slid off his barstool and Linda followed.

"You gonna talk to Sam?"

"It's a possibility."

"It's not him, I'm telling you. Sam's been coming in here for years. Quiet guy, not your hookup type either. And definitely not a killer."

"Thanks," said Linda. She threw a ten dollar bill on the bar. "Keep the change."

They left Robert standing there wondering if he'd served a drink to a murderer in the last three days and if he should sound some kind of alarm. Heading back out to 58th Street, Kyle stopped on the sidewalk and mulled over the information they had, which was next to none.

"So," Linda said.

"So … Vic comes here to meet Sam, Sam doesn't show up."

"Do they text? Do they call?"

"The police will know, if they have Vic's phone. That's not the kind of information they put in news reports."

"Should we leave it up to them, then? The police?"

Kyle looked at her. "There's no time," he said. "For all we know Vic wasn't the first victim."

"Sam was. He didn't show up. It's possible there's some connection between the three of them—Vic, Sam and the Killer."

"Possible, yes. We have to look at everything as possible, although I have my doubts. It doesn't fit this killer's pattern, but neither does disappearing for three years."

"So you want to go to the Met?"

"Yes," said Kyle. "The museum, not the opera."

"But we don't know what Sam Paddington does there."

"Someone will tell us."

Kyle stepped to the curb and held up his hand. A taxi heading west pulled up within seconds, and they drove off after Kyle told the driver they were going to the Metropolitan Museum of Art.

CHAPTER 16

D was uncharacteristically anxious. It was another thing that had changed since he was last in the hunt. First there had been the curious disappointment with killing Victor, as if he'd lost interest in the one thing he'd been most passionate about in his life. And now this anxiety, this impatience. He refused to believe he was *nervous*—that was for novices and people unsure of themselves. D was supremely confident in everything he did. This was more like a general anxiety, and it had gotten the best of him as he'd waited in the store, checking his watch every fifteen minutes. Finally, at 3:15 p.m., he'd told Jarrod he was feeling just a little under the weather and he wanted to go home and lay down for a bit.

"Is it something you ate?" Jarrod asked, concerned for his boss. He'd noticed a change in Mr. K since his return from Germany. He attributed it to the loss of his mother. Jarrod's mother had passed away six years ago, and he knew how difficult it could be. He'd learned that grief was not linear, that it came and went in waves. He suspected a wave had overtaken Mr. K and he just needed to be alone.

"No, I'm sure that's not the cause," D replied. "But thank you so much for asking, Jarrod. You're a true friend. I just want to rest awhile. I'll be fine in the morning."

D had left the store then, walking the three blocks to his townhouse. He wanted to center himself before meeting Scott. He was worried Scott, too, would not be the one, and he would find himself in a rush to identify a replacement. Rushing was dangerous. People who hurried made mistakes, and he could not be one of them. He walked briskly north toward home, wanting to get there quickly. He knew he would feel better once he was there—and not in his bed, as he had told Jarrod, but in his basement.

When D first bought the townhouse the basement had been dank and empty. It seemed people in New York had no imagination, no ability to see an empty cellar as anything but a place to put boxes or washing machines. D had taken a look and seen potential. It was one of the reasons he bought the place. He knew when he first descended the stairs that he could turn this space into something special. First to go were the rickety stairs. They were narrow and wooden and *looked* dangerous. The last thing he wanted anyone to think when they headed down the stairs was that something dangerous was waiting for them. No ghosts, no cobwebs, no rodents. New York City was full of rodents, D thought. Most of them with office jobs and cell phones to their ears.

He'd replaced the stairs with wider planks and had them carpeted. Carpet was essential in his redesign: it absorbed sound. It was also comfortable to walk on, and he wanted his victims to feel very comfortable when he took them downstairs.

Essentially the basement was whatever D needed it to be when he was chatting up his victims in the living room. He was adept at determining their pastimes and passions. One man was a wine connoisseur and, lo and behold, so was D! In fact, D had an impressive collection of wines in his basement, in a temperature controlled room. Come, I'll show you. Another collected jazz records from the 1950s. Really? You'll never believe this, but I have a collection as well in my basement. Come, I'll show you.

Whatever it was they fancied—photography, art, sculpture, movies—D had just the thing to impress them, down a short flight of carpeted stairs, down beneath his townhouse, down where no one but D ever came back from alive.

He'd furnished the basement, of course. Large leather chairs and a sofa. A wide-screen TV. Even a computer on a large desk. All for appearances. It was an illusion he only needed to sustain for a short while. By the time they got down there they were already woozy from a special cocktail in the living room. Something to refresh them and dull their senses. He'd only had to struggle with two of them, but he was in shape and it had never been a real contest.

D got home and went directly to his basement. It really was a very comfortable space, and he sometimes spent an afternoon or evening here by himself. He might watch the news, or listen to some music. He might have a drink, but never before a meeting. Today he simply wanted to center himself, to sit awhile in his favorite environment and let his mind slow down. He didn't like his thoughts racing. They could get away from him, which is what had happened earlier. He'd grown so impatient in the store that he'd become agitated, and his basement was the perfect place to remedy that.

He slipped off his shoes and sat back on the brown leather sofa. He imagined Scott being the one, coming over the next evening for a quick visit before heading off to dinner. He imagined Scott liking old movie posters and discovering to his delight that D had several originals … in the basement. Greta Garbo, Humphrey Bogart. Signed by the illustrator, no less. Come, take a look.

He closed his eyes and luxuriated in mental images. Scott having a second drink … *here, let me freshen that.* Scott needing to sit a minute, feeling lightheaded. Scott wondering what was happening to him just as D came up behind the sofa, his special belt taught between his hands, slipping the thick black leather over Scott's head as Scott realized there had indeed been something very dangerous down those stairs, something deadly.

D smiled, opened his eyes slightly, and looked at his watch. One more hour.

CHAPTER 17

The Metropolitan Museum of Art is the largest art museum in the United States and one of the ten largest in the world. You can see its classical Greek columns as you approach its massive façade on Fifth Avenue, the steps leading up to the entrance crowded in good weather with tourists, students and sightseers from around the world. Banners heralding its exhibits drape down the front like giant flags. Founded in 1870 by a group of American businessmen, financiers, artists and leading thinkers of the day, the Met has been a must-see destination for people visiting New York City since its doors first opened.

The taxi pulled up in front of the museum, taking its place behind a long line of cabs dropping off and picking up passengers. Kyle paid the driver, noticing how much more expensive it had become to take a taxi. Just getting into the backseat will cost you $2.50, and if you go more than a few blocks you'll burn through $10 in the course of a very short conversation—your own, or the one the cab driver enjoys illegally on a cell phone plugged into his earpiece.

"Who was he talking to?" Linda asked as they headed up the museum steps.

"No idea," Kyle said. "I don't understand the language. And he's not supposed to be talking to anyone, it's against the law. Danny tells them to stop, but they all do it anyway."

Linda slowed down and looked up at the museum. She'd never been here and was as impressed as she was meant to be by the architecture. The museum had a Very Important Place feel to it and she was amazed by the sheer number of people on the steps, climbing up and down them, sitting on them, taking pictures and flowing into and out of the building.

"This looks like a museum you could spend a day in," Linda said as they entered.

"At least a day."

The main room was cavernous and even more crowded than the outside. Visitors herded in three directions, wandering with maps to the left, right, and up a wide set of stairs directly across from the front doors.

Kyle stopped once they'd cleared the entrance enough not to obstruct it. He'd had no plan and had not formed one on the way over.

"What are we going to do?" Linda asked.

"I'm thinking." Kyle looked around, wondering who to ask about a man named Sam Paddington. He worked here, but where? Doing what? The bartender at Cargill's said he might be a ticket taker. "Let's just get our tickets and figure this out."

They headed to one of several counters. This one was staffed by two young women who looked like they could be interns or volunteers, and an older man who appeared to be teaching them the ropes.

"Two adults," Kyle said, handing his credit card to the man. He knew the entrance fee was suggested (something most of the tourists didn't realize) but decided he would make the full donation and support his local art institution.

The man took Kyle's card and swiped it. Kyle pegged him as gay. It doesn't take that much to get the sensors reacting: a mannerism, a speech pattern. In this case, the man just seemed a little fussy. Kyle thought he was probably very good at his job—fussy is likely an attribute working at one of the most famous museums in the world.

"Excuse me," Kyle said, signing the credit card receipt.

"Yes?" said the man. "Did you need a map?"

"No, no. Actually, I'm looking for someone."

The man glanced around. "Good luck here, there are several thousand people to sift through. What does this person look like? I could keep an eye out for you, let them know you've arrived."

"Actually, I don't know what he looks like."

The man looked at Kyle, then at Linda, sizing them up. Probably one of those gay man/straight woman friendships, although Linda seemed like she could be family.

"I just have a name," Kyle said. "Sam Paddington. I'm told he works here at the museum."

The man's eyes widened. He cocked his head, most curious, then said, "I'm Sam Paddington."

"Seriously?" Linda said.

"Well, yes. Seriously, not seriously. Frivolously, depending on my mood. Why are you looking for me?"

Kyle took a moment to compose himself. People choose not to believe in coincidence, preferring the illusion of order only rarely disturbed by the unexpected, but coincidences happen all the time. Life, Kyle believed, was pretty much one long coincidence that appeared not to be.

"It's about Victor Campagna," he said.

Sam's expression froze. He looked quickly to the two young women at the counter with him. "Excuse me, Gina," he said to the girl on his left. "I'm going to step away for a few minutes."

"Please, Mr. Paddington, go right ahead, we'll be fine."

Sam Paddington walked out from behind the counter and led Kyle and Linda to the side, as away from the crowd as they could get, which was not far.

"I feel so terrible," Sam said once they were clustered in a corner. "I keep thinking, if I hadn't canceled on Vic …"

"So you did cancel," Kyle said. "The bartender at Cargill's didn't know. He just said you never showed up."

Sam looked aghast. "Of course I canceled! I would never just stand someone up, and certainly not a friend like Vic. I texted him saying I wasn't feeling well and I was going home early."

Kyle looked at him carefully. "But you feel fine now."

"It's been three days. I would hope I felt better by now. What are you getting at?"

"Nothing, Mr. Paddington, I'm just thinking out loud."

"Monday afternoon I was feeling … I don't know, food poisoning, but not that bad. Just an upset stomach, and I went home to my apartment in the Village."

"And that was it?" Linda asked.

"That was it."

"Did Vic text you back?"

"Yes, yes he did. He said he was going to buy a suit."

Vincent Campagna had told them the same thing, that his brother wanted a new suit for their niece's christening.

"Here," Sam said, taking his phone off his belt holster. "I still have it.

He went to his message screen, scrolled to Vic Campagna's name and held the phone out for Kyle to see.

No probs. Feel better. Headed to Keller and Whitman for a suit. Want the best for the baby. Call me later.

Sam's face darkened. "I never called him. I feel so terrible."

"You had no way of knowing," Linda said.

"Still … it would have been nice to hear his voice one last time, before …. before …"

"What is Keller and Whitman?" Kyle asked, not wanting to lose the thread of their conversation.

"It's a high-end men's store, clothing store, on the Upper East Side. I told Vic he shouldn't spend that kind of money, it's not like he'd be wearing the suit again any time soon. But he insisted, it was a big deal in the family."

Sam put his phone back on his belt. His hand was shaking slightly and Kyle realized how upsetting this was for him.

"Thank you, Mr. Paddington, you've been very helpful."

"Have I?"

"Yes, you have. We'll let you get back to your job now."

"Are you going to see the museum? You paid full price, not everybody does. I've had people pay a dollar. Seriously."

"We'd love to," Kyle said. "Linda's never been here and I'm sure she'd like to spend a day walking around the exhibits, but we just don't have time."

They waved goodbye to Sam Paddington as Kyle led them back out onto the front steps. As they descended, he said, "Something happened."

"Yeah, he got killed!"

"No, I mean something happened either before he got to this Keller and Whitman store, or after he left."

"Maybe something happened *at* the store."

"Right," Kyle said, a little too dismissively. "He goes into a fitting room and runs into the Pride Killer. I doubt that."

"I'm just offering ideas, Kyle. Something to think about."

"Good, really. We need ideas."

"So are we going there? To the store?"

Kyle led Linda to the taxi line. "Maybe tomorrow," he said. "We have dinner with Danny tonight. It'll give us a chance to think this all through."

"Can we afford to wait?" Linda was worried they could lose their momentum.

"If his pattern holds, his next victim will be Thursday or Friday night. That gives us tomorrow to kick this into high gear. I'll find out when this Keller and Whitman store opens and we'll be first in the door."

They got into a taxi and headed south on Fifth Avenue. No sooner had they pulled away from the curb than the driver began chattering in a low voice. He was not talking to himself.

"You said it's illegal," Linda whispered in the back seat.

"So is jaywalking, and look around you."

Kyle was right. New Yorkers all seemed to do as they please.

One in particular was about to do it again.

CHAPTER 18

Just as Kyle and Linda were heading home for dinner at the apartment, D was walking into Pianissimo, a piano bar on 46th Street in the Theater District. Pianissimo had been around since the mid-1960s and remained a favorite haunt of locals in the know, as well as a steady flow of tourists looking for real New York flavor. More than a few big names in the cabaret scene had developed their chops standing on its small stage, singing standards and the occasional original song they hoped would become one.

D had never been here. He was careful not to meet his candidates in bars where he would be recognized. Described, okay, if it came to that, but not someone known by name or habit. He'd chosen this place because it was on the west side, in a busy area where two men meeting for a drink would blend in with fifty others. He'd also chosen it because he knew it would be quiet, even if someone was at the piano—no video screens here looping dance music clips, no loud pop blaring from suspended speakers—and because it was not a place men their age would stand out. Many of the gay bars in Manhattan catered to a younger crowd and it would be too easy for a bartender or server to remember "the two old guys" sitting at a corner table.

Still, he took his time approaching the bar, looking at his surroundings. He liked to arrive early so he would be in place and he could observe the candidate as he walked in. A lot could be learned from a gait, the way a man carries himself. More than once D had passed on one of them, his instinct telling him this was not a perfect choice and might make the kill difficult. He did not like difficult kills.

He was pleased, then, when he saw Scott walk through the door five minutes late. D had been sitting at a small table along the wall that faced the entrance. He had a glass of white wine in front of him, and when Scott came in looking around at the two dozen customers, D waved at him.

Not bad, he thought, *not bad at all.*

Scott Devlin was fifty-three years old and conscious of his appearance: he was thin, with just a hint of middle-aged paunch. He was middling height, five-nine if one were to guess. He had close-cropped brown hair liberally sprinkled with gray. He was dressed well, in new-looking jeans and a blue-and-white striped shirt covered by a navy sport coat—a little warm for June, but it spoke of a man who wanted to make a good impression.

"Phillip?" he said, walking up to D.

D had accepted at the outset that the only time they would ever know his true name was when they would no longer be able to tell anyone. Sometimes he never did tell them and they died believing he was Phillip or David or Leo.

"Indeed it is," D said. He stood and shook Scott's hand. Firm, he thought, but not too. It was not the handshake of a man he would have trouble overpowering. "And you must be Scott."

"Nice choice," Scott said as he sat at the table. "I've never been here, but it's famous."

"A favorite of mine. I thought you might like it. There's no reason not to, really, and it's quiet enough to talk. That's always a plus."

"I like quiet, too," said Scott. A waiter came over and took his drink order: Scotch and water. A mature man's drink, thought D as he settled back into his chair.

"So tell me about yourself," D said, knowing everything he was about to hear might be a lie.

"Well, I'm between jobs right now. I don't consider myself unemployed, just in transition. It's all in the attitude."

"And what do you do? When you're not in transition."

"I'm a bookkeeper. I worked for the last eleven years at a large bakery in Long Island City that just closed down."

"I'm sorry."

"Don't be. It happens. At least I wasn't the only one let go. We all were."

"And where do you live?"

"I thought I mentioned that in my email."

"You probably did," D said. "My apologies."

"No need," said Scott, eyeing D and smiling. "A man as attractive as you must get quite a few responses."

D feigned embarrassment, shrugging. "It's not that at all. I just don't remember as well as I used to."

"You don't look old enough to be forgetting things yet."

"Call it early onset Chardonnay."

Scott laughed just as his drink arrived. He thanked the waiter and took a sip. "I live in Washington Heights."

"Quite a long subway ride."

"I'm used to it. And what do you do, Phillip?"

D hesitated.

"Are you in transition, too?" Phillip asked, sensing D's reluctance.

"No, not at all. I work with the dying."

Phillip was surprised. "Hospice?"

"Something like that."

D sipped his wine. He'd only had half a glass and intended to keep it that way.

"Listen," D said, "I was wondering if we could have a proper conversation over dinner tomorrow night."

"So I passed the test," Scott said. "I'm impressed ... that you're impressed! I'd love to have dinner, but I have plans tomorrow."

D was not happy with the information. He didn't want to have to start over, look for another candidate in such a hurry. Hurrying invites miscalculations.

"But I'm free tonight."

Free tonight, D thought. *That changes things without really changing them. It's not the schedule I had, the plans I'd made, but it will do.*

"Unless you're not, of course, and I would completely understand. There's always next week."

"No, no," D said, "next week is a week too long. I was only planning to finish up some work at home tonight. But if you'll indulge me an hour or so we can just stop there. I have magazines and books you can read, or watch the evening news if you like. I'll wrap things up and we can have a lovely dinner this evening. It just might be the dinner of a lifetime."

Scott was obviously pleased. He smiled and waved at the waiter, about to order another drink.

"Hold off on that," D said. "Let's have a second drink at my town-house. I have Scotch that's been sealed and waiting for you for seventy-five years."

"Seventy-five-year-old Scotch? You really shouldn't."

"Please, that's what it's for. I've been saving it for a special occasion, and something tells me that occasion has arrived."

D let his leg slide against Scott's under the table. Scott pressed back and a moment later D felt Scott's hand resting on his knee. *How easy they are*, he thought. *How easy.*

The waiter came over, expecting to fill another drink order. Instead, D said to him, "Check please," as he took out his wallet. Scott reached for his and D said, "This one's on me. Now think of where you'd like to have dinner and we'll decide in the taxi."

Scott couldn't believe his good fortune. Meeting Phillip had relieved him for an evening of his worries. No thoughts of being in "transition," no thoughts of dipping into his savings for months as he looked for another job, no thoughts of yet another night alone as so very many of his nights had been. He was feeling especially lucky as they stepped outside and Phillip raised a hand to flag a cab. Soon he would be sipping on Scotch that had waited seventy-five years for him to taste it! It was going to be an evening to remember.

CHAPTER 19

I t had been a long day for Danny, filled with more emotion than he was used to or would like. Nostalgia wasn't a weakness of his, but he'd spent the afternoon immersed in it: nostalgia for the years he'd been at Margaret's Passion, *with* Margaret. Nostalgia for a time in his life he knew was passing quickly into memory. Nostalgia, even, for the years he knew he could never get back. Time, Danny had learned, was a non-renewable resource, and the older we get, the less of it we have. Unlike anything else in our lives we cannot replace it. It left him with a sense of self-pity, and that was something he disliked in anyone, especially himself.

He was relieved to be at home, back in the apartment with their cats Smelly and Leonard, back with Kyle and their friend Linda. As he prepared the beet and goat cheese salad he reminded himself there were always people with something to truly be sad about. Linda's wife Kirsten was in Phoenix awaiting her arrival while she tended her mother in the final stage of her life. They'd both liked Dot when they met her at the women's wedding. She'd seemed robust enough at the time, but Danny knew cancer could come fast and furious, zero-to-sixty in a matter of months, and that's what had happened to Dot. According to Linda she wasn't expected to live out the month of July and Danny had already spoken to Kyle about going to the funeral if they were invited.

"I love scallops," Linda said. She was standing in the kitchen doorway watching Danny and Kyle prepare dinner.

"The trick is to not overcook them," Kyle said. Frying the scallops was his task and he watched them carefully in the pan, making sure they didn't turn to rubber.

The dinner consisted of scallops, sautéed spinach, baked potato and the salad. It was a rare treat for the men to have dinner at home with a guest. They ate at home often enough, but seldom with anyone else in attendance. It gave Kyle a chance to take out the small folding table they used for company and set it for three. Normally, he and Danny ate sitting on the couch in front of the television, or sometimes on bed trays while they watched something they'd recorded. Smelly and Leonard, too, were delighted to have a visitor. The activity interested them and they kept walking in and out of the kitchen, waiting for something to happen. Smelly was hoping for a scrap of some kind, which she would not get. Leonard, meanwhile, kept marking Linda's ankles with his teeth, sliding them against her as he walked back and forth.

Fifteen minutes later they were all seated at the table. Kyle placed it by the window overlooking Lexington Avenue. It wasn't all that scenic—the view was out over the avenue, and across the street they could see Baruch College. Street sounds drifted up, the occasional car horn, a shout now and then. Kyle hoped they could make it through dinner without the shrill interruption of a siren.

"So how's the party planning going?" Kyle asked Danny, referring to Margaret's going-away celebration.

"It's going fine," Danny said. "I'm just glad it's not a surprise. You can't keep something like this a surprise. Speaking of which …"

Kyle waited a moment for Danny to finish. When he didn't, Kyle said, "Yes? Speaking of surprises?"

"She gave us the building."

Kyle didn't understand. "What do you mean, 'gave us' the building?"

"As in ownership, Kyle. She signed the building over to us."

"That's amazing!" Linda said.

"In good ways and bad," said Danny.

"I still don't understand."

"It's pretty self-explanatory, Kyle. She gave us the deed to the building. Well, to me, but that's the same thing."

Kyle was stunned. They owned their apartment free and clear, but an entire building? What would they do with something like that?

Danny continued: "She said she doesn't need the money, she has that from the restaurant purchase. She can't take the building with her—her words—and she just … I don't know … *gave* us the building. Not sold us, not loaned us. Gave us."

"Oh my God," said Kyle. "What are we going to do with it?"

Danny looked at him. "We're going to become landlords, that's what. We're going to keep the restaurant open, and decide what to do with the building twenty years from now."

"Jesus." Kyle's mind was racing. He'd been worried Imogene might take a job in another city and leave him. He didn't want to work for someone else, didn't want to work in an office at all if it came to that. He'd wondered a hundred times what he would do if he lost his job. His photography was a pastime, not a profession. He was weary of being an assistant in his 50s. And now this—a landlord, a restaurateur. Maybe this was the path he was meant to take.

"This is a lot to think about," Kyle said.

"A lot," Danny replied. "But not right now. It was a long day. I've got a party to finish planning, a building to own, whatever that entails. So damn much. And I want a new suit, for Margaret's going-away."

"You've got plenty of suits," Kyle said.

"No. I want something new, something really expensive. Margaret deserves the absolute best, and I'll give that to her."

"You have a tuxedo."

"I don't want a tuxedo. I want Armani, or Versace, something stunning."

The subject of a new suit made Kyle remember the places he and Linda had been that day, the people they'd talked to. "I'm not sure where to start tomorrow," he said to Linda.

"I thought we were going to Keller and Whitman. That seems to be a vanishing point for Victor Campagna."

"What's Keller and Whitman?" Danny asked.

"It's a high-end men's clothing store," Kyle said. "I'm sure they sell some very fine suits. Would you like to go with us?"

"I can't. I've got an appointment in the morning with a florist for centerpieces. Then I have to help Chloe get out invitations. We should have mailed them a week ago. I think I was putting it off, you know, avoiding the whole thing."

"Well," said Kyle, "if we see any suits I think you'd like I'll take some pictures and email them to you." Then, thinking of the surprise Danny had dropped on them at dinner, he said, "A landlord. What the hell? We'll be like Fred and Ethel Mertz without a Lucy and Ricky. Maybe Linda and Kirsten would want to move in. I heard Linda does a mean Babalu."

"No, thank you," Linda said. "I like my little house in the woods, and Kirsten's gotten to like it quite a bit, too. Keep Manhattan, just give me that countryside."

"The parade Sunday might change your mind," said Danny. "It's not like anything you've seen before. The biggest party New York City throws every year."

"I won't change my mind, but thank you. I like New York City as a great place to visit. Let's keep it that way. I'm good for one big parade a year, in someone else's hometown."

Someone else's hometown. It made Kyle think about bodies in the river, the Pride Killer's return. New York City was the killer's hometown, too. He would have to put aside thoughts of owning a building, being a landlord and running Margaret's Passion. Somewhere out there was another man about to be lured to his death unless they moved quickly. He planned to be out of the apartment with Linda first thing in the morning, getting breakfast somewhere as they headed east to be first through the door at Keller and Whitman. He hoped whoever worked there would remember the young man who came in Monday looking for a suit, assuming he'd made it that far.

CHAPTER 20

D **didn't like** changes to his plans, least of all sudden ones. But what had really changed except the timing? He was careful to always be prepared. There was nothing he was going to do tomorrow night that he couldn't do tonight. And besides, it was too late, unless he wanted to call the whole thing off, and that was out of the question.

He let Scott babble on about looking for a new job, keeping his chin up, refusing to surrender to all the naysaying about the job market and older workers. He smiled and pretended to listen, nodding when he detected a pause, meanwhile having a conversation with himself in the privacy of his mind. Doubt had begun to seep in, and that was entirely new. He wondered if the time had come to stop, to make this his last Pride weekend killing spree and remain forever uncaught. He could become a legend—or more of one than he already was. He could become the most famous serial killer of them all ... the one that got away. He had to consider it. He'd made the foolish mistake of choosing Victor Someone from among his customers. Then he'd hailed a taxi in front of Pianissimo's, instead of walking Scott a block or two to keep from being seen outside the bar. What other mistakes might he make if he kept this up? He knew they weren't deliberate. He was not one of those sad sociopaths who wanted to be caught, to find themselves the subject of tabloid television segments, interviewed from death row. He assumed it was because he'd been out of the game for three years, but was it really a game he wanted to see to its conclusion?

He was deciding to have one last go of it and retire when he glanced out the window at a street sign. 78th Street, three blocks from his home. Better to get out now in case the police somehow found this taxi driver and the man remembered them.

"You can let us off here," D said, leaning forward to speak through the partition.

The cab pulled over. "I've got it," D said, taking a twenty dollar bill out of his wallet and handing it to the driver. He threw the door open and stepped out, not waiting for change.

"This is where you live?" Scott said, looking up at the apartment buildings.

"A couple blocks," D said. "It's such a nice night, let's get some air."

Scott was amendable to a short stroll and the two of them headed up Third Avenue. Five minutes later they turned onto 82nd Street and D led them to his townhouse.

"Upstairs or downstairs?" Scott asked, looking at the four story building in front of them.

"Oh, all of it," D replied, smiling. He could tell by the impressed expression on Scott's face that the seduction had begun. How easily people let down their guard in the presence of wealth, he thought, walking up the four front steps and letting them into his home.

Once they entered they stood in the front entryway, a long hall with dark wood floor planks as old as the house itself. D tossed his keys on an antique crescent table, above which hung a portrait of an elegant woman in a blue gown and raven hair sitting in a red high-backed chair. D had no idea who she was. "My grandmother," he said, nodding at the picture.

Judging by the wealth displayed in the painting, Scott decided money ran in the family and that he'd done quite well on this date. Very different from the last few he'd had. The men he met online were either older and still using profile photos from ten years ago, or younger and disappointed in him for a variety of reasons. He had all but given up dating, and was now glad he'd given it one more chance.

D led them into the living room, which might properly be called a sitting room. There was a television tastefully concealed in an oak cabinet. Along one wall was a fireplace with another portrait above it, this one of a gentleman from the late 1900s and a large dog at his feet. Another stranger D had been looking at for a decade and telling people he was related to.

"This is an amazing house," Scott said. He was afraid to sit on the couch, which looked well-kept but old and expensive.

D saw his hesitation. "Go ahead," he said. "It's made for sitting."

Scott eased down onto the couch, marveling at its softness. Was it velvet? He wasn't sure, and he ran his hand across the fabric. So soft.

D walked over and stood in front of Scott. He cocked his head slightly, curious at this specimen. Scott reached out and placed his hand on D's thigh. A handsome man indeed, thought D. Such a shame. Or such a prize.

D leaned down and kissed Scott. Not passionately, but enticingly. Just a taste.

"What can I get you to drink?" D said. Then, "Oh, wait, Scotch! Scotch for Scott!"

Scott laughed. He was feeling luckier by the minute.

"I happen to have that very old, unopened bottle. No ice, of course. One does not dilute seventy-five-year-old Scotch. I'll be right back."

Scott leaned back against the couch cushion. He watched D turn a corner into a dining room. He began to hum a song to himself, one among his few favorite love songs.

D stopped smiling the moment he turned into the dining room and was out of Scott's line of vision. He walked to his liquor cabinet, another antique he had no use for except as a prop. He leaned down and opened the door, looking into the bottles of rum, Brandy, Bombay Gin and Dewar's. It was not seventy-five years old, but he seriously doubted Scott would know. If he could tell the difference, he wouldn't have long to comment on it. D reached behind the bottles, into the back of the cabinet, and wrapped his hand around the bottle of Rohypnol. One of those and Scott would soon think any Scotch was the best in the world.

Rohypnol acts very quickly. Once Scott began to enjoy his Scotch, commenting on its remarkable flavor, which made D smile, there wasn't much time to get him downstairs.

"I have a wine cellar second to none," D said, watching Scott for any signs of fatigue. It would be coming soon. "At least not second to any I've seen."

"Very nice," Scott replied.

And? D thought. He wasn't expecting a dismissive "very nice."

"I'm not a wine drinker, definitely not a connoisseur."

"I'd still like to show you. It's not something you'll find in most homes, a world-class wine cellar. Come, we'll only be a minute. I imagine you're getting hungry and we should head out."

"I thought you had some work to do."

"I've decided it can wait. Dinner with such a nice gentleman has pushed any thoughts of work right out of my head."

"Well, I was hungry," Scott said. "Now I'm a little woozy."

"Seventy-five year old Scotch will do that to you. Now please, indulge me. I don't often have the pleasure of showing off my wines! You can bring your drink. Better yet, finish it and we'll take a quick trip downstairs."

Scott nodded, then tipped his glass back and drained the rest of the Scotch. He set his glass down on the coffee table, stood unsteadily and followed D toward a door just off the kitchen.

D opened the door. A waft of cool air rushed up at them. It was a welcome sensation for Scott. He was beginning to feel warm, helped by the June weather. Soon it would be hot in New York City, hot and sticky.

"After you," D said, standing aside and motioning down the stairs.

"I don't feel well," Scott said. "I normally hold my liquor quite well. Very strange. You'd think there was something in it …"

A look of dawning realization came over Scott's face. He was on the third step down when he turned back and stared at D, who was no longer smiling.

"What brand of Scotch did you say that was?"

"My own," D said. He stepped forward and with both hands shoved Scott down the stairs. He would not normally do this, but he knew Scott was growing suspicious and he had to act quickly. He did not want to break Scott's neck in a fall—that would ruin the fun—but neither could he risk a struggle.

"Hey!" Scott shouted just as he tumbled backward, down two steps, three, six, finally landing at the bottom of the stairs. His legs felt like rubber and when he flung his hands out grasping for the hand railing, the steps, anything to give him balance and stop his head from swimming, they simply flailed.

"What are you doing?" he managed, looking back up the stairs at D and trying to focus his vision.

D said nothing. The time for explanations had passed—and he never explained himself anyway. He bounded down the steps, leaping the last two over Scott and landing on the basement floor in front of him.

"Help!" Scott cried.

"No one can hear you," D said. "Not your calls for help. Not your screams when they come."

D grabbed Scott's collar and began to drag the now-helpless man across the cellar floor, into his special room. There was an examination table waiting, handcuffs, a state of the art Nikon on a tripod, and the special belt he used to strangle his victims when he was finally done with them. Sometimes it was twenty minutes, sometimes an hour. It all depended how exciting it was and how unwilling they were to have their deaths prolonged. The less they fought, the less he was interested. It was a paradox of the trade: a serial killer who only enjoys the ones who make it hardest to be killed! The easily defeated ones, the ones who went limp or imagined they would please him with passivity, were quickly disposed of. He liked them trying to shout, to call out hopelessly and strain against the bindings. He especially liked the ones who threatened him and told him what they would do to him once they were free. Freedom never came, only a last breath, an exhale of complete surrender. No one would hear that, either. No one except D himself, when he leaned down close, closer, listening to them as they gasped their final breaths.

"I can't hear you," D would say, turning his ear to their mouths. "You'll have to speak up."

He felt the old passion return as he managed to get Scott on the table and begin his inspection. Very nice specimen. He liked them in shape. Age was not a determining factor, and Scott had taken good care of himself.

D began to take his own clothes off. There was seldom much blood; he simply liked to look at himself as he went about his favorite pastime.

He bound Scott to the table, sorry the man was now unconscious. He would have to wake him up when the time came. He didn't go through all this to miss the best part.

The body slipped easily into the East River. They always did, giving out just a splash as they broke the water's surface. D got them there in his car. It's the only reason he kept one in the City. No one really needs a car in Manhattan, unless it's for leaving. D chuckled as he headed back to his Lincoln. He supposed the car *was* for leaving, but he was not the one heading off. It was men like Scott, and Victor Someone, and Kerry and Rafael. He didn't remember all their names. He didn't need to. The souvenirs brought their names back to him. He always kept something, and when he took them out of his bedroom safe he suddenly remembered each and every one in detail.

He reached into his pocket, whistling lightly as he walked. There, next to his own keys, was the set he took from Scott. Just a half dozen keys, to a half dozen locks Scott would never open again. One of them, D knew, was to the man's apartment. It was silent now, as silent as the night. It was a silence that would never be broken again by the sound of the apartment owner walking through the door.

Scott had proven especially defiant. It was a nice surprise; D had expected him to be one of his more pliable victims. He couldn't say why; perhaps he'd let old stereotypes color his perception. But he had been wrong—delightfully wrong—as he'd discovered once Scott regained consciousness.

It had tuned into a shouting match with only one of them shouting! No pleading, that was good, he didn't like the simpering ones. Plenty of struggle, with Scott thrashing this way and that, calling for help, his face so red D had feared a stroke might steal the moment from him. But fortune had been on his side once again and Scott had reminded him in every sensual, psychological, physical and emotional way, why he loved what he did so much. It had been both sublime and ecstatic. The only disappointment for the nearly ninety minutes he enjoyed with Scott was that it ended.

He felt fine as he walked to his car. Great, really. He was back in fit form. It had all gone fantastically. He would have to rethink this whole retirement business. Who retires anymore?

CHAPTER 21

Kyle had slept fitfully. The dinner had been lovely, followed by a walk around Gramercy Park and down to Union Square. He and Danny wanted to make sure Detective Linda saw plenty of sights on this trip. She hadn't come with a list of things to see and Kyle had not suggested one. He thought the best way to experience New York City was to just show up and go where your interests took you. Their visit to the Met had been ridiculously brief and Kyle meant to ask Linda if she'd like to go back and spend an afternoon there. They only had a few more days—her flight to Phoenix was scheduled for Monday morning. And before that there was the parade Sunday. So little time.

He'd tossed and turned most of the night, disturbed by dreams. In one he was jogging along the East River under a full moon. Jogging was something Kyle would only do in a dream. As he ran along he came upon a small child, a little girl in a frilly yellow church dress, pointing at the water's edge. She said nothing to him, he said nothing to her. Instead he stopped jogging and walked over to the riverbank. There, floating face up, was Danny. Wearing the same clothes he'd had on last night for their walk. Kyle stood staring down into the water, unable to scream, unable to speak. And then, floating into view, coming to rest next to his husband and best friend of nearly eight years, was Detective Linda. Face up, eyes dead, bloated.

Kyle had bolted up from the dream, sucking in his breath. He'd reached down to feel for Smelly, who always slept between them. She was there.

Danny was there. They were in bed. The clock read 3:00 a.m. It was only a dream. He'd managed to fall back asleep after telling Danny, who'd woken from the sudden movement, that everything was fine. It took an hour, but the last time Kyle glanced at the clock it was just turning 4:00 a.m.. A moment later he was back asleep, this time dreaming about cats, hundreds of cats in a house of rooms.

He finally got up as the sun began to blanket the sky with early morning light. He quietly went to the kitchen and made coffee for himself. Cup in hand, he padded quietly back to bed in his slippers, tossed them off and slid back onto the mattress. He turned the morning news on low. He knew Danny was awake, but it was one of their differences: Kyle could not stay on his back, staring at the ceiling, or on his side looking out into the dark room. Once his mind clicked on he had to move, even if he just got up for coffee and came back to bed. Danny, on the other hand, had no trouble staying put for another half hour or more.

The familiar faces of Channel 2 filled the TV screen. Kyle had imagined for years that the TV news people were his extended family. He'd had a crush on several of them—the weatherman from Channel 4, and an anchor named George from Channel 7 who had mysteriously vanished three years ago, surfacing in a much smaller market (Kyle kept tabs on them now that the internet made anonymity nearly impossible). He was watching, sipping his coffee, when a "BREAKING" segment came on. A young Asian woman, new to the channel, was reporting live from the East River.

Kyle immediately felt sick. He kept watching.

The name "Melissa Pang" appeared in the left corner, identifying the reporter.

"… the dead man has been identified as Scott Devlin. The information we have so far is that an early morning jogger noticed the body floating near the riverbank around 4:00 a.m. this morning. The jogger, whose name has not been released, immediately called police."

"Oh my God."

"What?" said Danny, sitting up to watch the news report.

"We made a mistake. A terrible mistake."

"What are you talking about?"

"Shhh!"

Kyle leaned in, focusing his attention on the reporter's words.

"Authorities refuse to say if this is the work of the Pride Killer until further determinations can be made," Melissa said.

"Of course it is!" Kyle shouted at the TV.

"That man was never caught and was believed to have died or left the area, but fear is beginning to spread in New York's gay community. As of this morning, the hashtag #PrideKiller has been trending on Twitter. Can social media solve what the NYPD has failed to for seven years?"

"Great," Danny grumbled. "Everything's a hashtag now."

"I wonder what he kept," Kyle wondered aloud.

"What?"

"A souvenir. The Pride Killer always keeps one."

"And you know this how?"

"They did a profile on him the last time, it was on NYNow. They were getting desperate, hoping to jog someone's memory in the public—and then he stopped. Or went away, or got bored, who knows. But he kept something from all his victims."

"Well, they're not going to tell you what he kept, if they even know," Danny said. "They hold that information back, in case they have a suspect."

"I have to tell Linda."

"Let her sleep, you can't do anything about it at this hour."

"No, she'll want to know."

"I'm already up," Linda said. She was standing in the open doorway, her brown bathrobe held closed with its belt. "I saw it, too."

There was a television in the spare room. Kyle watched sometimes when he was at his desk, and it provided company with something to watch if they wanted to be alone.

"We should have gone."

"Where, Kyle?" Linda said. "Where should we have gone? What should we have done? This isn't your fault. You had no way of knowing."

"But I did. I knew he kills in threes. I knew the second was coming, but not so soon."

Kyle hopped out of bed, sliding his feet back into his slippers.

"Where are you going?" Danny asked. He was up now, too. Luxuriating in bed was not to be his this morning.

"More coffee, and a plan of some kind. We have to move quickly."

Kyle walked past Linda and headed to the kitchen. She turned and followed him, with Smelly and Leonard bounding off the bed and giving chase.

Kyle popped another single serving cup into the machine. "What kind do you want? We have a selection."

Linda stepped past him and looked at the coffee carousel on the counter, deciding between dark Columbian roast and vanilla hazelnut.

"We need to go to that store," Kyle said.

"Keller and Whitman?"

"Yes. Vic Campagna either never made it there, or he left and met his killer shortly after. Maybe he said something to the staff, gave some indication where he was going."

"It's quarter after six in the morning," Linda said. She handed him the vanilla hazelnut pod.

"Yes, I know what time it is, and I want to be there the minute they open. In the meantime I want to watch the news, see if they come out with anything more. And I want to go online. Whoever this Scott Devlin is, he may have a website, or a profile. The more we know before we leave here, the sooner we might have some idea where to look next."

Linda stood quietly, letting Smelly circle her feet. She thought of the gun she'd brought with her, tucked in her suitcase. It had been her father's gun, the one he'd left at home when he went to the store all those years ago and was gunned down outside a corner market in a botched robbery. It was his service pistol from his time as Military Police in Vietnam, a Colt .45 Series 70 government model he'd used as a Cincinnati cop. Her mother gave it to her when she joined the New Hope Police Force but she had never carried it on duty. It was too special for that. She had had kept it, cleaned it, and fired it hundreds of times at a local range, and now that she was retired it was her protection. She did not travel without it—or her permit to carry it as a retired police officer—unless she was flying. At some point soon she would need to let Kyle know she had it, especially now that she intended to bring it with her. She had not believed in putting her safety in anyone's hands but her own since she was eight years old and learned it could be fatal.

CHAPTER 22

D ran his fingers over the keys for the hundredth time, feeling the metal with his fingertips, remembering the look of terror in Scott Devlin's eyes as he realized he was dying at the hands of such a refined man, a man of taste who kept seventy-five-year-old Scotch and a Class A wine cellar in his basement. Meeting strangers had always been a gamble, but nothing about D made anyone think he was the least bit dangerous. That was part of the thrill, really. Appearing to be someone so completely different from who he really was. And then, near the end, revealing himself. Surprise! How's that for failing to expect the unexpected!

He was lying in bed, propped up on pillows against the headboard, with his favorite bamboo bed tray across his lap. He'd made his morning tea and accompanied it with buttered toast—a special treat on a special morning. He looked at the clock: 6:00 a.m. The news came on and he watched as the same reporter told the same breaking news that Kyle and Linda were watching on the other side of town. A body had been found in the East River. Speculation was rampant. Something about a hashtag. My, D thought, that was fast. Was it a good sign? A bad sign? No sign at all?

He liked this young reporter; she was a rising star in the local TV news market and he would keep an eye on her, perhaps send her flowers when this was over and he disappeared for another year. He would be back, he had decided that. Retirement was not for him. The uneasiness he'd had after killing Victor Someone and feeling so little fulfillment had subsided.

Scott reminded him how good he was at it, how much it meant to him. No, he was not going away, just taking his usual long vacation. But first, there was the spree to finish. The Pride Killer—and by day's end everyone would be saying he'd come home to kill again—made his kills in threes. Three men. Three trips to the basement. Three bodies in the river.

There had to be one more, and as D remembered it clearly now, the third time was the charm. In fact, the hardest part of his yearly ritual was stopping! He made it to three, he enjoyed the escalating pleasure of each kill, and then, on Sunday, he went to the parade. Hundreds of thousands of proud gay men, lesbians, allies, all letters of that ever-expanding acronym marching and hooting and hollering their way down Fifth Avenue. And D, there on a corner, so very proud himself. He belonged to them, and they certainly belonged to him. Thank you, Papa, he thought, nibbling at his toast. Thank you for the photographs and the letters I never answered. Thank you for showing me there is a different way, a better way.

He had decided to find his third victim in a different way as well. The police would be stepping up their efforts. It did not serve the New York City tourism business to have the country's most successful serial killer back in action during one of the biggest celebrations of the year. They would be looking at postings on websites, men seeking men for all sorts of things. And nowadays everything was spied on, everything was filtered. He wanted to do what they would least expect and find his next candidate offline. Someone he met in his everyday life, as long as it was nowhere near the store. He hadn't cruised in a very long time, except twice his first year in Berlin when he was lonely and his mother, demented and taking much too long to die, had become insufferable. It had been more to get out of the house, away from her and the string of aides she hired and fired. He'd gone home with the men and talked, then fooled around just enough to frustrate them before heading back to the dreary reality of a dying mother.

He would cruise again, finding his third victim on a park path or in a Chelsea coffee shop. There were still plenty of gay men in Chelsea among the baby strollers and nannies. He could meet one there. Or maybe the Met or the Guggenheim! Museums were especially fun to cruise in, pretending to look at paintings and sculpture while you were really stealing glances at men doing exactly the same thing!

Whoever he met, and however he met him, it would need to be soon. He'd had to push up his schedule with Scott. The benefit of it was that it gave him more time. He did not have to rush now.

He finished half his toast, leaving the second piece on the plate as he watched the weather forecast for the next five days. It was going to be a perfect weekend. He would excuse himself that afternoon, telling Jarrod, who was coming in late this morning after a doctor's appointment, that he wanted to visit the church where his mother had loved to pray. He would light a votive candle and drop some money in the offering box. She'd never lived in New York City. There was no church, no favorite pew, no candle. Everything Jarrod knew about his boss was a lie. So he would lie again and wander out … cruise out into the world of Manhattan and see who caught his eye. Did he still have what it takes to seduce a stranger with just a smile and a wink? Why yes, he believed he did.

Perfect weather. Perfect plan. Perfect weekend coming soon. He felt so alive, so renewed, that he took the second piece of toast and ate it after all. Why not? He deserved it, and the world deserved him. It was a match made in hell.

CHAPTER 23

Kyle still marveled at how time slowed down the faster you wanted it to move. It was now 8:30 a.m. and they had another ninety minutes before Keller and Whitman opened for business. Kyle had done some online research and found nothing about the store that wasn't on its website. Founded in 1995, Keller and Whitman served an exclusive clientele, and also an older one. The few models on the site were mostly mature white men, with one African-American and one Asian thrown in to give it a veneer of diversity; Kyle suspected the only minorities who shopped there were moguls and bankers from Tokyo, Beijing or the safer parts of Mexico City.

The founders of the store were relatives, one Leo Whitman and his nephew Diedrich Keller III. Neither had a photograph on the "About" page, and there was a brief dedication to Leo, with the years 1944-2003 under his name. Kyle took that to mean Keller was running the store alone now. He would find out soon enough, since he and Linda planned to be the first customers through the door.

"What if Victor Campagna never made it there?" Linda asked. They were sitting on the couch as Danny prepared to leave for Margaret's Passion. It was a part of Danny's daily ritual Kyle rarely got to see, since he would normally be heading to his job by now and Danny usually left later in the morning.

"Then we'll know something—or someone—happened to him between the time he left Cargill's bar and the time he expected to be at the men's store."

"Maybe he met someone there. Another customer, or someone outside the store."

The Pride Killer was not careless; he may be stalking his victims first. For all they knew, Victor had been selected days or even weeks before his murder. It could be that the killer simply bided his time until the right opportunity arose for him to act.

"I've thought about that," Kyle said. "I'm starting to think Victor was followed."

Linda nodded; she'd considered the same thing. "And somehow, somewhere along his path, the killer got him to take a detour."

Danny came into the living room. He was dressed for work in black slacks, a light blue shirt and dark tie. He'd always been meticulous in his work appearance and had become more so since he owned the restaurant. The burdens of ownership were several degrees higher and heavier than simply managing the place, and he wanted to always be prepared for doing business, meeting clients as well as customers, and generally looking like he owned one of the best restaurants in Manhattan.

"I'm heading out now," Danny said. He grabbed a lint roller from several they had on a shelf just inside the kitchen. Cat hair was a constant in their home, and he rolled the latest batch from his pants legs.

"You're leaving early," Kyle said.

"More planning to do."

"How's that all going, by the way?"

"Fine, considering this is the one party I never wanted to have. We're whittling down the list, getting the invitations out. We've only got a month. Some people we knew were invited got a 'Save the Date' email a couple weeks ago. Is your mother coming?"

"No," Kyle said, secretly glad of it. There had been increasing friction between Danny and his mother-in-law since they'd been business partners and Kyle wanted this going-away party to be free of it. Sally might have suggestions for the seating plan, suggestions for the menu, even suggestions for who was being invited. Kyle was relieved she'd be on a cruise with her man-friend Farley somewhere in the Caribbean.

"That's right," Danny said, remembering. "She's taking a cruise. Good for her. Better for me." He put the lint roller back on the shelf. "Margaret suggested, now that we have title to the building, we could get a line of credit and buy your mother out."

Kyle hadn't given any thought to being landlords and didn't want to think about it now. But he liked the idea of buying out his mother. It could relieve a source of stress that had been in their lives the last six months.

"Margaret's a smart woman," Kyle said. "Let's talk seriously about that after her going-away party."

Danny nodded. He walked over to Kyle and kissed him goodbye. "Love you," he said. They always said this to each other when they parted, even when one was simply going across the street for milk. Life was unpredictable. People got hit by cars, they had heart attacks. Better to always say "I love you" and not wish later you had.

Danny leaned down and gave Linda a hug. "Please keep an eye on him," he said. "And yourself. One of these days you two are going to go after a killer who's smarter than you are."

It reminded Linda she needed to tell Kyle she'd brought her gun. She would do that as soon as they were alone. There was something about this killer that put her more on guard than usual.

"We'll be fine," Kyle said. "Safety in numbers."

"I'm not convinced 'two' qualifies for that," Danny said. "Bye everybody, bye cats." He waved at Smelly and Leonard. The cats glanced at him, uninterested, as the door closed.

Kyle looked at his watch. They still had over an hour. "Hungry?" he said.

"I could use some breakfast."

"I know a diner, the Moonrise, not far from where we're going."

"Sounds good." Linda got up from the couch. "Let me get my gun and jacket first."

"Your gun?"

"Well, yes. I've been meaning to tell you about that."

Kyle followed Linda into the guest room as she began to tell him about her father's gun—now her gun—and why she planned on bringing it along.

CHAPTER 24

Danny walked slowly along Lexington Avenue, south toward 23rd Street. It was only a six-block walk to Margaret's Passion and one he'd taken a few thousand times in the last eleven years. It was also one he knew he would take only a dozen more times before Margaret Bowman was gone. What then? He would get to the restaurant knowing she was not upstairs. And now it was his building! What would he and Kyle do with it? He needed to speak to the managing agent and see about keeping them on, arranging as seamless a transition as possible from Margaret's ownership to theirs. What of the tenants, too? Danny knew some of them. There was the older couple in the second floor apartment next to Margaret's, and the author who lived on the fourth floor and came in for lunch every Tuesday—a woman in her 50s who wrote a wildly successful series in the Young Adult fiction genre. Gladys Markowitz, although she did not write under that name. Danny was trying to think of her pen name as he turned left at 23rd. Tess Collins? Tess Collier? Something like that. Sold books by the hundreds of thousands to teenagers around the world.

Danny stopped on the corner and looked around him. He was acutely aware of how little attention we pay to our surroundings. New York was just a glaring example of it: everyone stumbled along with smart phones in their hands, ear buds shoved into their ears, or both. Texting, reading, typing, ignoring everything and everyone around them without realizing they would never, ever, encounter this moment again. He'd been guilty of it himself and had only stopped looking at his phone the last few months. Whatever emails were there could wait until he got to work. He and Kyle watched the morning news in bed every day, that was enough. He didn't need to read the New York Times in miniature as he shuffled along Third Avenue. It could all wait—which was exactly the opposite of how the world lived now. Most people thought *nothing* could wait anymore, not their Facebook updates, not the latest tweet from their favorite celebrity, not the endless stream of "click-bait" trying to grab their attention with headlines that would shame a high school newspaper writer at his most vulgar and juvenile. Danny had a dim view of the culture he found himself living in at fifty-six. Was it age? Or was it simply coming to see it all as flotsam clogging the surface of a sea of emptiness?

He smiled at that one, "a sea of emptiness." What did that even mean? He waved at the old man who ran the shoe repair store near the corner of 23rd and Third. He was surprised the store was still there. Almost everyone around it had gone out of business, replaced by other shops that would last six months, maybe a year or two, then they'd be gone as well. Flow and change.

A lot had changed in Danny Durban's life the last seven years. He was married. He owned a restaurant, and now the building it was in. His second mother, the one he loved as dearly as he loved his own, was about to move to Florida for the last few years of her life. But the shoe repair store was still there! Third Avenue was still there! Smelly and Leonard and Kyle were still there. He straightened up, smiled. The sun was out, the temperature expected to stay below 80. What a beautiful morning. So many beautiful mornings he'd missed, walking with his head down, staring at the tiny screen on his phone. No more. Today, and tomorrow, and the next day, he would look at the world around him. He would take comfort in what had *not* changed. He would cherish it all for every moment it lasted and not fall prey to sorrow, wondering when it would end.

He had a party to plan. He had a life to celebrate—Margaret's and his own. And the lives of his cats, and the lives of everyone he loved. His mother, his father, his sisters, his nieces and nephews, his husband, Detective

Linda and Kirsten, the old man in the shoe store and the bus driver and the mail lady. Celebrate all of them, celebrate each step he took as he walked along, celebrate being alive.

Yes, he thought, as Margaret's Passion came into view just a half-block ahead. Time for a new suit—literally and figuratively. Time to be alive.

He reached the restaurant and saw Chloe already there. He waved at her through the window; she waved back. Trebor the bartender was there, too, making everything look fabulous for the coming lunch crowd. He opened the door and just stood there looking around at his restaurant. His Margaret's Passion. He would make sure it always lived up to its name, and he would thank Margaret every day of his life for the passion she inspired in him. No time now for sadness, no time for mourning what had not yet passed. It was time to get to work, and do it with a song.

CHAPTER 25

Kyle loved diners. There had always been something about them that gave him comfort. He traced it back to his childhood, when he and his parents would go to breakfast on Saturday mornings in Highland Park, Illinois. The Chicago suburb was Kyle's home until he left for college. His father, Bert Callahan, an architect of some renown, died at his desk in the house—the same desk Kyle now used as his own. It was the only possession of his father's Kyle asked for when his mother moved to Chicago. But the memories of the diners had never faded, and he loved sitting in them, interacting with the waiters and waitresses who came by with coffee and an occasional attitude. He liked the feel of the leatherette booths and the paper placemats with advertisements on them for local businesses. Everything about a diner said *home* for Kyle, and they were a way for him to go there no matter where he was: diners on the road when they traveled, diners near their apartment, diners in other states, other worlds. Like comfort food itself, diners were consistent, reliable and soothing.

They'd taken a booth near the window facing Lexington Avenue. It was just nine-thirty and they were only a few blocks from the men's store. Linda was eating light, a fruit bowl with cereal, while Kyle had a Greek omelet, dry toast, no potatoes. He was now aware of the gun Linda carried in a holster beneath her jacket that would be visible only to the trained eye had she not told him about it. Being a retired detective allowed her to carry her firearm across state lines, provided she also had proof she'd qualified with the weapon in the past twelve months. Linda never failed to qualify.

"So here's where we stand," Kyle said, waving away their waitress who was making the rounds with fresh coffee. "We know Victor Campagna was at Cargill's where he was supposed to meet Sam Paddington, who never showed up."

"Sam's last communication with Vic was a text about going to look for a suit. If there were more we'll never know, since there's no phone."

"At least no phone we know about."

"Maybe the phone was the souvenir. You said the Pride Killer always keeps one."

"That's a distinct possibility. And I would guess, given how careful and successful this guy is, that if the cops have the phone, there's nothing on it that will lead them to him. Otherwise there might not be a second victim—they would have stopped him by now."

Kyle had blamed himself all morning for not finding some way to prevent the latest murder. It was useless guilt and fantasy—there was nothing more they could have done—but it troubled him to know the killer had acted outside his pattern. Did it mean he was escalating? That he was in a hurry for some reason? If that was the case he might be meeting his third victim as they spoke.

"No one ever heard from Victor again once he left Cargill's," Kyle continued. "That means he met the killer either before he got to Keller and Whitman, or very soon after. He was in frequent contact with his brother and I just don't think an entire afternoon would pass without another text, another phone call, something."

"Vinnie said Victor had a habit of turning his phone off."

"A bad habit, as it turns out."

Linda thought about it. "So the store is a turning point. But what if he never showed up there?"

"That's what we're going to find out." Kyle quickly finished half his toast and left the other piece on his plate, along with most of his omelet. He wasn't hungry.

"I wish you hadn't brought the gun," he said.

"It's perfectly legal," Linda replied, self-consciously patting her jacket pocket. She could feel the pistol under the cloth. If diners were comforting to Kyle, her father's Colt .45 was comforting to her. "Or are you one of those people who thinks guns are evil?"

"I didn't say they were evil. They just make me nervous."

"That's because you're never around them, Kyle. I've been around guns my entire life and I'd have to say they make the world a safer place. And there's just something about this Pride Killer that makes me want to be very, very careful."

"Fine, Detective, whatever you say."

"I'm a Republican."

Kyle stared at her a moment, not knowing what one had to do with the other.

"I just needed to come out, that's all. I came out as gay not very long ago, and I don't want to be in any closets. Not with my family, not with my social circle, small at it is, and not with you. And I gotta tell you, Kyle, coming out as Republican when you've got gay friends is very risky."

Kyle was silent a moment, then burst out laughing. "You think this is an issue for me? You think I've never voted for a Republican in my life?" (He hadn't, but would not tell her that.) "Pa-leeze!"

"I didn't know. We've never talked politics."

"Listen," Kyle said, as he motioned to the waitress for a check. "You're an ex-cop. You're a kickass lesbian. I am not surprised in the least that you carry a gun, or that you're a Republican. I would've guessed Libertarian."

It was Linda's turn to laugh. It gave them both a brief reprieve from the seriousness they'd been immersed in the last twenty-four hours.

"Let's just hope your aim is better than your judgment." Kyle winked as he pulled out his wallet. "Breakfast is on me."

Kyle took out several ones and placed them on the table for a tip, then grabbed the check and slid out of the booth. Keller and Whitman was scheduled to open in ten minutes and he had a lot of questions to ask there. A man's life could depend on the answers.

CHAPTER 26

D was distracted and wished Jarrod had not had a doctor's appointment. The morning after a kill was always like this, as if he couldn't stop reliving the pleasure and excitement of it: the helplessness and fear in his victim's eyes, the belt around the neck, the indescribable ecstasy of seeing life extinguished like a flame that has burned its last molecule of oxygen. Then the pictures—click, pose, click, pose, some flash, some natural lighting—and the disposal. He even enjoyed that last part, wrapping the body in a plastic sheet, getting it to the river undetected, and dropping it in. Splish splash! Then home, slowly, already savoring the sense memories of the last few hours. And now the morning.

He'd kept Scott Devlin's keys in his right pants pocket. He did that on his mornings-after, bringing his souvenir to work with him. He could feel the keys jangling against his leg. He slid his hand in his pocket, fingering the metal on his skin, the contours. He was seeing it all again, the terrible surprise on Scott's face, when he looked up and saw them through the front window. A man and a tall woman coming into the store. Very early. Of course, when you ran a store, there was no such thing as too early. You wanted customers as soon as the door was unlocked, and here were two of them. He took his hand out of his pocket and smiled at Kyle and Linda as they entered.

"Good morning," D said, stepping out from behind the counter.

"Morning," said Kyle. He'd talked over their approach as they walked from the diner. It would not be a direct questioning, at least not at first.

He wanted the chance to see what was here, to get a feel for the place and whoever worked at the store.

Linda went along, following Kyle a few steps behind. Both of them began to look around at the clothes as if they were regular shoppers, or tourists who'd heard of the store's reputation.

"How may I help you?" D said, smiling.

"Not really sure yet," Kyle said. "I'm looking at suits."

D was now standing next to Kyle at a small rack of very high-priced suits.

"Is there an occasion in mind? We could start with your measurements, go with something custom made."

"It's not for me." Kyle ran his fingers over a charcoal gray suit coat. "It's for my partner. He has a special event to attend but he's very busy. I thought I'd look around for him, save him some time."

"I see," said D. He glanced at Linda, who was standing ten feet or so away, appearing to look at a display of ties.

Something wasn't right here. D considered his instincts impeccable and there was something off with these two. Was it the way they appeared *too* casual? And why was the woman keeping her distance, as if she were listening and not really looking?

"What's the event?" D asked. His smile was still there, but the corners of his mouth had fallen slightly.

"A going away party," Kyle said. "He works at Margaret's Passion."

"The restaurant?"

"That's the one."

"I've heard of it, although I've never been there. Is he a maître d?"

"No, he's the owner."

"Oh, pardon me," said D.

"No offense taken," Kyle said. "There's nothing wrong with being a maître d! But no, we own the restaurant."

We. D relaxed slightly. This was indeed a man of means. Margaret's Passion was known as one of the best restaurants in the city. Like Keller and Whitman, its customers came from the upper echelons of Manhattan society. D's suspicion was quickly pushed aside at the thought of selling a most expensive suit—several if he did his best.

"My name's Kyle Callahan, by the way. And this is my sister, Linda." He waved Linda over.

"Good morning," Linda said as she approached the man.

"Very nice to meet you both."

"A friend told us this was the place to buy the best suit in town," Kyle said.

"Really?" said D. "How nice of your friend to speak well of us. We won't disappoint!"

Kyle took out the photograph of Victor Campagna. "Actually, you may know him."

This was the moment of surprise Kyle wanted. He watched D's facial expression, his body language, as he held up the picture.

"He was here three days ago."

D froze, but only on the inside. He remained casual, very careful not to give away any recognition of the photograph.

"No," D said, shaking his head. "I don't know this man. Do you always carry photographs of your friends?"

"Only the dead ones," Linda said.

"I see." D noticed the slight bulge against her jacket and knew there was a gun holster beneath it. "You're with the police?"

"For the most part," said Linda.

Hmm, thought D, *for the most part*. They must be private detectives, or one of them was. Why the charade? To see how he reacted?

"Take another look, please," Kyle said, holding out the photograph again. "He was found in the East River sometime between midnight Monday and early Tuesday morning."

D pretended to look closely, to scan his memory. "No, I'm sorry. Did he say he was here?"

"He said he was coming here."

"I wish I could help you, but I've never seen this man."

Kyle glanced around the store. "Do you work here alone?"

"I own Keller and Whitman," D said. "My name is Diedrich Keller. Mr. Whitman, my uncle, passed away some years ago. And yes, I work alone here, unless I need assistance. I have a part-time worker for busy days but Monday was not one of them. I was alone here all day. This man did not come in."

Kyle hoped his disappointment wasn't visible. He'd seen no indication in Diedrich Keller's reaction that he was lying. Somehow, somewhere along the way, as Victor Campagna traveled from Cargill's bar to this store, he was detoured. But why, and by whom?

"Thank you for your time, Mr. Keller," Kyle said, putting the picture of Victor back in his shirt pocket. He took his wallet out and pulled out a business card from Japan TV3. It listed his name, his title of Personal Assistant to Imogene Landis (she had insisted on this and Kyle still hated it after six years), with his office phone and cell number. He handed it to D. "If anything jogs your memory …"

"He wasn't here, I'm so sorry."

"Still, if anything comes up, or you hear of anything, please call my cell number."

"Will do," said D. Then, to Linda, "Are you a private detective, by any chance?"

"No," Linda said. "Retired homicide detective, from the New Hope police force."

"Pennsylvania?"

"Yes."

"I've never been to New Hope, but I've heard so many good things about it."

"Visit us sometime, everything you've heard is true. It's a great place."

Kyle and Linda headed for the door. Linda stopped as they were about to leave, turned back to D and said, "Why did you think I was a private detective?"

"I noticed your firearm."

Linda looked surprised.

"I'm a tailor by profession," D said. "I notice everything about a man's clothes. Or a woman's."

"Thank you again for your time," Kyle said. He opened the door and held it for Linda. A moment later they were out on the sidewalk.

D watched them walk south on Lexington Avenue. His smile vanished the moment they were out of sight. How did they know about Victor Campagna coming to the store? Who else knew? He had just been visited by a man tracing the steps of his victim, and a woman who carried a gun. Would they let it go and move on? Or would they come back, forcing him to act? And what exactly would he do if it came to that? Choosing Victor Someone from his customers was a stupid mistake. *Stupid, stupid, stupid mistake*, he thought.

He felt himself sweating despite the coolness in the air-conditioned store. This was bad. Diedrich Kristof Keller III never sweated. He would have to do something about this, he just didn't know yet what that was. He glanced at his watch: 11:00 a.m. Thank God Jarrod had a doctor's appointment that morning. He would be in soon, and D would need to take leave. He wasn't feeling well. Jarrod would understand. Such a good, clueless, devoted man Jarrod was. It would be a shame to kill him. Perhaps D could send him on a surprise vacation somewhere, in appreciation for his years of remarkable service. A sudden, surprise holiday somewhere far away.

If these two found him, the police might not be far away. Time had been on his side all these years. Time had been his friend, but now it was staring him down.

He would not blink.

CHAPTER 27

Kyle and Linda walked down a half block from Keller and Whitman. Kyle stopped near the corner and took a seat on a bus bench. It wasn't like any bus bench Linda had seen: a single, curved piece of aluminum with low handles strategically placed to create three seats. Kyle took one end, Linda the other.

"This is a bus bench?" Linda asked, wondering how uncomfortable it must be for anyone who didn't fit between the handles.

"It's the new thing in urban architecture," Kyle said. "You'll notice there's no enclosure, either. When it rains, you get wet. Bus benches designed for comfort and shelter have gone the way of pay phones. Now it's all about the homeless."

Linda looked down at the bench they were sitting on. "The homeless?"

"Think about it."

Linda quickly understood. The benches were impossible to lie on, being both spiked and rounded. Only an infant might be able to lie between seat handles. And the absence of any shelter made them distinctly temporary: you were meant to sit here, if you sat at all, only until the next bus came.

"New York has changed so much since I moved here thirty years ago," Kyle said. "It's for the wealthy now—at least Manhattan is, and good luck finding much affordable in the outer boroughs. They don't want poor people here, and the homeless are treated like pigeons. At least people feed the pigeons, but I think it's against the law. Pretty much everything is."

Linda liked what she'd seen of Manhattan so far and wasn't sure she would prefer it the way it had been. She'd read about the success the city had with Times Square, turning it from a dangerous playground for degenerates and criminals into a place you could bring a family. Was it better then, she wondered. Kyle thought so, but Linda had her doubts.

"What did you think of his story?" Linda asked, referring to Diedrich Keller.

"It wasn't much of a story. He said Victor never came in, and there's no reason to doubt him."

"So where did he go?"

"That's the million dollar question. He was at Cargill's, we know that. He left and headed here but never made it."

"And there was no more communication with anyone after that."

"We don't know that," said Kyle. "We don't have his phone. We don't know if anyone has his phone. The police might have it. The killer might have it."

"Or," said Linda, "he may simply have turned it off, or ignored it. I do that sometimes. I hate a vibrating phone, it's like Pavlov calling to his dog. Vic's brother said he liked to disengage. Anything could have happened that afternoon and evening."

"Correction," Kyle said. "Something did happen. Victor Campagna was killed. But he had to get there, wherever 'there' is. He had to go *somewhere* after he left Cargill's, and the most obvious direction for him to head was here, where he intended to go. I mean, for godsake, it's only six blocks!"

"Did you see the moving *Vanishing?*"

"What?"

"Vanishing," Linda said. "It was about this couple who stop at a gas station. The woman goes inside to buy something and never comes back."

"No, sorry, I didn't."

"Well, we seem to be looking at something like that. My point is that no one simply disappears. There's always somewhere they went, or someone who took them—willingly or not."

They sat in silence another minute. A bus came by and stopped in front of them, letting two people off. Linda gave a small wave to the driver and watched as an elderly woman with a cart on wheels climbed up into the bus and took a seat in front. The bus pulled away.

"Let's walk it," Kyle said.

"Walk where?"

"From Cargill's to here. Let's go back to Cargill's, imagine we're Victor and follow in his footsteps. We have his picture. I say we stop in every store and ask if they saw him, or if they saw him talking to someone."

Linda did a quick calculation in her head. "That's probably thirty stores, on one side of the street. Sixty if we hit both sides."

"We'll be logical about it. We'll go back to Cargill's, which is on the south side of the street. We take an immediate right, which most people would do. We walk up to Lexington, cross to the east side—the side we're on—and head north."

The directions meant nothing to Linda. She knew most of Manhattan was designed in a grid, which made navigating the city very easy once you understood the 'north, south, east, west' business, and the whole 'uptown, downtown' thing. Generally speaking, Fifth Avenue was the dividing line between east and west. She had no idea if there was one for north and south, but she knew if you were going downtown you were going south, and if you were going uptown you were going north. And to know you were going in one of those directions was as easy as looking at the street signs: the numbers only went up or down! Cargill's was near the corner of Lexington and 72nd Street. Keller and Whitman was on Lexington near 78th. Six blocks. Thirty stores.

They stood from the bench. Linda looked at it again, wondering who sat in a room and came up with the idea for bus benches that could only be endured for very short periods of time and could never provide comfort for the homeless or weary. Subtly sadistic. Maybe Kyle was right. Maybe New York was now a place that welcomed only money. She was beginning to be glad she hadn't come here for thirty-five years until last spring. She had no before-and-after comparisons to make. She knew only the magical city she'd been to with her parents when she was eight years old. That was the New York City she had wanted to remember. Now, all these years later, it was its own version of pristine. There was still garbage everywhere, and scaffolding covering what looked like half the buildings. But it did not feel dangerous anymore. Clearly the victims of the Pride Killer found out it still was.

Her hand unconsciously dropped down to pat the gun beneath her jacket. It was an automatic gesture, making sure it was still there, seeking comfort in its bulk and its lethality. Some people sought food for comfort, some sought booze, some sought the embrace of a lover for the night or a lifetime. Linda sought the grip of a Colt .45.

CHAPTER 28

D watched from the corner of the store. He'd seen them walk to the bus bench and sit down. He thought they might be going downtown, but then a bus pulled to the curb and they did not get on. They were talking. What were they talking about, he wondered. Were they comparing notes? Were they preparing to come back and ask him more questions?

They had not seen Jarrod enter the store just a few minutes after they'd left. And if they had, they would only think he was another customer. His luck was holding out and he tried to be soothed by it, even as an unfamiliar nervousness took root in him.

Diedrich Kristof Keller III believed himself destined to be remembered as the Pride Killer, among the most successful killers America has ever known. But unlike its most famous celebrity killers, he would not be caught. His murders would go unsolved. He would be the modern Jack the Ripper, as well known as any Hollywood star or politician, and with a reputation far outlasting most.

He had only been questioned once before, after his first victim. He'd met the young man through an advertisement in one of the gay newspapers that were stacked outside the bars. David was his name (a killer remembers his first victim the way he remembers his first love; they may well be the same). He called himself a "body worker" and only did outcalls. D thought at the time David probably lived at home with his parents, or a lover. For whatever reasons, he did not want his clients coming to his home, so he headed off to the Upper East Side to an address D had given him several blocks from his townhouse. When David arrived and was understandably surprised to see the man he knew as Leo waiting for him in front of an abandoned jewelry store, D told him it was a precaution. Body workers were not the only ones who took measures to protect themselves. Come, let's walk, D had said. Tell me about yourself. This way he had a chance to take the measure of this man and to keep him from knowing where he was really going. David might write down the addresses of his customers and D wanted no trail that could lead directly to him.

The questioning had been by accident. Two detectives, frustrated at a lack of progress, had canvassed the area where the cabbie said he'd dropped David off. Despite being several blocks away, they knocked at D's townhouse as they went door to door asking if anyone had seen the young man. No, D told them, he had not seen the man he had recently killed in his basement (leaving out that detail). Perhaps his wife had seen him, but she was gone at the moment with their daughter at an orthodontist appointment. Should he call her? They told him not to trouble her and headed on to the next building. That was as close as D had ever come to being found out, which was not close at all. Until this morning. Until the man and woman came into his store.

"I've seen flyers," Jarrod said. He was behind D, opening a shipment of cufflinks that had arrived late the previous afternoon.

It startled D out of his reverie. He turned around. "Pardon me?"

"Flyers, Mr. K, of that young man they found in the river. I saw several posted around the area."

This was news to D—bad news. It must be the man's family. They'd done it before, several times over the four years he'd been active before going to Berlin. Desperate posters with the faces of missing men and a toll-free number to call. All of them had taken their last breaths as he watched them, their eyes bulging out, their bodies convulsing. He had not seen these latest flyers and was worried now. He may need to think of moving after this. Yes, Keller and Whitman may need to close, the townhouse may need to be sold, and D may need to relocate to another large city. Maybe take a year off, then resume his trade. He would have to think it all through very carefully.

"I'm not feeling well, Jarrod," he said.

"Again? You might want to see a doctor, Mr. K."

"I'll be fine. I just need to go home and rest. I haven't been sleeping well. I'm just tired, really."

"By all means go home and lie down then. I've got the store."

"You always do, Jarrod. I've counted on you for a long time now, and you have never let me down."

D prepared to leave.

"What if someone comes in here asking?" Jarrod said.

"About what?"

"About that young man."

D stared at him. "What young man is that, Jarrod?"

"The one who's missing. The one on the flyers. I'm sure he was in here."

"Oh," said D, in as cold and flat a voice as his assistant had ever heard. "They were already here. I told them the young man had come in looking for a suit but had not seen anything to his liking."

"But I thought …"

"What, Jarrod? What did you think?"

A chill ran through Jarrod that froze his blood. He clearly remembered his boss talking to the young man, and in a very friendly tone. He hadn't heard their conversation, but he could swear the young man, the one whose face was now on flyers being put up around the area, had said, "See you later."

"Nothing," Jarrod said. "Nothing, Mr. K. I'm glad you told them whatever they needed to know. I won't worry about it. Now you just go home and rest. Take the day if you need to, I'll be here till closing."

"That's a good man. I'll call you if I'm coming back."

"No need to call. Just surprise me."

Oh, I'll surprise you, D thought. *When this is over, when it's time for me to quickly and quietly disappear, I'll have a very big surprise for you.*

"See you later then," D said. "Or maybe not. It will be a surprise."

D left the store, looking down the sidewalk as he did to see if the man and woman were still there. They were not.

Jarrod stood behind the counter absent-mindedly fingering the cuf-flink boxes. For the first time in his years of working for Diedrich Keller he had the sense that he did not know the man at all … and that he did not want to. Something was not right. He began to hope the police would come by again. He would be a good citizen, even though he knew there was noth-ing untoward about Mr. K's encounter with the dead man. He may have misheard their conversation. The young man may not have said, "See you later." But he would tell them and let them decide. He was just a sales clerk, a retail assistant. He did what he was told. Mr. K had not told him to *not* say anything. He decided he would pass on what he had heard and seen, *if* they came back. He would not seek them out. He would not call the police, but if they came in asking questions again, he would just politely tell them about Monday afternoon. There would be no harm intended, and surely none caused, but the man's family must be frantic by now to learn anything about his disappearance. Mr. K surely had nothing to do with that, but if Jarrod could help them in their search, then that was his duty.

CHAPTER 29

It was nearly noon and Kyle and Linda had managed to cover five blocks, stopping and asking store owners if they had seen Victor Campagna walking by on Monday afternoon. As he had feared, Kyle soon discovered how little attention people paid to each other in their daily routines. Most of the shop staff did not spend much time looking out their windows—they were busy watching the customers who'd come in, offering to help them find what they were looking for, or hovering nearby to make sure they didn't steal anything. They struck out at the dry cleaners, the shoe repair store, two diners, and a newly installed pinball arcade where the machines were for sale as well as play.

"I'm beginning to think he never left the bar," Linda said, as they walked north on Lexington just a block from Keller and Whitman.

"Or he didn't get very far from it." Kyle was disappointed, too, having placed his hopes on a sighting by someone along the avenue.

"Keep in mind it was the afternoon. People pay less attention then. They've been at work all day, they want to go home or out to play. They're thinking of themselves more than they are of passersby."

"True," said Kyle. He was feeling glum. There had already been a second victim, ahead of schedule. For all they knew the third victim was selected and might be heading to his death right now. The thought depressed and angered him. He kept thinking they'd missed something, that if they'd asked a different question at Cargill's, or in any of the businesses they'd stopped in, they could have jogged someone's memory.

"Should we keep going?" Linda asked. "We backtracked. Should we move forward now, stop in all the shops heading uptown?"

"I don't know. I just don't know."

There was a newsstand a half block from Keller and Whitman's. Just a hole in the wall, a narrow box of a shop where the owner sold a dozen newspapers, gum, candy, and sodas from a small back cooler. "Let's stop in here," Kyle said.

"Who reads newspapers anymore?" Linda asked as they entered the small store. She, like everyone she knew, got her news online now. She barely used her smartphone as a phone, except to call Kirsten. "Shit!" she blurted.

"What?" Kyle said, startled.

"I forgot to call Kirsten this morning. Listen, you talk to this guy and I'll wait outside. I call her every day. She'll be wondering what's wrong." She pulled her phone out of her purse. There were two messages in her voicemail. "Too late. She's called me. I had the damn thing on silent mode."

"Go," Kyle said. "I'll meet you outside."

Linda left the store to make her phone call. Kyle walked up to the man seated on a stool behind the counter. He'd watched them when they'd come in but had said nothing.

"No more cigarettes," the man said.

Kyle looked at the wall behind the man and was surprised to see an empty cigarette rack. "I don't smoke," he said.

"Gum? Candy? Not too many newspapers left, they go fast."

"Actually," Kyle said, taking out the photograph of Victor, "I was hoping you may have seen this man. Monday afternoon." He handed the picture to the shop owner. "What's your name, by the way?"

"You first."

"Kyle. Kyle Callahan. I'm trying to find my friend."

"Omar. I'm the owner here, twenty years. Everybody else come and go, but Omar stays."

The man took a pair of glasses from under the counter and perched them on his nose. He stared at the picture. "This is the one they found in the river, yes?"

"Yes, I'm sorry to say."

"Then you found who you are looking for."

Kyle couldn't tell if the man was being facetious or just literal. "Okay, then, I'm trying to find out where he went *before* they found him in the river. He was last known to be in this area."

The man peered again at the picture, then handed it back. Kyle felt his disappointment rising. He expected to hit another dead end among too many that day.

"Sure, I saw him."

"Really?"

The man, who Kyle now knew was named Omar, scowled at him. "What, you think I'm just saying it?"

"No, no, I believe you." Kyle glanced out the window and saw Linda talking on her phone. He wished she was with him to hear this.

"I was outside smoking—I smoke them, I just don't sell them—and I saw him come out of the store."

"Which store is that?"

"The men's store, the snooty one. Their customers never come in here. That's why I notice him. He leaves the men's store and comes in here to buy gum. He speaks to me. Not everybody does. Most just put what they buy on the counter, pay and leave. But this young man, he was very nice."

"What did he say?" asked Kyle.

"He say he's feeling lucky, or it was his lucky day, something like that. Maybe he felt lucky because he didn't buy a suit. Very overpriced, that place, I went there once. My brother's a tailor. You need a suit, I get you a good one at half what you pay there."

"Thank you, Omar. I don't need a suit but I'll keep it in mind."

Omar handed the photograph back. "I'm sorry about your friend," he said. "I guess it wasn't his lucky day after all."

Kyle took the picture and slipped it back in his pocket. He quickly picked out a pack of spearmint gum and tossed a ten dollar bill on the counter. Omar rang up the purchase and was taking out the change when Kyle said, "Keep it," and hurried out of the store.

Linda was saying goodbye as Kyle came out on the sidewalk.

"How's Kirsten and her mother?" Kyle said.

"I can't say fine. Dot's in the final stages, but they're keeping her comfortable. Kirsten thinks we're looking at a week, two at the most."

"I'm so sorry."

"It happens … to all of us. Some people just have the misfortune of dying in pain. My concern is getting Kirsten through this. I didn't tell her about the Pride Killer, that's not something she needs on her mind."

"Right."

"How did it go in there? Nothing helpful?"

"Oh," said Kyle, "to the contrary. It was very helpful. He saw Victor Campagna. They spoke."

"What did they say?"

"Omar didn't say anything, as far as I know. But Victor told him it was his lucky day."

It was an odd thing to tell a stranger, unless you'd just had a nice surprise. "I wonder what he meant by that."

"I don't know, but I know someone who might. Someone who told us he'd never seen Victor."

"Diedrich Keller."

"You guessed it. Omar—that's the store owner—said Victor had just come out of Keller and Whitman. He was there, and something happened that put him in a very good mood."

"I think it's time to pay another visit," Linda said. She slipped her phone back in her purse and the two of them began walking toward the men's store.

Kyle wondered what Diedrich Keller would tell them this time. Whatever it was, he knew it would be a lie.

CHAPTER 30

D had never suffered from claustrophobia and could not even define it, other than as the fear of confined spaces. Whatever people afflicted with it experience, he imagined it to be what he was feeling now: confined, boxed in, with the walls seeming to close in on him. He had miscalculated badly. He blamed it on being out of the game for three years—damn his mother! Damn Berlin! He had gotten cocky on his return, assuming his ability to remain not just un-captured, but unsuspected all these years, was the natural order of things. He felt invisible, as if he could simply choose his first victim from any man he met on the street, as if he could say to the world, Look, I am invincible, you see me but you don't! I can do this with impunity. And so he had chatted up Victor Campagna when he came into the store, giving no thought at all to Jarrod observing from the counter or across the room. Giving no thought to Victor leaving any kind of trail, no thought whatsoever to the police following that trail, and certainly no thought to a stranger and his sister coming in to ask questions.

Think, Diedrich, think clearly, he mumbled to himself as he paced his living room. They may have their suspicions, but what could they really know? No one on the police force had come to see him. No questions had been asked, except by the man and woman in the store that morning. There was no *proof*. He was overreacting. He needed to relax. He went to the liquor cabinet and poured himself a small snifter of brandy. Drinking was not something he allowed himself during the day, but his nerves were on edge and he needed to slow down, to relieve the sense that everything was about to come crashing down on him.

He was a world traveler. He had a valid passport, with stamps from a dozen countries. He could always go back to Germany. He'd learned enough of the language to get by for the time it would take to establish a new identity. And while he hated the time he'd spent there, it was just the sort of place he could vanish. He took his snifter to the couch, sat down and enjoyed the warmth of the brandy spreading through him.

A few minutes later he was slumped on the couch, enveloped by the cushions. So comfortable, so comforting. He'd finished his brandy and was contemplating a second glass as he let his memories wash over him. Each of his fourteen victims had sat on this couch. Each had been happy to have met such a nice man, such a refined man, who welcomed them into his home. Each had relaxed as he now relaxed, and soon, after a drink of their own, each had gone to his basement for the biggest, most spectacular and final surprise of their lives.

You knew it had to end sometime, Diedrich, he thought. *Even the best dreams end with the opening of an eye, the dull workaday world coming back into focus as the sweet dream recedes. It won't be long. Do what you need to do, then dream again.*

All would be well, he knew that now. The mind, once calmed, is the most powerful thing on Earth. Everything man has accomplished began in his mind. Every vision made reality, every towering achievement, every work of art. His life was a work of art, he believed that with all his heart. There had never been one like him, and there would never be one like him when he was gone. And he would go. He knew that now, too, in the clear calm of his soothed mind. It was all a fiction anyway, was it not? The townhouse, the paintings, the appearance of a life he'd built here, even the store. All of it had been manufactured to serve his one true purpose, and that was the only thing he lived to fulfill.

He was hungry now. He decided to have just a few more drops of the brandy, then head out for a nice meal. The only thing that eased a troubled soul more than a good stiff drink was fine food. He wanted some. He stood from the couch just a tiny bit unsteadily and headed back to the liquor cabinet. One more taste, one more slow, luscious swallow of the hot powerful liquid, and he would leave the townhouse. He would take a taxi, give the man directions, and head south.

CHAPTER 31

Jarrod saw the couple through the store window as they approached the door. The woman was taller than the man and quite striking, with her long hair and her navy jacket. They were deep in conversation and Jarrod wondered what they were talking about. He'd entertained himself for years by making up stories about people he saw, strangers, and the conversations they had with themselves. He imagined they were talking about a wedding they were planning to attend. The man needed a suit for the wedding but hated wearing suits. He did not strike Jarrod, upon first impression and from a distance, as the type who dressed up unless he had to. But weddings were special events, and the woman was telling him he had no choice. This was her brother's wedding—to a man, no less, something that gave Jarrod a special tingle while stirring his own sad longing for love. (He'd thought when he first met Mr. K there might be something there, but he'd been wrong and quickly let it go.)

Kyle and Linda walked into the store and Kyle noticed the man near the counter staring at them as he quickly pasted on his best may-I-help-you smile. It was not Diedrich Keller and Kyle guessed it was his assistant, the one they'd been lead to believe was rarely there. The man looked to be in his 50s, slim and stylishly dressed in dark pants and matching sport coat. He wore a thin gray tie with a small diamond tie-pin at its midpoint. His hair was artificially black, but not the sort of shoe-polish look that some young hipster types wore or that made some older men look ridiculous. Just clearly dyed.

"May I help you?" Jarrod asked.

"We were looking for Diedrich Keller," Kyle said. "We spoke to him earlier and were under the impression he would still be here."

"He didn't mention having help today," Linda added.

Help? Jarrod thought. Is that how they thought of him? Surely Mr. Keller had not referred to him that way. He was an *assistant*. An Assistant Store Manager, if one wanted to rely on titles. But not *help*.

"I'm here every day," Jarrod said. "Perhaps if he referred to the help he meant the cleaning crew that comes in on Sundays. But of course it's not Sunday."

"Of course not," Kyle said. He could tell Linda's comment rubbed the man the wrong way. This could work to his advantage if he made this man annoyed with his boss. "Surely that's what he meant, not you."

"Definitely not."

Kyle extended his hand. "I'm Kyle, by the way. Kyle Callahan, and this is my associate Linda Sikorsky."

Linda nodded, declining to extend her hand. She was remaining silent, waiting to see how Kyle played this.

"Jarrod Sperling. I've been Mr. Keller's assistant here—Assistant Manager, that is—for nearly seven years. I basically run the store when he needs to be out, which is fairly often. Are you looking for a suit? A nice ensemble of some kind?"

"No. We're actually asking around about a friend of mine." Kyle took out the photo of Victor Campagna and showed it to Jarrod.

"Oh, my," Jarrod said, and Kyle knew he recognized Victor. "I've definitely seen him before … on the news. It's terrible what happened to him. But are they sure he didn't fall into the river? It happens sometimes. People have too much to drink, they get too close to the water's edge."

"That's what we're trying to find out."

"Are you with the police?"

"Yes and no," Linda interjected. "I'm a private detective, hired by Victor's family."

Something was peculiar with these two, Jarrod thought. First they were "associates." Then they were friends of the poor young dead man. Now one of them is a private detective. His guard went up. What should he tell them? And should he tell Mr. K first? Had they been the police it would be different, but they were not. He did not want to do or say something that could get him in trouble. He liked his life, he liked his job, he liked his status as Assistant Manager in one of the city's finest men's clothing boutiques. This was not a boat he wanted to rock.

"Well," he said, "other than on the news reports and the flyers, I can't say I've seen him before." It was a lie and Jarrod could feel his face flush, hoping it was only something he felt and not something they saw.

"We'd like to ask Diedrich a few more questions," Linda said. "Might you have his home address?"

Something was definitely fishy now. What private detective worth her pay could not find someone's home address? And that information was private. Jarrod had never, not once, given our Mr. K's address or his phone number.

"He's at a meeting," Jarrod said.

Kyle: "A meeting?"

"With one of our suppliers."

"Do you know when he'll be back?" asked Linda.

"Um … no, I don't. Sometimes he doesn't come back until the next day. He doesn't need to come back. He has me here."

"Yes, of course," said Kyle, "his Assistant Manager." This had gotten them nowhere, and he believed Jarrod was hiding something.

Linda took out her business card and handed it to Jarrod. It was the card for her vintage store in New Hope that listed her cell phone number.

Jarrod read it and looked at her curiously. *"For Pete's Sake?"* he said, reading the store name.

"It's my cover."

"An undercover private detective. I didn't know there was such a thing."

"Just please call me if Mr. Keller returns. It's very important. The family is distraught and I've promised to do all I can to find out what happened to their son."

"Do you think Mr. K ... Mr. Keller, might know something?"

"That's what we'd like to find out," Kyle said. "Not that he had anything to do with the disappearance, just if he might remember something, anything, about seeing Victor walk by or perhaps stop and look in the window here. Please give us a ring if Mr. Keller returns, it's a simple request."

"Yes, yes, of course."

Kyle and Linda prepared to leave. They both felt they'd been stonewalled and that the first thing Jarrod Sperling would do when they left was call Diedrich Keller. Maybe this was a good thing: having been to his store twice in one day, they might have him on edge, thinking too quickly and ripe for making a costly error.

"By the way," Kyle said as they were about to turn and leave. "You said you ran the store for Diedrich Keller when he wasn't here."

"Yes," Jarrod said, stiffening proudly.

"Did you ever run it for him for an extended period?"

"Why yes, I did. I ran it for him for nearly three years."

Kyle stared at him. He felt as if a shadow had just come over them. "Three years? Really?"

"Mr. Keller spent time in Germany. Berlin, to be exact, taking care of his mother. He's only been back a few months. Why do you ask?"

"No reason," said Kyle. "Thank you for your time. And if you do hear from him, please call that cell phone number on the card."

They left the store and Jarrod stood by the window, watching them walk away. It had been a most unusual exchange. He'd lied because ... because ... he wasn't sure who they really were or what he should tell them. He prided himself on making decisions, being proactive. But this was a very different set of circumstances. A young man was dead—a man who had been in the store just three days ago. Mr. K was acting oddly and taking off more than usual. And now two strangers had come in asking questions he felt he could not answer, not without talking to Mr. K first.

He hurried to the phone behind the counter and dialed Diedrich Keller's home number. After four rings it went to an answering machine and Jarrod hung up. This was too important to leave a message and wait. He dialed again, this time Keller's cell phone. After two rings Diedrich answered. He would know it was Jarrod from the called ID.

"Yes, Jarrod?" he said.

Jarrod could not tell where his boss was, but he thought he heard traffic sounds in the background. Interesting; he had not gone home, or, if he had, he'd left again.

"Two people were just in the store," Jarrod said. "They claimed to have spoken to you earlier."

There was a moment of silence, then Diedrich Keller said, "Go on, Jarrod. What did they want to know?"

"They were asking about that young man who was murdered this week. I didn't tell them anything."

"Of course not, there's nothing to tell. Is there?"

Jarrod hesitated. He was questioning his own memory. Maybe he hadn't seen Mr. K talking to the young man, maybe it was a different young man entirely. "No, nothing to tell, Mr. K."

"What else did they want to know?"

"If you'd ever been away from the store for an extended period—you know, like your time in Berlin."

"And what did you tell them?"

Jarrod proceeded to inform Diedrich Keller of everything that had transpired with the couple—that the woman claimed to be a private detective, that they wanted his home address (which Jarrod did not give them), and that odd question about any extended absence.

D remained calm through it all. A sense of peaceful finality had come over him. He was glad Jarrod had not given them his home address. It was a home he would be leaving very soon, but he had one more task at hand, one more mission to accomplish. He told Jarrod he'd done well and that he would see him in the morning. It was a lie. He intended never to see Jarrod Sperling again.

CHAPTER 32

A peace had come over Danny since he'd arrived at Margaret's Passion that morning. He knew it was part of an inevitable acceptance—accepting that Margaret Bowman was leaving, accepting that a large part of the world he had known and loved was changing. Margaret had lived a long and fruitful life. She'd achieved her dreams and touched so many people's lives. She had loved her husband, Gerard, with the same passion that gave her restaurant its name. Danny had never met Gerard Bowman, who died in a freak traffic accident just outside the restaurant two years before Danny was hired. He'd been a smoker, something Margaret disdained but indulged provided he went outside. So several times a day Gerard Bowman could be seen on the side street smoking a cigarette. One day he stepped off the curb to stamp out his cigarette butt in the gutter, and a taxi came flying through the light to make it across before it turned red. The driver saw Gerard in the street, was startled by the sight and swerved, losing control of the taxi. Ten seconds later Gerard Bowman was dead.

Margaret had carried on. She met Danny, hired him, and eleven years later she was leaving him. That was the part—the feeling—he had finally managed to make peace with. She was eighty-one years old. She was more than entitled to spend her last few years with her sister who was almost ninety. The restaurant was Danny's, and now Margaret had completed the transfer of the only thing that had kept her here by deeding the building to him. She was passing it all on, saying, Here, it's yours now. I'm entrusting it to you. I know you'll make me proud.

Danny was thinking of that—making Margaret proud by surviving in the business, being a landlord soon, and giving the old woman the most amazing going away party New York City had ever seen—when a man walked into the restaurant. It was almost two o'clock. The kitchen stopped serving lunch at two, but Danny had never told a customer it was too late, not until the kitchen was actually closed. The man had fifteen more minutes, which meant he would be seated, he would be given a menu, and he would be served.

"Good afternoon," Danny said. Chloe was in the back room stocking shelves and Trebor was behind the bar. There were two women on stools finishing an early afternoon glass of wine. No one else was there.

"Good afternoon," D said. "I hope I'm not too late for a small bite. I've just come back from Berlin and I'm famished."

"No, no, not at all, please come in. Any table you'd like."

D chose a table well away from the window—unusual during the day, Danny thought, but some people didn't like the light. Danny walked with the man to a two-top near the bar and handed him a menu once he sat down.

"Your waiter will be with you in a moment. In the meantime, is there something you'd like from the bar?"

"Just water," D said. "Thank you."

D watched the man disappear around the corner of the bar. He didn't know if he'd bring the water himself or if a waiter would do that. He looked around the restaurant and was quite pleased with what he saw. He'd heard of Margaret's Passion, of course. One does not own a high-end clothing store with upper crust clients without hearing of the places they patronize. The Plaza. Elaine's, when there was an Elaine. The 21 Club. And Margaret's Passion. It was comfortable in a way newer eateries catering to the nouveau riche and the hangers-on were not. The trend these days, dismaying to people like Diedrich Keller, was for deafeningly loud restaurants where shouting was the only way to be heard by the person sitting across a small table from you. No, this was much more … classy. More stylish, for those who knew what true style was.

He watched the man go into the kitchen, then return looking perplexed. He spoke briefly to the bartender, retrieved a glass of ice water and returned with it to the table.

"I'll be taking your order today," Danny said. He'd gone back to find Clarence, the waiter he expected to still be on duty, but was told by the cook that Clarence had taken off early, expecting no one else to come in. Chloe was still working on the dinner set up and Danny didn't want to bother her, so he decided to take the man's order himself. Danny set the water glass down. "Have you had a chance to decide?"

"Not quite yet," D said. "By the way, my name's Diedrich Keller. And you are?"

Danny was embarrassed. Introducing yourself was the first lesson of table service, but he had not taken anyone's order in a very long time.

"Danny Durban," he said. "My apology for neglecting to introduce myself."

"No apology needed. Are you the maître d?"

"No, no. I'm the owner."

"Ah," said D. "I feel special now." He glanced around. "I'd foolishly assumed someone named Margaret would be the owner of Margaret's Passion."

"She was, until very recently. Margaret Bowman."

"Is she deceased?"

"No. I … my partner and I bought the restaurant from her. But she'll be moving away soon. The restaurant won't be the same without her. We'll survive, but there's only one Margaret Bowman."

D pretended that a thought had suddenly come to him. "You and your partner, you say?"

"Yes, his name's Kyle."

"What a small world! I met him just this morning. He said you were looking for a new suit."

Danny sighed. He remembered Kyle saying they were going to a men's store and assumed Kyle had taken it upon himself to suit shop for him. Kyle knew he was looking for something special for Margaret's party. "I am, yes," Danny said.

"Well then," said D, taking out a business card from his wallet. "I'm just the person for you. I'm a business owner myself. Keller and Whitman, clothing for the gentleman's gentleman."

The name rang a bell this time. Some of the customers at Margaret's got their clothes there—impeccably tailored suits, and shirts that cost enough as a dinner for four. It wasn't a place Danny would ever shop given the prices, and why he hadn't remembered it when Kyle said they were going there that morning.

"Here," D said, taking a pen from his jacket pocket and writing his cell number on the card. "I'll tell you what, call me anytime and we'll do a private fitting. I know this event is important to you—how could it not be?—and I'd like you to look your absolute best. I'll measure you myself and get you something done by the time of your party."

"It's a month from now," Danny said.

"Then we have plenty of time." D handed him the card. "Promise you'll call." Then, as if he'd just remembered something urgent, he said, "Oh, my …"

"What?"

"I have to leave for London Friday. I won't be back until August. I'm looking at store locations there. But I don't do the stitching myself, of course!"

"Of course not," Danny said.

"I could size you and get an order in before I go. How about this afternoon?"

Danny hesitated. He'd never met this man before, but he knew the store's reputation. And it would be amazing to show up at Margaret's party in a suit from one of the city's best men's stores. "I'm not sure, I was planning …"

"I'll give you a discount," D said, smiling. "A very deep discount."

How could Danny say no? It might even lift his spirits and put him in the frame of mind he wanted to be in: to view and experience Margaret's going away as a celebration, not a funeral procession or a wake.

Danny took the card. "It's a deal," he said. "Just let me get things wrapped up here and I'll call. Shall I meet you at the store?"

"Oh, no, Mr. Durban. This will be a private fitting. Just give me a call and I'll provide directions."

Danny put the card in his shirt pocket. "And now," he said, "order anything you'd like. Lunch is on the house."

"Very, very kind," D said, turning his attention to the menu. He was hungry now, and planned to eat a hearty meal before heading back to his townhouse to wait for a phone call. It was going to be an excellent evening, an intimate affair—his own going away party for two.

CHAPTER 33

Few things unnerved Kyle more than speeding through Manhattan in a taxi. The drivers obeyed few rules, except the ones that could get them ticketed, and even those they skirted as often as they could. Lanes meant nothing to them, and they would veer wildly from side to side, maneuvering at high speeds through a sea of cars, trucks and buses. Double parking was common, especially during the week, and the flow of vehicles often made him think of clotted arteries, with cars as blood cells making their way around stops and knots.

This afternoon it was the opposite problem that had him fretting in the back seat with Linda: the President of the United States was in town, and traffic had come to a stop. They were idling at the corner of 49th Street and Lexington Avenue as traffic cops held everyone at a standstill, their arms out stiff and their whistles blowing.

"What the hell is *that*?" Linda asked, as they watched the longest motorcade either of them had ever seen turn onto Lexington Avenue and head south. The avenue had been closed to traffic, with police cars and motorcycle cops stationed at every street crossing.

"That," Kyle said, "is the Presidential motorcade." He knew this because his boss Imogene was scheduled to do a segment for Tokyo Pulse from a gala at the New York Public Library that night, with the President as the featured guest. Had he been working he might have been able to go as her assistant, but even the President of the United States couldn't keep him from taking time off to spend with Detective Linda. After all, there would always be another president.

They waited nervously in the back seat as the motorcade seemed to go on forever. Even the cab driver was impressed, gawking at block after block of black SUVs, many with SWAT types perched in the open backs, ready to jump out and fire in the event of an attack.

"What do we do now?" Linda asked, resigned to waiting for the motorcade to pass, the way one sits at a railroad crossing watching freight cars go by in a crawl.

"We re-group," Kyle said. "We go back to the apartment, we talk it through."

"When do we go to the police?"

"Today, I imagine. I just want to consider everything. I don't want to accuse a man wrongly, I don't want to assume that just because he spoke to Victor he killed him."

"But that's what you think."

"That's what I think, yes. If he didn't do it, if he's not the Pride Killer, then he's involved somehow."

"You mean he doesn't work alone?"

"It's not unheard of. And remember, if we move too quickly, we tip our hand. Who knows what might happen then. He might vanish again and we'd never catch him."

Kyle watched as the end of the motorcade finally passed by. They waited awhile longer as the traffic slowly started up again. Kyle felt his foot twitching furiously—they'd lost precious time waiting for the most powerful man in the world to pass by in one of those dozens of black SUVs (surely not the sedan with the Presidential flags flying from the hood, that had to be a decoy).

"It takes them awhile," the driver said, sensing his passengers' impatience. "They block all these streets, then they have to open them again, maybe five more minutes. You in a hurry?"

"Yes," they both said from the back seat.

"Let's just walk," Kyle said. "We can talk along the way. It's good for the thought processes."

"But it's twenty blocks."

"This is New York City. Twenty blocks is like walking across the street. Come on, we can bounce ideas off each other."

Kyle told the driver they were getting out. He handed a ten dollar bill through the plastic divider separating the front and back seats and opened the door. They could walk almost as quickly as the cab would get them there, especially if there were any more delays. And they could talk. They had the Pride Killer in their sights with one good shot at him and could not afford to miss.

CHAPTER 34

Danny's usual routine was to go home for the break between lunch service and dinner. The bar at Margaret's Passion remained open starting at noon, but meals were only available for the two sittings. It had always been this way at the restaurant and always would be. Bar food was for bars, and Margaret's was definitely not in that class.

Once the kitchen closed each day, Danny would walk the fifteen minutes it took him to get home around two-thirty in the afternoon, then return at five to oversee the beginning of the dinner shift. He did not stay the entire evening—he never had, he was the day manager for all those years before he became the owner—but he liked being there for an hour or so ahead of time, especially now that Margaret's was his. His night manager, Patrice, did a terrific job and had been Danny's right hand for six years now. Combined with his recent promotion of Chloe to day manager, the pair gave Danny the level of comfort he needed with the business.

He couldn't hear Margaret upstairs; the staff had never been able to hear the Bowmans in the apartment above them. But he knew she was there, puttering around, most likely starting to slowly pack for the move to Florida. He thought about going up to see her for a few minutes, but he'd been upstairs once already today and didn't want to be a nuisance. Besides, he knew the impulse to spend time with her would only become more frequent as the time drew closer for her to leave. He thought about calling Kyle to let him know he was going for a private fitting but decided against it. The last text he'd had from Kyle was an hour ago, when they were canvassing an Upper East Side neighborhood to see if anyone recognized the photo they had of Victor Campagna. Poor Victor, Danny thought, as he stared another moment out the window onto 3rd Avenue. Poor Vinnie! The brothers were very close. The entire Campagna family must be in terrible distress. There'd been nothing more on the news about the two murders. Danny wondered if the Pride Killer—assuming that's who was behind this—would once again slip into the shadows.

"A penny for your thoughts," Chloe said, startling him.

Danny turned around to see her drying her hands on a towel. Chloe had not changed a bit since her promotion. She would still bus a table if needed, bartend or wash dishes. It was in her nature.

"A penny won't get you much anymore," Danny said.

"A dollar then."

"Just sad, that's all. But it'll be this way for the next month until she's gone." He nodded at the ceiling. "And for quite some time afterward, I imagine."

"Is there anything I can do? Short of talking her into staying."

"Nothing, but thank you." Danny took the business card out of his pocket. "Say, listen, I'm going out for a fitting …" Chloe looked at him curiously. "For a suit."

"Ah."

"If Kyle calls, don't tell him. It want it to be a surprise. He went looking for a suit for me, you see, and I … oh, never mind. Just tell him I'm running some errands. I'll be home by five. We're having dinner out tonight with our friend Linda."

"Will do."

Danny took the card in hand, pulled out his cell phone and dialed the private number Diedrich Keller had written on it. He figured two and a half hours was plenty of time to get to where Keller lived, be fitted for a fabulous new suit, and make it back to Gramercy Park by five.

Keller picked up on the second ring.

CHAPTER 35

D had barely settled into his living room after a taxi ride home when his cell phone rang. He looked at the caller ID and saw Margaret's Passion listed. He let it ring twice before answering, staring at the phone as his smile grew wider. He'd been successful in enticing Danny Durban with his gracious offer of a private fitting. He'd been imagining it all the way back in the cab and here it was, about to become a reality.

"Diedrich Keller," he said, putting the phone on speaker so he could hold it in his lap.

"Yes, Mr. Keller, this is Danny Durban, from the restaurant."

"Mr. Durban! Let me guess, you'd like that fitting after all. And that deep discount! I'm so glad you took me up on my offer. Unless of course I'm mistaken and there's some other reason you're calling."

"No, you're absolutely correct. I've just finished up for the afternoon here and I was wondering if this would be a good time to stop by."

"Let me check my calendar," D said. He counted to five, then said, "Fortunately, I have nothing going until this evening. How soon could you be here?"

"As soon as a taxi can get there. By the way, I'll need to know where 'there' is."

D thought about it moment. Should he stick to protocol and give this man a false address several blocks away, then feign stupidity and walk him back? Or did it not matter, considering he would be on a plane by midnight? Danny, unlike like all the others, would not be in the East River but left in the basement as a grand farewell—he'd decided to let them find out who he was, who he *had been*. This was his pièce de résistance, his big going-away, after which he would be leaving for Europe. First stop: Berlin. He'd already checked into flights and booked one late that night. Yes, he hated Berlin. He hated the country, the people and the language, but he was no fool. He'd survived as the Pride Killer for seven years—albeit three in absentia—and he would reemerge again, somewhere, when the time was ready. But this was his last hurrah in a city he'd grown tired of, his curtain call as Diedrich Keller, owner of Keller and Whitman, master of etiquette and the slow kill.

"Do you have a pen handy?" D said. Danny said yes, and D gave him the address of the townhouse. Not two blocks away, not transposed or inverted. The real address of the real home where the very, very real Diedrich Keller lived and so many others had died. He intended for Danny to join them soon, after which Diedrich Keller would vanish, leaving behind him nothing but a ghastly mystery.

CHAPTER 36

Kyle and Linda walked into the apartment exactly twenty minutes after leaving the taxi. They'd talked everything over on the walk and both were convinced the key to finding the killer was Diedrich Keller. Neither was certain yet it was Keller himself—he didn't seem the type to be killing men and dumping their bodies in the East River. But, Kyle wondered, is there such a thing as a serial killer type? Most of the good ones—*successful* ones, he corrected himself, as he closed the door and set his keys on the small table in their entryway—did not look like serial killers. They looked like neighbors, co-workers, even fathers and favored sons. Once in a while they were daughters!

Smelly and Leonard had heard them coming down the hallway and were waiting at the door. They never ran out into the hallway, seeming to think it led somewhere dreadful and scary for curious cats, but they would perch close enough to make opening the door a challenge.

"That's odd," said Kyle, shooing them away with his foot. "Danny always gives them treats when he gets home in the afternoon." Then, to the cats, "What's up, kids? Didn't Danny give you snacks?"

"I don't think he's here," Linda said.

She was right. The apartment was completely quiet. Normally, Danny also turned on the television in the bedroom to get caught up on the news with one of the cable channels. Today there was silence.

"He must've run errands. Or maybe he's visiting with Margaret," Kyle said. "I know he's been spending more time with her before she leaves."

He gave Danny's absence no more thought as they settled back into the apartment. Linda took off her jacket, exposing her gun in its shoulder holster, and sat on one of the two small couches they had in the living room. This one faced the window, and she could see a nearly identical apartment building facing them from across Lexington Avenue. New York City struck her as the perfect place to have a pair of binoculars, if you were given to seeing what your neighbors were up to without them knowing.

"Do you ever think about being watched?" she asked, peering out the window.

"Excuse me?" Kyle said. He'd gone into the kitchen to make them coffee. He'd also grabbed the small box of cat treats from a shelf and placed a half dozen of them on the floor, where Smelly and Leonard quickly gobbled them up. He could see Linda from where he knelt just inside the kitchen door.

"I mean, you can see into other people's apartments here. And they can see you. Does that ever bother you?"

"That's what drapes are for," he called back, standing and returning to the coffee. "Besides, you get used to it. After a while you don't think about it anymore. Are they watching? Are they not watching? Some people want them to, you know."

"The exhibitionists."

"Yes, and there's no shortage of those in New York City. It's see-and-be-seen for too many people living here. Danny and I don't give it any thought. Unless I'm naked after a shower and I suddenly realize it, and it's like, ooops, I'd better put a towel around me. Otherwise having people see into your windows is like background noise, you can't even hear it after a few weeks." Watching coffee drip into a cup, he said, "Let me see if I remember ... creamer, no sugar."

"Perfect."

Kyle finished making their coffee and brought the two cups into the living room. He set them on the coffee table in front of Linda and took a seat on the matching couch across from her.

"Let me just check," he said, taking his cell phone off his belt clip. He looked at the message icon. "Nope, no text. No email. I'm guessing he went to the grocery store. We ran out of milk this morning." He hooked his phone back onto his belt, then took a sip of his coffee. "So what do we know?"

"We know the Pride Killer has struck twice in forty-eight hours. That's the first and most important thing we need to keep in mind."

"Right. A third is coming very soon unless we get past speculation into action."

"But action and accusation are two different things," Linda said. "What else do we know?"

"We know Victor Campagna went to Cargill's for a drink with his friend Sam Paddington, but Sam never showed up. He then left Cargill's and made his way to Keller and Whitman to look for a suit."

"Diedrich Keller said he was alone there that day—something I don't think we can take as gospel truth—and never saw Victor."

"But the bodega owner *did* see him," said Kyle. "And he saw him come out of Keller and Whitman's.

"Maybe Jarrod was working by himself that morning, we haven't considered that."

"So why would Keller say he was there alone?"

"To cover for Jarrod. We don't know what their relationship is outside work."

"Jarrod as the Pride Killer? The man seems like too much dust would unnerve him."

"Could be a front. Never assume there's a type in these cases. It's also possible the bodega owner was mistaken. Or lying."

"He'd have no reason to lie," said Kyle.

"For his moment of fame? Maybe he wants to be on the news. But I doubt it. I think he was telling the truth. I think the one lying here is Diedrich Keller. But is he lying to protect himself, or someone else?"

"Maybe he doesn't want to get involved. Saying he saw a dead man just before the dead man's trail grows cold could bring a lot of suspicion."

"So," said Linda, sipping her coffee and setting it back on a coaster. "Do we confront Diedrich Keller, or do we go to the police with what we think?"

Kyle considered it for several seconds, then said, "I think we have one last conversation with Keller, but we take him by surprise."

"How's that?"

"We go to his home. He won't be expecting us, and it will throw him off his game, if he's playing one."

"And it will get us inside that house ... or apartment, whichever it is. I'd like to see it for myself, get a sense of the place."

"Any secrets it might be hiding."

Linda instinctively touched her gun. Secrets could sometimes be fatal.

"There's only one problem," Kyle said. "We don't know where he lives. I tried finding an address with my cell phone but there's nothing listed. There's really nothing about Diedrich Keller at all online, except the store. That's quite an accomplishment in the digital age."

"Let me make a call," Linda said. She reached down and took her cell phone from her purse on the floor.

"You're calling Information? Does that even exist anymore?"

"Not the kind of information you're thinking of," she said. "Remember, I'm a retired cop, with friends on the force."

"In New Hope, Pennsylvania. This is Manhattan."

"It doesn't matter. When it comes to digging up information, nothing gets it done like a call from a police department."

"I hope you're right ..."

Linda held her finger up to her lips, silencing Kyle. "Hey, Marty, what's up?" she said into her phone. "It's Linda Sikorsky. Listen, I'm trying to get an address on someone who doesn't want to be found. Can you help me out?"

She listened carefully as her ex-colleague on the other end of the line went about trying to help her.

Kyle finished the last of his coffee and took their cups back into the kitchen, followed closely by the cats. It was they, and not the person giving them treats, who decided how many were enough. Kyle fished several more out of the pouch and put them on the floor.

After several minutes, Linda thanked Marty and walked quickly into the kitchen. "Got it," she said. "He's on East 82nd Street. No apartment number."

"Probably a townhouse," Kyle said. "The Upper East Side is full of them."

"So let's go. He'll never expect to see us on his doorstep."

Kyle rinsed out the coffee cups and left them in the sink. He led Linda to the door, grabbing his keys from the stand. "I have to let Danny know where we are," he said as they hurried into the hallway.

"Call him from the taxi. We're definitely not walking this time."

Kyle felt a slight annoyance with Danny for not sending a message. On the other hand, Danny knew Kyle was with Linda and probably thought they were still out somewhere on the trail. Danny wisely kept his distance from the chaos Kyle and Linda always found themselves in. He thought it was dangerous and preferred not knowing to worrying constantly. Kyle would call him once they were on their way. The very least he owed Danny was letting him know they were okay.

CHAPTER 37

"This is quite a nice home you have," Danny said. He'd arrived at Diedrich Keller's townhouse ten minutes earlier after a surprisingly quick cab ride from the restaurant. Synchronized green lights had gotten them twenty blocks without a stop; the rest was unusually light traffic for a Thursday afternoon.

"Thank you, Mr. Durban," D said. He was standing to the side, watching as Danny took in the living room with its fireplace and paintings.

"Please, call me Danny."

"Danny, then."

"Is that your grandfather?" Danny was looking at the same painting Scott Devlin admired the day before. D had bought the painting at a flea market for $50.

"My great uncle, actually. When the family still had its fortune, before ... well, everything comes and goes."

"I'm sorry," said Danny, not sure why he would be. Judging from the townhouse, Diedrich Keller was not poor and probably never had been. But Danny knew from working with wealthy customers that for many of them, being down to their last million dollars meant destitution was not far off.

"May I offer you a drink?" D said, still watching Danny from behind. He decided he'd made a good choice, both in terms of his victim and in his plan. He would have an afternoon to remember—and to be remembered by—then he would cease to exist for all intents and purposes. The memories would be his forever, and he would start anew, as another man, another killer. The anticipation was nearly too much for him to contain.

"I don't normally drink in the afternoon," Danny said. He turned from the painting.

"Please, have a seat." D motioned to the plush couch. Danny walked the few steps over and sat down.

"Very comfortable."

"I hope so. And even more comfortable with a glass of Chardonnay."

"I really shouldn't."

"It can't possibly hurt. We'll visit a while, enjoy some wine, then I'll take your measurements and show you my private catalog. You'll be on your way in less than an hour and the finest suit you've ever owned will be yours in a week. I promise."

Danny thought a moment more about it, then said yes, a glass of wine would be nice. The last few days had been especially stressful, with the party planning, the emotions of Margaret's leaving, and now having Detective Linda visiting for Pride weekend. Danny and Kyle weren't much into the annual festivities and had not been to a parade in years, but Kyle wanted Linda to have a good time, something to remember before going to tend to her dying mother-in-law. Danny would not let the strain of it all show—at least not to Linda.

D went to the liquor cabinet. A small refrigerator was tucked in beneath it. He reached inside and took out an unopened bottle of the best Chardonnay he'd been able to find. Two minutes later he'd poured them each a glass, with something special in Danny's. He took the glasses back to the living room and found Danny still seated on the couch, admiring the chandelier hanging over him.

"This really is quite a home," Danny said, taking the glass from D.

"Can you believe I got it for a steal? When I bought here, prices were still low and the Upper East Side was not the place to be. They practically begged me to buy this house. So I did. I made it my own, fixed everything up, and now it's worth three times what I paid for it. Are you looking to buy?"

"No," Danny said, laughing. "Kyle and I are apartment people, at least as long as we live in New York. Someday we may head out to suburbia, or maybe the New Jersey countryside—we love it there—but not townhouses in Manhattan, thanks anyway."

Danny began to feel just a bit dizzy. "I knew I shouldn't have had a drink this early."

"It's nothing. Just the first flush of a good wine." D took a sip from his own glass. "Speaking of which, I have some remarkable wines in the cellar. I know Margaret's Passion only serves the best of the best. Might you be interested?"

Danny was definitely feeling the wine now. "I'm always looking for the finest for my customers. Cuts of meat, staff, tea, and certainly wine. We have a sommelier, I should probably have her take a look at your collection."

"Excellent idea, we can set something up as soon as I return from London. In the meantime, come, have a look yourself. It's quite an extensive wine cellar, one of the best in the city, I've been told."

Danny wasn't a wine connoisseur but he'd always been fascinated by the subculture of those who were. The temperature controlled rooms, the obscene prices paid for a single bottle of fermented grape juice. One of his favorite shows on the Food Channel featured an obnoxious host named Claire Cracken who went around the world telling people their $2,500 bottle of 1865 Chateau-Something was worthless and tasted like vinegar. He couldn't pass up the chance to see what Diedrich had in his basement.

"Sure," Danny said. "Then the fitting! I haven't mentioned to Kyle that I was coming here, it's a surprise. It was sweet of him to go suit shopping for me, but I'm very particular. Don't tell him I said that."

"I won't say a word."

Could the situation be more perfect? He now knew what no one else did: Danny Durban had come to his home without telling anyone where he was going. Perhaps the stars were shining on him, right here, in broad daylight in Manhattan, to make up for the near-fatal mistake he'd made with Victor Someone. He was being repaid, he thought, and quite handsomely.

"Let's take a quick look at the wine cellar, perhaps select something you can take to your sommelier as an example, then we'll come back up for the fitting and you'll be on your way."

"Excellent," Danny said, as D led the way to the basement door. Danny had gone from feeling lightheaded to giddy as well, and decided there would not be a second glass of wine.

D opened the basement door and flipped on the light. A set of carpeted stairs lead down. The entire basement was carpeted for soundproofing, except for his special room, his *real* fitting room. He'd wanted the floor in there to be easy to clean. He felt the thrill course through him as the killing time ticked closer by the second.

"Please," D said, holding the door for Danny. "You first."

Danny handed his glass of wine to D, saying, "Hold this please, I feel a little woozy," and started down the stairs.

D looked at the glass, seeing it was nearly empty. He smiled as broad a smile as had graced his face in months. He waited until Danny was nearly at the bottom of the stairs, then he closed the door and followed.

CHAPTER 38

"That's odd," Kyle said, as the taxi rolled through 34th Street heading north. "Danny's not answering his phone."

Kyle had sent a text message as soon as they'd hopped in the cab in front of the apartment building. Danny was always very good at responding. Kyle texted again, "Where are you?" and heard nothing back. Finally, he did something he rarely did since the normalization of texting and emails: he dialed Danny's phone number. After four rings it went to voicemail.

"Maybe he's indisposed," Linda said, meaning perhaps Danny was in a men's room somewhere.

"No, he always responds. This is weird. I'm going to call the restaurant."

Linda watched out the window as they passed 38th Street, then 42nd, counting as the numbers slowly went up. She calculated they would be at Keller's townhouse within ten minutes, probably sooner.

"Chloe?" Danny said into his cell phone. "Is Danny still there? I can't get him to reply to my texts or calls."

Chloe proceeded to tell him that Danny had left an hour ago. As she'd been promised to secrecy by Danny she did not say where he went, only that he had some errands to run and he'd be home by five.

"Listen, Chloe," Danny said, "if he comes back or he calls, tell him to call me ASAP. It's very important."

The urgency in Kyle's voice made Chloe hesitate. "Is anything wrong? Are the cats okay?"

"Smelly and Leonard are fine, but I need to find Danny. If he comes back in or calls ask him to reach me immediately."

"Kyle, listen," Chloe said. "You didn't hear this from me, but Danny went out for a suit."

Linda saw Kyle's expression change.

"A suit?"

"Yeah," Chloe replied, her voice tinny through the phone.

"Hang on, Chloe, I'm putting you on speaker." A second later they could hear her voice filling the back seat as Kyle said, "You still there?"

"I'm still here."

"So what's this about a suit?"

"Well, there was this guy who came in late for lunch, just about time to close the kitchen. You know Danny, he never turns anyone away unless he has to. So he served him."

"What did this man look like, Chloe?"

"Tallish. Handsome. Older for sure, in his forties. Said he'd just got back from Europe and he owned a suit store, men's store, whatever."

Linda mouthed the words, "Oh my God" and started to say something, but Kyle shushed her.

"So what happened then?" he asked

"Then? The guy left. He ate, gave Danny his card, and left."

"Chloe, thank you for the information. It's very, very helpful."

Kyle was about to hang up when Chloe said, "Kyle? Please don't tell Danny I told you. He wanted me to keep it a secret. About the suit, I mean."

Kyle laughed for the first time in two days. "Well, I knew you didn't mean about the man, Chloe. Danny's not the straying sort. His eye might wander, all eyes do, but that's as far afield as we go. And don't worry, if this is the man I think it was, Danny will be very relieved you told me."

Kyle hung up. The taxi was now at 72nd Street and they had a decision to make.

"Do we go to the store instead?" Kyle said. "Danny left an hour ago, he's probably there now."

Linda was undecided: should they veer from their plans and head to the store, or stay on mission. The store wasn't that far from the townhouse, they could do both, but first she wanted to make sure Keller wasn't home.

"Let's stay on track," she said. "We'll go to the townhouse, have the taxi wait outside while we see if Keller's home, then make a beeline to the store. If Keller's the Pride Killer, he's not claiming his victims at a highly visible store on Lexington Avenue. If Danny's there, he's safe for the moment."

Kyle sighed—a deep exhale of anxiety and adrenaline. He was perched on the very edge of the backseat now. They were just a block away from the townhouse. He leaned up to the partition, handed the driver a $20 and said, "Listen, we need you to wait when we get there. Keep the meter running. If no one's home we have a second stop. If this person *is* home, just keep the change and go."

"Fine," said the driver. It was the only word he'd uttered in fifty blocks.

CHAPTER 39

Danny listened in horror as his cell phone buzzed. He kept it on vibrate at the restaurant, and now, helpless, he heard it shaking and rattling just out of reach. He knew it must be Kyle—Chloe and the others at Margaret's only called him in cases of emergency, knowing he needed his away-time from the demands of the job.

He had no idea how long he'd been unconscious. Obviously long enough for Diedrich Keller to get him to a gurney and secure him with straps. He was still fully clothed, which was a very minor relief. He also knew he had fallen into the trap of the man known for years as the elusive Pride Killer. How could he be so stupid, he wondered. How could he not have realized that while there were coincidences in life all the time, having Diedrich Keller come into the restaurant for lunch just hours after Kyle and Linda spoke to him was not one of them? Had his judgment been dulled by all the emotions of the past few months? Had he let his guard down so far he had no instincts left—if he'd ever had them at all? How, exactly, did he allow himself to be lured into this position, which may well prove to be his last?

"It's your husband," D said, glancing at the phone and seeing Kyle's name on the caller ID. "Shall I answer it?"

Danny knew the man was toying with him. He wouldn't be surprised if he answered the phone to torture Kyle with the knowledge of what was about to happen. Danny said nothing, hoping his silence would keep Keller from taking the call.

"No," said D, letting the phone ring a fourth time and go into voice-mail. "Better he and that bitch he's with find out about you when it's too late."

"What are you going to do?" Danny said, his voice hoarse as his wits slowly came back to him.

"Do you know who I am?"

"You're the Pride Killer."

"Then that answers your question."

Danny felt himself growing damp with sweat, yet the basement was nearly cold from an air conditioner he could see mounted in a small blacked-out window in a far corner of the ceiling. He forced himself to become fully alert, lifting his head as far as he could—there was a restraint of some kind lashed across his forehead. A belt? A strap? He couldn't tell, but he was able to bend his head up just a bit, and turn his neck slightly from side to side.

He was not in the main basement room, he was sure of that. He'd made it to the bottom of the stairs … it was coming back to him now. He'd felt his knees begin to wobble as he got down the stairs and into the well-furnished cellar. Diedrich Keller had taken pains to make his killer's lair as deceptively arranged as his townhouse. There was a large leather couch and two matching armchairs, Danny remembered that. There was some kind of artwork on the walls, imitation modern art that reminded Danny of Pollock and Warhol, one above the couch, another above a low ebony cabinet. There was indeed a wine cellar of sorts, with rows and rows of dark bottles carefully stacked in a waist-high rack that ran along the back wall. Danny had been about to comment on the comfort of the room when he realized the wooziness he'd been feeling was not natural. His legs began to buckle and he lunged for the couch, saying, "What did you do to me?" as he fell face-first onto the cushions.

"What I did to you," Danny remembered Keller saying just before he lost consciousness, "is nothing compared to what I'm going to do."

Then all was blackness, and now this. In a separate room. Cold but sweating with fear. Knowing Kyle had been trying to call, knowing rescue was just beyond his arm's reach. Watching as a sadistic, very successful serial killer hummed to himself and stood in front of a tray, his back to

Danny, inspecting tools that Danny could see just on the periphery of his vision. Torture tools. The kind of instruments from hell the living only see as they are about to die.

The taxi pulled up in front of Diedrich Keller's townhouse. Linda was out immediately, hurrying up the steps with Kyle a moment behind. The cab idled at the curb as promised.

Kyle caught up to Linda at the top step as Linda pushed the door buzzer and waited. After a long minute without response, she pushed the buzzer again.

"He's not here," Kyle said, taking Linda by the arm. "Let's go to the store."

"Wait just a minute, I'm not so sure …" She cocked her head and listened.

"What are you …"

"Shh!" She listened carefully, as if she heard a very small voice on the wind. She slowly turned her head, looking for the source of the sound. Kyle followed her line of sight, first up, then to the side, and finally down. There were basement window wells, and in one of them a small air conditioner could be heard humming.

"There," Linda said. "An air conditioner."

"In the basement. Why would he have an air conditioner in the basement?"

"And why would it be on if he wasn't home?" She pushed the door buzzer again, this time hard enough that Kyle thought she might push it through the wall.

D heard the buzzer upstairs. So did Danny, though he tried to keep any trace of hope or excitement off his face.

"I'm very well equipped down here," D said, turning back from his tray. He held what looked like an X-Acto knife in his hand. "You know, I've always been quick about it, preferring a belt or garrote of some kind—not for mercy, but for the mess. I mean, really, who needs the clean up? But I've

gone to some trouble for you, acquiring a few extra toys just this morning."
He held up the knife. "Art supplies, indeed." He then nodded to another
corner of the room, behind Danny. "You can't see it from where you are,
but there's a small monitor mounted in the corner. I can see whoever's at
the front door. Would you like to know who it is?"

Danny swallowed hard, afraid of the answer. Was it the police? Would
this madman simply ignore them and hope they went away? *Please, please
don't go away*, Danny prayed, licking his drying lips.

"It's your husband and the bitch. She's looking around. My mistake!
She probably heard the air conditioner."

Danny discovered in that instant that hope and despair can be felt at
the same time. He hoped Kyle and Linda would not go away, that they
would know something was happening in this house of horrors. Yet he de-
spaired they would leave and he would never see his husband, his friends,
his cats, anything that mattered to him, ever again.

D put the knife back on the tray. "I'd better go see what they want
before they call in reinforcements," he said. "Don't worry, Danny. I'll be
back." He took a roll of duct tape from the tray and hurried over to Danny.
Peeling off a piece and cutting it with the knife, he taped Danny's mouth.
"Can't have you shouting out now, can we?" he said.

Taking a deep breath, D composed himself. Danny watched in fascinated terror as Diedrich Keller's face changed, softening, smiling, becoming the face of an innocent man caught up in something he had nothing to
do with. "This won't take long."

D left the room, humming to himself. Danny could hear the hum fade
as the man who was very close to taking his life climbed the basement
stairs and quietly closed the door behind him.

"He's here," Linda said. "I know he is." She rang the bell one more time.
If Keller did not answer the door she was prepared to find a way in. Then,
to their surprise, the door opened. Diedrich Keller stood in the doorway,
feigning sleep, as if he'd been woken from a nap.

"Yes, Mr. Callahan, and Brenda, was it?"

"Linda Sikorsky."

"Right. I'd say it was nice to see you again but I've just been sleeping! I nap sometimes in the afternoon."

"May we come in?" Kyle asked. "We'd like to ask a few more questions."

"Certainly," said D, as he stepped aside, waving them into his home.

The three of them entered the foyer, tastefully furnished with an ebony crescent table and mirror just inside the door. Soft classical piano music played in the living room. Kyle identified it as Chopin, among his late father's favorites. "Let's head into the living room and sit," D said, leading them down the short hallway into his expansive living room.

Kyle looked around, taking in each detail. The paintings, the fireplace, the soft suede furniture. There were a number of photographs lined up on the fireplace mantel. Kyle wandered over and looked at them. He had the strange sensation no one in the pictures was related to Diedrich Keller. "Family?" he asked.

"Distant," said D. "Won't you have a seat?"

Linda eased down onto the couch. D could see she was still wearing the gun holster. His smile fell an inch or two. He remained standing as Kyle took a seat in the matching chair, forming a small triangle with Linda on one side, Kyle on the other, and Diedrich Keller standing by the coffee table.

"Now," D said. "May I get you something to drink?"

Danny could hear movement upstairs. The floorboards in the townhouse were old and original, and they'd warped over the years as old wood does. The constant shifting of cold to hot, damp to dry with the changing seasons, created curves in the boards. No matter how well they were kept up, they always creaked. He heard voices, too, but muffled. He recognized the timbre of Kyle's voice, speaking in short sentences. It elevated his agitation to a nearly unbearable level. Would Keller kill them, too? Would they all be found dead in this basement days from now, or be buried under the floor?

He tried to free his hands. His arms had been fastened with straps to the metal bars along the side of the gurney. His legs were bound with a belt and strapped down. There appeared to be no way to free himself, but he kept trying, wriggling his right hand back and forth. He told himself over and over to relax, just relax. He'd always been fascinated by escape artists, and he knew the key to extricating oneself from restraints was not to fight against them, but to surrender to them. Deep breaths. Let the body become fluid. Finally, after a full five minutes of letting himself become smaller and smaller, his right hand came free. At first he didn't realize it, but he felt the space that had opened up around his wrist, just enough empty space to allow him to slide his arm up and out. He raised his hand and stared at it, as if he couldn't believe what he was seeing. Then he quickly grabbed the tape on his mouth, yanked it off and screamed.

Kyle and Linda both declined D's offer of a drink. They did not want to waste time while he made coffee or tea, and they certainly were not having alcohol in the middle of the afternoon. When he'd made the offer, Linda glanced at Kyle with the very slightest shake of her head: no. Kyle read into it everything Linda wanted him to. Keller was stalling. Keller was up to something. Whatever he offered someone to drink in this house, it was a drink they regretted.

"We visited your store again," Kyle said.

"Yes, I know," D said. "Jarrod called me. He was afraid I might be in some danger."

"Danger?" said Linda.

"With this Pride Killer person on the loose, and apparently some connection to my store I'm completely unaware of. I realized after speaking with Jarrod that I had seen that young man, looking in the store window. He never came in, though. Do you suppose this killer is stalking his victims? Perhaps he followed the man, approached him outside my business, and that's where the trail went cold, so to speak."

"I think you know more than you're telling us," Kyle said. "I think it's time for us to go to the police and suggest they have a conversation with you."

D stared at them. "I have to ask you to leave now." His voice was cold, his smile gone and replaced by a flat, hard expression.

That was when they heard it: a loud scream from beneath them. A man shouting, "Help me! Help me!" And that man, Kyle instantly recognized, was Danny.

"Oh my God, he's here!" Kyle shouted. He jumped up from the couch. "Where is he?"

Without waiting for Keller to respond, Kyle hurried through the house, looking for doors, calling out, "We're here, Danny! We're here!"

Keller was alone in the living room now with Linda. Just as she rose from the couch he lunged at her, shoving her back into the cushions. She was a tall woman, but Diedrich Keller was taller, and stronger. He shoved his forearm against her throat. When she reached up with both hands to free herself, gasping, he grabbed her gun from its holster. Stepping back from the couch, he pointed the pistol directly at Linda's chest and said, "Stop right there."

Danny had not been successful in freeing his other arm. He'd also stopped relaxing, fighting frantically against his restraints. He heard the door open and footsteps rushing down the stairs. He looked up, shocked and relieved, to see Kyle running into the room.

Kyle hurried over to him. He didn't know what was going on upstairs, but he knew they had little time. He had to free Danny from the gurney. He stood over Danny, trying to determine where the buckles were on the straps.

"The knife," Danny said, nodding at the tray where Keller had his instruments of pain and pleasure. "Use the knife."

Kyle grabbed the X-Acto knife, turned back to the gurney and began slicing the straps. The knife wasn't meant to cut leather, but Kyle was determined. He cut himself slashing at the straps and a gush of blood began flowing from his fingers. He didn't care. He kept cutting, furiously digging with the knife blade. Finally the strap gave way and Danny was free. He slid off the gurney. He wanted to embrace Kyle, to fall into him, but there was no time. They were both about to run back upstairs when they heard the voice behind them.

"Let's all just stay in the basement, shall we?" D said.

Kyle turned around and saw Linda in front of Diedrich Keller, who was holding her gun, calmly and evenly, prepared to shoot her in the back.

"It will be so much easier to clean things up down here."

Kyle and Danny watched in horror as Keller raised the gun back over his shoulder. In a quick, savage arc, he brought the gun butt smashing against Linda Sikorsky's skull. She collapsed in an instant, as if she'd been inflated and all the air inside her suddenly released.

Kyle ran to her, fearful of the worst.

"I doubt she's dead," D said. "Probably just unconscious. She's in for quite a surprise when she wakes up again."

Timing was everything, Kyle knew. Decisions had to be made so quickly sometimes they could not be called decisions, but reactions, instincts. He was in a crouch over Linda. He still had the knife in his hand, and without thinking, without knowing what would happened next, he threw himself at Keller and thrust the knife into his leg.

Keller screamed. Kyle pulled the knife out and plunged it in again, causing Keller to collapse on the floor beside Linda.

Kyle scrambled for the gun. They two men struggled—Diedrich Keller was not giving up without a fight. Danny watched, terrified, as his husband and the man who had been close to killing them all rolled and wrestled on the floor. What could he do? Should he jump in and try to subdue Keller? Then he saw it: Keller had gotten the knife and was raising it over Kyle's back. He was going to bury it in Kyle's neck! Danny screamed, "Nooooo!"

Then a gunshot. One single, roaring gunshot. Danny feared the worst. It had come to this. Kyle and Linda's obsession with criminals, their repeated forays into the worlds of the depraved. His very worst nightmare had just become reality. He had to do something. He had to survive and do what he could to help them all. He turned to the instrument tray and grabbed a small, stainless steel hammer. With enough force it could be lethal. He turned back and the sight stunned him. Kyle standing up. Kyle rising slowly. First to his knees, then to his feet. Linda Sikorsky's gun was in his hand. Diedrich Keller was dead.

Kyle had never fired a gun in his life. He'd never held a gun. And yet, here he was in the basement of a townhouse owned by one of the most vicious and elusive serial killers New York City had ever seen. That killer was dead, and Kyle had killed him.

Linda stirred, moaning on the floor.

"She's alive," Danny said.

"He's not," said Kyle, looking into the open, lifeless eyes of Diedrich Keller. And then he said, simply, "Call the police."

CHAPTER 40

Kyle wished it had been a dream. He lay in bed, staring up at the ceiling, afraid to look at the digital clock by the television. A muted sitcom re-run played on one of a hundred channels, the light from the screen flickering into the room. Danny was asleep beside him. Or at least he was pretending to be. Kyle stayed silent, not wanting to know if Danny, too, was wide awake on his side, reliving the last moments of the night before.

Kyle was consumed with guilt. Not for killing Diedrich Keller—lives had been saved by that gunshot, immeasurable pain had been spared his victims and his victims' families. But guilt for chasing killers in the first place. It had become a pastime for him, a way of amusing himself. Bo Sweetzer at Pride Lodge, Kieran Stipling from the Katherine Pride Gallery, Charlotte Gaines at CrossCreek Farm, and now the deadliest of them all, Diedrich Kristof Keller III. Dead by Kyle's own hand in an air-conditioned basement.

He'd thought the interrogations would never end. He, Linda and Danny spent most of the night at the police station giving statements, reliving what had happened, and answering over and over why they had not gone to the police with their suspicions. What was he supposed to tell them? *That it was too much fun chasing killers on their own?* That was the real answer, the answer that shocked him, like realizing something about ourselves we would never tell anyone and had not wanted to know.

It had to stop. Now was as good a time as any, too. So many things were about to change. So many shifts and rearrangements in life. Now was his chance to turn away from the dark side, to just be a personal assistant, amateur photographer, friend and husband. To live a normal life. Could he do it? Would he do it?

The answer is what had him awake at 3:00 a.m., blinking in the darkness. The answer was no.

Epilogue

July came and went without the kind of heat Kyle was accustomed to in New York's summer months. On the whole it was shaping up to be one of the coolest summers they'd had in a decade. He was fine with that; the heat, stench and humidity of Manhattan between June and September were usually overwhelming. But not this year. This year had been different in so many ways.

He had killed a man. He'd pursued murderers before, but never had it come to this: struggling with someone who was determined to end his life in a feverish bid to save his own, wresting Linda's gun away, and then ... without thinking about it, without even intending it, shooting Diedrich Keller in the heart. He didn't know he'd shot him in the heart until later, when an autopsy was performed. But he knew immediately Keller was dead, and he knew he had killed him when he lifted himself up from the floor, with Danny behind him and Linda just beginning to regain consciousness. It was a scene he would relive in his mind for years to come, perhaps for all the years he had left on the planet.

It was now August. The Pride parade had snaked down Fifth Avenue over a month ago and displayed its explosion of color without them. Linda would simply have to visit again, or find another parade to go to, although Kyle suspected she never would. For her, too, the memory of what happened had quickly become a stain. There was no way any of them was going to a parade after the events of that Thursday in the basement of an

Upper East Side townhouse. By Friday morning everyone knew the Pride Killer was dead. The police knew. The media knew—including Kyle's boss Imogene, who for once in her life had the good sense not to press him for an exclusive interview. At least not until the following week. He turned her down.

The three of them gave exhaustive statements. The detectives they met took a very dim view of them pursuing a serial killer on their own. There was also the issue of Linda's firearm. New York City was famous for its gun laws and the whole thing had left them in a gray area. Kyle was the one doing the shooting. Kyle was not licensed to have, hold, shoot, or own a gun. But Kyle had somehow gotten the gun from Keller and ended the career of a killer who had confounded the NYPD for seven years. At the mayor's prodding, any idea of charges concerning the weapon were dropped. Kyle was hailed as a hero, a position he never sought or wanted to hold. It had made for a stressful, dreadful weekend, with the time they had to spend with Linda its only saving grace.

Linda Sikorsky had no problem with a dead serial killer. She also did not envy Kyle's sudden fame as the man who stopped the Pride Killer—a claim he would never make anyway. She had encountered many terrible things in her years as a cop and was able to put most of her feelings aside, down where she kept the fear she'd known on the job, the doubt, and the sorrow of having told so many people their loved ones were dead. She also had bigger concerns. Her wife was waiting for her in Phoenix with her dying mother-in-law. Life did not stop because a madman died quickly and deservedly in a New York City basement.

The three of them spent the rest of that weekend going around the city. They shopped, they sight-saw, they even went to a Broadway show for Saturday matinee. None of it made them forget what had happened, but it helped. Nothing could be changed, but Linda's time with them was limited and they spent it having as much enjoyment as they could. Then, early Monday, they said goodbye on the curb outside their apartment building as Linda got into a taxi and headed to the airport. Nothing would ever be quite the same.

In the six weeks since, parts of their world had shifted dramatically. Margaret Bowman had her going-away party, and it was a huge success. Also a very tearful one, as guest after guest toasted the old woman and offered anecdotes about what Margaret's Passion meant to them—a first date, a wedding anniversary, the signing of a contract to star in a movie. Danny did not buy a new suit after all and doubted he would be suit-shopping anytime soon. He gave the last toast of the night.

Two weeks later they got a call from Linda. She was still in Phoenix with Kirsten, making funeral arrangements. Dot McClellan had died the night before, quietly, as is usually the case with someone riddled with cancer and pumped full of opiates. All in all it had been a cool but very hard summer.

Now Linda and Kirsten were back in their small house in rural New Jersey. Linda was back at her vintage-everything store. Kirsten was taking pottery classes and wondering what she wanted to do now that she'd sold her real estate business. One thing she knew: she never again wanted to stand in anyone's living room but her own, selling a prospective buyer on the neighborhood and the schools. She wanted something new, something very different in her life. She had Linda, they had the house, and the future looked interesting since she, too, had spread her wings and taken a leap into the unknown.

The four of them were talking, in very early conversation, about going on vacation together. A belated, delayed double honeymoon. They'd not decided where, but were hoping to finally arrange it the following spring. As they found themselves living again, laughing, letting the immediate past move further and further away, they thought a shared vacation might be just the thing to really give them distance from it all. In the meantime, Kyle had much to do—learning to be a landlord at the building they now owned, soothing his mother's feelings over being bought out (she took the deal, knowing it was best for them all), and somehow becoming the man he had been before he ended Diedrich Keller's life. He wasn't sure that was possible, but he hoped. Death had come up to him, looked him in the eye, and walked away. It was time to live again.

About the Author

Writing is the one thing I have done consistently all my life, whether it was being expressed in short fiction, long fiction, poetry, prose, plays, or children's television scripts. It is the one thing I've always felt compelled to do. Day jobs come and go, but the keyboard is forever. One day, hopefully far in the future, they'll find me dead with my head on the space bar, having passed on to the Great Word Processor in the Sky doing what I loved to do.

Thanks to anyone and everyone who has spent some time with Kyle and the gang. I hope you'll stop by again on their journeys, meet a new traveler or two, and keep me getting up before the sun to bring you more.

As for my personal life, I live in New York City with my husband Frank Murray and our dwindling family of cats. We have a house in the rural New Jersey countryside where we plan to move permanently someday ... maybe.

Mark McNease
www.markmcnease.com